THE SECRETS OF LORD GRAYSON CHILD

A CYNSTER-CONNECTED NOVEL

STEPHANIE LAURENS

ABOUT THE SECRETS OF LORD GRAYSON CHILD

#1 New York Times *bestselling author Stephanie Laurens returns to the world of the Cynsters' next generation with the tale of an unconventional nobleman and an equally unconventional noblewoman learning to love and trust again.*

A jilted noblewoman forced into a dual existence half in and half out of the ton is unexpectedly confronted by the nobleman who left her behind ten years ago, but before either can catch their breaths, they trip over a murder and into a race to capture a killer.

Lord Grayson Child is horrified to discover that *The London Crier*, a popular gossip rag, is proposing to expose his extraordinary wealth to the ton's matchmakers, not to mention London's shysters and Captain Sharps. He hies to London and corners *The Crier's* proprietor—only to discover the paper's owner is the last person he'd expected to see.

Izzy—Lady Isadora Descartes—is flabbergasted when Gray appears in her printing works' office. He's the very last person she wants to meet while in her role as owner of *The Crier*, but there he is, as large as life, and she has to deal with him without giving herself away! She manages— just—and seizes on the late hour to put him off so she can work out what to do.

But before leaving the printing works, she and he stumble across a murder, and all hell breaks loose.

Izzy can only be grateful for Gray's support as, to free them both of suspicion, they embark on a joint campaign to find the killer.

Yet working side by side opens their eyes to who they each are now—both quite different to the youthful would-be lovers of ten years before. Mutual respect, affection, and appreciation grow, and amid the chaos of hunting a ruthless killer, they find themselves facing the question of whether what they'd deemed wrecked ten years before can be resurrected.

Then the killer's motive proves to be a treasonous plot, and with others, Gray and Izzy race to prevent a catastrophe, a task that ultimately falls to them alone in a situation in which the only way out is through selfless togetherness—only by relying on each other will they survive.

A classic historical romance laced with crime and intrigue. A Cynster Next Generation-connected novel—a full-length historical romance of 115,000 words.

OTHER TITLES BY STEPHANIE LAURENS

To Distraction

Beyond Seduction

The Edge of Desire

Mastered by Love

Black Cobra Quartet

The Untamed Bride

The Elusive Bride

The Brazen Bride

The Reckless Bride

The Adventurers Quartet

The Lady's Command

A Buccaneer at Heart

The Daredevil Snared

Lord of the Privateers

The Cavanaughs

The Designs of Lord Randolph Cavanaugh

The Pursuits of Lord Kit Cavanaugh

The Beguilement of Lady Eustacia Cavanaugh

The Obsessions of Lord Godfrey Cavanaugh

Other Novels

The Lady Risks All

The Legend of Nimway Hall – 1750: Jacqueline

Medieval (As M.S.Laurens)

Desire's Prize

Novellas

Melting Ice – from the anthologies *Rough Around the Edges* and *Scandalous Brides*

Rose in Bloom – from the anthology *Scottish Brides*

Scandalous Lord Dere – from the anthology *Secrets of a Perfect Night*

THE SECRETS OF LORD GRAYSON CHILD

THE SECRETS OF LORD GRAYSON CHILD

Copyright © 2021 by Savdek Management Proprietary Limited

ISBN: 978-1-925559-48-4

Cover design by Savdek Management Pty. Ltd.

Cover couple photography by Period Images © 2021

First print publication: July, 2021

Savdek Management Proprietary Limited, Melbourne, Australia.

www.stephanielaurens.com

Email: admin@stephanielaurens.com

The names Stephanie Laurens and the Cynsters and the SL Logo are registered trademarks of Savdek Management Proprietary Ltd.

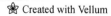 Created with Vellum

CHAPTER 1

WOBURN PLACE, LONDON. JANUARY 2, 1852.

*L*ord Grayson Child stepped down from the hackney he'd instructed to halt at the southern end of Woburn Place, at the northernmost corner of Russell Square.

Gray glanced around, then paid the jarvey and waited until the cab pulled away before crossing the busy thoroughfare, at that hour thronged with traffic, and continuing into Bernard Street.

As Corby, Gray's gentleman's gentleman, had assured him, he found Woburn Mews a block along on the left. Thrusting his hands into his greatcoat pockets and dipping his head, Gray confidently strode up the mews, consciously projecting the image of a man who knew where he was going.

His bootheels rang on the cobbles. He adjusted his stride and placed his feet more quietly; he didn't want to draw unnecessary attention. With the time nearing five o'clock, the encroaching winter evening progressively deepened the shadows that draped the western side of the street along which he was pacing.

As the street's name indicated, the area had once played host to the homes of the well-to-do. While pockets of private houses wreathed in quiet gentility remained, with the university so close, many residences had been converted to lodging houses for scholars and faculty, and other buildings had been taken over by businesses catering to academe.

The eastern side of Woburn Mews played host to several such establishments—a paper supplier, a purveyor of artists' supplies, and the

Molyneaux Printing Works, which produced the popular gossip rag *The London Crier*.

From the opposite side of the street, Gray surveyed the printing works' façade. Two stone steps led up to a neat, white-painted, half-glass-paned front door with the words "Molyneaux Printing Works" etched into the glass and highlighted in gold.

To the left of the door, a tall, wide window, uncurtained and stretching from approximately waist height to what must nearly be the ceiling, presumably allowed daylight to strike deep into the large workshop beyond.

Gray's eyesight was excellent; through the window, he could see a long counter that ran across about half the workshop's width, running parallel to the window and separated from it by a narrow space—a foyer of sorts. Behind the counter, deeper within the lighted interior, several figures moved about, busy and absorbed with their tasks.

Noting that, Gray strolled on. After the wide window, a more normal-sized window, currently with blinds unhelpfully drawn, faced the cobbles; the window belonged to a narrower room separated from the printing works' foyer and workshop by a wooden partition. Behind the screening blinds, a lamp burned brightly.

Gray eyed his target—the office in which he hoped to find either the proprietor of *The London Crier*, I. Molyneaux, or failing him, the editor of the gossip rag.

Surreptitiously, Gray glanced around, then slowed and stepped into a shadowy alcove before a padlocked door. Effectively hidden from sight, he settled to watch *The Crier's* door.

He'd learned of the threat *The Crier* posed when, the previous Saturday, while visiting his parents at Ancaster Park, his ancestral home, he'd been reduced to reading the gossip rag and, on the front page, had discovered a notice touting *The Crier's* upcoming exposé.

The words still rang in his mind.

From the Editor's Desk:
An Upcoming Exposé
Which scion of a noble house, after a lengthy sojourn in far-flung lands,
has recently returned to these shores a veritable Croesus, yet is being
exceedingly careful to hide his remarkable fortune from the eyes of the
world?
More details will be revealed in coming editions.

Unfortunately, given the festive season, his family's expectations, and various social obligations he had not wished to break, he'd had to remain in Lincolnshire to see in the New Year. Today—the Friday after he'd first seen the vexatious notice—had been the earliest he'd been able to come racing down the Great North Road.

On reaching London, he'd been irritated to discover that, being a weekly publication, *The London Crier* had released a new edition that day. A copy was jammed into his greatcoat pocket; he didn't need to consult it again to recite the substance of the latest titillating revelation.

Latest from the Editor's Desk:
As promised, we have an update on our most recent and highly secretive
Golden Ball, who continues to play least-in-sight, at least as far as
society is concerned. However, in this season, perhaps such retiring
behavior isn't to be wondered at or, indeed, discouraged, as our sources
assure us this long-lost son has spent the festive weeks being re-embraced
into the ducal fold. And that, of course, can only heighten society's
interest in him. Be assured that, as the Season approaches, your trusty
correspondent will reveal further insights into this elusive yet exceedingly
eligible gentleman.
More to come.

Reading that had hardened his resolve to ensure no further revelations were made. He had no wish to become the target of every matchmaker in London, let alone every Captain Sharp and purveyor of shady investments, all of whom would, inevitably, beat a path to his door. News of sensational and unexpected wealth invariably brought all three types running, hoping, respectively, to marry the money, acquire it via wagering, or extract it through convoluted business deals.

Gray failed to understand why such charlatans believed that anyone blessed with unexpected good fortune should be a fool readily parted from it, but so it was. And while he would take a certain delight in disabusing anyone of the notion that he was an easy mark, having to do so repeatedly would quickly become annoying and—even more irritating— potentially damaging with respect to the genuine business and investment relationships he'd begun developing and nurturing.

In his opinion, having money brought with it a certain responsibility, and that meant *The London Crier's* proprietor was going to have to find some other scandalous morsel with which to titillate his audience.

In the distance, the city's bells pealed, melodiously tolling for five o'clock. Gray detected renewed movement inside the printing works, then the lamps deeper in the workshop were extinguished, with only one lamp, on the long counter, left turned low.

Gray glanced at the office. As he'd hoped, that lamp continued to burn brightly. He had no wish to identify himself to the printing works' staff and was counting on the owner or editor being the last to leave.

The door opened, and a young woman—laughing at something—emerged, followed by two men in their twenties, another slightly older man, and two middle-aged men. All were garbed as respectable workers. The last man to leave, a burly, broad-shouldered individual with graying hair, pulled the front door shut, but didn't lock it.

In a loose group, the printing works' crew walked toward Bernard Street and were joined by workers emerging from the neighboring shops.

Once the printing works' staff were two doors down the street, Gray left the shadowed alcove, crossed the cobbles, and climbed the steps to the printing works' door. He grasped the handle and opened the door. A bell above the door tinkled loudly as he stepped inside.

He shut the door and walked slowly along the counter, taking note of the metal monstrosity looming in the dimly lit space beyond the barrier; he assumed it was the printing press. A scent drawn from ink, metal, and oil teased his nostrils.

The single lamp left burning at the end of the counter had been turned so low that, other than the shapes of two worktables and cabinets along the wall, he could distinguish little else in the body of the workshop. Closer to hand in the foyer, wooden benches ran along the front wall below the wide window, and a shorter, more comfortable bench sat against the side wall between the counter and the door.

No doubt summoned by the bell, brisk footsteps approached from inside the office. As he'd thought, wooden panels separated the office from the rest of the workshop. A half-glazed wooden door stood open, affording him a view across the brightly lit office to a wall of well-stocked bookshelves.

A woman appeared in the doorway.

With the bright light behind her, she initially appeared as a silhouette. A very attractive silhouette—tall, slender, yet nicely curved, with a well-shaped head topped by fashionably coiffed dark hair, a pale oval face, and a long, swanlike neck. Her gown was of some dark material, fashionably cut yet subdued in style.

She stepped into the foyer and, abruptly, halted. Then she stared.

Gray's eyes adjusted to the poor light, and her features—stunned and shocked—came into sharp focus.

He blinked and stared back.

His senses hadn't lied. She was definitely a lady.

Barely able to believe his eyes, he struggled to get his tongue to work. Eventually, he managed, "Isadora?" He felt as if his mental feet had been knocked from under him.

Lady Isadora Descartes couldn't stop staring, but as the apparition had spoken, he wasn't a figment of her imagination. Warily, she responded, "Grayson?"

He kept staring, and so did she—as if they couldn't get enough of seeing the other. The seconds stretched, and his gaze seemed to grow more intense, almost...hungry.

So much had changed, yet so much hadn't. Her leaping senses informed her he was just as tall as he'd been ten years ago, but he was carrying more muscle on his long frame, and even in the dim light, his hair seemed brighter—more burnished. His skin was more tanned than she remembered it ever being, and his features possessed a hard, harsher, sterner edge.

His amber eyes still held a glowing warmth she could drown in, yet the intellect behind those lovely eyes was, she sensed, significantly sharper.

A frown slowly claimed his face. Although he seemed to have to fight to do it, he forced his gaze from her and, frown deepening, looked over her shoulder into the office.

From where he stood, all he could see were the bookshelves filling the opposite wall.

He refocused his frown on her. "What are you doing here?"

The suspicion in his eyes and tone wasn't surprising but served to snap her wits into place. Coolly, she met his gaze and, challengingly, raised her chin. "More to the point, what are *you* doing here?"

What possible business could have brought him there?

He was the last person she would have expected to walk through *The Crier's* door, and beyond question, he was the very last person she wished to encounter there, let alone speak with.

He didn't immediately answer. His still-confounded gaze raked over her again, this time comprehensively, taking in her ungloved hands with their ink-stained fingers and the severe plainness of her slate-colored day dress, specifically selected to conceal the smudges she invariably picked up while moving about the workshop.

He stirred and prowled closer.

Her senses skittered and leapt; that stalking walk was infinitely more predatory, more powerfully impactful than before. Locking her eyes on his, she fought to ensure not a whit of her instinctive reaction showed.

Four measured steps, and he halted directly before her. He searched her eyes. "I'm looking for I. Molyneaux, the owner of *The London Crier*. Or failing him, the editor."

You've found them both.

His nearness was sending distracting frissons of sensation up and down her spine. She frowned and eased back a step. "Why?"

His amber eyes narrowed to shards, and he took another step.

Instinctively, she backed away, then caught herself, locked her spine poker straight, and halting squarely in the doorway, raised her chin and narrowed her eyes warningly.

He halted mere inches away and peered around her, surveying the office, and she realized she was holding her breath.

She knew what he would see—to his left, before the window, twin armchairs flanking an occasional table, then opposite the door, the book-shelves packed to bursting with a jumble of volumes, and to his right, the large desk, its surface strewn with articles and layout sheets illuminated by two banker's lamps, and most notably, the chair behind the desk and the two armchairs before it, all empty.

Weighted with increasing suspicion, his gaze returned to her face.

Lips compressed, she met his gaze.

He searched her eyes. "I. Molyneaux. That *I* wouldn't happen to stand for Isadora, would it?"

She held her nerve and his gaze and, as coldly as she could, responded, "What is your business with *The London Crier*?"

He scanned her face, then his tone flat and faintly menacing, said, "*The Crier* has recently commenced touting an exposé that...greatly concerns me."

She did her own searching. "Why would that—"

"Concern me?" He studied her eyes, and his incipient glare faded to a puzzled frown. "Obviously, I don't appreciate having my—"

Comprehension struck; he saw it leap in her eyes, saw dawning realization lighten her expression, and belatedly pressed his lips shut.

She nearly laughed; she didn't need further confirmation. Unable to conceal her mirth, she grinned. "Really? *You* have just returned from abroad and are as rich as Golden Ball, too?"

"Too?" He dropped all pretense, letting his aggravation show, along with his confusion. "Who else…?"

His face wasn't all that easy to read, but she'd once studied his expressions avidly, and that long-ago knowledge stood her in good stead; she knew he'd accepted that he'd irretrievably given himself away and also that he at least suspected who the intended target of her exposé was.

His gaze locked with hers. "Who is *The Crier's* supposed Golden Ball?"

"Ah, now—that would be telling. Buy the next few months' editions, and you'll find out, along with the rest of the ton."

"Izzy—"

The sound of her nickname, falling from his lips in that half-pleading, half-threatening way, sent her whirling about and walking purposefully to her desk and around it. She gathered her skirts, sat in her chair, and waved him to one of the chairs facing her.

While he subsided into it with the graceful elegance he'd always possessed, she reminded herself to be careful in how she dealt with him. He could make life exceedingly difficult for her, her family, and all at *The Crier*. With little effort, he could destroy all she'd worked to establish and build since they'd last met.

As for their past association, that was water long under the bridge— and all the way out to sea.

She folded her hands on her blotter, met his gaze as it returned to her face, and succinctly stated, "Suffice it to say that the gentleman referred to isn't you."

His amber gaze roamed her face. "How many 'scions of noble houses'—ducal houses, no less—have returned from 'far-flung lands' recently, much less as wealthy as Croesus?"

"Apparently, there are at least two."

"Indeed, and I know them both."

Gray hung onto his temper, admittedly one of the lesser emotions feeding the unprecedented tumult churning through him. "Permit me to assure you that neither of us will be delighted should *The Crier* proceed to wave our wealth like a red flag, alerting all society and bringing every matchmaker, trickster, and chancer in town down on our heads."

"I daresay not," she coolly replied. "Equally, there are those who would maintain that society has a right to know the status of those the hostesses welcome, and not least among that group are the hostesses themselves."

"Not to mention the matchmakers, although admittedly, they're often one and the same."

"Indeed."

Her serenity pricked his temper, but he bit back the words that leapt to his tongue; given their past, mentioning mercenary, husband-hunting females would assuredly cut too close to her bone, and from the awareness in her emerald eyes, she was half expecting him to attack on that front.

He shifted his gaze from those mesmerizing eyes to the wall behind her, which was covered with framed copies of *The Crier's* past front pages.

If he'd been clear-headed enough to formulate a strategy to undermine her and *The Crier's* intentions, he might, indeed, have used their past, but he was still inwardly reeling, buffeted by a maelstrom of roiling emotions evoked purely by seeing her again.

Hearing her voice, drinking in her features.

He'd had no idea the mere sight of her would affect him to such a degree, as if his mind and his senses were wholly immersed in discerning and absorbing every little detail, every change and nuance about her.

It struck him that he *yearned* for her more avidly and in myriad more ways than he had all those years ago.

He literally felt giddy as memory sucked him back to the last time he'd seen her. He'd been younger, naive, so eager and full of love, and she had been, too—or so he'd thought. Yet the very next day, he'd overheard her talking with her mother and her aunt about how many pounds he would have per annum, and her aunt had instructed her to bring him up to the mark in short order. He could still hear Izzy's voice as she'd blandly agreed. He'd been in her house, standing in the corridor outside the open drawing room door, and in that moment, something inside him had irretrievably smashed to smithereens.

He'd turned on his heel and walked away. Without a word; he'd never felt he'd owed her an explanation.

That had happened nearly ten years ago. They hadn't set eyes on each other since.

He told himself it was the shock of meeting her in a place and in a context he could never have foreseen that had pitched him so far off balance.

He knew she was waiting, using the moments to study him. In an effort to spur his wits into action, he pretended to scan the room, using the moment to draw in a breath. Then he surrendered to impulse and met her guarded gaze. "I still can't believe I'm having this discussion with you." He waved his hand about the office. "What on earth are you doing here, Izzy?"

When she didn't reply, he borrowed some of her calm and silently waited while she debated what to tell him; although her poker face had always been good, when arguing with herself, she had a habit of catching the inside of her lower lip between her teeth.

Eventually, she released her lip and raised her chin to an indomitable angle. "If you must know, I am, indeed, I. Molyneaux."

Izzy saw Gray's frown return, then his gaze fell to her left hand—to the plain gold band that adorned her ring finger—and she inwardly blessed her mother and their maid, Joyner, for insisting she always wear the ring when in her guise of Mrs. Molyneaux.

His frown darkened. "You're married?"

His almost-accusatory tone flicked her on the raw. "What did you expect when you vanished as you did?"

Her flash of fury momentarily rocked him.

Seizing the chance to avoid his question, she continued, "Where did you take off to, Gray? The East? Or was it America? I eventually heard that you were believed to be somewhere in America, although no one had any certain information."

His gaze rested heavily on her. "Those who needed to know knew where I was."

Clearly, the silly female who'd believed they'd reached an under-standing and that she stood on the cusp of entertaining a proposal of marriage hadn't been among that number, but instead, had deserved to be left in complete ignorance of his change of heart and mind.

It took effort to rein in her temper, but she managed and coldly responded, "I see."

The hurt and pain she'd buried all those years ago started to rise, and determinedly—desperately—she shoved it back down, deep, where neither he nor anyone else could ever see it.

She drew in a steadying breath; she couldn't afford to indulge in emotional catharsis no matter how good telling him what she thought of him might feel. Besides, she was past all that—over him entirely—and with him sitting before her, potentially poised to wreak havoc on her life, she needed to keep her wits about her.

There was no sense revisiting their past. No sense remembering that while her elders—her aunt in particular—had approached the matter of her prospective husband in a calculating and mercenary way, she had steadfastly refused to do anything other than follow her heart, and when she'd met Grayson Child and lost her heart to him, nothing had mattered more to her than following what she'd believed had been her fated path into marriage with him. Given her family's need at the time, that he'd been wealthy had seemed like Fate's blessing.

Then he'd vanished.

Just vanished.

Leaving her bereft and without a heart to gift to anyone else.

She wasn't going to say another word, wasn't going to allow her anger and her hurt to tempt her into any further revelation. Her gaze steady on his face, she waited.

He waited, too, but eventually, his features hardened. They were significantly more spare, more chiseled and austere, as if the years had pared all softness from him.

He glanced at the doorway. "Where's Molyneaux, then?" He returned his gaze to her face. "Or is this somehow wholly your province?"

She allowed a slight smile to curve her lips. "I'm"—*masquerading as*—"a widow."

Gray had thought he'd got his emotions corralled, but his instant and intemperate response to that knocked him sideways again. Predatory eagerness shot through him—a widow being fair game—but in the next heartbeat, that was drowned beneath welling concern that, as a widow, she was facing life alone.

Normally, he was even-tempered, in control, and completely sure of himself; being battered by such countervailing compulsions was unnerving.

Shoving aside the contradictory impulses, he managed a bald "I see." Not that he did, but he needed to refocus on what he'd come there to achieve. "In that case, my business here is, indeed, with you." He met her emerald gaze. "I'm here to demand you cease and desist with your current exposé."

He watched her face for some hint of reaction—in vain.

Her gaze level, her tone measured, she informed him, "As I've already told you, *The Crier's* upcoming exposé has nothing whatsoever to do with you."

He held her gaze. "If your new Golden Ball is Martin Cynster, then your exposé is most definitely of concern to me."

A faint frown in her eyes was the only sign that he'd guessed correctly.

Feeling on surer ground, he smiled, all teeth. "We're friends."

"Of course you are." She lightly tapped the blotter with a fingernail, a gesture he recalled as indicating she was thinking rapidly. Her gaze remained on his face; he had no idea what she hoped to read there. "Regardless," she said, "as the exposé doesn't concern you personally, then—"

"Do you seriously want to bring down the wrath of the Cynsters on your enterprise?" He arched his brows high. "They might not yet have noticed your pending exposé, but soon enough, one of them will, and they'll realize who your target is, and then you'll face far more pressure than an evening visit from me."

To his surprise, she appeared unmoved. "Actually, I'm willing to wager the Cynster ladies have already noted the upcoming exposé. They all take *The Crier*, you know."

That was said with a certain pride. And *of course*, the Cynster grandes dames would pore over *The Crier*. Virtually all were active ton hostesses, and not a one was above playing matrimonial games.

"My information," Izzy went on, "is that they are, at present, blissfully unaware that their prodigal son is anywhere near as wealthy as he is. He's kept the extent of his fortune a close secret." Her gaze refixed on him. "As have you."

"Indeed, and perhaps you should dwell on why that might be."

"To keep yourselves off the matchmakers' most-eligible lists?"

"Business."

She frowned. After a moment of regarding him, she invited, "How so?"

He was happy to enlighten her. "Martin and I are carefully— cautiously—investing the wealth each of us, independently, brought back to this country." He paused, marshaling his thoughts, then went on, "In making business investments and, even more, acquisitions, having the other side know you're sitting on a veritable pile of gold is not helpful. Instead of being reasonable and naming a price that has some relation to the asset's value, any business owner or company chairman is going to push for an exorbitant sum, and far from negotiating down to something sensible, they'll stick to that high price or even seek to inflate it further."

Presumably through owning the printing works, she'd gained some degree of business acumen; from her expression, she understood the scenario he was describing.

"And that's just the legitimate businesses Martin and I might be interested in. If you imagine matchmakers are the worst we have to fear, then you have no idea of the avariciousness of the men who seek to part those with great and unexpected good fortune from their money." Candidly, he added, "I would rather face the ton's matchmakers en masse than have to wade through the importunities of every last shyster in Britain. And if such men gain an inkling of the wealth Martin and I possess, they'll descend on us like locusts."

She held his gaze for a long moment, then grimaced. She searched his face, seeking he knew not what, but from the quality of her frown and the fact she was biting the inside of her lower lip, he assumed she was debating whether or not to believe him.

Eventually, she asked, "Is it truly that bad? Or are you painting a dramatic picture in an attempt to sway me?"

Her suspicion—more, her lingering distrust—brought a hard and unyielding emotion to the fore. Obeying the promptings of his inner demons, he stated, "If I was at all inclined to indulge in drama, then all those years ago, when I overheard you, your mother, and your aunt assessing my suitability as a husband in terms of pounds per annum, instead of turning around and quietly leaving the house, I would have stormed into the drawing room and told you what I thought of young ladies who valued a man purely on the basis of his wealth."

Long before he got to the last word, her eyes—her whole expression —had filled with a creeping horror that, he suddenly realized, he didn't understand. She made no attempt to deny his description. How could she? It was the truth, and they both knew it, yet she'd paled until her complexion resembled alabaster, and the shock and dismay in her eyes were entirely genuine.

He searched the deep pools of her emerald eyes, drowning in distress, and once again felt shoved off balance.

Some part of him had wanted the truth of their past stated and clear between them. He couldn't comprehend why him describing an event she knew in every detail had so shaken her.

In an attempt to regroup, he forced himself to evenly state, "As you're aware, I didn't react in any histrionic manner then, and neither am I being overly dramatic in describing how much damage having Martin's and my wealth broadcast to all and sundry will cause—how much of a threat the exposé you propose to run poses to our respective futures."

Her expression had shuttered; he could no longer glean any hint of what she was thinking, not even in her usually expressive eyes, which now seemed dull and opaque.

When she remained silent, he hardened his tone to one he used in tense business negotiations. "You owe me, Izzy, and I'm calling in the debt. Halt your exposé. It hasn't gone too far yet."

She stared at him. He wasn't even sure she was seeing him and not some ghost from the past, then she breathed in and shook her shoulders slightly, as if throwing off the shackles of memory. Her gaze refocused on his face, then she winced. "It's not that simple. I can't just"—she gestured —"cancel the exposé. If I do, I'll never be able to use the ploy to generate interest, drive distribution, and boost sales again. And we—*The Crier*— can't afford that. Our advertisers would leave in droves."

"Be that as it may—"

"The only way around it would be if I could find something even more compelling to report."

He studied her. "A scandal?"

She shook her head impatiently. "We don't do scandals or, at least, not the sort you're thinking of. Whatever it is needs to be more fascinating and engrossing than that. Something that would enthrall your mother and sister-in-law yet still be an incident they could freely share at an at-home."

He arched his brows. "What about something royal? They always seem to be gossiping about them."

She met his eyes. "I shouldn't invite the wrath of the Cynsters, but instead, you suggest I invite the ire of the palace?"

"Victoria and Albert and their brood aren't the only royals about."

She tipped her head consideringly. "True." After a moment, she looked at him. "Do you know of anything I can use in place of the exposé?"

He frowned. "Not off the top of my head, but surely we can find something." He met her gaze. "How long do we have before your next issue?"

"I would need the copy by Wednesday at the latest."

She still looked troubled—worried and concerned—and he felt an absurd yet impossible-to-deny impulse to help, to wipe the evidence of underlying anxiety from her features.

Features he remembered as being so wonderfully full of life and love—

He shifted, and she looked up, then glanced at the clock on the bookshelf to her right. He followed her gaze and saw it was a minute before six o'clock.

"Good Lord!" She pushed back her chair and rose, bringing him to his feet. "It's late."

She bent and rummaged in a drawer, then straightened, a black reticule in her hand. She rounded the desk, crossed the office to the hat stand beside the still-open door, and reached for her coat. "I need to get home."

Why? Do you have children waiting for you there?

Automatically, he'd followed her. He took the coat from her hands and held it for her.

She shot him a wary look before thrusting her arms into the sleeves. After settling the coat and looping the reticule's strings over her wrist, she lifted down a plain silk bonnet, put it on, and swiftly tied the wide ribbons.

He watched as she returned to her desk and turned off both lamps.

He had no idea why, but instinct prodded, and as she walked back to where he waited by the doorway, he asked, "Why don't we see what we can drum up together to replace the exposé? I can ask around the clubs and see what I turn up."

Briefly, Izzy met his eyes; she was still reeling in the aftermath of his revelations. But he was offering an olive branch and a way to end this encounter. She nodded. "All right. I'll be here tomorrow—we open for the half day."

She needed to get away from him, needed time to work through what he'd said and decide what it meant.

She waved him through the doorway ahead of her, then followed and drew the office door shut. As she always did, she looked down the length of the darkened workshop toward the rear door, then stepped past the end of the long counter to scan the area—her fiefdom—one last time.

He came up beside her. "Is that the printing press?"

His gaze was fixed on the metalwork monstrosity that was *The Crier's* pride and joy and principal source of income. "Yes. It's steam driven." She looked deeper into the workshop, toward the boiler that powered the belt that ran the press. "We don't just print *The Crier.* We produce lots of booklets and pamphlets for the scholars at the university and for the museums and other institutions."

"I wondered if that was why *The Crier's* offices were located here."

"Indeed. We have relationships that Fleet Street doesn't." She scanned the area one last time and noticed the sign on the darkroom door was set to Occupied.

"Damn! Quimby's still here." She set off across the dimly lit floor.

"Quimby?" Gray's long strides quickly caught up with hers.

"Our photographer." She pointed to the yellow-lettered sign. "That means he's in there, fussing with his photographs."

Separated from the rear wall of her office by a space half the workshop's length, the darkroom had originally been the nearer of two offices nestled in the rear corner of the workshop. The other old office, located between the darkroom and the workshop's rear wall, was used for storage.

She halted before the darkroom door and rapped sharply. "Quimby?"

She waited, but heard nothing—certainly not the grumpy roar she'd expected. She frowned. "That's odd."

Gray reached past her and thumped a fist rather more forcefully on the solid wooden panel.

"Quimby!" she called, exasperation and command in her tone.

Silence answered.

"The room's not that large, and while he's an irascible old coot, he's not deaf." She reached for the doorknob and rattled it vigorously. "Quimby!"

Even she heard the rising anxiety in her voice.

When nothing happened, she bit her lip and glanced at Gray. "Usually, the threat of anyone walking in brings him roaring to the door."

Gray didn't need better light to see the apprehension in her face. Apparently, Quimby was old enough for her to fear he'd had a seizure and collapsed. Feeling slightly grim himself, he nudged her sideways, gripped the knob and turned it, then slowly pushed the door open.

Nothing happened. He stepped into the strange dimness created by a low-level, red-shielded lamp. He halted and, while his eyes adjusted, scanned the area. Filing cabinets lined the wall to his left, with a large, white enamel sink in the far corner. A high, narrow table ran down the middle of the room, and a raised bench stood along the right side.

Scattered along the bench was a conglomeration of photographic implements and supplies, including numerous trays, bottles, and jugs, and there was an untidy pile of glass plates strewn on the central table. The plates looked to be the treated glass photographers used to capture their images. Gray estimated over fifty or more plates lay haphazardly discarded in the pile.

What he failed to see was any man who might be Quimby. "There's no one here. Perhaps your Quimby simply forgot to reset the sign when he left."

Crowding close, Izzy peered around him. "That would be even more odd. Quimby's a stickler about using that sign."

Her hands splayed on his back and tentatively pushed.

He stepped to the right, allowing her into the room.

She paused beside him, scanning as he had, then she gasped. "Great heavens!" She rushed to the table and the pile of glass plates.

"Oh no!" She reached out to touch one, but stopped before she did. "His daguerreotype plates!" She leaned closer, squinting at the plates. "Good Lord—they're all scratched and ruined!"

She looked at Gray, then glanced around wildly. "What on earth happened?"

Her gaze snagged on several partially open cabinet drawers. "Why would he—"

Her voice suspended.

Moving down the other side of the table, Gray glanced at her.

She was staring at the space before the sink. Even in the poor light, her face was deathly pale, and a mask of horror had overlaid her features.

"Oh, my God!" She rushed forward. "Quimby!"

Gray swore beneath his breath and strode along the narrow table. He rounded the end to see Izzy crouched beside the slumped form of an older man in a dun-colored dustcoat, presumably Quimby. The photographer appeared to have staggered back against the wall, then slid down to a sitting position with his legs half stretched before him.

"Quimby? Can you hear me?" Izzy lightly patted one of Quimby's cheeks.

His head lolled forward.

"Here! Let me help you up." She lowered her hands to Quimby's sides, then froze.

She drew back her right hand and stared at the palm. Her expression stunned and stricken, she looked at Gray and held up her bloodied palm. She swallowed. "He's been stabbed." Dragging in a shaky breath, she looked back at Quimby. "I think he's dead."

Gray stepped around the photographer's legs, bent, and gently gripped Izzy's shoulders. He drew her upright, then eased her aside. "Let me look."

Once he was certain she was steady on her feet, he released her and crouched before the fallen man.

Even in the weak red light, it was plain the fellow was beyond mortal help. Nevertheless, Gray checked, but there was no pulse to be found. As far as he could tell, Quimby had been stabbed very close to the heart. Just one blow. But what made the hairs on Gray's nape rise was that the body was still warm, the blood still sluggishly oozing, only just turning sticky.

He rose and drew in a deeper breath. The photographer had been killed while Gray and Izzy had been in the office.

What if I hadn't been here? Izzy would have been alone...

Thrusting aside the thought, he turned to her, taking in her stricken expression and stunned, helpless eyes. He was shocked, too, but he'd seen death—even violent death—before and in much uglier circumstances.

He stepped across, blocking her view of the body, and urged her toward the darkroom door.

She made an incoherent sound and tried to turn back to the dead man, but inexorably, Gray steered her on. "Yes, he's dead. We need to summon the police."

CHAPTER 2

*A*fter relighting the lamps on her desk, Gray settled her in the armchair he'd previously occupied. When she stared mutely at her bloody palm, he fished out his handkerchief. "Here. Wipe it with this."

With a wooden nod, she took the linen square.

He recognized shock when he saw it. He didn't want to leave her, but the police had to be informed. "Where are your keys?"

She blinked up at him.

"I want to lock you safely inside while I go and fetch the police."

Without a word, she hunted in her reticule, drew out a set of keys, and handed them over.

Suppressing his concern—meek wasn't a label he'd ever thought of applying to her—he quit *The Crier's* offices, locked the door, and strode quickly to Bernard Street. With no convenient policeman in sight, he walked the short distance to Woburn Place. The major thoroughfare still buzzed with evening traffic, and as he'd hoped, a bobby was idly pacing its pavement.

Gray hailed the fellow and, in a few short sentences, explained that a man had been found dead, stabbed, in the offices of *The Crier* on Woburn Mews and unblushingly used his title to demand the attendance of an inspector from Scotland Yard.

Having been back in the country for only three months, he wasn't sure how the police force currently operated, but the bobby accepted his demand for a denizen of Scotland Yard without argument.

The excited constable left hotfoot to report to his local station, and Gray returned to *The Crier's* offices.

He arrived to find Izzy sitting exactly as he'd left her, staring down at her now mostly clean palm, his stained handkerchief crumpled in her other fist. She hadn't even looked up at the jingling of the bell above the door. He'd hoped she would have eased out of her shock; seeing her as she was bothered him on some fundamental level.

He walked into the office and halted beside her, but she didn't lift her head. Reaching down, he eased the stained linen from her fingers, then tucked the crumpled ball into his greatcoat pocket.

"Thank you," she murmured.

The response was automatic—ingrained good manners.

He thought, then asked, "Is there somewhere the staff make tea?"

Strong tea was the standard prescription for ladies under stress.

She raised her gaze to his face, then waved vaguely toward the workshop's rear. "Go past this side of the press, all the way back to the rear wall. There's a bench, a sink, a small stove, and tea things there."

He returned to the foyer, turned up the lamp on the counter to full, then went hunting and discovered all he needed. He filled the tin kettle, boiled the water, then poured it into the plain brown teapot, over a large quantity of leaves.

While he waited for the tea to steep, he looked around. To his right, close to the water supply, was the coal-fed boiler that generated the steam that apparently drove a wide belt connected to the printing press.

He glanced the other way and noticed a door set into the rear wall, not far from the open doorway of what was plainly a storage room. On impulse, he wandered across and tried the door. It opened easily and silently.

Stunned, he looked out across a narrow lane. He stepped into the doorway and glanced about; he could see up and down the lane, to Bernard Street at the southern end and to some other street to the north.

He closed the door and stared at the handle. After a moment, lips compressed, he returned to the tea, poured a cup, then hunted and found a canister of sugar and a bottle with milk still fresh enough to drink and doctored the cup. Milky and sweet was recommended for shock.

He noticed a clean rag and dampened it with warm water, then carried the cup and rag to the office.

"Here." He offered Izzy the cup. "Drink up—it'll make you feel better."

She accepted the cup and saucer and took a tentative sip, then a bigger one. "Thank you." Her voice was low and hoarse, as if she were holding herself together via sheer will alone.

He was cravenly grateful she was making the effort; emotional females—especially those of his class—made him nervous.

He reached for the other armchair, angled it beside hers, and sat. "Give me your hand." Judging by the way she held the saucer, the sensation of dried blood on her skin was bothering her.

She balanced the cup and saucer on the chair's arm and extended her hand, delicate and pale with the long, slender fingers he remembered.

Cradling her hand, palm up, in his left hand, he ignored the sensation of her skin against his and gently wiped the last traces of blood from her palm and fingers.

There was a spot of blood on the very edge of her coat sleeve. Deciding that her maid would know better than he how to remove it, he left the spot untouched.

Once he was satisfied her skin was clean, he straightened and released her hand, unnerved to discover that he had to force himself to do so.

She cleared her throat, whispered, "Thank you," and resumed sipping her tea.

He rose, took the pink-stained rag back to the sink, rinsed it clean, and returned to the office, wondering when the police would arrive.

He settled in the armchair beside her. She'd unbuttoned her coat; he hoped she was recovering her customary poise. He glanced at her face and was unsurprised to see a frown haunting her eyes. "I checked the rear door and found it open. Should it have been locked?"

She grimaced. "Quimby has—had—a key to that door and usually came in that way. He didn't work regular hours. He traveled about the city, searching out scenes to photograph for *The Crier* and his other clients. Neither I nor the staff could be sure when he would be here, hence the absolute adherence to the darkroom sign. If it was set to Occupied, he was in there, working. As for the rear door, he was supposed to lock it if he was the only one still working, but I suspect he often didn't."

"*Other* clients. So Quimby wasn't an employee solely of *The Crier*?"

"He wasn't an employee at all. He and I had an arrangement. He needed a darkroom and didn't have one, and *The Crier* had one, but no photographer. So we struck a deal—Quimby got unfettered use of our dark-room in return for supplying three photographs of scenes about London for us to run in each week's edition." She paused, then added, "He provided his own supplies and stored most of his equipment and what have you here."

A hammering on the front door made her jerk.

She set her empty cup on the desk, and he rose. "I'll see who it is."

He strode across the foyer, opened the door, and hurriedly stepped back as three constables barreled in.

"Where is it?" the first belligerently demanded. With a ruddy face and thinning greasy hair, he appeared to be the oldest, carrying a paunch and the attitude of being in charge.

He looked around wildly, then swung to Gray. "The dead body!" he barked. Then he actually looked at whom he was confronting, swallowed, and more temperately added, "Sir."

With the faintest of cold smiles, Gray replied, "It's 'my lord.'" He rarely used his title, but in such circumstances... "And you are?"

The man stiffened into a semblance of attention. "Senior Constable Perkins, m'lord, from the Guildford Street watchhouse."

"I specifically asked that an inspector from Scotland Yard be summoned."

Perkins and his compatriots nodded.

"Indeed, my lord," one of the others responded. "A message has been dispatched."

"But see, we can't tell how long it might be before an inspector gets here." Perkins thrust out his chest. "So we're here to see what's what."

Perkins's gaze deflected toward the office. Gray glanced that way and saw Izzy standing in the doorway, pale as a ghost and all but wringing her hands.

"In that case," Gray stated, "you'll find the dead photographer in the darkroom."

All three constables peered uncertainly down the long workshop.

Surreptitiously, Gray signaled to Izzy to retreat into the office, then stepped forward. "Come—I'll show you."

The three started to follow, then Perkins paused and hissed at one of his juniors, "Stay by the door and make sure no one leaves."

By "no one," Perkins meant Izzy. Gray wondered how difficult the man was going to be.

Gray picked up the lamp on the end of the counter and, raising it, carried it with him, dispelling the shadows as he led Perkins and his remaining junior to the darkroom door.

Nearing the door, he pointed to the Occupied sign. "That was what attracted our attention as we were about to leave for the day. It indicated that Mr. Quimby, the photographer, was inside. We knocked and called, and when we couldn't raise him, we went in and found him dead."

Gray halted before the darkroom door. "The only light in there is from a special red-shielded lamp. If you like, I'll hold this lamp in the doorway so you can more easily see."

Perkins nodded agreement, and Gray stepped to the side. Perkins opened the door and stared into the room.

Gray held the lamp high and waited.

He'd expected both constables to go inside and look around, but after staring at the dead man for a full minute, Perkins huffed and backed away. "He looks dead as dead."

"He is," Gray confirmed. "I checked. He's definitely dead."

"Well, then." Perkins retreated another step. Distinctly pale, he gave a jerky nod and turned away. "Nothing we can do until the inspector gets here. Best leave the scene undisturbed."

Relieved, Gray closed the darkroom door and trailed the two constables back to the foyer.

"Right, then." Perkins tugged his belt higher on his paunch. He'd recovered his color along with his attitude. "Until Scotland Yard get here, I'm in charge. So"—he turned his beady eyes on Gray—"if you would, sir—my lord—who was it found the body?"

"Mrs. Molyneaux and myself. We were about to leave when Mrs. Molyneaux noticed the Occupied sign on the darkroom door, and we went to check on Quimby."

"Well, then, sir—my lord." Perkins looked toward the office. "Perhaps we'd better join the lady and get the formalities out of the way."

Gray inclined his head in acquiescence and led the way.

Izzy had returned to the armchair, and he sat in the chair alongside her.

Instead of fetching a chair for himself, with his feet planted wide, Perkins took up an aggressive stance before them and dragged a dog-eared notebook from his pocket. He licked his finger and turned several pages, then pulled out a pencil and fixed his gimlet gaze on Gray. "Right, then, my lord. And you are?"

It seemed that, knowing he would be relegated to less exciting duties the instant the Scotland Yard inspector arrived, Perkins was intent on stealing whatever limelight was to be had before his more exalted colleague arrived.

Unimpressed, Gray replied, "My name is Lord Grayson Child. My father is the Duke of Ancaster."

Perkins's pencil stalled on the second piece of information, but then he scribbled something down and, eyes narrowing, shifted his gaze to Izzy.

"And this," Gray smoothly continued, "is Mrs. I. Molyneaux, proprietor of *The London Crier*."

"Heh?" Perkins looked confused. "You...own this place, ma'am?"

Izzy nodded. "I do."

Perkins's gaze darted between Gray and Izzy; Gray suspected the man was leaping to unwarranted if predictable conclusions. Faced with Gray's impassive stare, Perkins cleared his throat and consulted his notebook. "And when did you arrive here, my lord?"

"At a minute or so after five o'clock. I heard the bells tolling as I approached and saw a group of staff leaving. I arrived and met with Mrs. Molyneaux in this office."

Gray felt Izzy's gaze on the side of his face. She'd picked up his selective retelling and was wondering at his reasons.

"So"—Perkins continued scribbling—"you came in at five. Was anyone else here?"

Gray replayed what he remembered of those moments in the foyer, but his attention had been locked exclusively on Izzy. "I honestly can't say if anyone was lingering in the workshop. The lamp out there was turned low. I turned it up later, while we were waiting for the police to arrive. Mrs. Molyneaux came to the office doorway, greeted me, and we came in here and sat." Gray waved at the desk. "We had business to discuss."

From the corner of his eye, Gray saw Izzy glance at the papers on her desk. She still appeared dazed, very far from her usual, rapier-witted self. Protectiveness welled, too definite and determined for him to quell.

Perkins directed a piggy-eyed, almost-malevolent look Izzy's way. "Right, then, Mrs. Molyneaux." Perkins stumbled over the pronunciation. "Your husband about?"

Izzy raised her gaze to Perkins's face and baldly stated, "I'm a widow."

"Ah—I see." Perkins's tone suggested he saw something else entirely.

"And you manage the newspaper?" Incredulity rang in his tone. He might as well have sneered *Pull the other one.*

"I *own* the paper, Constable." A touch of steel had crept into her tone. Gray was relieved to see her emerald gaze sharpen on the hapless Perkins.

"So who manages the place?"

"I do."

Perkins's eyes narrowed to muddy shards. "So it was you hired the photographer chap?"

"I arranged for his services, yes." She opened her lips to say more, then thought better of it. It seemed she'd taken Perkins's measure and didn't like what she saw any more than Gray did.

"His name?" Perkins demanded.

"He is—was—Mr. Horace Quimby."

"And how long's he been working for you?"

"For over two years." She thought, then amended, "Nearly three."

"Address?"

She frowned, then rubbed her forehead—another sign Gray remembered, indicating difficulty recalling something. "He has lodgings not far away…" Her face cleared. "Winchester Street in Pentonville. Number twelve."

Perkins scribbled away. "And he was often here, in that room—the darkroom—at that hour of the evening?"

"He often came in about five o'clock, around the time the others leave. It was his habit to develop the negatives he'd exposed that day and hang them to dry overnight, then come in the next day and see what they looked like and print any he thought were good enough to satisfy me or his other clients."

"Other clients?"

"I don't know them all, but several other newspapers took photographs from Quimby. He was widely known."

"And how did you feel about that, heh?"

Ignoring the suggestion in Perkins's tone, she replied, "Our arrangement wasn't exclusive. He was free to sell photographs to whomever he chose, as long as *The Crier* had the rights to publish the three photographs we include in each edition."

Perkins didn't bother writing that down. "Did you know he would be in today?"

"No, but that wasn't unusual. He doesn't—didn't—come by the office.

He had a key to the rear door and always came in that way and went straight to the darkroom, shut himself in, and got to work." She blinked several times, as if using the past tense had brought Quimby's passing home.

"So how did you and his lordship here come to go into the darkroom and find him?"

"As I said, when he came in late in the day, he developed his negatives and left them to dry. That normally took him about half an hour, and he would leave as he'd come in—via the rear door. But it was six o'clock when we"—she tipped her head Gray's way—"started to leave, and I saw the darkroom sign still said Occupied. That meant Quimby was still in there. That seemed odd—he wouldn't normally have been there so late—and I went to check if everything was all right."

Silence fell as Perkins labored over his notes, then he raised his head and looked with open suspicion at Izzy before shifting his gaze to Gray. "When you arrived, your lordship, was Mr. Quimby already on the premises?"

"I don't know. As I said, when I arrived, the lamp in the workshop was turned very low, and I didn't know about the darkroom. I'm afraid I didn't look that deeply into the shadows."

Perkins's gaze returned to Izzy, and he eyed her aggressively. "So, Mrs. Molyneaux"—Perkins continued having trouble wrapping his tongue around the name—"before his lordship arrived, you were here with Mr. Quimby."

Izzy blinked. "I really can't say, Constable. I have no idea when Mr. Quimby arrived. For all I know, it might have been after his lordship came in."

"Ah, but it could have been before!" Perkins all but pounced. Leaning closer, with a certain relish, he declared, "Quimby could have been working away in that darkroom—just like you said—and you could have gone in and killed him. Stabbed him to death before coming back out to your office for your meeting with his lordship."

"What?" Izzy looked at Perkins as if he were demented. "No! Why on earth would I kill Quimby? I need his photographs for *The Crier*. We don't have another photographer we can call on, and our readers expect their photographs."

Straightening, Perkins bounced on his feet. "Maybe so, maybe so, but perhaps Quimby learned something about you. A widow owning and running a business like this, you have to have secrets. Or no! Wait!

Perhaps Quimby was your lover and wanted a piece of the business, and you had to kill him to stop him. Yes, that could be it!"

From the fire flaring in Izzy's eyes, Gray knew she teetered on the brink of losing her quite spectacular temper.

"Constable!" As Gray had intended, the single word, imbued with the authority only centuries of forebears accustomed to absolute rule could confer, hauled Perkins back to earth.

He blinked at Gray.

Gray caught the man's piggy-eyed gaze. "That is enough. I suggest we wait for the inspector from Scotland Yard before you attempt to further prosecute such a fanciful fiction."

Izzy drew breath and, with a valiant effort, reined in her temper. "Such a *nonsensical* fiction. I most definitely did not murder Mr. Quimby." She shut her lips and glared haughtily at Perkins.

A fraught silence descended, and she felt as if, finally, her mind had cleared enough to think. Perkins was the sort who would be only too happy to arrest her for Quimby's murder, even in the teeth of contradictory evidence. He patently felt that her owning *The Crier* was an indication of malfeasance, and was predisposed to concoct and pursue the wildest suggestions implicating her.

Eyeing Perkins irefully, she hoped the inspector from Scotland Yard proved to be more rational.

Perkins didn't know what to do with himself. He drifted closer to the door, then the framed front pages on the wall behind the desk caught his eye.

Izzy relaxed a touch, and her awareness of Gray, seated beside her, rose in her mind. Whether intentionally or otherwise, he was exuding a comforting aura of calmness and power.

She glanced his way and discovered him waiting to catch her eyes. She searched his amber gaze, drawing strength from the warmth therein, and fractionally inclined her head in thanks. He'd known she'd been about to lose her temper, which was the last thing she needed to do.

Indeed, the more her thoughts settled, the clearer it became that she would need to be exceedingly careful over what she revealed during the next hours. She couldn't afford to have her true identity exposed, especially not in relation to murder.

Not five minutes later, the bell above the door tinkled, heralding the arrival of a burly man of average height, followed by a tall, lanky, rail-thin individual. The pair entered, and the thin man closed the door, then both men stood stock-still and, with a professional air, surveyed the scene.

Perkins came alert. He shot a glance at Izzy and Gray, then with a muttered "Stay here, if you please," went to stand in the office doorway.

When the newcomers' gazes reached him, Perkins snapped to attention. "Sir! Senior Constable Perkins from Guildford Street, sir. I've taken charge of the scene pending your arrival, sir."

Looking past Perkins, Izzy saw the burly man, who possessed a jowly, well-worn face reminiscent of a comfortable bulldog's, nod equably. "Perkins. I'm Inspector Baines, and this"—he indicated the lanky man —"is Sergeant Littlejohn." Baines looked deeper into the workshop. "So what have we here?"

"A photographer, sir, stabbed in his darkroom." Perkins jerked his head toward Izzy and Gray. "Found by this pair here."

"Oh?" Baines glanced past Perkins at Izzy and Gray and offered a polite nod, then returned his sharp gaze to Perkins. "Right, then. Let's see the body. The surgeon will be along shortly—best we get a look in now, before he lays claim."

Perkins waved down the workshop. "Along here, sir." He led the way.

Izzy listened to the heavy footsteps head toward the darkroom.

Gray murmured, "One can only hope Baines has more sense than Perkins."

She grimaced. "Indeed."

They waited in strangely companionable silence.

About five minutes later, the three policemen returned to the foyer and paused there, conferring in low tones, Baines with his hands in his pockets and Littlejohn with a notebook in his hand, judiciously jotting while Baines questioned Perkins, who had his own notebook out and was flicking through the pages as he answered.

The bell over the door tinkled again, and a dapper-looking man carrying a medical bag walked in.

"What-ho, Baines!" The surgeon grinned. "What have you got for me?"

Baines nodded in greeting. "Cromer. A stabbing victim, not long dead." He tipped his head down the workshop. "In a darkroom back there." Baines looked at Perkins. "Senior Constable, you'd best conduct Dr. Cromer to the body and remain with him to render whatever assistance he requires."

Perkins's shoulders sank. He glanced longingly at the office, but obediently murmured, "Yes, sir," and proceeded to usher Cromer to the darkroom.

Baines and Littlejohn watched the pair go, then exchanged a glance—a wordless communication that suggested they'd worked together for years—and turned toward the office.

Baines tapped on the door frame—a meaningless formality, perhaps, but nevertheless, he did—and after meeting both Izzy's and Gray's gazes, walked in.

He halted in the middle of the office, glanced swiftly around, then looked at Izzy and nodded politely before focusing on Gray. "Lord Child?"

Gray inclined his head.

Baines transferred his gaze to Izzy. It was a kind-enough gray gaze, holding none of Perkins's instant suspicions. "Mrs. Molyneaux?"

Izzy copied Gray, and Baines introduced himself and Littlejohn, who, notebook in hand, half bowed. Baines concluded with, "We're from Scotland Yard, sent in response to his lordship's request." Baines's gaze shifted between Izzy and Gray. "I believe the pair of you found the body. Together?"

Gray nodded.

"Indeed," Izzy said.

Baines focused on Izzy. "I understand you own and run the paper, Mrs. Molyneaux. Have you been here all day?"

"Since eight in the morning."

Baines looked faintly surprised. "Is that normal?"

"Yes. It's Friday. For us, that's distribution day, when we send out this week's edition. I'm always here for the entire day, issuing invoices and approving last-minute orders and so on."

"I see." Baines's gaze rested on her. "You're a widow, I hear. How long is it since your husband died, ma'am?"

She had to think quickly, especially with Gray sitting beside her—also plainly interested and knowing something of her past. "Eight years." She raised her chin. "I bought the printing works seven years ago."

Baines glanced at Littlejohn, confirming he was writing down the information. Izzy could only hope that the police didn't think to look for a marriage license or a death certificate for the fictitious Mr. Molyneaux.

"Right." Baines looked back at her. "You own and manage *The London Crier*, and it's produced and printed here." Baines shifted his gaze to Gray. "And you, my lord. What brought you here today?"

Calmly, Gray replied, "I wished to speak with Mrs. Molyneaux concerning a piece she's considering publishing."

Baines's brows faintly rose. "I hear you arrived at five o'clock—a trifle late for a business call, wasn't it?"

Gray's lips curved fractionally. "I preferred my discussion with Mrs. Molyneaux to be conducted in private, Inspector."

Baines nodded. "So you waited until the staff left before coming in?"

"As I approached, the bells tolled for five, and I saw what I took to be most of the staff leaving. I had assumed they would, hence my arrival at that time. The staff were only a matter of yards down the street when I walked in, and before you ask, I have no idea whether Quimby was in the darkroom at that time."

"Had you met Quimby before?" Baines asked.

Gray shook his head. "Aside from Mrs. Molyneaux, I haven't met any of those who work here."

"I see." Baines turned to Izzy. "Did you know Quimby was in the darkroom, Mrs. Molyneaux?"

Izzy shook her head. "As I explained to Constable Perkins, Quimby came and went as he pleased. I wasn't surprised when I saw—or rather, realized because of the Occupied sign—that he'd come in, but I did think it odd that he was still in the darkroom given it was six o'clock. He was usually gone by then."

"Do you often remain here until six o'clock, ma'am?" Littlejohn put in.

"Not often, but sometimes, it's six before I leave."

Gray had been keeping an eye on the foyer. He was keen to learn what the surgeon had found, and just then, the dapper Dr. Cromer reappeared, juggling his black bag while he shrugged on his overcoat. He turned toward the office, while two other men bearing a stretcher with a sheet-covered body upon it went past him, heading for the front door.

Alerted by the footsteps, Baines turned, saw the surgeon, and grunted. "Cromer—what can you tell me?"

Settling his collar, Cromer walked into the office. "Dead as a door-nail, old son. Cause being a sharp blade thrust just above the heart. Double-sided narrow blade—perhaps a dagger of some sort, but definitely narrow."

The bell over the door tinkled faintly as the men ferrying Quimby's body to the morgue departed with their burden.

"How long's he been dead?" Littlejohn was scribbling madly.

Cromer hesitated, and Gray judged it time to volunteer, "When we found him, the body was still warm. Almost normal temperature—barely cooled at all. And the blood was tacky, but not fully congealed."

Cromer's eyes lit with interest. "What time was that? Do you know?"

Gray inwardly smiled. "Right on six o'clock."

Cromer nodded eagerly. "That fits with what I'm thinking." He looked at Baines. "I rarely see bodies so fresh. I'd say this one was killed between five and six for certain, with my inclination as to the exact time being close to the half hour."

Littlejohn paused in his scribbling to throw the surgeon a sharp look. "Could it have happened at five o'clock? Close to? More or less on the hour?" Littlejohn's gaze slid to Izzy; apparently, he—and presumably Baines—had been infected with Perkins's fanciful conjecture.

Cromer frowned, plainly deliberating, but to Gray's relief, the surgeon slowly shook his head. "I really can't see it. Admittedly, the room isn't heated, but neither is it cold enough to delay the signs that much." Cromer thought, then sighed. "Five is really, really stretching it, but that said, I can't definitively rule it out." He threw Baines a sharp look. "But if I were you, I'd want some much better evidence as to the deed being done at that time before I tried to put a case with death at five o'clock before any judge."

Baines grunted.

Before Cromer could turn away, Gray said, "There didn't seem to be that much blood about the body. Would the murderer have been splattered, do you think?"

Cromer's expression declared his delight at being asked intelligent questions. "That's another interesting point. In most cases of stabbing, there's a quantity of blood, usually more than enough to mark the murderer, but with this particular blade and the placement of the wound and the way the body fell, most of the bleeding was internal. It doesn't look as if much leaked out, except on the blade, which I presume the murderer took with him?"

Cromer looked at Baines and Littlejohn inquiringly, and the latter replied, "No one's found the weapon yet."

"Can't say I'm surprised," Cromer said. "If it is a dagger, as I suspect, my money would be on him taking it with him." He nodded to Baines. "You'll have my report on Monday."

Baines raised a hand in acknowledgment, and with an abbreviated bow to Gray and Izzy, Cromer left.

Baines's expression had turned thoughtful. He regarded Gray and Izzy and, as if coming to some decision, asked, "If you have no objection, my lord, Mrs. Molyneaux, would you show me your hands?"

Gray inwardly sighed and extended his. Baines examined them closely, but of course, there was nothing to be seen.

Shifting to stand before Izzy, Baines studied the backs of her slender, delicate hands, then asked her to turn them and scanned the palms. Baines grunted and started to straighten.

Gray was about to release the breath he'd held when Baines froze.

A second later, Baines straightened fully and pointed to the tiny dab of blood on Izzy's cuff. "Care to explain why you have blood on your cuff, ma'am?"

Izzy raised her right arm and calmly examined the tiny spot. "It must have happened when I tried to help Quimby to his feet." She looked at Baines, her expression open and entirely unperturbed. "The light in the darkroom is permanently shuttered with red, and in that light, all I could see was Quimby slumped against the wall. I thought he'd taken ill and collapsed, so I put my hands to his sides to help him up…" Her voice quavered, and she blinked several times.

Baines retreated a step. "I see."

Evenly, Gray stated, "Mrs. Molyneaux had blood on that hand, where she'd tried to grip Quimby's left side, thinking to assist him to his feet. After finding a constable and sending him running for you, I returned here and wiped her hand clean with a cloth—you'll find it in the sink against the rear wall." In case Baines had failed to get his point, he added, "She was in shock at the time."

"Yes, quite." Baines looked at Littlejohn, and a silent communication of some sort passed between the pair, then Baines cleared his throat and glanced at Gray before setting his sights on Izzy. "I can't say I like Perkins's theory, but at the present moment, it's the one that best fits. It seems reasonable to suppose that you, Mrs. Molyneaux, killed Quimby at close to five o'clock, in the few minutes between the departure the rest of the staff and his lordship's arrival."

Gray looked at Izzy and bit back his own protest. She was staring—coldly—at Baines and, in her most haughty, earl's-daughter's voice, inquired, "Inspector Baines, can you explain to me why I—the owner of *The London Crier*—would want to kill the photographer I rely on to provide the photographs that are critical to the success of every edition of my publication?"

Baines shifted uneasily, instinctively reacting to her tone, but although he colored faintly, he persisted, "Perkins has suggested that Quimby had learned some secret and was blackmailing you."

Izzy arched her brows. "Indeed?"

That single word carried enough icy weight to have Baines rushing on, "Perkins is sure that if we look, we'll learn whatever it was. But you must see that, as matters stand, you're the only one who could have killed the man."

Izzy frowned, but before she could respond, Gray calmly said, "I take it Perkins hasn't yet discovered that the back door, which gives access to the rear lane, was unlocked throughout the relevant period."

"What?" Baines scowled and glared at Littlejohn. "What back door?"

Littlejohn looked as annoyed as Baines. "I'll find out."

He left the office. Izzy caught Gray's eye, and they both sat back, apparently relaxing in the armchairs. She resisted the impulse to exhale with relief. Her heart was still thundering.

I can't be taken up for murder!

Minutes later, Littlejohn returned, all but dragging a now-reluctant Perkins.

Grim-faced, Littlejohn nodded at Baines. "A few details Perkins forgot to mention, sir." Littlejohn tipped his head toward Gray. "Like his lordship said, the back door opens to a lane that runs behind this row of buildings, all the way along the block from Bernard Street to Great Coram Street. Seems that door was unlocked the entire time, and Cromer found the key on a ring with others in the deceased's waistcoat pocket."

Baines glared at Perkins, who had the sense to look cowed.

"Right." Baines turned back to Izzy and Gray. After a second of inner debate, Baines bowed to her. "My apologies, Mrs. Molyneaux. Obviously, someone could have come in from the lane—"

"Or," Gray interjected, "Quimby could have brought a friend or acquaintance with him."

Baines looked like he'd just sucked a lemon, but inclined his head and went on, "And whoever killed Quimby could have left by the back door, unseen and undetected, as well."

Izzy was not happy that Perkins was still hovering. Although she didn't look directly at him, she was aware his beady eyes remained locked on her.

Baines drew in a breath, then let it out. "Let's see if we can't get straight in our heads exactly what happened with the pair of you and

Quimby this evening." He looked at Gray. "You said you arrived here at five o'clock?"

Gray nodded. "The bells pealed, and in less than a minute, the door opened, and the staff streamed out. I saw them walk down the street as I approached. They were walking past the third property along when I opened the door."

Baines looked at her, then back at Gray. "Was this an arranged meeting?"

She left it to Gray to say, "No. I wished to discuss an upcoming article with Mrs. Molyneaux and wanted to catch her at a time when we might talk with some degree of privacy. She appeared to be the only one about when I arrived, but if Quimby had been in the darkroom, I wouldn't have noticed."

"If Quimby arrived before the other staff left, they would know." Izzy gestured toward the workshop. "You've seen the place. There's no chance he could have entered via the back door and reached the darkroom without someone noticing him. They all knew him."

Baines focused on her. "Where were you when the staff left?"

She waved at her desk. "Here, reconciling the accounts for the past week."

Baines noted the clutter on her desk. "Right, then. What happened when his lordship came through the front door?"

"Well, the bell tinkled, and from my chair behind the desk"—she tipped her head that way—"I couldn't see who had walked in, so I got up and went to the doorway to find out. I expected to see one of the staff who had forgotten something."

"But instead," Baines said, "it was his lordship."

Izzy's wariness increased, but she nodded. "Indeed."

Baines was looking shrewdly from Gray to her. "But that wasn't the first time you'd met."

A guess, no doubt fed by observation; she and Gray hadn't been acting like complete strangers who had only just met. "His lordship and I are acquainted, but we haven't seen or spoken to each other for..." She glanced at Gray and arched her brows. "It must be close to ten years."

He nodded. "Almost a decade."

Baines glanced at Littlejohn to confirm he was jotting that down, then returned his gaze to her and Gray. "So what happened then?"

"After the usual greetings, we came in here. I sat behind the desk, and

Lord Child sat where I am now, and we discussed the article he'd come to see me about."

Baines glanced toward the workshop. "Did you close the office door?"

Both she and Gray shook their heads. "No," Gray stated. "It remained open throughout the time we were in here."

"I shut it when we left," she said, "but before that, it was as it is now."

"And," Baines continued, "you both remained here, together, until you decided to leave?"

Again, they nodded.

"So what happened when you ended your meeting?" Littlejohn asked.

"I put on my coat and bonnet"—she gestured to the black bonnet sitting on the desk—"then we went out into the foyer. I shut the office door and, as I always do, glanced one last time down the workshop. That was when I noticed the darkroom sign was set to Occupied, and that meant Quimby was in there." She paused, then went on, "Quimby was obsessive about that sign. He never left it up if he wasn't in the darkroom, because he'd drummed it into everyone's head that if the sign *was* up, then he was definitely in there working with his negatives and on no account was anyone to open the door, much less go in." She glanced at both policemen. "If light fell on his negatives at the wrong time, they would be ruined."

Littlejohn grunted. "I've heard about that." He glanced at Baines, then at Perkins, still hovering by the door. "Perkins said you told him Quimby often worked late. So what made you go and check on him if him being there wasn't unusual and he had his own key to the back door?"

She sighed and repeated what she'd earlier told Perkins.

"So," Baines summed up, "Quimby coming in around five wasn't unusual, but him still being here at six was strange?"

She nodded. "Exactly."

"So you went to the darkroom, knocked, but received no answer, and went in together." Baines looked at Gray for confirmation.

"Yes, together," Gray evenly supplied. "I entered first, and Mrs. Molyneaux followed. She went along the left side of the table, stopped to exclaim over the ruined daguerreotype plates, then saw Quimby and rushed to help him. I was on the table's other side, so I was a split second behind her. Quimby was already slumped on the ground before we came in, or I would have seen him straightaway." Gray shrugged. "The rest you know."

Littlejohn glanced up. "That pile of photographic plates—daguerreo-type plates, you called them? All piled up and scratched and—you said—ruined. Was that normal?"

"Not at all." Izzy sat straighter. "I'd forgotten about them. And no—Quimby would never have destroyed his work like that."

Puzzled, Baines studied her. "Are you saying that the killer stabbed Quimby, then hung around and scratched up those plates? Or might they already have been like that when Quimby arrived?"

Izzy felt a phantom chill slide over her nape. "It must be the former." She glanced at Gray. "If Quimby had walked in and found his plates in a pile like that, scratched and wrecked, he would have erupted out of the darkroom, roaring like a lion. But he didn't." She looked at Baines. "The plates couldn't have been like that when Quimby arrived, ergo, the killer must have taken the time to damage them after he killed Quimby."

Baines frowned. "Are those all the...whatever-they're-called plates Quimby had? Or were there others he kept somewhere else?"

She frowned. "I can't say for certain, but all the plates he had here, he kept in those cabinets in the darkroom."

"*In* the darkroom," Littlejohn confirmed.

She nodded.

"And he didn't take any away?" Baines asked.

"Not that I know of. He told me he preferred to store them in the darkroom, and I know for a fact that ours was the only darkroom to which he had access."

Gray stirred; plainly, it was time to do a little more directing. "That the killer took time to destroy Quimby's photographs surely suggests that the motive for his murder might well lie in something Quimby saw and photographed, presumably something the killer didn't want anyone else to see."

"If so," Izzy pointed out, "the killer certainly wouldn't have wanted the photograph printed and distributed in *The Crier* or any of the other papers Quimby supplied."

From his position by the door, Perkins spoke, not quite aggressively yet certainly pointedly. "You'd be the person most likely to know what Quimby photographed. Perhaps you didn't want him to print one, and you and he argued—"

"Constable!" Baines flung Perkins an aggravated look.

Perkins glowered. "Well, it's true."

Izzy regarded Perkins with a contemptuous air. "Actually, your premise is false. I had no idea what Quimby would photograph—that wasn't how he operated. He knew what sorts of scenes we at *The Crier* wanted, and every week, he would take at least three photographs of those sort of scenes—in Hyde Park, along the avenue or the lawns or Rotten Row, along Regent Street or Oxford Street, or St. James's Park, that sort of society picture. I never gave him specific instructions about who or what to photograph, and I seriously doubt any of his other clients did, either."

Baines frowned. "I see."

In the distance, the city's bells tolled for eight o'clock.

Baines glanced at Littlejohn, then looked at Gray and Izzy. "I suggest we leave any further questions for tomorrow. We'll be back in the morning to speak with the staff. We need to find out if they saw Quimby arrive and if they know anything more about him and any enemies he might have had."

Izzy inclined her head, and Gray followed suit. Littlejohn closed his notebook and tucked it and his pencil away.

With half bows to Gray and Izzy, the Scotland Yard duo turned toward the doorway, only to have Perkins bar their way.

"But, sir!" Perkins exclaimed.

"What?" Baines grumpily demanded.

Perkins darted a look at Izzy. "Aren't we going to take the widow in, sir? She's the only suspect we have, and she might have done it!"

Baines heaved a weary sigh. "How?"

Perkins blinked. "How, sir?"

"Yes, Perkins, *how*. It's one of those pesky pieces of evidence we need to prosecute a case—opportunity to do the deed. Yet Cromer is clear Quimby was knifed *between* five and six, and Mrs. Molyneaux was with his lordship the entire time."

Izzy—and, she was sure, everyone else in the room—could see that the overeager Perkins quivered on the cusp of suggesting that she and Gray had conspired together to murder Quimby, but even Perkins seemed to understand that voicing such an accusation would be one step too far. Instead, he said, "Perhaps she had an accomplice? Yes—that's it! She knew Quimby would be in the darkroom and that the back door would be open—well, she probably has a key to that herself, so could make sure it was—and she hired someone to come in and bump the man off."

Baines sounded unimpressed. "Why?"

But Perkins believed he was on surer ground with that. "Plain as a pikestaff, sir. Quimby learned something about her she didn't want to get around. A woman running a place like this? A female *owning* a business like this? I mean, there must be something havey-cavey going on, and if we look, we'll find it, but meanwhile, we should take her in, or she might leg it."

Perkins looked at the long-suffering Baines, transparently expecting the inspector to agree.

At that point, the notion of "legging it" rather appealed to Izzy.

While one part of her brain was panicking over the police uncovering all she was concealing—more than enough motive for her to kill anyone who found out and threatened her with exposure—on another level, she was starting to feel sufficiently distanced from the incredible events of the evening to find Perkins and his views oddly entertaining.

Sternly, she told herself laughing wouldn't help.

She wasn't the only one who jerked to attention when Gray, his aristocratic tones cutting and cold, said, "Inspector Baines, I feel I should remind you that Mrs. Molyneaux and I are—as we've mentioned—very old friends. I and others will take it very badly should her standing be in any way adversely affected by unwarranted speculation being bandied about by members of the police force."

Fascinated, Izzy stared at Gray, who had leveled his gaze on Perkins, but as she watched, Gray shifted his gaze to Baines's face and inquired, "I trust I make myself plain?"

Baines and Littlejohn had stiffened at Gray's first words and swung to face him. Baines moistened his lips and bobbed his gray head. "Indeed, my lord." He flung a sharp, warning glance at Perkins, then looked at Littlejohn and jerked his head toward the door.

The sergeant dipped his head, caught Perkins by the arm, and made for the foyer, forcibly taking the constable, hissing in protest, with him.

Meanwhile, Baines focused on Izzy. "My apologies once again, Mrs. Molyneaux. It'll be me and the sergeant, both of us from the Yard, who'll be pursuing this case. You won't have to deal with Perkins again."

She decided it behooved her to be gracious and inclined her head civilly. "Thank you, Inspector. That might be for the best."

Baines cast a cautious glance at Gray, then returned his gaze to her. "As I said, ma'am, Littlejohn and I will return tomorrow to speak with your staff. I take it you'll be open?"

"For the half day only. We close at midday."

"Duly noted. We'll be here around midmorning, I expect."

After bowing to her and to Gray, Baines strode out of the office.

Izzy watched as the inspector and his sergeant collected Perkins and his compatriots and bundled them out of the front door.

When the door shut, she heaved a heartfelt sigh of relief.

Then worry and concern swamped her. She couldn't afford to have the police scrutinize *The Crier* and its owner overmuch. She was safe from a cursory examination, but if they delved deeper...

She felt Gray's gaze and glanced up to find him regarding her in a direct fashion she hadn't previously encountered in him. Quite what he was seeing, she wasn't at all sure, but his scrutiny reminded her that she really didn't need him getting too close to Mrs. I. Molyneaux, either.

Smoothly, she rose, bringing him to his feet. "Finally, we can leave." She rebuttoned her coat, picked up her bonnet, and settled it in place. After loosely tying the ribbons, she swiped up her reticule and turned off the twin desk lamps. As darkness engulfed the office, Gray led the way into the foyer, still well-lit by the lamp the police had returned to the counter.

She stepped into the light and shut the office door.

It seemed strange to be going through the same motions, the same small tasks she performed most evenings. Fishing in her reticule for her keys, she realized Gray still had them and halted. "My keys?"

He drew them from his pocket and handed them over. She took them and walked down the workshop to the rear door. As she'd expected, it was still unlocked. She found the key and locked it, then started back toward the foyer.

Gray had followed her as far as the darkroom. He stood in the doorway, scanning the interior in the light thrown by the lamp on the counter. She halted beside him and glanced inside. The red-shielded lamp had been turned off, and the pile of glass plates remained on the central table, more or less as they had been earlier.

"I know nothing about photographic processes." Gray caught her eye. "Do you?"

She shook her head. "But our young printer's devil—our lad-of-all-work—has been working as Quimby's assistant for months. He'll know more." She studied the wrecked plates and grimaced. "Given the police brought unshielded lanterns in here, I doubt anything in that pile will be salvageable."

Gray grunted and followed her to the counter. She doused the last lamp. Guided by the glow from the streetlights, they crossed to the door and, finally, stepped outside.

The night air was cold and refreshing.

She shut and locked the door, tucked the keys into her reticule, and extracted her gloves. Pulling them on, she glanced at Gray, who was still hovering. "My house isn't far."

He frowned. "You walk?"

"As I said, it's not far, and usually, I'm not this late."

He didn't look reassured. He glanced down the street. "I'll see you home. Which way?"

She resisted an impulse to protest. He'd always exhibited a certain chivalrousness—except for the time he'd vanished from her life without word or excuse; despite that incident, apparently, his compulsion to protect women hadn't changed with the years.

From beneath her lashes, she scanned his features. They had changed, becoming starker, more austere. This was definitely not the younger version of Grayson Child, the man she'd thought had loved her as much as she'd loved him, until he'd deserted her. This older version was a lot harder, more decisive and sharper edged.

She didn't bother mounting even a token resistance. Despite the risk of having him step further into her life, given she still felt distinctly unsettled, she was and would be grateful for his company.

How very easily they'd slid back into their previous ways of dealing with each other. They weren't the same people, and their interaction wasn't quite the same, yet still...

She waved toward Bernard Street. "The house is in Woburn Square."

She started walking, and he fell in beside her.

They maintained a steady pace down the mews and into Bernard Street, slowed to negotiate the traffic and cross Woburn Place, then walked along the northern edge of Russell Square. All the while, Gray scanned their surroundings. He was neither overt nor covert about it; indeed, it was as if it had become second nature for him to remain aware of all around him.

Once, she'd loved the man he had been, and she had to own to a burgeoning fascination to learn about the man he now was.

At the northwestern corner of Russell Square, she turned right, up the short street that opened into the elongated Woburn Square. The so-called square was so narrow, there were no houses at the far end, where it met Byng Street. But the terrace houses lining the east and west sides were well-kept respectable residences, precisely the sort of house a widowed newspaper proprietor might be expected to inhabit.

She led Gray along the western side and, eventually, halted on the pavement before the steps leading up to the blue-painted door of Number 20. The twin lamps burning on either side of the door lit the steps and the area in which she and Gray stood.

As she turned to face him, she'd never been more thankful for the solid façade of her Mrs. Molyneaux persona.

She offered her hand. "Thank you, not only for walking me home but for all that came before that. Perkins would have gladly clapped me in irons had you not been there."

He grasped her fingers, and his amber eyes caught hers, and for an instant, time fell away. A frisson of sensation streaked through her, all the way to her toes, just as it had the first time they'd met, all those years ago.

His muscles tensed as if to raise her hand to his lips—as he had in that long-ago ballroom—and she froze, and so did he.

To cover her reaction—both their reactions—she said, "Your family— especially your brother and sister-in-law—are going to hate your name being associated with a murder, even if only in passing."

His gaze remained on her face. She studied his, but couldn't read the expression in his eyes, and his features were significantly more difficult to read than they once had been.

Then his lips curved wryly. "When have I ever cared what people— especially Roddy and Pamela—think?"

She tipped her head, acknowledging that. He'd always been one to go his own road.

He released her hand and shoved both of his into his greatcoat pockets. "I'll drop by tomorrow, and we can talk more about dropping the exposé."

She frowned. "We hardly need to discuss that further. This murder is going to dominate our news for the next weeks, and by that time, our readers will have forgotten that I ever mentioned a secretive Golden Ball."

His lips twisted cynically. "Glad to know that even in your readers' eyes, murder trumps matchmaking." His gaze hardened. "Nevertheless, I'll call tomorrow and see how the land lies."

She inwardly sighed and nodded. "Very well. I'll see you then. Again, thank you for your escort home."

She forced herself to turn and climb the steps to the front door. She gave a light rap, and the door was opened by the housekeeper, Doyle.

Aware of Gray still standing on the pavement, his gaze on her, Izzy stepped inside, nodded at Doyle to close the door, and waited in the dimly lit hall for several seconds. Then she went to the narrow window beside the door, shifted the lace curtain a fraction, and peered out.

Gray was walking away, head down, thinking.

She sincerely hoped he wasn't thinking about Mrs. I. Molyneaux.

She let the curtain fall and turned away, expecting to feel relieved. Instead, her emotions were…scattered. Uncertain.

"Isadora?" A quavering voice came from the front parlor. "You're awfully late tonight."

Izzy smiled. "One moment, Agatha."

She glanced at the waiting Doyle, who smiled and assured her, "I'll tell Fields to fetch the carriage, my lady."

"Thank you. I'll just have a quick word—I won't be long." Izzy walked to the open parlor doorway and into the warmth and light.

Mrs. Agatha Carruthers, an elderly widow, sat swathed in rugs and shawls beside the fire.

Izzy bent and kissed Agatha's lined cheek. Agatha's halo of soft white curls brushed Izzy's bonnet. She straightened and, taking Agatha's hand, gently squeezed her crooked fingers. "I am rather late. Some unexpected business came up that I couldn't ignore."

She saw no reason to burden the old lady with news of murder.

Agatha patted her hand. "Well, late as it is, you mustn't let me keep you."

"Fields is getting the carriage, so I have a few minutes." Izzy drew a footstool nearer and sat. "Now tell me, how was your day?"

She spent the next minutes chatting with Agatha about the undemanding highlights of the old woman's day, then bade her a goodnight and went to the kitchen, where Doyle was preparing her mistress's nightcap.

Doyle looked up and smiled. "Fields will be ready and waiting."

Izzy smiled back. "Thank you." With a wave, she headed for the back door. "I'll see you in the morning."

She opened the door, stepped outside, then closed the door and checked that the lock had properly engaged. Only Agatha and Doyle lived in the house, and Izzy's coachman, Fields, who spent most of his days there, helped out with the heavier work.

Izzy walked down the paved path to the back gate, opened it, and stepped into the lane where Fields sat on the box of the smaller Descartes town carriage. Izzy pulled the gate closed, waved at Fields to remain where he was, walked to the carriage door, opened it, and gathering her skirts, climbed in.

She leaned out to pull the door shut. "Home, Fields—at last!"

The coachman grunted and, the instant the door clicked shut, gave his horse the office. The strong chestnut stepped out, and the carriage rattled down the narrow service lane, then slowed and emerged onto Montague Street. The pace picked up as the wheels bowled along the west side of Russell Square, then Fields turned right onto Great Russell Street.

By the time the carriage was traveling west along Oxford Street toward Lady Isadora Descartes's home in the leafy streets just north of Hyde Park, Izzy's perceptions of her day had shifted, reflecting the transition from Mrs. I. Molyneaux, owner and editor of *The London Crier*, who, to all appearances, lived at Number 20, Woburn Square, to Lady Isadora Descartes, unmarried elder daughter of the late Earl of Exton and elder sister of the current earl, who lived exactly where the ton expected her to live, on the fringes of Mayfair.

As she frequently did at that moment in her journey, Izzy gave thanks for the stroke of luck that had prompted her brother, Julius, to marry Dorothy Barton and thus gain as a grandfather-in-law the wise and canny Silas Barton.

Silas had become Izzy's mentor in all things business. He had overseen her purchase of the old printing works in Woburn Mews and guided her transformation of the business into the profitable enterprise it now was. It had also been Silas who had insisted on and instituted the careful façade of Mrs. I. Molyneaux. Mrs. Carruthers was an old friend of his, and through his good offices, they'd arranged that, for a small monthly stipend, Isadora could use the house in Woburn Square as her staging post —where, every evening, she stepped from being Mrs. I. Molyneaux into the carriage of Lady Isadora, and in the morning, reversed the process.

Consequently, should anyone follow Mrs. Molyneaux, the trail would lead to Woburn Square and nowhere else.

Certainly not to the home of the Dowager Countess of Exton and her lovely daughters, the elder, Isadora, a confirmed spinster, and the delightful Lady Marietta, who had made her come-out last year.

With her gaze fixed unseeing on the façades slipping past, Izzy renewed a pledge she'd made when she'd signed the contract that had

made the printing works hers. She would not allow—could not allow—
any difficulty in her life as Mrs. I. Molyneaux to touch her family.

The image of Quimby slumped lifeless against the darkroom wall, the
slimy feel of his blood on her hand, and most of all, the shock and threat
of Perkins's suspicions lingered in her mind.

As the skeletal canopies of the trees in Hyde Park replaced the buildings on the carriage's left, Izzy forced herself to draw in a deep breath and
push all the horror away.

She hadn't expected to see Grayson Child—certainly hadn't expected
her pending exposé to bring her Molyneaux self face-to-face with him—
yet regardless of the unwisdom of them interacting in any way, she
couldn't help but thank God he'd been there.

CHAPTER 3

*I*zzy barely slept a wink, too agitated by the multiple threats thrown up by Quimby's murder as well as the potential ramifications of Grayson Child re-entering her life.

She walked into Woburn Mews at five minutes to eight and immediately spotted Gray leaning against the wall by *The Crier's* door.

Her stride hitched, then she raised her chin and resumed her steady pace.

As she neared, she couldn't resist observing, "I was under the impression that you—and indeed, your peers—never rise this early."

He straightened from the wall and followed as she climbed the shallow steps and unlocked the door. "I got used to doing so during my time abroad."

Opening the door, she glanced at him, conscious, again, of curiosity stirring, then led the way into the foyer.

Ignoring her inquisitive look, Gray shut his lips on the words *For most of the years I was away, I didn't have anywhere to lay my head that remotely resembled a bed* and followed. Along with all the rest of his acquaintance, she didn't need to know anything about that time in his life.

He ambled in her wake and waited in the office doorway while she hung up her coat and bonnet. When she crossed to take the chair behind the desk, he went to the armchairs they'd used the previous evening, rearranged them before the desk, and sat in the one farther from the door.

She glanced up, saw what he was doing, and nodded. "Thank you."

She'd barely re-sorted the papers on her desk when the bell above the door jangled and several men Gray vaguely recognized as staff came in.

They were all smiles and morning chatter. Those who noticed him were curious, but were more intent on shrugging off their coats and hats and hanging them on pegs on the other side of the office wall.

Gray heard Izzy sigh, then she rose and walked out.

He got to his feet and went after her. He halted in the doorway and, propping a shoulder against the frame, watched as she was greeted with good humor and smiles, which faded as the five men and one younger lad took in her somber expression.

She surveyed the group, then said, "I'm afraid I have some disturbing and rather bad news, but I'll wait until Mary arrives."

The two older men—one stocky and appearing as strong as a bull, the other tall and reedy—exchanged concerned glances, then the thin one volunteered, "She won't be long. Just stopped for a quick word with our landlady. She should be on my heels."

Izzy nodded.

The lad stood still as a statue, his face a mask of growing anxiety.

The three younger men shifted on their feet, then one asked, "Is it bad news for *The Crier*, ma'am? Will we be stopping production?"

"Oh no," Izzy assured them. "It's nothing like that. It's bad news, but not of that sort. In fact, I suspect our circulation will go up once the news gets out."

That reassured but also puzzled everyone, then the bell rang again, and a fresh-faced young woman came hurrying inside.

She saw them all waiting, and her footsteps slowed. "Oh." She scanned the faces. "Is something wrong?"

"In a way, yes, and I'm about to explain." Izzy waved the girl—Mary, Gray surmised—to the counter, and she slipped past and went behind it and started to shrug off her coat.

"Now." Her fingers twining, Izzy raised her head. "I'm sorry to have to tell you that Mr. Quimby was murdered last night."

"What?"

"Never!"

"Where?"

"Oh, heavens," Mary breathed. "Don't say it was here!" Horrified, she looked toward the darkroom. "He was here when we left yesterday."

"Was he?" Izzy paused, then admitted, "We weren't sure if he'd arrived before you all left, but sadly, yes. He was stabbed in the darkroom."

"Cor!" the young lad looked simultaneously horrified and fascinated.

"I know he could be a grumpy old sod, but whyever would anyone want to murder Quimby?" the thin man asked.

The stocky man stepped forward. "Was it you who found him, ma'am?"

Izzy's fingers gripped tighter. "Unfortunately, yes." She pulled her hands apart and gestured at Gray. "Luckily, Lord Child had dropped by to discuss a business matter, and he was leaving with me when I noticed the sign was still up on the darkroom door. We knocked and called, and when we got no response, we went in…and found him."

She paused to draw breath, then went on, "Lord Child arranged for Scotland Yard to be informed and stayed with me and helped deal with the police when they arrived. The surgeon came and took away the body. His lordship and I were in the office and heard and saw nothing, but the back door was unlocked—"

The thin man snorted. "I reminded Quimby it was supposed to be locked before we left, and he said he had. I should've checked. Far as I know, he never did lock it when he came in late, not until he left again." He paused, then in a quieter tone, added, "He always said it wasn't important."

Gravely, Izzy shook her head. "The killer must have come in that way. I wanted to warn you that the police have said they'll be around later this morning to speak with you all, to learn if Quimby arrived before you left, and if you know of anyone who might have wished him harm."

From the looks on the staff's faces and their murmured comments, it was plain they hadn't known of the murder before this, nor could they imagine why the photographer had been killed.

"One thing," Izzy said, reclaiming everyone's attention. "From now on, I would like you all to make sure the back door is kept locked at all times, and during those moments it needs to be open—when you take out the rubbish or get in coal—that there are at least two of you there throughout the period the door is unlocked." She sighed. "It might be shutting the door after the horse has bolted, but better safe than sorry."

There were nods of agreement all around.

The stocky man asked, "Beggin' your pardon, ma'am, but are we planning on running an edition this week?"

Izzy nodded. "I want to run an obituary at the very least, and perhaps a special section on Quimby's work and what a loss to us he and his talents will be."

Everyone seemed to think that was appropriate.

"In that case"—the stocky man turned to the others—"we'd best get on with our usual chores." He cocked a questioning brow at Izzy.

She nodded. "Yes. I think we should keep on as best we can."

The staff moved off, deeper into the workshop. The thin man paused to pat the young woman, Mary, who looked pale and stunned, awkwardly on the back. He said a few words, to which she nodded, then she went to the counter, and the man moved along the far side of the printing press to where narrow tables set end to end ran down that side of the room.

Izzy watched her staff settle to their tasks, while Gray watched her.

Eventually, she turned and walked toward him. She waved him into the office. "They don't need us watching over them like mother hens."

His lips twitched, and he remained lounging in the doorway. "Who are they? Start with the stocky man. If I'm to be hovering for a while, it'll help to have some names."

She halted and frowned at him. "Obviously, the exposé will not now go ahead, so there's no reason for you to linger."

"Much as it pains me to contradict a lady…" When she huffed, he hid a grin. "I was here when the body was found and during the time of the murder. While the police have thus far focused on you, who's to say they won't, at some point, fasten their beady eyes on me?" He arched his brows, daring her to argue. When she merely grimaced, he half smiled and added, "Aside from all else, I'm curious to see in which direction Baines takes his investigation. Telling me who your staff are won't hurt."

She stared at him as if debating what was in her and her staff's best interests, then crossed her arms and swung to face the workshop. "Mary Maguire is my assistant copywriter and also acts as receptionist. The tall, thin man is William Maguire. He's our senior typesetter and also Mary's father. The stocky man is the printing works manager, Henry Lipson. It's he who oversees the running of the press."

He was tracking each individual as she named them. "Lipson looks strong enough to turn the press by hand."

"He is and, on occasion, does. Of the younger men, the stockier one with reddish-brown hair is Tom Lipson, Henry's second son. The other young man working on the boiler is Gerry Horner. He's specifically responsible for keeping the boiler in perfect condition. The man wearing spectacles and working alongside William at the typesetting tables is Jim Matthews."

"And the lad?"

"Our printer's devil, Digby Crew."

Gray eyed the towheaded youngster, about fifteen years old, skinny and scrawny and all big eyes. Lipson Senior was watching over the lad and keeping them both busy, poking about the huge printing press. "He—your young devil—is the one who's been working as Quimby's assistant?"

Izzy nodded. "Quimby was here often enough during work hours, and Digby was always hanging around, asking questions. I think, at first, Quimby took him into the darkroom simply to keep him quiet. Then Quimby realized how useful Digby could be."

She drew in a breath and, lowering her arms, faced him. "And now, like everyone else, I need to get back to work."

With an equable smile, he moved out of the doorway.

She shot him a narrow-eyed look and sailed past.

Hiding a smile, he returned to the armchair and relaxed into it.

His real motive in remaining within her orbit was to ensure Baines didn't opt for the easy course of making her a scapegoat, but he wasn't stupid enough to say so.

Baines and Littlejohn came through the front door not long after.

Izzy glanced at the clock. "It's barely nine—hardly the generally accepted idea of midmorning."

Gray could have told her the early arrival was a ploy to catch Izzy and her staff off guard. Instead, he rose as she did and followed her into the foyer. She intercepted the Scotland Yard pair, then at their request, called the staff to gather again in the space at the end of the long counter.

Once everyone was there, she named the staff, mentioning their roles, then introduced Baines and Littlejohn and stepped back to stand by the office wall beside Gray as, with Littlejohn taking notes, Baines commenced his questioning.

Dipping his head, Gray murmured, softly enough that only she would hear, "It's notable that they're interviewing the staff as a group."

She glanced at him. "It is?"

"It suggests they don't suspect the staff of having anything to do with the murder."

She frowned slightly. "That's good, isn't it?"

"Not if it means they've reverted to suspecting you."

He had a nasty feeling that supposition would prove true.

Baines confirmed that none of the staff knew Quimby socially, that, indeed, none had ever met him anywhere other than at the printing works. Likewise, none of the staff had any idea who might have killed the photographer or why.

Watching closely, Gray concluded that none of the staff were hiding anything; they were an honest and open bunch. He was pleased to hear them confirm everything Izzy had said of Quimby.

The one new piece of solid information was that on the previous evening, at a few minutes before five o'clock, Quimby had entered the printing works via the rear door—his usual means of access—grunted at everyone as was his wont, and gone straight into the darkroom, as he usually did.

The printer's devil, Digby, who had been told to scarper off home by Lipson a few minutes early and had left via the still-unlocked rear door, had passed Quimby in the lane. "He was coming down from Great Coram Street—his lodgings are somewhere up that way. I passed him a little way down from the corner and nodded, polite-like, and he nodded back, and we went on our ways."

That seemed clear enough, as was Lipson's tale of locking the back door after he'd shooed Digby off, and Maguire's report of knocking on the darkroom door and warning Quimby the others were leaving and asking if he'd relocked the rear door. Quimby's response, heard by several others, had been clear, namely that he'd taken care of it.

"Shouldn'ta listened," Maguire said. "I shoulda gone down to the door and checked. We knew he wasn't the sort to bother, but he was usually off again in a half hour or so, so it didn't seem worth the argument."

Littlejohn looked up. "Who has keys to the back door?"

"I do." Henry Lipson nodded at Izzy. "Mrs. Molyneaux has a key, and Quimby, of course."

"Only the three?" Littlejohn asked, busily scribbling.

"Yes," Lipson said. "And I was already at the front door when we remembered Quimby, and William here went back to ask."

"So he told you it was locked, and you had no reason to believe he was lying, even though you suspected he might be." Baines nodded. "Perfectly understandable. So you all left then, at the same time?"

The staff looked at each other as if confirming who was there, then nodded.

"We left in a group," Lipson stated. "All except Digby, who'd left earlier, and Quimby, who was in the darkroom."

"And Mrs. Molyneaux," Baines pointed out. "She was in the office, I believe?"

The staff looked at Izzy and nodded.

"At her desk," Lipson confirmed. "It being Friday, she was doing the invoices and accounts, like always. We all called goodbye."

"Right, then." Baines glanced at Littlejohn. "I think that establishes all we need as to movements leading up to the incident." He focused on Lipson. "Can you or anyone here tell us whether the plates left on the table in the darkroom are all the plates Quimby had? Or are there others stored somewhere else?"

All the staff looked at Digby, who colored but, encouraged by nods from Lipson and Izzy, cleared his throat and said, "None of us have gone into the darkroom. We don't usually go in there, not unless Mr. Quimby tells us to. It's—was—his place." Digby blinked, then went on, "So I don't rightly know what plates you're talking about, but if they're about this size"—he held up his hands about nine inches apart, moving them to indicate a square—"and have a black-and-silver film on them, then I reckon they'd be Mr. Q's daguerreotype plates, and he kept all of those in the cabinets inside the darkroom. Safest there, you see."

Baines and Littlejohn digested that, then Baines asked, "If we took you to look in the darkroom, would you be able to tell if all those plates have been taken out and left on the table?"

Eyes rounding, Digby nodded.

Baines looked at Littlejohn and tipped his head toward the darkroom. "Take him in and let him check."

Littlejohn pocketed his notebook and, with a kindly expression, waved Digby ahead of him. "Come on. Let's take a look."

Everyone watched the pair go down the workshop and into the darkroom. Digby insisted they put up the Occupied sign and closed the door.

The others looked at each other and shifted, but otherwise waited in silence.

After quite a few minutes, the door opened again, and Digby, paler than before, emerged, escorted by Littlejohn, who shut the door behind him.

Digby returned to Lipson's side.

Littlejohn resumed his position beside Baines and drew out his notebook. "The lad and I looked through all the cabinets, and there weren't any other plates like those on the table left stored away. The lad did a quick count, and he thinks all the plates Quimby ever had are on the table, and the lad is quite certain they're all useless now."

Digby nodded. "Wrecked, they are! Poor Mr. Q would be roaring..." He broke off and looked down, then mournfully shook his head. "To have all his work ruined like that. Senseless, it is."

Gray suspected that, far from being senseless, wrecking the photographic plates had been the murderer's principal aim.

Baines thanked Digby for his help, then thanked the staff as a whole, ending with, "I doubt we'll need to question you again, but we might be back to check on this or that."

Lipson looked at Izzy. "Best we get back to work, then."

At Izzy's nod, the staff drifted away, returning to what they'd been doing before.

After a murmured comment to Littlejohn, Baines turned to Izzy. "If we might have a word, ma'am?"

"Of course." Izzy briefly met Gray's eyes as she led the way into her office. He wasn't surprised to see flaring concern in her emerald gaze.

He followed on her heels, not about to be shut out of the coming exchange. While Izzy returned to her chair behind the desk, he reclaimed the armchair he'd previously occupied and waited to hear what Baines had to say.

Littlejohn shut the office door. Along with Baines, Littlejohn remained standing.

Baines hadn't expected Gray to be there; he shot him a wary glance, then, rather uncertainly, faced Izzy. "Mrs. Molyneaux, this morning, the superintendent was asked to review the evidence in this case. Littlejohn and I were called on to report our findings from yesterday and, once we return, will add what we've learned this morning from your staff." Baines glanced briefly at Gray, then returned his gaze to Izzy. "I have to warn you that there's pressure mounting from the local force for the Yard to make a quick arrest. The locals feel there's evidence enough regarding who might have done the deed, and despite what I admit is very tight timing, you, ma'am, remain the principal suspect."

Apparently unmoved, Izzy stared at Baines, patently waiting for his next pronouncement.

Gray nearly laughed. "She isn't going to run."

"Heh?" Baines looked at him, then faintly colored.

Gray smiled a sharklike smile, then turned to Izzy. "It's an old trick. If you have a person you decide is guilty but have insufficient evidence to prove it, you suggest that they are about to be arrested and wait for them to try to flee. If they do, you have all the proof you need—they've made the case for you."

Izzy's emerald eyes hardened. Her expression severe, she trained an adamantine gaze on Baines and, enunciating excruciatingly precisely, inquired, "You didn't just try to make me incriminate myself, did you, Inspector?"

Baines turned several shades of ugly red, but to his credit, didn't deny the accusation. He shifted his weight and when, brows arching haughtily, Izzy waited, conceded, "There's a lot of pressure to close this case, ma'am."

Before Izzy could respond, Gray coldly stated, "If we're to speak of pressure regarding this case, Inspector, you might wish to ponder the fact that Mrs. Molyneaux has friends in what are generally termed high places, and they, like myself, will take a very dim view of Scotland Yard attempting to prosecute a case against Mrs. Molyneaux without any sound evidence beyond the circumstantial linking her to the crime. Miscarriages of justice tend to turn very messy for the policemen involved."

From the look on Baines's face, he knew that was true. Nevertheless, he asked, "Are you threatening me, your lordship?"

Gray smiled. "Good heavens, no, Inspector. I'm merely drawing your attention to an irrefutable truth."

He was increasingly certain that Baines—much less his superiors—had no idea they were proposing to arrest an earl's daughter. She might be Mrs. I. Molyneaux, yet she was still Lady Isadora, daughter of the late Earl of Exton and sister of the current earl. Arresting her on the flimsiest of evidence would create a furor few would forget. Yet from Izzy's refusal thus far to own to her title and the warning looks she was casting him now, it seemed clear she didn't wish that side of her identity to be revealed.

Given she was now the proprietor of a gossip rag, perhaps that was understandable.

On top of that, having been absent for the past decade, he didn't know how the land lay between her and her family. For all he knew, they might be estranged. He couldn't quite imagine that, yet regardless, making unnecessary assumptions at this point wouldn't be wise.

Baines and Littlejohn were trading unhappy looks while Izzy was still staring warningly at Gray.

Acknowledging the wisdom of winning the Scotland Yard officers—neither of whom seemed all that keen to prosecute the case against Izzy—to her side, Gray ventured, "Perhaps the best way forward for all concerned would be to search for further clues as to who entered the workshop via the back door Quimby left unlocked. That person—the killer—must have left via the same route, so at two separate times between the hours of five and six o'clock yesterday evening, he was walking along the rear lane."

Baines and Littlejohn recognized an olive branch when it was waved in their faces. Baines looked at Littlejohn. "We should ask the businesses in the lane if they saw anyone walking past around the time of the murder."

Littlejohn nodded. "We can do that now, and later, I'll ask around my snouts in case any of them have heard a whisper about someone wanting a photographer killed."

Gray suppressed a satisfied smile. "Meanwhile, Mrs. Molyneaux and I will see if there are any other clues to be found in the darkroom or elsewhere in the workshop."

Baines might be suspicious of Gray being so helpful, but he was also relieved. He half bowed to Izzy and to Gray. "We'll leave you to that while we get on with our inquiries."

Baines made for the door, and with a nod to Gray and Izzy, Littlejohn followed.

Gray waited until the pair disappeared down the workshop, presumably making for the lane, then looked at Izzy. "I assume you would very much rather the police don't realize you're an earl's daughter?"

She met his eyes. "You assume correctly." She paused, then admitted, "No one here knows."

"You do realize that if they learn of it, they'll assume Quimby had as well and was blackmailing you—or had threatened to blackmail you—over that?"

"Regardless, for reasons that I'm sure are obvious to you, I do not intend to reveal my connection to the Earl of Exton."

He inclined his head in acceptance. "That being the case, I suggest we take a more active hand in the investigation."

Izzy appreciated how adroitly he'd steered the police into pursuing other avenues. "While I'm grateful for your help and agree that the easiest way to avoid being taken up for Quimby's murder is to find the real killer, I confess I have no idea how to do that."

The prospect of the situation ruining everything she'd spent the past eight years building, let alone dragging her family through the mire as well, threatened to overwhelm her, but something inside her rose and faced down the specter. She hadn't got to where she now was without dogged and sometimes ruthless determination, and she was not about to allow some nameless, faceless killer to rip away all she'd worked so hard to achieve—not without a fight, without doing her damnedest to avoid that disaster.

Her last comment had set Gray frowning. He grimaced. "Despite what I told Baines, I can't see any obvious way forward other than hunting for some sighting of the killer, as he and Littlejohn are doing." He met her eyes. "However, that the killer took time to ruin Quimby's photographic plates suggests the motive for the murder lay in those plates—"

"But they're ruined, so we can't use them to identify the motive or the killer."

"True." He tapped a finger on the chair's arm, then his features firmed. "While the police focus on the killer, let's focus on Quimby. There must be some reason he was killed." He glanced at her. "Baines asked your staff about Quimby's movements, but he didn't ask about the man himself. Why don't we see what your staff know of him? There might be some clue there."

She arched her brows. "Why not?" She couldn't think of anything else they might do. She rose, and he followed her out to the workshop.

She halted just beyond the end of the counter and clapped her hands. "If you can all leave what you're doing for a moment, his lordship and I would like your help. We need to learn as much as we can about Quimby himself, enough to get a better picture of the man in the hope that something about him will lead us to his killer."

The staff readily downed tools and, once again, gathered in a loose circle.

Leaning against the office wall, Gray got the impression the staff often met for meetings with Izzy like this; there was a comfortableness in the way they crowded around, eager to listen.

Izzy slanted him a glance, but with a dip of his head, he indicated she should lead the discussion.

She turned to the staff. "Let's pool everything we know about Quimby and see what sort of picture we can paint of him as a person."

Gray settled against the wall. It was apparent the staff at *The Crier* thought highly of Izzy; their respect was evident in their eagerness to help, to alleviate the burden of Quimby's death. Initially led by Lipson and Maguire, but with the younger members soon chiming in, the group pooled their knowledge of the dead photographer, creating an image of a gruff, often irascible and outright grumpy yet relatively harmless, solidly professional man, not wealthy but sufficiently well-to-do to be able to afford the necessary equipment and supplies to pursue his chosen career.

Importantly, despite having worked alongside Quimby for nearly three years, no one had caught even the slightest hint of any of the customary vices.

"No chance he would have gambled," Matthews observed, "not with the way he was always saving for the latest new invention."

The others all nodded; "saving for the latest new invention" had clearly been a frequent Quimby refrain.

"He didn't really drink, either," Horner said. "We asked him to join us often enough, but he never was interested."

Lipson pulled a face. "I don't think he even had friends, not close like. When it came down to it, all he ever thought about—all he ever talked about—was photographs and the equipment to take them."

The others nodded, and Maguire summed up, "You could say his one vice was photography. That was his passion—all he ever wanted to do was take more photographs."

"You're right." Gray straightened from the wall and walked forward to halt by Izzy's shoulder. He briefly met her gaze, then looked at the others. "In light of all you've said, we've been asking the wrong questions. What if the reason Quimby was killed had nothing to do with him per se, but was because of something he photographed?" Curiosity leapt in everyone's eyes, and he went on, "Normally, a killer does the deed and immediately flees the scene, but Quimby's killer spent ten or more minutes destroying all the daguerreotype negatives he could find."

Gray paused, imagining the scene. "The killer must have heard us"—he tipped his head toward Izzy—"talking in the office. The door was open, and we were speaking normally. The rest of the place was silent, so the killer must have known we were there." He met Izzy's eyes, seeing them widen in understanding. "Yet the killer took the risk of us coming out and seeing him, or coming to the darkroom and cornering him there, in order to wreck those negatives."

Izzy blew out a breath. "So wrecking the negatives was his true aim, and the question we should be asking is what did Quimby photograph that the killer didn't want published—in *The Crier* or anywhere else?"

Lipson was nodding. "That makes more sense than anything else, but would it have been an exposure he took recently or one sometime back?"

"Recently," Maguire answered. "In fact, most likely something he'd photographed that day." The typesetter looked at Izzy and Gray. "Quimby worked on a weekly system. Most of the exposures he took in weeks past would already be published, either by us or the other papers he supplied. He only ever did as many as he needed—as he was contracted to supply. Three for us and however many for the others. The process is expensive, after all."

"And," Gray said, "he was always saving for the next piece of equipment."

Maguire nodded. "Exactly. He'd go walking around town during the week, getting ideas for the scenes he needed to produce that week, then on Thursday or Friday, he'd go out and take the shots, usually all in one day. He once told me that way, he could develop them in a batch, all together, and so save on the solutions and such."

"That's how he worked," Digby put in. "He liked to take his photographs and develop them all in one day, so if any had to be retaken, he'd have time before he needed to submit them."

Izzy glanced at Gray. "So most likely Quimby took the photograph that led to his death sometime yesterday."

"The killer probably saw Quimby taking the photograph," Lipson said. "He had to set up his camera and tripod, so he would have stood out."

"But," Maguire went on, "the killer wasn't close enough to stop Quimby taking the photograph, so he followed him and—perhaps—tried to get Quimby to sell him the photograph—"

"Which Mr. Quimby would never do," Digby averred. When everyone looked at him, he blushed and offered, "It's one of those things about professional photographers."

Not unkindly, Tom Lipson ragged him, "And how would you know about that, young devil?"

Digby glanced at Izzy, and when, clearly curious, she looked at him inquiringly, he offered, "Mr. Q took me around to the Society of Photographers—he introduced me as his assistant. He said 'cause I was interested, I should learn about things from people who knew. Seeing as I was only an assistant, the president said I could join for just a shilling a year, and Mr. Q paid that, so I've been going every week—the society meets every Sunday afternoon and every second Tuesday—and listening and learning." He looked at Tom. "And that's one of those things I learned—that professional photographers always give their clients the photographs taken for them and never give the photographs to anyone else, no matter what's offered."

Izzy nodded. "Yes, I see. It's a matter of honoring the contract."

"Yes," Digby said, "that's how they describe it. Honoring the contract."

"All right." Gray was starting to see how the murder might have come to be. "Let's say we're right, and Quimby took a photograph the killer, for whatever reason, didn't want anyone to see. The killer approaches Quimby, offering to buy that exposure from him, but Quimby refuses."

"He'd be gruff and dismissive about it, too," Lipson Senior said.

Gray nodded, feeling increasingly sure of their hypothesis. "And let's say that in rejecting the killer's offer, Quimby mentions that the photographs are destined to be published in various papers."

"Ooh, the killer wouldn't have liked that." Mary's eyes were round.

"Exactly," Gray agreed. "In fact, the killer might have had reason to fear that, and so felt he had no alternative but to follow Quimby, kill him, and then ruin all the exposures he could find, just to make sure he ruined the one he didn't want anyone to see."

Gray glanced at Digby. "I imagine that to people who know nothing about photography, all daguerreotype plates look alike?"

Digby nodded. "Can't tell one from the other until they're developed and the image stabilized."

"Put together," Izzy said, "that makes more sense than anything else as to why Quimby was murdered, but with all Quimby's plates destroyed, how are we to tell which photographs he took yesterday, much less which was the critical one that set the killer after him?"

She wasn't surprised to see most of the others, including Gray, grimace, but Digby looked confused.

When he saw her observing him, he shifted nervously and looked even more unsure.

"Digby? What is it?" she asked.

Still looking uncertain, he replied, "I haven't searched the darkroom, ma'am—I only looked at the plates and to see they'd all been pulled out and wrecked, like the policeman said. But I didn't see any of the calotype negatives, and I didn't look in the drawer." He glanced at the others. "I only looked around quick-like, but it seemed that Mr. Q had come in, put the day's negatives safely in the drawer like he always did, then set about making up the solutions."

Digby returned his gaze to Izzy's face. "So did the man who wrecked the plates ruin the calotype negatives as well?"

For a moment, Izzy stared—along with everyone else—then asked, "Digby, what are these 'calotype negatives'?"

"They're the ones Mr. Q uses—" He broke off and amended, "Used these days. They're the latest thing, see? Well, they have been for a few years, 'parently, but in England, you have to pay a license fee to some man to use them, so not many photographers do. But Mr. Q sprung for the license the beginning of last year, and he's been using the new calotype process ever since. The negatives aren't glass plates—like with daguerreotypes. They're more like thick paper." He glanced toward the darkroom. "And I didn't see any of them in the mess."

"Are you saying," Gray asked, "that Quimby was using a different system—that the photographs he took yesterday would have been on some sort of paper and not on glass plates?"

Digby nodded. "Those plates were all his old work. They were best stored in the darkroom, so he kept them all there. The calotype negatives, once they're developed and the image fixed, are stable in light." Digby tipped his head toward the cabinets that lined the wall between the back of the office and the front of the darkroom. "All his calotype negatives are in those cabinets, but if you want to look at the photographs he took yesterday, like as not the negatives are in the drawer, waiting to be developed. It didn't look like he'd finished making the solutions when...when the killer came in. And Mr. Q wouldn't have roared if the door opened then, because he'd have known his day's work was safe in the drawer—it's light-tight, you see."

"So," Gray said, "he wouldn't have been instantly furious, but he would have been surprised." He caught Izzy's eyes. "That explains why he didn't call out—the killer surprised him at his work and gave him no chance."

Izzy was still struggling to make sense of Digby's revelations—and even more importantly, the implications. She focused on her young printer's devil. "So you think Quimby's photographs from yesterday—the negative calotype papers—are still in the darkroom, waiting to be developed. Will they still be useable?"

"Oh yes." Digby answered with complete assurance. "Long as they're in that drawer, they could wait for days, possibly even weeks."

Izzy held her breath. "Digby, do you know how to develop the images and treat them? Print them so we can see the pictures Quimby took?"

Digby nodded, again with certainty. "Mr. Q's been having me make up all the solutions, and he's had me developing and printing some of our photographs all on me own, so I'd know how to do it."

God bless Quimby's well-hidden heart of gold.

"Perhaps before we get our hopes up"—Lipson placed a massive hand on Digby's shoulder—"we should check that drawer you mentioned." Lipson glanced at Izzy and Gray. "Just in case the killer took those calo-type negatives away with him."

"Excellent idea." Gray nodded to Lipson. "Why don't you go into the darkroom with Digby and take a look in this drawer."

"We'll need to close the door and put the red light on," Digby warned as he turned and readily led the way.

Everyone else remained where they were, waiting on tenterhooks to learn what Lipson and Digby discovered in the drawer.

When the pair re-emerged from the darkroom—Digby zealously turning the Occupied sign over—Izzy couldn't wait any longer. "What did you find?"

Lipson's wide smile gave her the answer. "There are seven papers in the drawer, and"—he glanced at Digby—"our young man here says they're all in good nick, and he can print the photographs off all of them."

Digby looked hopefully at Izzy. "If you'd like me to, ma'am?"

Izzy could have kissed him. "I think that would be another excellent idea." Then she glanced at the clock. "But it's already past eleven." She returned her gaze to Digby. "How long will it take you to develop the negatives, then print a set of photographs? Can it be done in a day?"

Digby screwed up his face in thought, then nodded. "It'll take 'til about five o'clock, but if I use the stove to help dry the prints, I could easily do it all today."

Gray glanced at Izzy. "We should probably get three sets of prints made—the police will want one."

She nodded. "And it would be wise to have an extra set in case anything goes wrong." She refocused on Digby. "How much longer will it take to do three sets of prints?"

"Oh, only minutes, ma'am. Not much more time to do three prints as one. The time's all in the setting up, see?"

Tentatively, she asked, "Are you free to work longer today, Digby? I know your mama counts on you at home, so if you have anything you need to do, we can wait until Monday."

To her relief, her young devil was already shaking his head. "No trouble, ma'am. I can stay and get it done today." He sobered, and for an instant, sorrow shadowed his natural exuberance. "'Sides, I want to do whatever I can to help catch the beggar what killed Mr. Q."

"We'll do your usual chores," Mary volunteered, and Gerry and Tom nodded. "So you can start straightaway."

Digby looked to Lipson for approval, and the manager nodded. "Off you go, lad. We all want to see the blighter who did for Quimby strung up, and it sounds like the clues the police'll need are in those photographs."

That, Izzy thought, summed up the situation perfectly. They all stood and watched Digby set the darkroom sign to Occupied again, then disappear into the darkroom and shut the door.

The rest of the staff looked around, then returned to the usual Saturday morning chores, most of which revolved around cleaning the press and its plates, and cleaning and re-sorting the type into the appropriate boxes Maguire and Jim used when they set the type for a page.

Izzy remained at the end of the counter, looking over the workshop and thinking. Gray hovered beside her, his gaze on her face. After reviewing what awaited her in the office, she said, "As I'll be staying until Digby emerges with the photographs, I'll have all afternoon to take care of everything on my desk. Given the staff lost so much time with the police and then with our deliberations, I'm going to help them with their tasks so they can get away at twelve as usual."

Pushing up her sleeves, she walked to where Lipson was poking at something under the big cylinder of the press. When he glanced up at her, she asked, "What can I do to help?"

He grinned. "Why don't you help Maguire and send Matthews to me. I could do with another pair of hands here, but yours are too small."

She laughed and went to do his bidding.

Seconds after she settled with a pile of type-filled blocks from the previous edition to pick apart into their component letters, Gray appeared on her left. He pulled up a stool, sat and watched her for several minutes, then reached for a spare bodkin tool and pulled one of the boxes to be disassembled toward him.

Without looking up, she murmured, "You don't have to help—you don't have to stay."

He made a dismissive sound. "If you imagine I'll leave before we see those photographs, you're dreaming."

She grinned; she hadn't imagined any such thing. In his place, she'd be curious, too.

They settled companionably side by side to complete the finicky task.

By the time twelve o'clock came around, all the usual chores had been completed.

"We only got done thanks to you lending a hand." Lipson shrugged on his coat. "Or hands, as the case was."

Izzy noticed he included Gray in his grateful nod.

The others got ready to leave, somewhat reluctantly; it was plain all were keen to see what Digby produced. As usual, they left in a group, calling their farewells—in which they all included Gray.

Hmm.

Izzy knew very well that, at that point, trying to get rid of him would be wasted effort. Instead, after checking that the rear door was locked, she walked back to her office, sat behind her desk, and immersed herself in the neglected accounts.

Gray watched her with a far-too-understanding smile curving his lips, but said nothing. He sat in the chair opposite, stretched out his long legs, folded his hands on his chest, and closed his eyes.

Glancing up from beneath her lashes, she confirmed his eyes were truly shut, swallowed a humph, and got on with her work.

CHAPTER 4

*I*zzy completed every last scrap of outstanding paperwork, then tidied her desk. With everything in place, she looked hopefully at the clock; it was barely two-thirty.

She listened, but could hear no movement in the workshop. Digby must still be in the darkroom.

The lad had emerged at just after twelve o'clock, saying the developed calotype negatives were fixing and assuring her and Gray that the images were nice and sharp and would print well.

Gray had just returned from buying pies and drinks, and she and he had already consumed theirs. She'd given Digby the pie bought for him. He'd wolfed down the meat-filled pastry and gratefully accepted the bottle of ginger beer Gray had handed him. From the way Digby had savored both pie and drink, she suspected he didn't get to taste such treats often, if at all.

After tendering his thanks, Digby had retreated to the darkroom to print the three sets of the seven photographs they'd decided they would need.

He'd said it would take three hours at least.

Izzy looked around the office, searching for something to do.

Inevitably, her gaze landed on the one object she'd been attempting to ignore. Gray was sunk in the armchair he seemed to have claimed, his long legs stretched before him and his hands loosely clasped on his chest.

His chin rested on his neckcloth, and his eyes were closed. He hadn't moved for some time; she assumed he'd fallen asleep.

This seemed the perfect opportunity to look her fill and sate her curiosity, her fascination with this "new" him. If she studied him for long enough, perhaps she would no longer feel the constant need to examine his every expression to see if his reactions had changed from what they'd been before.

The long, angular planes of his face were at ease, yet even when relaxed, there was no hiding the patrician cast of his features. His broad forehead, well-set eyes, and lightly arched brown brows could have been chiseled by some artist, so ineffably aristocratic were they in line and form, yet his well-shaped lips and the slight cleft in his chin softened the image to something more human and infinitely more appealing.

That she still found him so was an unwelcome realization.

As she let her gaze roam, studying, examining, drinking in all she could see, she couldn't help wondering what might have been.

Unsurprisingly, that led her to dwell on what had actually happened back then. Courtesy of his revelation of yesterday, she now had a more accurate idea, yet from her perspective, questions remained. Even though the incident and their connection of that time were in the distant past and undoubtedly irrelevant now, she still wished she knew the whole story.

Even with his eyes closed, Gray was acutely conscious of Izzy's scrutiny—as, he now accepted, he would always be alert to everything to do with her. If she was in his orbit, his senses locked on her. No matter what else he might be doing, no matter what other distractions presented themselves, he would always be aware of her.

He wondered what she was thinking. What was going on behind those lovely emerald eyes? If anything, their vibrant hue seemed more intense than in his memories.

Deciding the moments of quiet waiting was an opportunity too good to pass up, without stirring, he asked, "How did you come to own *The Crier*?"

Her attention snapped to his face. She studied it for a second, then replied, "I needed to make money, and believe it or not, this is a nicely profitable business."

He opened one eye and met her gaze. "I always understood that income from advertisers was notoriously unreliable."

"Indeed it is, which is why the printing works' profit doesn't rest on income from *The Crier* alone."

He opened both eyes and waited for her to elaborate.

Leaning her elbows on the desk, she obliged. "While *The Crier* generally covers its costs, the bulk of our profit comes from our printing for the university, several museums, and various other institutions, for faculties, private scholars, and scholarly societies. All want a printing works that understands what they need and doesn't charge exorbitantly. These days, most printing presses are so large it's uneconomical to do short print runs or print small documents like pamphlets or guides. We can and do handle such projects, and over the years, we've made a name for ourselves supplying those orders on time and with excellent finish."

"So you offer a service few others can replicate."

"Exactly." She clasped her hands before her. "Now I've answered your question, you can answer one of mine. How did you amass your amazing newfound wealth?"

"I visited the Californian goldfields and picked up a nugget. A large one."

She widened her eyes at him. "And that was all it took?"

He grinned and straightened in the chair. "That nugget was worth a lot, but I took the money and invested in a succession of enterprises and, over the years, built my fortune into what it is now."

"Why did you come back?"

He'd answered that question for others, and the answer leapt to his tongue. "Because, believe it or not, I decided I'd had enough adventure, and once I sat back and contemplated life, I realized I missed England."

"Our green and pleasant land?"

"Indeed." After a second's hesitation, he added something he'd shared with no one else. "I also realized that the ultimate challenge I faced was creating a satisfying life, and my vision of that was anchored here, in this green and pleasant land." He lightly shrugged. "So I came back."

To make the most of his life—to create the best life he could; that had been the motive that had driven him for the past nine years. That and, in more recent times, a desire to live up to his name and make his family proud to own him.

He shifted to better face her. "You said you started this endeavor because you—and I assume that means your family—needed the income. Yet you could have easily married money, more than enough to be comfortable for the rest of your life." He paused, then candidly observed, "I wasn't the only ducal sprig hovering. Why didn't you seize one of them?"

Izzy held his gaze and her tongue...then decided to throw caution to the winds. It no longer mattered, after all. "You're correct in that I could have married several others, but after you left, I took stock and decided that, if I didn't *actively* wish to marry a particular gentleman, it would be better for everyone concerned if I didn't and, instead, pursued other avenues to support the family—avenues I felt happier pursuing." Just in time, she remembered to add, "Molyneaux intervened, but"—she gestured about her—"here I am."

She was perfectly content to allow Gray to assume she'd married Molyneaux for love.

A faint frown shadowed his amber eyes; she couldn't tell what he was thinking.

A door opened, and footsteps, light and eager, hurried toward the office.

Both she and Gray looked across at the doorway.

Digby appeared, wearing a gray dustcoat several sizes too big and carrying a sheaf of photographs.

His gaze had been locked on the photographs. He paused in the doorway, looked at her and Gray, and smiled delightedly. "I think they're good. All of them!"

Smiling, she waved at the cleared expanse of her desk. "Come and show us."

Digby crossed to the desk and eagerly set out the prints. Gray stood and looked down on the images.

"I made three copies like you wanted." Digby arranged the prints in three long rows of seven. "I had to get the stove going to dry them, but the lines are nice and sharp, and there's lots of different grays as well as black and white, just like Mr. Q said there should be."

Izzy scanned the prints. "These are as good as any I've ever seen. The focus is excellent." She picked up one and examined the details more closely.

Gray picked up a different print. "You said you expected three scenes a week. Which of these are the three for *The Crier*?"

She waved the print in her hand. "This is taken in Regent's Park, showing people walking the lawns and paths. That's the sort of scene we use, so I would say this is one Quimby would have offered me."

She scanned the row of prints nearest her and pulled three more out of the line. "These two"—she tapped her finger on the first and second —"are scenes in Hyde Park, but I wouldn't have taken both. One, certainly, but not both." She considered the third print she'd selected, the last in the line of seven. "This is Fleet Street, I think, and it's the third photograph I would have taken for *The Crier*." She glanced up and met Gray's eyes. "We use scenes of people about town."

He nodded. "So these other three...?"

"Most probably, Quimby would have offered them to other newspapers." She peered at the other photographs. "With a scene like this one"—she tapped the sixth print—"the forecourt before the museum with the museum in the background, he might even have had an arrangement with some don or the university to supply such an image. That's the sort of photograph we see in some of the booklets we print for the university faculties and colleges."

Digby pointed a stained finger at another of the prints. "I'm pretty sure that building is near the new station."

"So"—Izzy scanned the photographs—"we have two of Hyde Park, one of Regent's Park, one in Fleet Street, one of the museum, one near the new station, and lastly, a scene of ships clustered about a dock along the Thames."

Digby stared at the picture of the docks. "He musta taken that one from London Bridge—you can see some of the people walking along by the railing, and there's a bit of a carriage, too."

She studied the photograph, then glanced over the seven prints. "There are people in all of them."

Gray was examining the seven prints lined up on his side of the desk. Of the Hyde Park scenes, one showed several groups of ladies strolling the snow-dusted lawns, while the other featured clusters of riders on and about Rotten Row. The Regent's Park picture was of multiple couples and groups taking the air, while the one in Fleet Street was a view, taken from the other side of the street, of a conglomeration of men on the pavement outside a coffeehouse. The photographs of the museum courtyard, the building by the new station, and the docks likewise included multiple people.

"Not just people," he said, "but a lot of people, and given the clarity of these prints, all those people will be recognizable to anyone who knows them." He met Izzy's eyes. "It's not hard to imagine that someone might have had reason not to want one of these photographs to be published in a newspaper."

She nodded. "Our theory that Quimby was murdered because of one of these photographs seems sound."

Gray noticed Digby sneaking a glance at the clock on the bookshelf and dug into his waistcoat pocket for the sovereigns he'd put there earlier. "You've done well, Digby. I'm sure Mr. Quimby would be proud of these photographs, and with any luck, we'll be able to use them to track down his killer."

Digby blinked. "You think?"

"We do," Izzy assured him.

"Here." Gray held out two shiny gold coins. "From me and Mrs. Molyneaux for all your hard work."

Digby's eyes widened to saucers at the sight of such largesse. "Oh my!" He glanced at Gray, then at Izzy. "But I only did what Mr. Q taught me."

"You gave up your Saturday afternoon to help catch Mr. Quimby's killer," Izzy said, "and we wouldn't have even known to find the negatives for these if it wasn't for you working so closely with Mr. Quimby. He wasn't the easiest person to get along with, but you happily worked alongside him for months, and I know he thought highly of you."

Gray caught Digby's hand, turned it upward, and placed the two coins in his palm. "My advice is to put one away for a rainy day and use the other to treat yourself and your family."

Digby stared at the coins resting in his palm. "Oh, sir!"

Gray went on, "You did something no one else could have done, Digby, and you've helped us enormously. Thanks to you, we—and the police—have clues to follow, and follow them we will. But you've done your part for today. You'd best be off to enjoy your reward."

Izzy smiled at Digby. "Your mother must be wondering where you've got to. Off you go now, and take a well-earned rest tomorrow, and we'll see you on Monday morning."

Digby slowly smiled and ducked his head. "Yes, ma'am." He turned to leave, then swung back. "And I've cleaned the darkroom like Mr. Q would have wanted."

"Thank you, Digby," Izzy replied. "I appreciate that."

Still standing before the desk, Gray watched the lad happily doff the dustcoat and swap it for a threadbare jacket, then cross the foyer to the front door.

Once the door had shut, Izzy looked up at him. "Thank you for paying him. He's the sole provider for his mother and sister, and that will allow them to have a few nice things."

Gray reclaimed the armchair. "He seems a likeable lad—very eager to please."

"He always tries hard." She looked at the photographs. "And clearly, he's taken in a lot of what Quimby taught him."

Gray also refocused on the prints. "These really are excellent photographs."

She nodded, but was already scrutinizing the scenes again.

He gathered one set of prints and did the same, then shook his head. "I've been away too long. I can't identify anyone. Can you?"

"Three of the ladies walking in Hyde Park, two of the riders, and two ladies and three gentlemen in the Regent's Park picture. I can't see anyone else I recognize, but Mama and Marietta might be able to put more names to the faces."

To his ears, she didn't sound all that certain. He tapped the prints he was holding against his fingers. "I know someone who will likely be able to put names to most of those in the society scenes—the ones in Hyde Park, Regent's Park, and possibly even the one of the museum."

He caught Izzy's eyes when she glanced up. "I'll go and ask—" He broke off and grimaced. "I've just remembered they're in the country." He tipped his head. "That said, they're not that far away. I could drive north tonight, see them and pick their brains tomorrow, then hie straight back."

Izzy wasn't sure whether to encourage or discourage him. Who was it he planned to ask? Would they know of her?

But he'd been back in the country for only a few months, and it was January. It was highly unlikely he'd made the acquaintance of any of the significant matrons of the ton as yet. "Is this a crony of yours?"

"So to speak. They live near Ancaster Park."

His parents' property. "Well, we definitely need the information." She just hoped he didn't mention her, and really, why would he, at least not in the sense of questioning her identity? As long as he referred to her as Mrs. Molyneaux, all would be well. She nodded. "Very well. You see what you can learn of the people in the photographs, and I'll do the same."

He rose, and together, they sorted the photographs into three sets. He reached for his greatcoat, shrugged it on, then picked up one set and slid it into the coat's pocket. Meanwhile, she locked the second set in the central drawer of the desk, then picked up the last stack and eased it into her reticule. "Right." She drew the reticule's strings tight, pushed back from the desk, and rose. "You search, I'll search, and we'll pool what each of us learns."

She glanced at him as she went to fetch her coat. "When do you think you'll be back?"

He followed, lifted the coat from her hands, and held it for her. "Late Sunday. I'll meet you here on Monday morning, and we can pool our findings and see where that leads us."

She allowed him to settle the coat on her shoulders, then after sliding the strings of her reticule over her wrist, put on her bonnet. She waved him through the doorway, then followed and drew the door shut.

Automatically, she glanced down the workshop, her gaze coming to rest on the darkroom door. "I daresay Baines will return on Monday, and I would dearly like to have something with which to distract him when he does."

Turning to Gray, she caught the smile that flashed across his face, then he glanced at her, reassurance in his eyes. "Don't worry. We'll find something."

She wished she could be as confident.

They left the printing works, and she allowed him to walk her "home" to Woburn Square. They didn't exchange words along the way, but there was comfort and support in their companionable silence. She was increasingly aware of the degree of reassurance she drew simply from his presence, and the relief she felt in knowing he would be with her on Monday, when the police came calling, was almost seductive.

As they walked along the boundary of Russell Square, she told herself that a large part of the allure of having him beside her was simply that—that it had been such a long time since she'd shared her day-to-day experiences with anyone. From that realization, it was a short step to warning herself not to get too accustomed to him being by her side; doubtless, once the killer was caught, he would be satisfied and move on...perhaps even sooner if clues proved thin on the ground and he lost interest.

She shouldn't count on having him there, a shield of sorts against the world. While he might be intent on helping her out of this mess, she shouldn't forget that his reason for doing so was to ensure that the news of the murder replaced and distracted all attention from her proposed exposé.

As they turned up the short street to Woburn Square, she inwardly frowned. She might not have been acquainted with Grayson Child for the past decade, yet burying the exposé seemed an exceedingly flimsy motive for his continued efforts on her behalf, his unabating insistence on protecting her.

That left her pondering the unsettling question of what else was keeping him pacing so determinedly beside her.

After seeing Izzy into the house in Woburn Square, Gray walked back to Woburn Place and hailed a hackney to take him into Mayfair.

He walked into his lodgings in Jermyn Street just after five o'clock.

His gentleman's gentleman, Corby—who had instantly given notice and returned to Gray's service as soon as Gray reappeared and hunted him down—came hurrying from the nether regions to take his greatcoat. "Good evening, my lord. I trust your day went well?"

"Well enough." Gray surrendered the coat. "At the very least, it was interesting, apropos of which, I'll be leaving for Ancaster within the hour."

"Indeed, my lord. For how long should I pack?"

That was one of the things Gray appreciated about Corby; he was the epitome of unflappable. "Just one night. I'll be back tomorrow, albeit quite late. Tell Sam to fetch the curricle and the grays from the stable and tell him he'll be going with me."

"At once, my lord." Corby turned away as Gray headed for the small parlor.

Then Gray halted and spoke to Corby's departing back. "Corby, send Tom in. I have a job for him, and you'd better come and hear of it, too."

Corby looked faintly intrigued. "Yes, my lord. We'll be with you in a moment."

Gray went in and sat in his favorite chair by the fireplace. A cheery blaze warmed the room, reminding him of how cold it would be on the drive north to his father's principal estate. At least it would be a fairly direct run, more or less straight up the Great North Road.

While he was away, however...

Two minutes later, Corby opened the door and came in, followed by Tom, Corby's nephew. Tom, a more strapping version of his uncle, closed the door, then took up station beside Corby and nodded a greeting to Gray, then grinned, dispelling his until-then-bland expression. "You wished to see me, my lord?"

"Indeed, Tom. I intend to head to Ancaster Park shortly and won't be back until tomorrow night. However, there's a matter I'd like you to take care of while I'm away—say from seven o'clock tomorrow morning to seven o'clock in the evening." Gray paused, eyes narrowing in thought, then grimaced. "Actually, I need two of you—I have two different places I want watched."

He looked inquiringly at Corby and Tom. "Do you know of any likely lad who wouldn't mind earning a few shillings keeping watch on a different place over the same hours?"

Corby and Tom exchanged glances, then Corby looked at Gray. "Young Bill would be happy to help out, we're sure. He's my other sister's youngest lad."

Corby came from a large family, each member of which, barring only Corby, seemed to have had multiple offspring. Gray arched his brows. "How old is Young Bill?"

Tom, who was all of twenty, replied, "Seventeen, my lord. A good lad, if a bit tall and gangly still."

Corby nodded his agreement with this assessment.

"Very well. I'll leave it to you both to organize Young Bill. I want him to keep watch over the Molyneaux Printing Works, which is also the office of *The London Crier*. It's in Woburn Mews, just a bit up from Bernard Street."

Tom nodded. "We'll find it, my lord. It being Sunday tomorrow, will there be anyone there?"

"There shouldn't be anyone inside, but it's possible the police will have thought to put someone on watch. Unlikely, but Bill needs to bear that in mind and not let any other watcher spot him."

Tom grinned. "I'll explain that, my lord."

Gray went on, "I'm not anticipating any action, but if Bill should see anyone attempting to break in, he should alert the nearest constable—he'll probably find one in Woburn Place. The local police know that the premises in question was the scene of a murder yesterday, so they should act with all the promptness we might wish."

"Indeed, my lord," Corby said. "You can count on us to take care of that."

Gray inclined his head. "Now, Tom, I want you to watch a house not far from the printing works—Number twenty, Woburn Square. It's off the northwestern corner of Russell Square."

"Aye—I know it, my lord," Tom said.

"I want you to make sure you're not noticed by any of the occupants of that house, and if the owner, a lady, Mrs. Molyneaux, goes out, I want you to trail her—hanging well back so she doesn't spot you. I want you to keep her in sight and follow her wherever she goes, even if that means catching a hackney. However, if she goes anywhere, it's likely to be to the local church or, possibly, the printing works, which she owns." Gray focused on Tom. "If she does appear there, she'll have a key to the door. Make sure Bill knows that and doesn't raise any alarm."

"Of course, my lord," Tom said. "How will I know her?"

"She's a trifle taller than average, a slender lady with dark hair. She's a widow, so usually wears dark colors, and her customary bonnet is black silk. Wherever Mrs. Molyneaux goes, I need you to keep her in sight at all times and take note of anyone who approaches her, especially if she doesn't appear to know them. I don't believe she's in any danger at the moment, but if, for instance, some man attempts to force her into a carriage or in any way harm her, you are to do whatever you can to keep her safe."

Tom straightened to attention. "You can count on me, my lord. And Young Bill as well."

"I'm sure I can." Gray had Tom repeat his orders, then nodded and rose. "My thanks in advance to you and Young Bill."

Both Corbys stepped aside as he made for the door. "Corby, let's see about that packing."

"Yes, my lord." Corby fell in at Gray's heels as he started up the stairs.

As Gray led the way to his bedroom, he sifted through the possibilities; as far as he could see, he'd covered every eventuality that he could.

Fifteen minutes later, with his greatcoat flapping about his top boots, he strode out of the house, climbed up to the box seat of his curricle, took the reins from Sam, and set his grays trotting for the Great North Road.

CHAPTER 5

*A*fter catching a few hours' sleep at Ancaster Park and spending half an hour with his parents, Gray rode his hunter across the snowy fields to Alverton Priory.

Despite his ten-year absence, the Priory staff hadn't forgotten him; he left his horse in the stable and entered the house via the side door, then made his way to the front hall, where he found Edwards, the butler.

He greeted the man, asked for the earl and countess, and was directed to the family parlor.

Gray walked quietly into the parlor and grinned at the sight of Devlin, Earl of Alverton, and his countess, Therese, stars in the firmament of the haut ton, sitting on the carpet before a roaring fire and playing a complicated battle of toy soldiers with all three of their youthful brood.

Gray drank in the sight and inwardly acknowledged that the comfort of home and family inherent in the scene embodied the essence of what, ultimately, he wanted to secure for himself.

Then the boys—Spencer and Rupert—saw him. With shouts of "Lord Grayson!" they leapt to their feet and came pelting across to seize his hands and tow him farther into the room.

Laughing, he allowed them to lead him to where, abandoning the game, Devlin and Therese were getting to their feet, little Horry, their daughter, in Devlin's arms.

Horry ducked her head under Devlin's chin and smiled shyly at Gray;

she'd yet to decide if he was an acceptable person, which suited him, as he had no idea how to respond to a female of her age.

Hoping for the best, he smiled and tapped Horry's nose, which surprised her, then made her chortle, then he looked down at her importuning brothers. "Yes, I rode over on Smoke and Mist."

"He's in our stable?" Spencer, the elder, asked, eyes wide.

"Well, it's a bit cold to leave him wandering the lawns, so yes, I left him with Wallace."

Immediately, Spencer and Rupert turned identical beseeching looks on their parents.

"Can we *please* go and see Smoke and Mist?" Rupert begged.

Devlin shot a questioning look at Therese. She nodded, and the boys cheered.

Devlin held up a finger. "But you can only go near if Wallace is with you. If he can't watch over you, you are to come straight back."

"Yes, Papa," the pair sang.

Devlin held the boys' gazes for an instant, then nodded. "All right. Off you go."

With an exuberant whoop, the pair thundered off.

"But be back in time for your luncheon," Therese called after them.

She met Gray's eyes as she reached for Horry, and Devlin handed the little girl over. "At the moment, for those two, horses trump every other topic."

Gray smiled. "Devlin and I were the same."

"Into our late teens," Devlin confirmed.

"Good Lord!" Therese looked struck. "Is that what I have to look forward to?"

Gray and Devlin grinned.

Balancing Horry on her hip, Therese humphed. "Let me find Horry's nursemaid. Don't say anything interesting until I return."

She headed for the door, and Devlin waved Gray to the comfortable old sofa and dropped into a well-worn armchair opposite.

Being very old friends and mindful of Therese's admonition—knowing she definitely meant it—while they waited for her to return, they exchanged comments about the road from London and the likelihood of more snow.

Wintry light washed through the mullioned windows, bathing the scene in a pearl-gray glow. The warmth from the fire was soothing, reminding Gray of afternoons long gone. He glanced around. "I have a lot of fond memories of this room."

Devlin nodded. "We spent a lot of our childhood here."

"Playing and plotting." Gray smiled. "Good times."

Devlin smiled back.

Therese returned, sans Horry, and sank onto the other end of the sofa. "So what brings you here? Your mother wasn't expecting you, so I take it something specific has brought you our way."

Gray sobered. "You surmise correctly." He proceeded to explain about the exposé. It transpired that Therese had seen the notice but, as he had, had assumed it referred to him.

He shook his head. "No—or rather yes, it would apply to me, but in fact, the intended target was your brother, Martin."

"Really?" Therese stared at Gray, then shifted her gaze to her husband. "I knew Martin had 'made his fortune,' so to speak, but I had no idea he was that wealthy."

Devlin tipped his head. "I know no more than you, but I suspected that might be the case." He looked at Gray. "Did you know?"

"Not exactly, but given his stated direction business-wise, I did wonder, enough that learning he was the target instead of me wasn't a huge surprise."

Therese was frowning. "If none of us knew of Martin's wealth, how did *The London Crier* learn of it?"

Gray admitted, "I didn't ask. I concentrated on making the case— Martin's and mine as well—that exposing our wealth to all society would not just bring the matchmakers down on our heads but would also severely compromise our abilities to invest and generally do business. Luckily, when I explained all that to the proprietor, Mrs. Molyneaux, who turned out to be Isadora Descartes as was, she saw the light and agreed not to run the exposé and, instead, substitute some other sensation."

"What?" Therese's shocked exclamation brought Gray up short.

Before he could ask what had so exercised her, she leant forward and, her eyes locked on his face, demanded, "Did I hear you aright? *Isadora* owns *The London Crier*?"

Slowly, he nodded. "That's what I said."

Therese sat back, her expression suggesting she was flabbergasted— not something that often occurred. She stared unseeing across the room. "How exceedingly...*bold* of her."

Starting to sense he was missing something, Gray added, "She's the chief writer as well."

Therese's gaze returned to his face. She was still plainly stunned. "Good heavens! I had absolutely *no* idea!"

That she was stunned by the fact she hadn't known something made perfect sense to Gray; a glance at Devlin saw amused appreciation in his expression as well. Therese prided herself on knowing absolutely everything that went on in ton circles; to have been completely ignorant of two juicy pieces of gossip, one concerning her own brother, would, naturally, set her on her heels.

Then her expression grew puzzled. "But why Mrs. Molyneaux...oh!" Her face cleared. "Of course! To conceal her identity. Obviously, she wouldn't want that known."

Gray frowned. "No, because she married Molyneaux and is widowed—"

He broke off, because Therese was now staring at him with amazed eyes and a very strange expression.

If Lady Isadora Descartes had married, Therese would know. It was beyond impossible that she wouldn't.

Gray stared at Therese, while in his chest, something moved in a disconcerting way. "Izzy didn't marry, did she?"

Therese shook her head. "Not only is there no chance in Heaven that I would have missed an event such as the wedding of Lady Isadora Descartes, I met Isadora and her mother and sister at Lady Hitchen's ball a few months ago, just before we left town." Therese blinked, then added, "And of course, Molyneaux is the dowager countess's maiden name—she was the last of the Suffolk Molyneaux."

Gray was stunned, not only by the discovery but even more by his visceral reaction to the news that Izzy hadn't married. That she hadn't been some other man's...

He hauled his mind from that unsettling tack and refocused on what he'd come there to do. "Well, that's interesting, but it's really neither here nor there with respect to what's brought me to your door." Although Izzy's deception in portraying herself as a widow only increased the potential for Quimby to have been blackmailing her, Gray accepted that her true marital status needed to remain concealed at all costs.

Glancing at Therese, he realized she was debating whether to allow herself to be distracted from the intriguing news of Izzy's unexpected ventures, and he firmly stated, "There's been a murder. While Izzy and I were in the office of the printing works, talking about replacing the exposé, the photographer who worked for *The Crier* was stabbed to death in the darkroom, mere yards away."

That proved sufficiently dramatic to distract even Therese. "Good Lord!" Her hand rose to her throat. "Is Isadora all right?"

"In general, yes. However..." He described the situation in broad strokes, explaining that the police plainly needed assistance to find the killer.

At that point, they were interrupted by Edwards with the news that luncheon was ready to be served whenever they wished.

Therese invited Gray to share the meal, and he readily accepted, and they adjourned to the smaller dining room.

"So," Devlin asked, once they'd served themselves and settled to eat, "what are you doing to help the police?"

Gray gathered his thoughts, then said, "One thing that seemed notable was that despite almost certainly knowing Izzy and I were there, talking only yards away, after killing Quimby, the murderer took the time to find and wreck all the photographer's daguerreotype plates—the originals of the photographs he'd taken. That suggests that the motive for the murder lay in the photographs Quimby had taken."

Therese frowned. "If the photographs are all wrecked... Did the photographer keep a record of what he'd taken?"

Gray blinked. "That's an interesting notion, but sadly, we haven't learned of any such record as yet. However, after the police left the work-shop yesterday—they came and interviewed the staff—Izzy and I met with the staff and talked things over, and we learned that Quimby had changed the way he takes photographs, and the photographs he'd taken on the day he died were still safe in the darkroom. His young assistant printed up copies, and those are what's brought me to you."

Therese's eyes were wide. "How can we help?"

"There are seven photographs in all—seven scenes about London. Our working hypothesis is that there's something in one of those photographs that the killer doesn't want others to see. All seven photographs could have ended up published in a newspaper—*The Crier* or others—and that's what the killer was prepared to murder to prevent."

Devlin was nodding. "That seems a reasonable argument."

"So we think." In between talking, Gray had cleared his plate. He laid down his cutlery, dabbed his napkin to his lips, and set it aside. "The thing is, there are lots of people in the photographs—ladies, gentlemen,

men, women—and we need to identify them all. Izzy and I know a few, but naming the others was beyond us."

Therese pushed her empty plate away. "You've brought the photographs with you?"

Gray tapped his coat pocket. "We had the assistant make three sets of prints. Izzy has one set and is consulting her mother and sister. Meanwhile, I thought I'd come and consult you."

Therese's face lit. "An excellent notion!" She looked at Devlin. "Shall we return to the parlor?"

They did. Therese sat in the center of the old sofa, with Devlin on her left. Gray drew out the stack of seven prints and handed them to Therese, then pulled out a small notebook and pencil and sat on her other side.

Therese flicked rapidly through the prints, then returned to study the first closely.

Gray glanced across; it was the photograph of the riders in Hyde Park.

"That's Lord Compton." Therese pointed to one rider. "And that's Frederick Ashfield."

Between them, she and Devlin named almost everyone in the Hyde Park and Regent's Park photographs; Therese even identified the two nursemaids pushing perambulators in Regent's Park, at least in the sense of which household they worked for.

Of the other four scenes, they picked out two gentlemen in the scene of the museum's forecourt, one of whom was tooling his carriage along the road, and in the Fleet Street photograph, Devlin was fairly certain the well-dressed gentleman standing before the coffeehouse and speaking to another neatly dressed but portly individual was something to do with some government office, but couldn't remember more.

Neither Devlin nor Therese recognized any of the people in the picture of the building near the new station or the view from London Bridge.

While Therese looked over the photographs again, Devlin sat back.

Gray noticed his old friend was frowning at the photographs.

Then Devlin raised his gaze and, over Therese, met Gray's eyes. "You know Drake Varisey, don't you? Winchelsea?"

When, puzzled, Gray nodded, Devlin continued, "He's taken up where his father left off."

"Wolverstone?" Gray clarified.

"Yes. And I suspect"—Devlin shared a glance with Therese—"that Drake might be interested in this murder of yours."

Therese nodded decisively. "Even if it's not something in his baili-wick, Drake will want to know of it, and he wields a lot of clout with the authorities."

We might need that. The thought popped into Gray's head. A second later, he caught himself and wondered at that "we."

Glancing at Therese, Devlin smiled. "And if Therese's reaction on learning that Isadora is the proprietor of *The London Crier* is anything to judge by, Louisa—Louisa Cynster who is now Drake's wife—will fall on your neck and drag you inside and avidly listen to all you have to say, which means Drake will as well."

Therese added, "If anyone can guess what in these photographs might have moved someone to murder, it'll be Drake."

Gray dipped his head in agreement. "I'll contact him. It can't hurt." He accepted the photographs from Therese and slipped them into his pocket.

He glanced at her, then ventured, "While investigating the murder, I'm obviously going to be associating with Isadora, with whom, you might recall, I was acquainted before I left the country. What can you tell me about her life now?"

He was absolutely certain that, despite the years, Therese would remember exactly how close he and Izzy had been. In truth, it hadn't been only Isadora who had been expecting him to propose.

When Therese arched her brows, he acerbically added, "I don't want to find myself stumbling over further misconceptions."

She grinned. "I suppose I have to thank you for the news about Isadora owning *The Crier*—and please do assure her that neither Devlin nor I will breathe a word of that to anyone."

He nodded and looked at her pointedly.

Still grinning, she settled into the cushions and waved airily. "Fire away. What do you want to know?"

Voicing his questions would expose his interest. Nevertheless, he knew of no better source for the sort of information he needed to know.

Over the next twenty minutes, he confirmed that, despite a veritable horde of suitors who had swarmed about Isadora after he had left, she'd never come close to encouraging, let alone entertaining, an offer. "That drove the grandes dames quite to the brink," Therese said. "Even when the truth of the family's finances started to leak out, on birth alone, Isadora still ranked as a highly eligible young lady."

Therese explained how, in the way such things happened, word had slowly seeped through the ton that the late earl had all but bankrupted the family. "The situation became obvious when they were forced to sell the Mayfair house." She frowned. "That must have been the year after you left."

When Gray inclined his head, she continued, "Sometime after that, Isadora's brother, Julius, who had succeeded to the title—I believe he's younger than her by a year or so—contracted a marriage with the grand-daughter of a wealthy millowner."

Gray was surprised.

Therese saw it and nodded seriously. "Indeed. It had come to that, and the union bought the family some respite, and by all accounts, the marriage has proved a happy one. Nevertheless, not long after that, Julius sold the family estate, which had been in the family for generations but, courtesy of his late father, who had secretly broken the entail, was mort-gaged to the hilt."

Therese's gaze roved the comfort and solidity of the walls around her. Without prompting, she went on, "As far as I know, Isadora currently lives with her mother, Sybil, Dowager Countess of Exton, and her sister, Marietta, who was presented last year, in a town house in Norfolk Cres-cent, just north of Hyde Park off Edgware Road." Therese met Gray's eyes. "To all intents and social purposes, the Exton ladies go on well enough. I don't know what more I can tell you."

Gray inclined his head. "That's a great deal more than I knew before. I've been picking my way through incidental comments Isadora's made and guessing. Knowing the situation will make dealing with her much easier."

And that's possibly the most massive understatement I have ever made.

Thinking over all Therese had said, he frowned. "I'm surprised Julius —now he's the earl—hasn't cut up rough over Isadora being the owner and active manager of *The London Crier*."

The look Therese bent on him was openly patronizing. "You are speaking of Isadora Descartes. In that family, she was always the leader, the one who took care of everyone else. Even while her father was alive, Julius, Marietta, James—her younger brother who's at Eton now—and Sybil all took their lead from Isadora. While they will always support her—and staunchly—I can't imagine any of them being of much practical help. They are all very nice people, but not the sort to act on their own—they are not in Isadora's league and will always look to her for guidance." Therese met Gray's eyes. "Consequently, Julius wouldn't dream of getting in Isadora's way, much less censuring her."

Gray nodded. "I see." And indeed, he did. Izzy didn't have anyone she could turn to in the current fraught situation—or at least, no one she would turn to for active help and assistance. He knew her well enough to feel certain that, rather than involve those she loved, she would keep her worries close and carry any burden herself.

Apparently, Therese had been dredging her memory. "As I recall, Isadora wasn't initially happy with Julius's decision to marry the millowner's granddaughter, but once she came to know the girl, Isadora changed her tune and approved and supported Julius's suit. And that, I must tell you, was critical to having the marriage more or less accepted within the ton. The grandes dames might not always approve of Isadora's actions, but they definitely respect her intelligence and her opinions. Once she accepted Julius's marriage, they did, too. Mind you, Julius and his wife—I believe her name is Dorothy—rarely come to town. I understand they prefer their life in the country and are quite content raising their children and managing their acres."

The clocks in the house chimed for three o'clock, and Gray stirred. "I should ride home. I have to be in town in the morning."

He and Devlin rose.

"I'll have your horse saddled and brought around." Devlin went to tug the bellpull and summon Edwards.

Gray gave Therese his hand and helped her to her feet. "Thank you for the information. I don't suppose you remember what number in Norfolk Crescent the Exton house is?"

She smiled brightly. "It's Number six."

He smiled in thanks, and they walked to where Devlin waited.

Gray shook hands with Devlin, thanked him for his assistance, and confirmed that he would definitely inform Drake about the murder, then Edwards arrived to say his horse was waiting, and Devlin and Therese walked out with him.

The pair halted on the front porch and watched Gray go down the steps and accept the reins from the groom.

Gray swung up to the saddle, raised a hand in farewell, then wheeled his horse and rode down the drive.

Therese and Devlin watched him go, and Devlin heard Therese murmur, "Who knows?"

He decided he didn't need to inquire further as to what she was specu-lating upon; he was fairly certain he knew.

Then the love of his life turned her bright eyes his way. "I have to say, I'm quite envious of Isadora and her creation at *The Crier*." More pensively, she added, "I wonder how it all works."

He managed to hide the horror her words—and even more her tone—evoked and mildly replied, "Indeed." He turned her in to the house and artfully asked, "I wonder what the boys are up to? They've been quiet for hours. Maybe we should check."

That galvanized her into action. With his fingers metaphorically crossed, Devlin followed her up the stairs.

∼

Gray reached Ancaster Park and rode straight to the stables. There, he found Sam and gave orders to have the grays put to, then strode to the house to fetch his bag.

During the ride from the Priory, he'd had time to digest all he'd learned and was now intent on driving back to town.

As he hauled open the side door and strode into the corridor, he muttered to himself, "To beard the lioness in her true den."

∼

At seven o'clock the following morning, Gray strode up the steps of Number 6, Norfolk Crescent. He paused on the semicircular porch and glanced around. The house faced west, across the neat street from a small, half-moon-shaped park ringed with black iron railings. The park hosted several trees that, in spring and summer, would make a pretty scene.

The terrace houses lining the crescent were relatively new and in pris-tine condition, and at this hour, there was no traffic about to compete with the birdsong.

All in all, it was one of the nicer spots in London to live. Not quite holding the cachet of Mayfair, but it would certainly pass in society as a "good address."

Turning to the glossy dark-green door, Gray plied the bronze knocker and waited.

During the drive to town, he'd dredged his memory for the names of the Exton staff, and when the butler opened the door, Gray greeted the man with an amiable smile. "Good morning, Cottesloe."

Gray stepped forward, and taken completely by surprise, the butler gave way.

"My lord?" Cottesloe blinked several times, then managed, "Forgive me, but it is Lord Child, is it not?"

"Indeed." Gray handed Cottesloe his hat, which the bemused butler accepted, and shrugged off his greatcoat. "I'm here to see Lady Isadora. I assume she's at the breakfast table?"

"Ah…" Instinctively, Cottesloe accepted the heavy coat Gray held out. "I…ah, believe she is, my lord."

"Excellent." Guessing the most likely direction, Gray started down the corridor that ran beside the stairs. "It's this way, is it?"

"Yes, but…" Weighed down with coat and hat, Cottesloe trotted after him. "My lord…that is…"

Gray caught the scent of toast and followed it to a sunny breakfast parlor at the rear of the house. Through the open door, he caught sight of Izzy, sipping from a teacup as she stared through the window at the small, winter-drab garden.

Without altering his stride, he walked into the room.

Alerted by his footsteps, startled, she looked around, then her eyes flared, and she stared at him as if she couldn't believe her eyes.

He smiled, intently, at her and circled to draw out the chair with its back to the window, the one directly opposite her. "Good morning, Izzy. I thought I'd find you here." He sat and held her stunned gaze.

Cottesloe hurried in and dithered by her elbow. "My lady, I didn't know if or, rather, whether his lordship—"

She waved aside his words. "My apologies for not warning you, Cottesloe." She glanced at the butler. "It's quite all right."

Cottesloe looked from Gray to her, his expression stating that to his way of thinking, the situation was far from satisfactory.

"Perhaps," she glanced at Gray, "his lordship might like some breakfast."

Gray smiled at Cottesloe. "I've already eaten, but a cup of coffee would be welcome."

With something acceptable to do, Cottesloe drew himself up and half bowed. "Of course, my lord."

Gray watched as the butler, spine rigid, disapproval in every line, departed, bearing away Gray's coat and hat.

"What the devil are you doing here?"

Shifting his gaze back to Izzy, he noted that the look she was leveling at him over the rim of her teacup was not so much aggressive as wary. He opted for the fastest way to convince her that he knew all. "The people I visited yesterday to consult over the names of those featured in Quimby's photographs were the Earl and Countess of Alverton."

Izzy closed her eyes and softly groaned. "Therese Cader—I might have known."

"Indeed, you might. I grew up with Alverton, after all."

She shook her head and opened her eyes. "I'd forgotten the connection." She paused, then met his gaze directly. "I assume that means you know everything about my current position in society and the... subterfuge, for want of a better word, I have in place to keep the two halves of my life separate."

He held her gaze for a heartbeat, then replied, "As to whether I know all...that's impossible for me to say. But I certainly know a great deal more than I did on Saturday." He circled a finger in the air. "Enough to understand about here."

Enough to be a very great nuisance and an even bigger threat.

Rationally, Izzy knew that was so, yet she felt not the slightest threat emanating from him. Irritation at having been taken in by her subterfuge and a certain grimness, too, but nothing that triggered her well-honed defenses.

He remained committed to helping her solve Quimby's murder and wouldn't let her down.

While that knowledge was comforting, that she felt so certain of him was itself unsettling.

As if confirming her assessment, he added, "Therese told me to assure you that neither she nor Devlin will breathe a word of your situation to anyone." His lips twisted. "Truth be told, she seemed rather envious of your achievement in setting up *The Crier*."

Izzy suppressed a snort. She knew Therese well enough to be unsurprised by that.

Cottesloe reappeared, bearing the silver coffeepot. He poured Gray a cup, then took up his customary position by the sideboard.

Izzy caught Gray's eyes with a look of warning. Any words spoken before Cottesloe would find their way to her mother within hours.

Gray lowered the coffee cup. "I learned the names of several people in the photographs. Did you get any further with your inquiries?"

That, she could safely answer. "Mama, Marietta, and I had a quick look at the prints before we went to church. Marietta recognized a few faces, and after lunch, she and I strolled in the park, wracking our brains, then returned to pore over the photographs with Mama again. We've put names to most faces in the Hyde Park and Regent's Park photographs, and a few of those in the museum scene, and we think we know two of the ladies on the edge of the London Bridge picture."

He nodded. "When we reach the office and write everything down, we'll have names for most of the members of the ton who feature."

Izzy interpreted the comment as a statement of intent, namely that he was going to accompany her to the office and, presumably, continue by her side, at least as long as it suited him.

Normally, such high-handed interference in her day would provoke immediate resistance, but she wasn't averse to him being at the office when the police returned.

"Indeed." She drained her teacup. "Once you finish your coffee, we can go."

The smile that curved his lips was more predatory than warming. He drained his cup, set it down, and waved. "Lead on."

She rose and sent Cottesloe to summon the carriage, then walked with Gray to the front hall.

He helped her don her coat. "Your mother and sister?"

"Are rarely seen downstairs before eleven o'clock." She settled her bonnet on her head.

He shrugged on his greatcoat. Cottesloe returned to hand him his hat and open the door.

She'd left her reticule on the hall table. She picked it up and led the way outside.

Fields, her coachman, stood beside the carriage, holding the reins and the open door.

She informed him, "Lord Child will be accompanying us this morning."

Fields's surprise showed only fleetingly, then he bowed to Gray. "Your lordship."

Gray nodded back, grasped Izzy's elbow, and steadied her up the carriage steps.

She felt the imprint of his long fingers through the two layers of fabric.

His hand slid away, and she gathered her skirts and sat, and he climbed into the small carriage and settled on the seat opposite. Fields closed the carriage door, and the body dipped as he climbed to the box.

Until that moment, she hadn't felt claustrophobic in the carriage—hadn't even noticed it was that small—but with Gray shut in with her, she felt as if air was in short supply.

Breathless. She felt breathless.

The carriage jerked into motion, then settled and rolled smoothly along.

They both had long legs and sat angled to accommodate each other in the cramped space, leaving his trousers brushing her skirts.

She drew in a constrained breath and was almost grateful when, his gaze on the passing streetscape, he said, "Therese, of course, knew only about the ton side of your life." Shifting his gaze to her face, he said, "Tell me about Woburn Square."

She debated spinning him some tale, but he was too intelligent to bamboozle. "A Mrs. Carruthers owns the house. She's an elderly lady, the relict of a country squire and an old friend of Silas Barton, my brother's grandfather-in-law." She met Gray's amber eyes and smiled. "Silas was an unexpected benefit of Julius's marriage. He's a self-made man—a wily, wise, and sound one—and he befriended us all. You might say that, in our time of need, Silas was a godsend.

"With respect to *The Crier*, he's acted more like a godfather to me. It was he who helped me acquire the printing works and rebuild what was an ailing business into the profitable enterprise it now is. Woburn Square was also Silas's idea—he insisted that, if I was to go into the newspaper business, it was imperative that I conceal my identity, and using Mrs. Carruthers's house as a staging post when going there and back ensures no one can readily follow me from the paper to Norfolk Crescent."

Still smiling, she added, "In true Silas fashion, me dropping in on Mrs. Carruthers twice every workday—I almost always stop to exchange a few words while passing through the house—gives the old dear something to look forward to." She refocused on Gray. "That gives you some idea of Silas's character."

Gray shifted restlessly. "Therese explained something of what happened with your family. I hadn't realized, back then, that your father had left the family so deeply in debt."

"For obvious reasons, we concealed as much of the impact as we could, but there was no avoiding the reality. We sailed very close to the rocks in the years immediately after Papa's death. With James still in the nursery, Julius at Oxford, and Marietta in the schoolroom, it was left to Mama and me to cope as best we could, riding out the storm of creditors. That dragged on for several years. It turned out Papa had mortgaged everything he could to fund his gambling, and there really wasn't anything left."

Gray straightened. "He was a gambler?"

"Indeed. With him, it was mostly horses." Even she heard the caustic tone the years of bitterness lent her voice. "He was addicted by the end. He couldn't bear to know a race was being run anywhere in the country on which he hadn't wagered. It was ludicrous, the lengths to which he went just to scrape up a few more pounds to lay on the nags. It wasn't even about winning, by then. It was purely the thrill of having so much riding on the race. The deeper the debt, the greater the risk, and the more fevered he became. The experience became his drug."

She glanced out of the window, but could feel Gray's gaze on her face. "You can imagine how relieved Mama and I were that Julius has never shown the slightest sign of being interested in wagering on anything."

Gray's gaze shifted.

After a moment, she glanced at him and saw he was staring blankly into space, then he blinked, saw her watching, and offered, "Sometimes, that's the way of it—personally experiencing the damage gambling does, not just to the gambler but to everyone around him, sends people in the opposite direction."

"Whatever the reason for Julius's aversion to gambling, we're sincerely grateful."

"Where is James, incidentally?"

"At Eton. That was one thing Julius and I—and Mama—were adamant about, that James has the education and opportunities he should have."

"Who funds that?"

"Partly Julius, from what is now the earldom's estate, and partly the business."

Gray forced himself to think—and to acknowledge how rattled he was. From Therese's report, he'd assumed the late earl had lost his fortune through poor investments or something of that sort; learning that Izzy's father had gambled the family more or less into destitution had shaken him to an extent he didn't want Izzy to see.

He cleared his throat. "If I've understood everything correctly, you—

with help from Silas Barton—set up the Molyneaux Printing Works and *The London Crier* in order to keep your family in the manner to which you're accustomed."

She tipped her head from side to side. "That's partly correct. The income from the printing works pays all the bills for Norfolk Crescent and for Mama, Marietta, and me." Briefly, she met his eyes. "Even though both Julius and Silas have made standing offers to assist, it's important to Mama, Marietta, and me that we are not a burden on anyone."

He had no difficulty believing that and understood the pride underlying the sentiment.

The carriage turned down a narrow service lane bounded by the rear fences of two rows of houses.

"We're nearly there." Izzy gathered her reticule and shifted forward on the seat.

The carriage drew up beside the rear gate of a property. Gray leaned across, opened the door, and stepped down to the lane, glanced briefly around, then handed Izzy down. "Number twenty, Woburn Square, I take it."

"Indeed." She led the way through the gate and up the garden path.

Following her, Gray closed the gate and heard the carriage rattle away. "What happens with the carriage?"

"Fields drives to a nearby livery stable and leaves the horse and carriage there for the day, then returns here and helps out about the house until I'm ready to leave for home again."

He glanced at the houses on either side as he drew level with Izzy, who had paused on the back step. "What do the neighbors think of your visits?"

"Doyle, Mrs. Carruthers's housekeeper, is friendly with the housekeepers on either side. Apparently, everyone around believes I'm a very devoted friend."

Gray said nothing more, but followed her through the back door into a cozy kitchen.

There, he found himself introduced as Lord Child to the Carruthers staff—a surprised-looking Doyle, Millie the cook, and a young scamp called Freddy. All three regarded him warily, but seemed to accept Izzy's airy explanation that he was helping her with business.

He was then led to a breakfast parlor where he was presented to an ancient old lady. She examined him through shrewd blue eyes and, when Izzy explained his presence, simply nodded and stated, "Good."

With that, she waved them off. "I know you have to hurry, my dear. You can tell me more this evening."

Gray felt Mrs. Carruthers's gaze dwelling on him as he fell in behind Izzy. Even on such abbreviated acquaintance, he'd received the distinct impression that the old lady was very fond of Izzy and, moreover, was nobody's fool.

They left through the front door and, at a brisk pace, set out for the printing works. He glanced around, noting how very few denizens of the neighborhood were in evidence.

Izzy threw him a glance. "It's a very quiet and genteel neighborhood. At the times I tend to go in and out, there's rarely any people about."

He was starting to appreciate just how well organized the subterfuge truly was—how canny Silas Barton had been in arranging for Izzy to use the Carruthers house.

Gray owned to being increasingly keen to meet Mr. Barton. Aside from anything else, he felt he owed the man his gratitude. Izzy had been forced to deal with a terrible situation more or less on her own, and Silas had been there and had helped when...

When I thoughtlessly ran away.

And left Izzy to shoulder the burden of taking care of and protecting her family entirely on her own.

Neither saw a need to talk as they walked. Unfortunately, that left Gray a prey to his thoughts. He knew what he'd heard that fateful afternoon, knew why he'd fled, but...he now had to consider the possibility that the words Izzy had uttered had, in the context in which she'd stood, been more a statement of fact than of feeling.

The long and short of it was, he *had* intended to offer for her, and he *had* been wealthy.

But he'd heard what he'd heard and felt as he'd felt, and he'd reacted and walked—run—away.

Now he knew that while he'd been adventuring, taking risks, gambling like a fiend, and eventually, recklessly losing every last penny and landing in a gutter, only to have Fate lift him out of it and grant him one last chance...while he'd been doing all that, constantly pursuing life to the fullest, living high and low and taking no responsibility for anyone but himself, Izzy had been dealing with the horrendous situation in which her father's gambling had landed the earldom, making difficult decisions, managing as best she could, and shouldering the responsibility for all her family.

Until today, he would have described some of his past years as rough and hard. He had a sneaking suspicion that in comparison to Izzy, he didn't know what the word "hard" truly meant.

He knew he wasn't responsible for the troubles that had beset her, but equally, he would have made her life infinitely easier had he stayed.

Had he honored the unspoken promise that had lain between them.

As they turned onto Bernard Street, pacing beside her, he forced himself to draw in a deep breath, then slowly let it out.

From now on, he would keep his eyes open, take in all he saw, and properly reassess.

Not just their past but their present.

And not just her but himself as well.

They reached the door to the printing works a few minutes before eight o'clock. Izzy fished in her reticule, hauled out her keys, unlocked the door, and led the way inside.

From the reports Gray had received the previous night from Tom and Young Bill, he knew that, although the police hadn't seen fit to post any watch, no one had tried to break into the workshop, at least not during the day.

Reassuringly, everything was as it had been when he and Izzy had left on Saturday.

Izzy went straight to the office and hung up her bonnet and coat, then headed for her desk.

After scanning the workshop, Gray ambled for the office while, in the distance, the city's bells tolled for eight o'clock.

He'd just hung up his coat when the bell above the door tinkled. He looked across to see the staff arriving.

Izzy rose and walked past him, into the foyer. She greeted the staff who were doffing their coats, and they gathered around.

Gray lounged in the office doorway.

Once everyone had arrived, Izzy explained about the photographs Digby had printed, again thanking him for his excellent work. The others beamed and patted the lad's shoulder, leaving him blushing and bashfully ducking his head.

"So what are the photographs of?" Lipson asked.

Izzy described the seven scenes and the progress they'd made in identifying the people in them. "I'm sure the police will return sometime today, and we'll explain our thinking and give them the extra set of prints Digby made. They might see something in the photographs that we haven't. Meanwhile, however, I've decided we should go forward and publish this week's edition, including a section on Quimby and his murder."

The relief in the staff's faces was apparent; their expressions suggested the news gave them heart.

"Not to cast a spanner," Maguire said, "but what will we do for photographs? Do you want to use the three Quimby did for us last Friday?"

Izzy frowned. "I'm not sure we should, not if they're somehow linked to Quimby's death. That doesn't seem"—she wrinkled her nose —"appropriate."

"We could use photographs from before—like from early last year," Digby suggested. "Even though we've used them once, the punters aren't likely to remember, and the backgrounds will be winterish."

"That's true enough." Lipson nodded approvingly. He looked at Digby. "Do you know where they are?"

Digby tipped his head toward the cabinets lining the wall between the office and the darkroom. "They're in there." He glanced at Izzy. "I could pull out some of last winter's scenes and show you, and you can choose which to run."

"That will do for now," Izzy said. "At least until I can secure the services of a suitable photographer."

Gray listened as the staff joined in a discussion of what articles should be written and run. All agreed that an obituary was called for as well as a lead story reporting Quimby's strange murder.

"Might seem a bit crass," Matthews observed, "but the readers will love it."

All nodded their assent, and the meeting broke up, and everyone dispersed to their various tasks. Izzy started for the office, saw Gray, and halted, staring at him, then she swung around. "Gerry?"

The young man turned back. "Yes, ma'am?"

"Can you bring me seven clean sheets of printing paper, please?"

"'Course, ma'am. I'll fetch them up for you right away."

While Gerry strode off to the storeroom, Izzy swung about, waved Gray back, and walked into the office. She returned to her chair behind the desk, sat, and pulled several sheets of notes toward her.

Gray sank into his customary armchair as she stated, "I have to write the lead story and Quimby's obituary, but first"—she glanced at him —"we'd better make a note of all those in the photographs we've already identified."

Gerry arrived, bearing seven large sheets of blank printing paper. "Here you are, ma'am."

"Thank you." Izzy received the sheets and laid them on her desk. She dismissed Gerry with a nod, and he left, hurrying back to his work.

Izzy wrestled her set of prints from her reticule, rummaged in a drawer and drew out several pins, and pinned the top photograph—the one of riders in Hyde Park—in the middle of the first sheet. "Right." After setting the rest of the prints aside, she picked up a pencil and drew a line with an arrow indicating one of the riders. "I know who this gentleman is."

As she wrote down the name, Gray dragged the armchair around, leaned over, and tapped another rider. "That, I'm told, is Lord Compton."

"It is, indeed." She noted that down.

They progressed through all seven photographs, pinning each to a blank sheet and noting all the names they'd gathered.

The last print they addressed was the one taken from London Bridge, for which they had only a few suggested identities, none of which were certain.

When Izzy sat back and frowned at their combined effort, Gray glanced at the clock and discovered the hour was already after ten. "Therese and Devlin suggested that we take the photographs and the story of Quimby's murder to Drake Varisey." He looked at Izzy and saw understanding dawn in her emerald eyes. "I take it you know about Drake's...occupation?"

Calculation infusing her expression, she nodded.

"Devlin and Therese strongly recommend consulting him, but of course, that means his wife, Louisa, will likely learn about this as well. Indeed, I understand that she's the best possible source for the identities of those in the photographs—those of the ton we've yet to name." He paused, then said, "I left a note to be delivered to Wolverstone House at eight this morning, asking Drake for a meeting at ten-thirty. I didn't mention your name or *The Crier*, although the paper will obviously feature in what I tell Drake."

He studied Izzy's face, but her expression was now shuttered; he couldn't tell what she was thinking. "Do you want to come with me? I think it would be best if you did, but if you don't wish Drake and Louisa to know your secret, I'll do my best to avoid mentioning you other than as Mrs. Molyneaux." His gaze on her face, he quietly said, "Your choice."

After several moments, her gaze rose to meet his. He could see in her eyes that she was deeply reluctant to go; if Therese had been curious, it seemed Louisa would be even more so, and for Izzy, the more people who knew her secret, the greater the risk to all she'd built over the past years, and the greater the threat to her and her family's security, both financial and in society.

Then her gaze sharpened, and her features firmed. She nodded. "I'll go with you."

She looked down at the sheets, each with the relevant photograph attached, and quickly and efficiently folded them into a packet, pushed back from the desk, retrieved her reticule, and carefully pushed the packet inside.

Then she looked across the desk, determination in every line of her face. "Catching Quimby's murderer is too important not to do everything I can. Until we know why Quimby was murdered, we can't be certain the killer won't come back or that he doesn't have some sort of twisted vendetta against *The Crier* itself and Quimby was only his first victim."

Gray came to his feet as she did and followed her to the coatrack. "I hadn't thought of that." He helped her don her coat, then caught her eye. "And it's a truly horrifying proposition."

She threw him a speaking look and, settling her bonnet on her head, led the way out of the door.

CHAPTER 6

"*H*ow well do you know Drake and Louisa?" Gray asked as the hackney he'd hailed rattled south toward Grosvenor Square.

Seated beside him, Izzy stared at the passing streetscape. "I meet them socially, so we know each other in that way, and Louisa and I have always moved in similar circles, even if we're not close."

She sighed and glanced at him. "I can't see any way to hide my ownership of *The London Crier*, not from Drake and Louisa. They're both as sharp as the proverbial tack. If we want their help—and I agree with Therese and Devlin's assessment that consulting both Drake and Louisa would be the sensible thing to do—then I'll need to be open with them." She gestured vaguely. "It's the only way."

That she was prepared to risk all in pursuit of the killer could not have been clearer. Gray said, "From what I've gathered, Drake—and Louisa as well—must, of necessity, be very good at keeping other people's secrets."

"There is that."

"With luck, nothing adverse will come of this meeting."

She grimaced faintly. "I can only hope."

The hackney bowled along the north side of Grosvenor Square, then slowed and pulled up outside Wolverstone House.

Izzy grasped Gray's hand to step down from the hackney, waited while he paid the jarvey, then raised her skirts and climbed the steps to the imposing mansion's front door.

Gray rang the bell. A magisterial butler opened the door and, when Gray gave their names, bowed them into the front hall, took their coats and hats, then conducted them to the drawing room.

Izzy had visited the house often enough over the years to feel entirely assured, yet for a disconcerting second as she crossed the tiled hall, she wasn't sure which persona she should be projecting—Lady Isadora Descartes or Mrs. Molyneaux.

The point was clarified when the butler announced them as Lady Isadora Descartes and Lord Grayson Child, and she drew in a fortifying breath, and side by side, they moved into the room.

Louisa, who'd been sitting on one of the twin sofas, saw her, blinked, then all but sprang to her feet. "Isadora!" Louisa's pale-green gaze flicked from Izzy to Gray and back again.

Izzy dipped her head. "Louisa."

Drake had been standing with one arm resting on the mantelpiece; he straightened and, equally curious, came forward. "Isadora."

She halted and inclined her head. "Drake."

Drake's gaze deflected to Gray. "Child."

Gray held out his hand. "Please, just Gray."

His lips lightly lifting, Drake shook hands. "Drake. I remember you from Eton—you were in Alverton's year."

Gray grinned. "For my sins."

Releasing Gray's hand, Drake turned to Louisa. "My wife, Louisa, although I expect you've met before."

Gray grasped the hand Louisa offered. "Years ago. I believe you'd only just been presented when I left the country."

Louisa nodded. "I think we met only once, at some ball." She continued to glance back and forth between Izzy and Gray.

Drake also looked curiously at Izzy.

Calmly, Izzy caught Louisa's eye and waited.

Recalled to her hostessly duties yet patently still burning with curiosity, Louisa waved at the other sofa. "Please, sit, and tell us what brings you here."

Izzy walked to the sofa, sat, let her reticule fall to the cushion beside her, and started to pull off her gloves. As Gray sat beside her, she looked at the pair settling themselves on the sofa opposite. "Perhaps I should commence our revelations by explaining that I'm here in my role as proprietor of *The London Crier*."

When dealing with powerful people, it helped to knock them off balance from the start.

Judging by the astonished looks both Drake and Louisa fixed on her, she'd achieved her objective.

"*You* own *The London Crier*?" Then Louisa's expression cleared. "Well, of course you do—that explains so much! I've always wondered how they got their information. And your anecdotes are always so wickedly accurate."

Izzy had to admit she enjoyed surprising Louisa, who was generally held to be all-knowing, at least as pertained to those in the ton.

But before Louisa could launch into the myriad questions clearly forming in her busy brain, Drake drily said, "With that now established, what brings you to our door?"

Izzy glanced at Gray, and he obliged.

"Murder."

Drake's eyes widened. "This gets more and more interesting. Who was murdered?"

Between them, they told the tale of Quimby's murder, including the involvement of the police, then explained their theory that the motive for the murder lay in the photographs Quimby took that day—that the killer had tried to destroy—and the subsequent discovery of the unmarred negatives and their efforts to identify what it was in the photographs that might have led to Quimby's death.

By the time Izzy extracted the photographs, each wrapped in its individual information sheet, from her reticule, Drake and Louisa could barely wait for her to unfold the sheets and lay them on the low table Drake fetched and set between the sofas.

As soon as she smoothed out the sheets, Drake and Louisa leaned forward and pored over the prints.

After several seconds of Louisa muttering names beneath her breath, Drake said, "Let's take these one at a time." He lifted the sheet with the photograph of the riders in Hyde Park attached and spread it on top. Both he and Louisa studied it. "I agree with all the names you have," Drake said.

"And that gentleman"—Louisa pointed to the single man they'd yet to name—"is Louis Kilpatrick."

Izzy pulled a pencil from her reticule and wrote down the name.

"Right." Drake set that sheet aside, revealing the next—the scene in Regent's Park. "What about this one?"

Louisa brought her excellent memory to bear, and soon, they had the names of all the people in that photograph and the second Hyde Park scene and most of those in the view of the museum courtyard.

When it came to the print of the building near the new station, neither Louisa nor Drake could name anyone. "They're ordinary people going about their business." Drake scanned the print. "I seriously doubt there's anything in this scene that might have triggered the photographer's murder." He set the sheet aside, revealing the view taken from London Bridge.

Louisa leaned close, peering at the two young ladies just visible along the bridge's railing. Then she stabbed her finger at the stationary carriage, a section of the back of which had made it into the photograph. "That's the Duchess of Lewes's carriage. Such a ramshackle old thing, but she insists she finds it comfortable. And the two young ladies are the duchess's granddaughters."

Louisa rattled off names, and Izzy promptly added them to the sheet. "My mother thought as much, but wasn't sure."

Louisa nodded and re-examined the print. "I don't think there's anyone else we need to identify on that one."

Izzy agreed, and Drake shifted the sheet to lie with the others beside the table.

Louisa studied the final print, the one of the scene outside the coffee-house in Fleet Street. After a long moment, she shook her head. "I don't know anyone in this one." Her tone was almost forlorn.

Drake tapped his finger on the image of the largish, well-dressed gentleman, who was talking to a shorter, rotund, and rather nattily dressed man on the pavement before the coffeehouse. "His name's Duvall. I've seen him around the corridors of Whitehall, but I can't recall which department he's with."

Gray nodded. "Devlin said much the same, but couldn't remember which department, either. At least we now have a name."

On the sheet, next to Devlin's "government" comment, Izzy wrote "Duvall, Whitehall?" and drew an arrow pointing to the man.

Drake lifted the other sheets and laid them on top of the one on the table, then all four sat back and regarded the stacked sheets.

"The critical question," Louisa said, "is why would someone kill to stop any of these apparently innocuous pictures being published?"

Silence reigned, then Drake stated, "The next logical question is what is it that we don't know?" After a moment, he went on, "I accept your thesis that Quimby was killed because of something one of these photographs reveals. That means the motive is staring us in the face, but as yet, we don't know enough to recognize it."

After a further moment of silent cogitation, Louisa shifted her gaze to Izzy's face. "I read *The Crier* every week, so I know the owner is listed as I. Molyneaux—ah." Her expression lightened. "Molyneaux is your mother's maiden name, isn't it?"

Izzy admitted it was. "I took that name to conceal my involvement with the paper."

"Well, I certainly won't tell anyone." Louisa directed a sharp glance at her spouse. "And neither will Drake."

He glanced at her and smiled, then looked at Izzy. "I won't tell, but I admit I'm already thinking of what use I might have for a paper with a certain circulation and an understanding proprietor."

Amused, Izzy shook her head at him, then Louisa, plainly curious, asked how Izzy actually ran the paper. "What, exactly, do you have to do?"

Izzy saw no reason to withhold such information. She described how each edition took shape, more or less going through her week's work day by day.

Louisa and Drake listened avidly, occasionally posing questions, which Izzy duly answered.

She'd reached the point of describing how the distribution of the paper was handled, when Louisa's expression suddenly lit, and she flung up her hands. "Wait—wait!"

Everyone, her husband included, stared at her. From her expression, she was following some mental trail, then she refocused on Izzy and beamed. "I know how to catch the murderer!"

Drake viewed his wife with undisguised trepidation. "How?"

Louisa kept her gaze trained on Izzy. "I'm sure you're intending to report on the murder in the next edition. I assume that will be this week's?"

Izzy nodded. "It'll go out this Friday." Cynically, she added, "Having a murder on the premises is a sure way of gaining the public's attention."

"Just so," Louisa returned. "And what if you state that it's believed the reason your photographer was killed lies somewhere in the last photographs he took?" Louisa waved at the sheets. "Publish all seven and tell the readers that the vital clue to identifying the murderer lies in the pictures. Can they spot it?"

Enthused, her face alight, Louisa leaned forward. "Print the photographs in the paper and ask your readers for any information or insights they have. For instance, who are the people in the photographs—the people we don't know?"

Drake stirred and also sat forward, studying the uppermost sheet, then he flicked through the stack and examined the others. "That just might work. These are all clear enough, detailed enough—it would be a pity not to use them." He looked at Izzy. "And offer a reward. It doesn't have to be much—ten or twenty pounds would do it."

Izzy's mind was whirling. She felt Gray's gaze and glanced his way.

"That's an excellent idea," he said. "I'll put up the reward."

His eyes said: *Especially as this will banish all memory of the exposé from the minds of your public.*

She smiled and nodded.

"You'll need to state that the reward is for new information that actually leads to the killer, but"—eyes bright, Louisa met Izzy's gaze—"this will be just like an old-fashioned hue and cry. All we're doing is adapting the concept to the modern age by using a newspaper rather than the town crier…" She laughed. "And how appropriate it is that a newspaper called *The London Crier* will run the piece."

Izzy continued to nod as the possibilities firmed in her mind. "We'll include a photograph of Quimby himself—I'm fairly certain we have one—and ask if anyone saw him on Friday, especially if he was with any others."

Drake inclined his head. "That's a very good notion."

They discussed the ins and outs and the potential wording of their appeal to the readers. Izzy took notes, and it was plain all four of them had been completely won over by the idea of a modern-day hue and cry.

The jeweled clock on the mantelpiece chimed melodically, indicating that it was half past twelve. Louisa glanced at it, then looked at Izzy and Gray. "Please say you'll stay for luncheon. We can continue our discussions over the table. I'm sure we'll come up with more good ideas if we give ourselves the time."

Izzy looked at Gray. "There's nothing that requires my immediate attention at the printing works."

He nodded and looked at Louisa. "By all means, we'll stay and keep working on this idea."

"*My* brilliant idea." Louisa rose and went to tug the bellpull. "And because it was my idea, I'm going to demand to know all the details of how Izzy plans to execute it."

Izzy laughed and, as it truly had been a brilliant idea, gracefully inclined her head in acceptance, then the butler arrived and confirmed that luncheon was ready to be served, and they rose and adjourned to the dining room.

With Drake, Gray followed the ladies, who despite the disparity in their heights, had their heads together, planning and plotting.

Eyeing the pair, Drake shook his head. "There'll be no stopping them now, but I do think a hue and cry edition will be the fastest way to flush out the murderer."

Louisa led them to what was plainly a personal dining room; the table was round and would hold only six at a pinch. They sat, with Izzy opposite Drake and Gray facing Louisa. The butler served the soup, and after swallowing her first mouthful, Izzy glanced at Drake. "In bringing our problem to your door, I hope we haven't hauled you away from any pressing concerns."

Drake shook his head. "In fact, I'm pathetically grateful to have a mystery into which I can sink my teeth. It's been rather dull of late—in this season, political intrigue tends to take a holiday."

"For which, I'm sure, we can all be grateful," Izzy responded.

The conversation flowed freely. Courtesy of his recent return, Gray was the one with least to contribute, so he listened as three of arguably the keenest observers of the ton traded quips and comments as they entertained themselves and him.

As Lady Isadora, Izzy effortlessly fitted into this milieu. This was her true station, something Drake and Louisa—of similar station, as was Gray himself —instinctively recognized, unquestioningly accepted, and automatically responded to. The observation fed Gray's appreciation of just how remarkable her performance as Mrs. Molyneaux was. At the printing works, she was accepted as the owner and manager, and he was quite sure not a single person there suspected her of being an earl's daughter who regularly appeared in the major drawing rooms of the haut ton. Whether it was her innate confidence or an acquired knack, she had mastered the art of dealing with people as people regardless of social rank, without relying on her inherited status.

His attention caught, he watched more closely, studying her in this incarnation, one he hadn't seen since returning to England. This Izzy was the mature version of the young lady he'd left behind, and her poise and self-assurance were impressive, even judged against Louisa's mercurial brilliance.

The more Gray observed of Louisa's and Drake's responses to Izzy, the more it was borne in on him that, for an aristocratic spinster of her age, she occupied an unusual position of acceptance within the ton. After some cogitation, he decided the reason had to lie in the grandes dames and those like Louisa and her ilk knowing, or at least suspecting, more of the family's true history than he had known.

It appeared the haut ton had come to view as laudable, rather than as a matter for censure, Izzy's decision not to marry and, instead, devote herself to protecting her mother and siblings and successfully guiding the family through the minefield of severely straitened circumstances to an easier time.

Of course, one of the talents members of the ton had historically excelled at was fully comprehending yet never referring to the reality of living in straitened circumstances. Within the ton, appearance was all, and he suspected, for ladies of Izzy's rank, their instinctive reaction on viewing her situation would be along the lines of "there but for the grace of God go I."

By the time they reached the end of the meal, all four had grown even more enamored of the notion of their modern-day hue and cry.

Rising from the table, Izzy caught Gray's eye. "I need to return to the printing works to get things rolling for our hue and cry edition."

He nodded, and Drake dispatched a footman to secure a hackney.

Together, they strolled into the front hall, and after promising to keep Louisa and Drake informed of any developments, Gray and Izzy took their leave, and he led her down the steps to the waiting hackney.

They set off, with Izzy apparently mentally planning her upcoming front page. Gray smiled to himself; he was entirely satisfied with the outcome of their morning. As for the rest of the day, he planned to stick to Izzy's side and ensure nothing, as the Americans would say, threw a wrench in her works.

Gray held open the printing works door, and Izzy glided through, her gaze already focusing farther down the workshop.

"Lipson? Everyone? We have news and a change of plans."

The staff looked up, then downed tools and came forward to gather in the usual spot.

Izzy walked into the office, set her reticule on the desk, then undid and removed her bonnet and shrugged off her coat. Gray took her coat and bonnet and hung them with his coat on the rack, then followed her out to where the staff were waiting.

"Before you start," Lipson said, "you should know you just missed the police."

"Oh." Izzy looked from Lipson to Mary and Maguire. "What did they say? Anything to the point?"

The responses to that question were distinctly contemptuous. Gray, who had taken up his usual stance leaning against the office wall, concluded that the police had struggled to find sensible questions to ask and had retreated empty-handed and, if the staff were to be believed, empty-headed as well.

"They didn't have a clue—not one," Lipson said. "Just wasting their time and ours, they were."

That seemed the general consensus.

"Well"—Izzy waved at Gray—"his lordship and I have just come from meeting with some others, people connected with the authorities, and it was suggested that we run what might be termed a hue and cry edition."

She described what she envisaged, enthusing about the possibilities and verbally painting a graphic picture of what she wanted to achieve.

The staff, one and all, fell in love with the idea and readily threw themselves, minds, hearts, and hands, into its execution.

Eventually, the majority of the staff returned to preparing the press for action once the pieces were written and ready to set and print, while with Lipson and Mary, Izzy retreated to her office.

Gray lingered in the workshop long enough to be impressed by the staff's commitment to the latest idea; he overheard Tom Lipson, helping Horner and Matthews clean the massive drum of the press, saying that getting out the upcoming edition and, through it, catching Quimby's killer could be their parting gift to Quimby.

Maguire and Digby were sorting type like dervishes, their hands moving so fast they were almost a blur, all the while with grins on their faces.

Reassured, Gray ambled into the office to find Izzy, Mary, and Lipson gathered about the desk, leaning over it as they sketched, wrote, altered, and redrew, entirely absorbed with thrashing out ideas of how they would create a sensational front page.

For Gray's money, the subject matter was all that would be needed to attract the public's interest. As long as the word "murder" appeared, preferably in large capitals, the fickle public would flock to pick up the paper and read.

The banner headline of "Hue & Cry" was a forgone conclusion, but as Gray stood listening, debate raged over what to run below that. Lipson proposed featuring a picture of Quimby and a description of the crime, while Mary was all for the description, but felt that a picture of the deceased might be considered in poor taste, at least on the front page.

For her part, Izzy didn't seem convinced by any of the suggestions; she stood with arms crossed, frowning down at the roughly sketched headline.

Gray cleared his throat. When the three looked at him, he offered, "A hue and cry doesn't necessarily mean murder. You need to make that very clear. 'Murder Most Foul' run under the banner would do it. Then keep the words to a minimum on the front page—you want people to buy the paper to read more. Run Quimby's picture by all means—that'll help to make the victim real—but keep the rest simple. Just something along the lines of 'Respected photographer stabbed to death in his darkroom. Help us find the killer!'"

Izzy's eyes came alight, and she seized a pencil and started scribbling ferociously. "Oh yes! That will do nicely."

Mary and Lipson smiled at him delightedly, then went back to conspiring with Izzy as she sketched in the elements for their front page.

Gray felt a warm glow over having made a contribution.

"We'll need to make sure we have a decent picture of Quimby," Lipson said.

Still aimless, Gray spoke up. "Digby would be the one to ask, wouldn't he? Shall I go and see what he can find?"

Izzy threw him a grateful smile. "Please. That will allow us to get on with our second page."

Gray left them to it and went in search of Digby.

He found the lad still working alongside Maguire, cleaning individual pieces of type. When Gray asked about a photograph of Quimby, Digby said he knew of a few.

When the lad looked to Maguire, the older man grinned and tipped his head. "Best you go and find them. Mrs. Molly will want to see a rough of the front page, and if that's going to be on it, we'll need to work it up."

Gray hid a grin over "Mrs. Molly" and followed Digby to the cabinets along the far wall. He watched as the lad ferreted about in the drawers, moving from one cabinet to another.

"I know they're here somewhere," Digby muttered. He glanced over his shoulder at Gray. "Mr. Q used himself as a model when he was experimenting, changing his settings or using different developing solutions." The lad all but stuck his head in one of the bottom drawers, then emerged with a triumphant "Here they are!"

He straightened with a folder clutched in his hand.

Gray had been leaning against the table that Izzy had said was used to assemble the elements for each page; he stood as Digby laid the folder on the table and opened it.

Inside lay various photographs of a middle-aged man, possibly nearing fifty, of medium height and build, sporting wiry sideburns and curly, grizzled hair.

Gray had seen Quimby only in death. The photographs gave the man more depth and brought him alive in a way that, to Gray, he hadn't previously been.

Digby was sorting through the prints, setting some aside. "These are the older ones—done with daguerreotype. We don't have the negatives for them no more. But these"—Digby pushed forward a set of five photographs—"are more recent, taken using calotype, so we can use any of them."

Gray studied the five prints. "Actually, we might want to use two. This one"—he tapped a classical portrait that showed Quimby full face, from the waist up—"because it shows his face most clearly, and this one." He picked up a full-length image of the photographer, facing the camera from across a narrow street with the steps of a building behind him and two other men walking along the pavement. "It gives a better idea of how tall he was, and if we want people to remember if they saw him out and about, that picture is more likely to jog memories."

Digby agreed unreservedly.

Gray tipped his head toward the office. "Why don't we take these two to the office and explain why we think they should be the ones used?"

Digby gathered up the folder and, carrying the two selected prints in his hand, went with Gray to the office.

After contributing to the discussion over which photographs of

Quimby would be used, Gray trailed Izzy as she and Lipson moved to the table used to lay out the page designs and commenced doing just that. They called Maguire over to discuss the size of type to be used for the various headlines, then blocked in the areas for the articles, notices, and photographs.

Gray found his opinion solicited regarding where best to place the announcement of the reward and was fascinated by the degree of understanding of their audience's reading habits displayed by Izzy, Lipson, and Maguire. Once blocks of space for the various sections of text had been allocated, Maguire returned to his type while Izzy and Lipson surveyed the twelve individual pages, noting down all the blank spaces.

Pencil in hand, Izzy consulted a notebook, then stated, "I make that seven medium advertisements and a grand total of eighteen smaller." She cocked a brow at Lipson.

He nodded. "That seems right."

"How many slots have we already got filled?"

Gray realized she was talking about advertisements.

Lipson tipped his head from side to side. "We could fill them all right now, but given this is such a special edition and will get much greater circulation…" He looked questioningly at Izzy.

She nodded decisively. "Indeed. We should call in the advertisers and discuss a higher fee." She tapped the pencil to her lips. "We could offer a special deal. A significantly higher fee for running in this edition"—she glanced at the rough layouts—"especially for the medium slots on the pages with the main story and the ads on the pages with the photographs and the notice of the reward, but as part of the deal, we'll agree to revert to our previous rate for the following two editions, which will also benefit from the increased circulation." She looked at Lipson. "What do you think? You're the one who'll be making the argument."

Lipson nodded decisively. "They'll all go for it. Once word about this hue and cry edition gets out, we'll be beating off new advertisers with sticks, and our regulars are smart enough to know that."

"Right, then. I'll leave you to get cracking with that. Meanwhile"—Izzy looked at Gray—"I have a lead article and an obituary to write."

She left Lipson making notes off the layout sheets and strode for the office.

Gray followed, but when Izzy—with a stern frown as a warning not to distract her—settled at her desk to write, he wandered out into the workshop again.

Lipson was standing behind the counter, working on a list, while Mary was perched on a stool farther along and busily writing. Izzy had mentioned that Mary wrote some of the pieces run in the paper, and she seemed to be working on an article of some sort.

Rather than interrupt, Gray ambled deeper into the workshop. He noticed that the darkroom door was propped open and glimpsed Digby inside, filling containers with solutions. Gray wondered when and from where Izzy would find another photographer. He skirted the huge, hulking printing press, still being crawled over by Tom Lipson and Horner, and came again to where Maguire, now assisted by Matthews, was preparing his type for setting the new edition.

Maguire gave Gray an encouraging smile. "The printing business new to you, then?"

Gray glanced at the press. "I know the basics—that you set the type into frames and those get inked and paper rolled over them in the press." He looked at Maguire. "I also know that Friday is distribution day, and Mrs. Molyneaux and Mary are both hard at work writing their pieces for this Friday's edition. But I'm curious. How does the work progress day to day?"

"Ah, well." Maguire's quick fingers didn't pause in sorting the tiny type. "If we start on Saturday, that's clean-up day. Then today, Monday, is get-ready day." He tipped his head toward the press and the men climbing over it. "Gerry and Tom go over the press and the boiler, and Jim and I get all our type cleaned, sorted, and ready to go. Then tomorrow, Tuesday, that's layout day. Mrs. Molly, Lipson, and our Mary finalize the layout for all twelve pages, and Jim and I get the formes for each page set up, ready for dropping in the type boxes for each article and advert. That's all done in the morning, and in the afternoon, Jim and I get started on setting the adverts and the articles as they're finalized."

Maguire reached for another shallow wooden box divided into segments and pulled it closer. "Wednesday is what we call drop-dead day. Articles have to be finalized by midday so we can get them set, ready for printing on Thursday. Digby knows what we need for the photographs, but as there'll be seven—no, nine all told—in this edition, that's going to be a challenge. It's lucky Quimby took the time to teach Digby all he did, otherwise, we'd be in difficulties."

Again, Gray glanced at the press. "So on Thursday, the press runs."

"Aye." Maguire grinned. "Can't hear yourself think, and we're all busy, collating sheets. We run tests first, of course—a few sheets pushed out by hand so we can read over it and spot any errors. Sometimes, we get to proofreading on Wednesday afternoon, but regardless, it has to be done. But on Thursday, once we're all happy everything's right, the boiler's fired up, and the press rolls."

"You enjoy it," Gray stated.

Maguire nodded. "Gets in your blood, it does." He glanced at Jim. "Heh, Jim?"

Jim raised his eyes from his task and smiled. "It does, indeed." He, too, glanced at the press. "I was just thinking that it's lucky this is one of our quiet spells."

Gray glanced around. "This is quiet?"

Maguire chuffed. "At times, we're like a beehive in here, everyone rushing and doing at once. But right now, with the university term just started, we don't have much by way of pamphlets, booklets, and such that we do for the faculties and societies and the like."

"We were rushed off our feet all through December," Jim explained. "It's always like that. Toward the end of one term, all the lecturers and secretaries start thinking of what they need for the next."

Maguire nodded. "So right now, we're quiet, which means we can concentrate on *The Crier* and doing what we can to help to catch Quimby's killer."

After a moment, Gray asked if he could help. Maguire glanced at Gray's coat, then nodded to where a number of leather aprons hung. "Best get one of those on, or you'll end with ink smudges everywhere."

Gray donned an apron, then sat on a stool opposite Maguire and was soon engaged in sorting type. That was, he reflected, something he was actually qualified to do.

Half an hour later, with the clock inexorably ticking toward five, Izzy decided she'd got as far with the main article and Quimby's obituary as she could that day. For the article, she needed to step back and let her thoughts settle, and she needed more details about Quimby to lend color to the obituary.

She rose from the desk and stretched, then walked out to the workshop.

Lipson saw her and came to show her his list of advertisers and confirm he would spend the following day visiting them and explaining about the special edition and the new rates for advertising in it.

After approving the list and the increased rates, Izzy checked with Mary and went over what she'd written—an article they'd had in mind for some time, focusing on the good work of the nearby Foundling Hospital. Izzy had decided to suspend their usual lighthearted articles on the foibles of those in ton society. She hoped the piece on the Foundling Hospital, being serious but also uplifting, would strike the right note to balance the sensational and, of necessity, rather dark account of murder she was penning.

Reassured that Mary had the piece well in hand, Izzy turned from the counter and spotted Gray, wearing a typesetter's apron, sorting type and chatting with Maguire and Jim.

She blinked several times to confirm she was neither dreaming nor hallucinating.

Before she could investigate the unexpected sight, the big clock on the workshop wall above the counter chimed for five o'clock, and the staff paused, assessing their work, then downed tools and headed for the pegs on which their coats hung.

Izzy remained at the counter, smiling and returning farewells. After doffing the apron, Gray came to stand beside her, plainly intending to dog her steps as he had for the past several days.

She didn't react, but somewhat to her surprise, she noticed that the nods directed his way as the staff filed toward the door were not just accepting but also approving. To a man and a woman, her staff were pleased that she had someone like him by her side.

She might have sniffed dismissively at that, only she was, in truth, grateful. She wasn't silly enough to be otherwise, regardless of their past.

Consequently, when she stepped onto the front steps, locked the door, and started down the street and he fell in beside her, she accepted that attempting to dissuade him from escorting her would be hypocritical.

They walked to Woburn Square, spent a few minutes chatting with Mrs. Carruthers, then left via the rear door and, in the rear lane, climbed into her carriage.

As they traveled the streets toward Norfolk Crescent, she reviewed the events of the day and acknowledged how much of a help he had been. She slanted a glance across the carriage; he was idly watching the houses slip past.

He could have been much more of a nuisance, but instead...

The carriage turned onto Edgware Road, and the familiar weight of social obligation settled more definitely on her shoulders. She shifted, drawing his gaze. "Would you care to dine with Mama, Marietta, and me —perhaps tomorrow evening?" She hadn't mentioned his reappearance in her life to her mother and sister, but there was a reasonable chance that, by now, Cottesloe had done so. "If you're free?"

In the poor light, she couldn't make out his expression, but he straightened his legs and inclined his head. "I am free, and I would be honored to dine with you and your family."

She nodded as the carriage drew up outside her home.

He descended first and handed her down.

On gaining the pavement, she caught his gaze. Slightly breathless, she retrieved her hand from his unsettling clasp and waved at the carriage. "Fields can drive you home if you like." She assumed he was living somewhere in nearby Mayfair.

Gray glanced briefly at Fields, but shook his head. "I can easily catch a hackney on Edgware Road."

"Very well." She nodded a dismissal to Fields.

As the carriage drew away, she looked at Gray.

Smiling, he tipped his head toward the front door, plainly waiting to see her safely inside.

She inwardly sighed, walked up the steps, knocked on the door, and turned back as if to say, "Are you satisfied?"

His smile widened, but he dallied until the door opened, then he raised a hand and saluted her before finally turning away.

She paused on the porch, her gaze lingering on his broad shoulders until he neared the corner, then before he could glance back and see her, she walked inside.

Cottesloe shut the door behind her.

She paused to unbutton her gloves. Gray hadn't mentioned whether he intended to turn up again tomorrow morning, but... Stripping the leather from her hands, she glanced at Cottesloe. "Did you happen to mention my morning visitor to my mother?"

"No, my lady. I assumed you would explain to her ladyship in good time."

"Indeed, I'm about to do just that. However, so that you're not caught out, I won't be surprised if his lordship appears tomorrow morning at the same time. If he does, please admit him, and unless my mother has other plans, he will also be dining here tomorrow evening."

"Very good, my lady." Cottesloe accepted her gloves and bonnet, then the coat she shrugged off. "I will inform Mrs. Hagen that we will have another at table, both for breakfast and dinner."

Izzy nodded and made for the drawing room door. Johnny, their young footman, hurried to open it, and she glided through to find her mother seated by the fireplace in her favorite wing chair and Marietta relaxing on the sofa.

Both looked up with smiles of welcome.

Izzy smiled back and took a moment to drink in the sight of the pair looking so unconcerned and at ease, then she sat beside Marietta and said, "I have news."

That, of course, was a massive understatement, given that she hadn't, until then, told them about Quimby's murder. When she'd requested their help identifying the people in the photographs, she hadn't explained why she'd needed the information, and accustomed to her researches, they hadn't asked.

As she related the tale of how the notice of her upcoming exposé had brought Gray to her office, and how, together, they'd subsequently found Quimby's body, her sister's eyes grew rounder and rounder. Even her mother, not one to show her emotions, looked aghast.

Izzy didn't give them time to exclaim but rolled on, outlining what happened next and Gray's assistance, both on that fateful evening and subsequently.

"I need to warn you that, in seeking information about the people in the photographs, Child consulted the Alvertons—Therese and Devlin—so they now know my secret, and today, Child and I visited the Winchelseas —Drake and Louisa—so they know, too. However, all four have sworn themselves to absolute secrecy on the issue, so"—she shrugged fatalistically—"we have to trust in their discretion, and realistically, there was nothing else we could do."

Without waiting to be asked, she described the idea of the hue and cry edition and explained that, with the staff's active assistance and Gray's support, it was well underway.

"So," she finally said, "given all that, I felt obliged to invite Child to dine tomorrow evening." She looked at her mother. "If you approve?"

Her mother had slumped back in her chair, her hand at her throat, regarding Izzy in faintly stunned fashion, but at the question, she regrouped and declared, "Of course I approve, dear. Why, if his lordship hadn't been there... Well, it really doesn't bear thinking about."

"No, indeed." Marietta blew out a breath, her expression suggesting she was rapidly regaining her usual sunny equilibrium. "How fortunate that Child thought the exposé was about him and so was there to be your alibi for the murder." She grinned at Izzy. "You do have the most amazing adventures, Izzy."

"While I will agree it's been amazing, I assure you it hasn't been pleasant." She rose and waved at her day dress. "I need to go and change. I'll see you at dinner."

"Yes, of course, dear." Her mother smiled benignly. "You'll feel much more the thing once you've washed and changed."

With a wave and "I'll be down shortly," Izzy left the room.

Sybil, the dowager, listened to her elder daughter's firm footsteps ascend the stairs, then sank back in her chair, a pensive expression overtaking her soft features.

Marietta studied her mother's face. After a moment, she asked, "Lord Child—isn't he the gentleman Izzy had her eye on all those years ago? And then he vanished, simply upped and disappeared, and the why of it was a mystery to everyone, his family included?"

Her gaze distant, Sybil nodded. "Yes, that was he."

Marietta narrowed her hazel eyes on her mother's uninformative countenance. "And am I right in thinking that after Child vanished, Izzy never looked at another gentleman—not in any meaningful way?"

Sybil refocused on her younger daughter's face and faintly smiled. "Exactly so."

Marietta held her mother's gaze and, after a moment, smiled, too.

CHAPTER 7

*G*ray knocked on the door of Number 6 Norfolk Crescent at seven o'clock the following morning and almost blinked when the door was opened by a beaming Cottesloe, who bowed and welcomed him inside.

When Gray entered the breakfast parlor, Izzy didn't turn a hair.

He pulled out the chair opposite her. "I assume you warned Cottesloe to expect me."

"I told him to admit you if you should call." She fixed him with a direct look. "So why are you here so bright and early?"

Gray paused as Cottesloe came in with the coffeepot and made a production of pouring Gray a cup, then the butler asked, "Will there be anything else, my lord?"

"No, thank you, Cottesloe." Gray lifted the cup, sipped, then smiled genially at the butler. "This will suffice."

Cottesloe bowed and departed.

Gray lowered the cup and returned his gaze to Izzy. "Yesterday, you speculated that the killer might be pursuing a vendetta against *The Crier*. Given it's a gossip rag, it's not difficult to imagine that a motive for such an action might exist in some man's mind. While we've fixed on Quimby's photographs as providing a more likely motive, it occurred to me that, regardless of whether the killer's motive lies in Quimby's photographs or in something *The Crier* has previously printed, the killer might, from the first, have had you in his sights as well."

His eyes locked with hers, he went on, "You were in the office and should have been alone that evening. He might have intended to attack you as well, but hadn't counted on me being with you. If so, whatever his reasoning, he might still view killing you as a part of his campaign. More, if the photographs are, indeed, the source of his motive, once he learns of the special edition and that you mean to publish the photographs he thought he'd destroyed, he might well try again to stop their publication, and in that respect, you are as much of a target as *The Crier* itself."

From her arrested expression, she hadn't thought of that.

Ruthlessly, he pressed the point home. "With you dead, *The Crier* would simply stop—cease publication—at least for a while."

She frowned.

He glanced at her crumb-strewn plate, then waved his cup. "Finish your tea. We can work out what to do for the best once we reach the printing works."

Izzy met his gaze, then raised her teacup and drained it. He was right; her being a potential target for the killer was a subject better discussed far from household ears.

She rose, and he set down the coffee cup and joined her. Within minutes, they were bowling along the streets toward Woburn Square.

She spent the journey deep in thought, weighing what he'd said and trying to marshal arguments with which to refute his prognostication, but in the end, she let it lie unchallenged. Who could say with any certainty what their killer presently thought?

They transited through the Woburn Square house and walked briskly on to the mews. Although they were the first through the door, the staff arrived on their heels, all eager to get working on the special edition.

Far from having any time to think, much less discuss the prospect Gray had raised, Izzy found her hours claimed by a succession of issues that required her immediate attention. Because of the edition's unusual nature, several situations demanded different solutions from those she and the staff routinely employed.

In between answering various questions, she worked on the lead article and Quimby's obituary. Regardless of her occupation, she was incessantly aware of Gray, either by her elbow or seated in front of her. In the end, she took to consulting him on this and that and discovered that having another pair of intelligent eyes attached to a brain with a similar grounding in life as hers was a boon.

Especially given that mind was one she trusted...

She pulled herself up at the thought, surprised and somewhat taken aback, but there was no denying that assessment was accurate. Mentally shrugging the realization aside, she buckled down to complete her article; she wanted it done by the end of the day.

At ten o'clock, the bell above the main door jangled, heralding the return of Lipson, who had been out meeting their advertising clients, explaining about the hue and cry special edition and soliciting advertisements to run in it at the special, higher rate.

Izzy raised her head, wondering... She'd recognized Lipson's heavy tread, and as she'd expected, other footsteps followed him into the foyer.

From behind her desk, she couldn't see who had entered, but Gray, sitting at his elegant ease before it in the chair with its back to the bookshelves, had an unimpeded view. Quietly, he informed her, "It's Lipson, followed by four gentlemen, who I suspect are your major advertisers."

She sighed and put down her pencil. "I was expecting them."

Having left the four men waiting in the foyer, Lipson rapped on the open door, then came in and shut it. He looked at Izzy and wryly smiled. "As we could have predicted, Belkin, Kennedy, Simms, and Morrison wouldn't come on board, at least not for me. But all four are insisting we 'honor our contract' with them regarding running their ads. Silly beggars, but they won't take any argument from me."

Izzy nodded and rose. "As you say, that's no more than we might have expected." She went to the filing cabinet against the wall, pulled open a drawer, rummaged through the contents, then straightened with four slim folders in her hand. She shut the drawer and looked at Lipson. "I'll see them one by one—best start with Belkin."

Lipson glanced at Gray. "Do you want me in here as well?"

She reclaimed her chair. "Yes. They need to accept that what you tell them comes from me—that you speak with my authority." She looked at Gray and said to Lipson, "You can show Belkin in."

She set the folders on the desk and, the instant Lipson stepped out of the office, said to Gray, "I don't suppose you'd like to go for a wander around the workshop."

He held her gaze. "No. I'd rather remain here."

She sighed. "Just try not to distract them."

He arched a laconic brow. Both she and he knew him not distracting the men wasn't possible.

She sorted the folders, then Lipson ushered in a florid-faced gentleman who looked ready to breathe fire.

Assuming a relaxed and pleasant demeanor, Izzy rose and waved the man to the vacant armchair before the desk. "Mr. Belkin. How kind of you to call. Do sit down."

Belkin had intended to storm inside and bluster, but the sight of Gray, watching with undisguised interest, had taken him aback. As Izzy resumed her seat, he came forward cautiously and, on walking into the chair, caught himself and slipped into it.

Izzy hid a sigh; she'd known this was going to happen. Briskly, she said, "Mr. Belkin, I understand Mr. Lipson has explained the situation regarding the advertising charges for our special hue and cry edition."

The words succeeded in bringing Belkin's attention back to her, and he only just restrained himself from leaping to his feet. "Indeed, he did, Mrs. Molyneaux, and I must protest—most strongly! Belkin Emporium has a contract with *The Crier*, ma'am, and it stipulates quite clearly the rate for each advertisement run. I must and will insist that contract be honored. To the letter!"

"Indeed, sir. I am entirely of similar mind." She smiled calmly at the temperamental man. "That, in large part, was the reason behind Mr. Lipson's visit this morning. We felt honor-bound to offer longstanding regular advertisers such as the Belkin Emporium first chance to secure slots in our special edition. I have a copy of your contract here."

She opened the topmost folder, extracted the bound sheets of legalese, and turned back the first two pages. "As you will be aware, at clause six, the contract states that the agreed rates stated within the contract apply only to advertising in regular editions of *The London Crier*, and that inclusion in any special edition at such rates is specifically excluded, and further, that should inclusion in any special edition be offered, such inclusion will be subject to whatever advertising rates *The London Crier* deems appropriate at that time."

She raised her gaze to Belkin's now-much-paler face. "Given that, sir, I had thought that a business such as the Belkin Emporium, keen to gain sales from ladies everywhere, would have leapt at the chance to secure prominent placement in an edition all but guaranteed to have a significantly larger and wider distribution. As everyone knows, a murder gains interest, but a hue and cry, with a reward offered, will be a sensation."

Belkin's expression had grown first calculating, then alarmed. He cleared his throat and ventured, "So our contract doesn't cover advertisements in special editions?"

Izzy replaced the contract in the folder and clasped her hands on the cover. "No."

"Ah. I see." Although he hadn't again looked at Gray, Belkin all but twitched with the impulse to glance at the elegant personage seated only a yard away. Doing his best to appear unaware, Belkin glanced the other way—at the foyer, where others who might snaffle the prime advertising spots waited.

Belkin snapped his gaze back to Izzy. "As to the rates for this special edition…what are you asking?"

Izzy smiled and got down to negotiating.

After the application of a few judicious strokes to his ego, when Belkin left the office ten minutes later, after having agreed to a hefty increase in fees for three placements in the special edition, he was almost preening.

The other three merchants waiting in the foyer, seeing Belkin's overweening satisfaction, almost came to blows over who would be next to offer to enrich *The Crier's* coffers.

When the last, Simms, departed, shown out by Lipson, who was eager to return to setting up the press, Izzy gave a contented sigh and rose to replace the folders in the filing cabinet.

Gray observed, "Whoever drew up those contracts had a good head on their shoulders."

Izzy shut the cabinet, turned, and met his eyes. "I drew them up."

He dipped his head. "As I said." To his mind, her performance managing the four businessmen had been masterful.

She resumed her seat behind the desk and rapidly tallied the figures she'd jotted down during the negotiations.

He noticed she added the figures once, paused, then repeated the exercise.

Finally, she laid down her pencil and fixed her emerald eyes on him. "Despite not saying a word throughout, by virtue of the unsettling effect you had on our local gentlemen of commerce, you greatly assisted in more than tripling the printing works' income from an average edition of *The Crier*."

Smiling, he arched his brows. "I'm delighted to have been of service."

She huffed, then glanced at the clock, pushed back her chair, and rose. "I need to see to the layouts. Now we have the major advertising settled, we can finalize those."

Gray rose and ambled after her. He was increasingly fascinated by all the various aspects of the business and what each aspect revealed of her and her unexpected talents.

The discussion with Lipson and Maguire over the layout table displayed her grasp of her readers' preconceptions and vanities and how those influenced the way said readers interacted with the pages in their gossip rag of choice.

Gray found the various arguments enlightening; he doubted he would look at a newspaper in the same way again.

Finally, all was settled, and leaving Lipson to start setting up the frames—known as formes—that Maguire would eventually fill with type, Izzy returned to her desk and the article and obituary she was still polishing.

Gray trailed after her and sat in the armchair he was coming to regard as his.

Not long after, reminded by the emptiness of his own stomach, he walked out, chatted to Lipson, then stuck his head into the office and informed Izzy that he was going out to fetch sandwiches and cider for everyone.

She was deep in writing and glanced up, gaze unfocused, then waved him off and went back to her work.

He grinned, left, and following Lipson's directions, found the nearby bakery nestled beside a shop selling bottled drinks of all sorts.

Twenty minutes later, he returned to the printing works, set his offerings on the counter, and invited everyone to partake, which they all did. Izzy came out and nibbled on a sandwich, poured cider into a mug, and carried it with her back to her desk.

After helping Mary clear away the detritus remaining after the staff had finished, Gray returned to the armchair and settled.

"Stop watching me," Izzy ordered.

He laughed and closed his eyes.

Several minutes later, Mary knocked on the door frame and, when Izzy looked up, came in, carrying several sheets of paper.

"My article." Mary brandished the sheets. "It's as polished as I can make it."

Izzy set down her pencil and held out her hand for the sheets, and Mary handed them over. Izzy glanced at Mary's effort, then looked at her own work—the lead article for the hue and cry edition. She hesitated, then looked at Gray. "While I read over Mary's work, perhaps you could read over mine?"

Genuinely delighted, he smiled and held out his hand. "I'd be happy to."

Izzy's lips pressed tight as she fought to hold back an answering smile. She gathered her writing and handed the pages across, then picked up another two sheets and offered them to Mary. "Sit"—Izzy waved toward the other armchair—"and look over these. They're my notes on the obituary. We'll need to finalize it by tomorrow morning at the very latest. You'll see I've noted several pieces of information we should find and add in."

Mary took the sheets and sat, and in the next second, all three of them had their heads down, reading.

After a time, Gray reached out, snagged one of the many pencils rolling about on the desk, and made a note in the margin of her article. She glanced up, gaze sharp, but after a moment, went back to her perusal of Mary's work, on which she was making corrections.

By the time Izzy had reached the end of Mary's article, Gray was on the last paragraph of the lead article, and Mary was finished with the obituary.

The instant he looked up, Izzy held out her hand and wiggled her fingers. "Let me see."

He smiled and handed over the sheets. When she queried what his cryptic note meant, he explained, and after some discussion, she amended the ambiguous phrasing that she hadn't, until then, realized could be read in two diametrically opposing ways.

"Here." She thrust Mary's article at him. "I think this is as perfect as it gets, but see what you think." She then handed Mary the main article. "And you can take a look at that while I work on the obituary."

They settled in comfortable silence, broken only by the soft scrape of Izzy's pencil and the rustling of paper.

Eventually, she was satisfied with what she had thus far for the obituary. She set down her pencil and stretched out her hands. "We're still missing information I think should be there—for instance, where he was born—but we can squeeze that in if we manage to learn it in time."

She caught Gray's gaze and nodded at Mary's article. "How's that?"

"Excellent." Gray glanced at Mary. "You have a flair for describing places in a way that brings them to life."

Mary all but glowed at the praise.

Izzy smiled at Mary and, taking the pages from him, offered them to the younger woman. "Done! You can take those to your father for typesetting for the proofs."

"Thank you." Mary beamed. "Both of you." She rose and took the pages and, with a spring in her step, left the office.

Izzy watched her go, an almost-maternal smile on her face. "She's coming along nicely. And yes, I agree. She does have a gift for depicting places."

Which, Gray thought, was one of the reasons you suggested the Foundling Hospital for Mary's piece. Sitting back, he waved at the pages beneath Izzy's hands. "Let me take a look at the obituary."

She handed the pages across. She watched him as he started to read, then said, "I'm still not sure I have the tone right. I don't want to sound too distant. I want it to be clear that there's a connection to the paper, that Quimby was one of the team that put together what the readers have been enjoying over the past years."

He nodded. "You want the emotional connection to show."

"Yes, and of course, we usually write in quite the opposite way—as impartial commentators."

He read through to the end of the piece, then made several suggestions. Izzy took the sheets, made various changes, then handed them back. "Does that work better?"

After reading the piece through again, he said, "I think it's better, but it's really in the way it sounds, so..." He started to read the piece aloud.

Nodding, she sat back and listened.

He'd reached the final paragraph when the bell over the door tinkled. He looked across and saw Baines and Littlejohn come in.

The pair nodded at Mary, back at her station behind the counter, then headed for the office.

Gray stopped reading and lowered the sheets. "It's our friends from Scotland Yard."

Izzy sighed.

Baines tapped on the door frame and came in. He halted before the desk and nodded to Gray and to Izzy. "Your lordship. Mrs. Molyneaux."

"Inspector." Izzy conjured a bright smile and aimed it at Baines and Littlejohn, who had slipped into the room in his superior's wake. "Is there anything we can help you with?"

Baines sighed somewhat wearily, then said, "I don't suppose you've had a change of heart and would like to confess to killing Quimby?"

Izzy's features hardened, and her gaze turned stony. "No."

Baines's lips tightened, then as if forced to say the words, he stated, "I'm here to warn you, ma'am, that as of this moment, you remain the sole suspect in the murder of Mr. Horace Quimby."

Gray inwardly sighed. "Inspector, what evidence do the police have that implicates Mrs. Molyneaux in Quimby's death?"

Baines looked pained. "At this moment, none. But as others have been quick to tell me, such evidence will surely be found if I look hard enough."

His tone made it clear that he was being pressured by others and didn't like it one bit.

"I see." Gray's lips curved, but the gesture held more warning than humor. "I continue to hope that you and your superiors at the Yard will not be so unwise as to attempt to inconvenience, much less detain Mrs. Molyneaux, nor spread any rumors that might damage her reputation and that of her business, unless and until you have incontrovertible evidence of her supposed misdeeds sufficient to lay formal charges before a magistrate."

"Not if I can help it," Baines muttered. He shot a plainly apologetic glance at Izzy, then straightened and said, "We've just come from Quimby's rooms. We searched, trying to find some hint of his next of kin, but as far as we can tell, he didn't have any." Baines focused on Izzy. "We came to ask if anyone here had ever heard him mention anyone."

"No," Izzy said. "I've already asked—I would normally mention that in an obituary." She glanced at Gray, then pointed at the pages he held. "Perhaps, Inspector, you would read through what we're intending to print, to ensure our facts are correct."

Gray handed Baines the pages. He took them, sat in the other armchair, and carefully read through the piece.

When he reached the end and paused, Izzy calmly inquired, "Is there anything you would like us to add to the obituary, Inspector?"

Baines glanced at her. "Actually, yes." He handed the sheets over the desk and, as Izzy took them, said, "Everything you have in there is accurate as far as I know, but it would be helpful if you could end with a note along the lines of 'there being no next of kin known to the authorities, anyone wishing to inquire regarding the deceased's estate should contact Inspector Baines at Scotland Yard.'"

Izzy picked up a pencil, swiftly wrote, paused to read what she'd written, then looked up. "Done."

"Is there much of an estate?" Gray asked.

"Not much," Baines replied. "A small amount in savings, the equipment he kept here, and some old camera bits he'd left in a wardrobe."

"So it's unlikely Quimby was murdered for his wealth." Pointedly, Gray caught Izzy's gaze. They needed to tell Baines about the hue and cry edition, and now seemed an opportune time.

Izzy set aside the obituary and leaned her elbows on the desk. "Do the police have any further leads, Inspector?"

Baines grumped, "No. That's what's brought us back to *The Crier*."

Izzy met Gray's eyes, then ventured, "Well, from our point of view, since we last saw you on Saturday, there have been some developments."

The change in both Baines and Littlejohn was marked. "Developments?" Littlejohn parroted.

"What developments?" Baines leaned forward, hope ringing in his tone.

Gray sat back and listened as Izzy explained about the new style of negatives Quimby had been using and how, courtesy of Quimby's assistant, they'd found the negatives Quimby had exposed on Friday and had printed the photographs from them.

Izzy unlocked and opened the desk drawer, drew out the third set of prints, and handed them across the desk.

Baines fell on them like a starving hound, and Littlejohn peered over Baines's shoulder as the inspector studied the seven scenes.

When, frowning, the pair looked up, Gray outlined the theory that, given the murderer had taken the time to wreck all Quimby's daguerreotype plates, presumably assuming that in doing so, he was wiping out the evidence he had killed to prevent Quimby making public, then the motive for Quimby's murder lay somewhere in the seven photographs.

"Seems reasonable," Baines allowed, and Littlejohn nodded.

"We've asked around among others of the ton," Gray went on, "and can identify more than half the people in the seven scenes, but as to the names of the others and what in the photographs might be a reason for murder, that, we've yet to unearth."

Baines stared at the photographs. "But that's the sticking point, isn't it? How are we to tell what it is about one of these pictures that set the killer after Quimby?"

"As to that"—Izzy exchanged a glance with Gray, then refocused on Baines—"we've decided that the best way forward is to run a hue and cry edition."

"A *what*?" Baines looked stunned and prepared to be appalled.

Izzy launched into a description of the special edition, detailing what would be included and what they would ask and mentioning the reward, while throughout, using her descriptive talents to paint the undertaking in an exciting light. "It will be a new and novel way of doing exactly the same thing as an old-fashioned hue and cry, but in this case, we'll be using the new medium of newspapers to reach a much wider audience."

Judging by Baines's and Littlejohn's expressions, they could see the possibilities and were sorely tempted, yet...

Baines grimaced, and his shoulders fell. "I can't see my superiors approving such a thing—not at all. You'll be laying evidence in a murder case before the public. They're likely to have conniptions over that."

"They don't have to like it," Gray said, "to allow it to go ahead, and I'm sure your superiors will appreciate that attempting to block an action that was initially suggested by the Marchioness of Winchelsea and, subsequently, gained the marquess's active support won't reflect well on them."

From their stunned expressions, Baines and Littlejohn recognized the significance of Drake's involvement.

Gray smiled his most sharklike smile. "I suggest that, if your superiors raise an issue with *The Crier's* upcoming special edition, you would do well to suggest that they take it up with Winchelsea."

Baines and Littlejohn both blinked, as if imagining such a scene.

Then Baines started to smile, and the rather lugubrious set of Littlejohn's features eased.

Izzy noted the changes and calmly stated, "So, gentlemen, as of this moment, our special edition is going ahead under the imprimatur of the marquess and is on track to be distributed on Friday."

Baines's entire disposition had brightened. "Friday, heh?"

She nodded firmly. "As usual—we can't easily alter our distribution arrangements, so Friday it has to be."

Baines looked at Littlejohn, and the pair exchanged a long glance.

Izzy suspected that they were eager to embrace all the possibilities that had fired her enthusiasm. Artfully, she asked, "Is there any information the police can share that will help capture and encourage the public's interest and involvement? For instance, what did the surgeon who examined the body report?"

Baines hesitated, then agreed to share that report and anything else suitable that the police came across. "On the proviso that Littlejohn and I get to see the—proofs, is it?—before your press starts to roll."

Izzy studied them, then inclined her head. "Very well—on that basis.

But if you have any information it would help to include, I'll need to see it by the end of the afternoon." She paused, then went on, "We can't make any changes once the formes are set, which happens late tomorrow. However, you're more than welcome to drop by earlier and view the proofs of every page—all the articles and photographs. If you come by tomorrow, any time after ten o'clock in the morning but at the latest by one in the afternoon, you'll be able to look over the entire edition."

She omitted any mention of them making any changes; why invite something she would resist?

Baines and Littlejohn agreed; both looked eager and quietly excited, a significant transformation from when they'd arrived.

"We'll leave you to it, then." Baines rose and nodded to her and Gray. "I'll send over the surgeon's report as soon as I get back to the Yard."

Baines headed for the door, and with a dip of his head, Littlejohn followed.

But on reaching the doorway, Baines paused, then turned back. "I've been thinking about that reward you're offering." He glanced at her. "I'd suggest you print all the names you've already got for the people in the photographs and make it crystal clear what the reward is for—additional names or other information that leads to the killer. You also need to detail everything we know about Quimby's movements on that Friday and say if anyone knows more, then get in touch, because that might lead us to the killer, too."

He met her gaze. "Trust me, if you don't do all that, you'll have half of London lining up to tell you things you already know."

Littlejohn grunted. "Let alone the other half who'll be lining up to tell you things they think you want to know, but which never actually happened."

"Thank you," she returned in heartfelt tones. She rose. "I'll make sure all that gets incorporated in our notice about the reward."

Baines nodded, and he and Littlejohn took themselves off.

Izzy followed them out of the office and went to speak with Mary.

As usual, Gray ambled in her wake.

He leaned against the counter while Izzy and Mary worked on the notice announcing the reward. Given some of those they wanted to entice to come forward might well belong to the more gentrified classes, he'd suggested fifty pounds as a reward, and Izzy had agreed.

"Good!" Izzy set the reward notice aside. "Now that's settled, after talking with Baines and Littlejohn, I've had a thought of how to end the lead article—namely, with a sub-article entitled 'What we know of Mr. Quimby's Movements on That Fateful Day.'" Her tone made it clear which words should be capitalized. She looked at the younger woman. "We need to set out the time line as we currently know it and ask anyone with further information as to Quimby's whereabouts to come forward. Why don't you write up a first draft, and I'll have a look at it tomorrow morning? We can finalize it then."

Mary eagerly accepted the commission. Leaving her already setting out fresh paper and picking up her pencil, Izzy turned, scanned the workshop, then walked briskly to where Lipson, Maguire, and Digby were working on blocking out the sections for the photographs, working from the sheets with the pinned prints, each annotated with the relevant accumulated information. After confirming that the trio were, indeed, intending to incorporate the information already collected beside each photograph, Izzy headed for her office, waving at Gray to join her.

He entered the office to find her with the obituary in her hand.

She looked up as he neared. "My lead article is in good shape, and this"—she tapped the obituary—"is as finished as it can be, but I would like to add a few personal touches."

He could guess what she was thinking and glibly suggested, "Perhaps we should take a look at Quimby's rooms. The police have finished there, so we won't be treading on their toes, and with any luck, the landlady or a neighbor might have a few of those personal snippets you're after."

She beamed at him as if she hadn't already thought of searching Quimby's rooms. "And who knows? We might stumble across something our intrepid duo missed."

He didn't think that likely—Baines and Littlejohn struck him as experienced and competent, at least when they weren't being backed into a corner—but waved her on.

She knew the address and how to reach it. Bundled up in their coats against the blustery day, they walked up the mews to Great Coram Street, where he hailed a hackney.

She directed the jarvey to Winchester Street. "You can drop us at the corner of Collier Street."

The hackney took off smartly, and soon, they were walking the cobbles of Winchester Street, a narrow street with row houses crammed cheek by jowl on both sides.

Izzy took note of the few numbers displayed, counting along, then halted outside a faded door. "This should be it."

Gray stepped up and knocked on the door.

It was opened by a pale, faded-looking woman of perhaps forty or so years, wearing a washed-out pinafore over a worn woolen skirt. "Yes?" Noting the wariness in the woman's eyes, Gray stepped back and allowed Izzy to take the lead.

She did so with a gentle, commiserating smile. "We're from *The London Crier*—where Mr. Quimby had his darkroom. He worked for us."

The woman nodded. "Yeah, he mentioned the place. I'm Ida Cummins, his landlady. I 'spect you'll be wanting to check that he hasn't anything of yours in his rooms here, then?"

Izzy's smile was all gratified understanding. "If it wouldn't be too much trouble. We won't take long."

The woman tipped her head inside and stepped back from the threshold. "Come on in, then. At least you're not all heavy-footed like those policemen who came this morning."

"Inspector Baines and Sergeant Littlejohn." Izzy followed the woman along a narrow corridor. "They told us they'd come and had finished their work here."

"Well, that's a relief." The woman started up a flight of wooden stairs.

At the top, she halted on a miniscule landing, opened the door to the right, stood back, and waved them inside. "These are Mr. Quimby's rooms."

Izzy walked in, and Gray slipped past the landlady and followed.

The term "rooms" was a misnomer. There was only one longish narrow room with a single sash window at the far end. A single bed sat at the nearer end, with a simple washstand and wardrobe tucked into a corner, while closer to the window, a wooden desk stood against the inner wall, with a single straight-backed chair before it. An armchair that had seen better days was positioned in the opposite corner by the window, angled across the room toward the desk. There was, Gray noted, no fireplace.

Izzy walked to the window and looked out; over her head, Gray saw that the view wasn't of any garden but a bare cobbled yard ending in a paling fence with a rickety gate.

When Izzy turned away and went to look in the desk drawer, he glanced around, confirming that there wasn't anywhere else bar the wardrobe in which something might be hidden; he crossed to it and opened the narrow double doors. Clothes met his gaze, not that many and all of middling quality. Not the best but not the worst, either. A single pair of worn slippers, neatly lined up together, were the only things on the lowest shelf. He checked the drawers, shifting aside the few clothes and searching for anything else, gradually working his way up to the top shelf, where he found an old knitted hat and scarf and nothing else.

He shut the wardrobe doors and turned to see Izzy frowning at the back of a printed card. "Anything?" he asked.

She glanced at him, then looked back at the card. "Not exactly, but reading between these lines…I wonder if Quimby hailed from Dorset."

She looked at Ida Cummins, who was leaning against the doorjamb. "Did Mr. Quimby ever mention where he hailed from? Or did he go for holidays to some particular place in the country?"

Mrs. Cummins nodded at the card in Izzy's hand. "Just there. Said it was the place he knew best. He went every year in summer for a week."

Izzy sighed and put the card back in the drawer.

"So"—Mrs. Cummins straightened—"did you find anything of yours? It's just the police went through everything—left the place in a right mess. It didn't seem decent to leave it like that, so I put everything back like he'd have wanted it. Quite particular he was."

Understanding from that that Mrs. Cummins probably knew every stitch Quimby had owned, Gray asked, "Did you happen to notice—not just in the last days but at any time before—any glass plates or special photographic papers? Did he keep anything like that here?"

"Don't believe so. He told me he kept all that sort of thing at his work."

Izzy nodded. "That seems to be so."

Mrs. Cummins gnawed at her lower lip, then with a jut of her chin, said, "Mind you, if he had brought something here over the last few days, that something—I don't know what, mind—might have been here when he died."

Izzy looked at the landlady and tipped her head. "Why do you think that?"

"Well, the day Mr. Quimby died—that Friday—he came back here late in the afternoon. Came straight up to his room here, but he didn't stay long. He went off after maybe five or ten minutes."

"Did he often do that?" Izzy asked. "Come home and go out again?"

"Oh, aye. He'd go back to his work, then he'd go and have his supper someplace and come home here about nine or so."

Puzzled, Gray asked, "So why do you think he left something here that day, when normally—I assume—he didn't?"

"Oh, it wasn't that—him coming and going—made me think so. When he didn't come down for breakfast on Saturday morning, I came up and looked in"—Ida Cummins stepped into the room and pointed at the window—"and that was open. Pushed right up it was, and I can tell you, in this weather, Mr. Quimby would never have left it like that." She snorted. "He'd never have had it open at all—all the warmth from the stove below would go straight out."

"This was before the police came?" Izzy asked.

"Aye—seven or so. They didn't get here 'til gone eight." Mrs. Cummins folded her arms beneath her ample breasts. "I shut it up tight again, o'course."

Gray moved to the window, noting there was no lock on the sash. He pushed it up, leaned out, and saw a shed with a flat roof directly below, only about three feet down.

Izzy had come to peer around his shoulder. She turned back to Mrs. Cummins. "Did you notice anything not as it should be—as you would have expected?"

"Well, I'd thought to find Mr. Quimby in his bed, of course, but it was obvious he hadn't been in all night. Other than that…well, the wardrobe door wasn't properly shut. That might seem a small thing, but Mr. Quimby was always very neat—everything exactly as it should be."

Izzy shot Gray a speculative look.

He shut the window, then turned to Mrs. Cummins. "Did you tell the police about the window?"

She snorted inelegantly. "Them! They said they was here to search his rooms and told me—ordered me, in me own house—to stay downstairs." She shrugged. "So I did. They didn't see fit to ask me anything. Just stuck their heads around the kitchen door to tell me they was leaving." She frowned, then looked at them worriedly. "Here—I won't get into any trouble, will I? For not telling them about the window?"

Izzy smiled reassuringly. "I wouldn't worry about the police not knowing. I don't think anything was taken."

But Mrs. Cummins had finally worked out what had happened. "But…someone broke in here, didn't they? Oh, my God!" She clapped her hands to her face. "Was it the killer? Is that why you and the police have come, searching for something like the killer already did?"

Her eyes flared wide. "Mercy me! Here, whoever he is, he won't be coming back, will he? I don't want to be murdered in me bed. Surely he found what he wanted?"

Gray confidently stated, "You're right, and it's highly unlikely you have anything to fear." His matter-of-fact tone had Mrs. Cummins instantly calming; he went on in the same vein, "As you say, if there was anything here, although we don't believe there was, but even if there had been, then whoever broke in would have found and taken it, and they'll have no further interest in this house."

Mrs. Cummins thought through that, then exhaled gustily. "Well, that's a bit of excitement I could've done without."

"Thank you for letting us see the room." Izzy gently steered Mrs. Cummins to the door. "I really don't think you'll have any further trouble."

Reassured, the landlady led the way downstairs, and with thanks, Gray and Izzy left the house.

Izzy paused on the pavement and pulled on her gloves. "Other than a tenuous link between Quimby and Dorset, I suppose the news of a break-in is a crumb we can offer Baines and Littlejohn if and when we need one, but it certainly puts paid to the notion of any clue being left in his rooms."

They started down the street, and Gray admitted, "While it seems unlikely Quimby had left anything photographic there, if there'd been any other sort of clue linking him to the killer—a letter or something similar —the killer would have taken it."

He walked on for a few paces, then said, "However, our foray there did confirm that there's no reason to suppose there are any other photographic negatives of Quimby's in existence, other than those at the printing works."

"True. He does seem to have kept everything photographic there."

"Except," Gray reminded her, "for the discarded bits of camera equipment that Littlejohn mentioned, which he and Baines must have removed, but clearly, the killer didn't want those, anyway."

"Exactly. That means our hypothesis still holds water. If the killer is desperate to keep the public from seeing something Quimby photographed on Friday, then the photographs we're printing in the hue and cry edition should contain the revealing information—whatever it is."

Gray nodded. "It's all about something in those photographs."

He hailed a passing hackney, and they returned to the printing works to discover Baines had been as good as his word and had sent over the surgeon's report.

Gray scanned it, then handed it to Izzy. While she retreated to her desk to finish the obituary, working in a reference to Quimby having a connection to the village in Dorset depicted in the printed card, before settling to incorporate the surgeon's grisly information into the lead article in a way that wouldn't shock the readers, Gray, too restless to sit, wandered around the workshop, chatting to the staff and filling them in on what he and Izzy had discovered in Quimby's rooms.

At one point, he stepped into the darkroom and found a teary-eyed Digby scrubbing basins in the sink. Gray pretended not to notice the tears, propped his hip against the central table, and talking to Digby's back, told him about their findings in Winchester Street, then asked about the use of the various basins, a topic which, as Gray had hoped, drew the lad from his sorrowful thoughts.

When it came to anything photographic, Digby was a font of eager information; it was clear Quimby had recognized a like mind and had gone out of his way to mentor and encourage the lad.

Finally, it was time for the workshop to close for the day. Izzy farewelled the staff, then declared that her own writing was as complete as it could be, and given Gray was dining in Norfolk Crescent that evening, neither of them dared be late.

By then, another issue had occurred to Gray. He halted in the office doorway, waited while Izzy donned her bonnet and coat, then asked, "The seven calotype negatives—where are they?"

She frowned. "Digby showed me where he put them. They're in the cabinet with the others."

He paused, then said, "What I said this morning, about you being a possible target? By extension, once the killer learns of the special edition —hopefully only after it goes out—and gets desperate, this place will also become a target. He doesn't yet know the negatives still exist, so won't as yet be seeking to destroy them, but one is a critical piece of evidence. We shouldn't leave them here, unsecured and unguarded."

Her lips set, and she waved him out of her way. "I'll fetch them. Can you look under the counter for an envelope big enough to hold them?"

He rummaged and found one. By then, she'd retrieved the seven negatives and carefully slid them inside the paper sleeve, then closed the top and handed it to him. "You can carry it, at least as far as Woburn Square."

They walked even more briskly than usual to Mrs. Carruthers's house. After spending a few minutes regaling the old lady with their day's adventures, they exited via the back door. In the rear lane, Gray helped Izzy into her carriage, then handed her the envelope.

She blinked at him. "Aren't you coming?"

He shook his head. "It's faster to head to Jermyn Street from here." He saluted her. "I'll see you tonight."

He shut the carriage door and nodded to the coachman, then stood and watched the carriage rumble away.

Then he started walking down the lane. He would find a hackney in Russell Square and be at his lodgings in good time to wash and change.

As he walked, he pondered the feeling seeping into his gut. It took him a while to identify it, for he hadn't felt the like in a very long time.

He was nervous. Keen and eager and strangely nervous over making a good impression on Izzy's mother and sister.

Nonsensical, yet…

He emerged into Russell Square, spotted a hackney, and waved it down, and just for a minute, allowed himself to question where he was heading with what was fast becoming his pursuit of Isadora Descartes.

Then the hackney halted beside him, and he shook the distracting question aside and climbed in.

He was, as usual, operating on instinct—just as he had for the past very many years.

And over all those years, instinct had never steered him wrong.

CHAPTER 8

$\mathcal{A}$n hour and a half later, Gray was admitted to the Norfolk Crescent house by a benevolently smiling Cottesloe. The butler took his coat and hat, then led Gray to the drawing room and formally announced him to the company.

Izzy was already on her way to greet him. "Good evening, my lord, and welcome." She was all sophisticated formality in a gown of pale-gray watered silk that made the most of her abundant charms, with the hue setting off her flawless complexion and lustrous dark hair to perfection.

Gray smiled, took the hand she extended, and equally formal, bowed over it. "Lady Isadora. It's a pleasure to be here."

She retrieved her hand and turned, gesturing to the four people gathered before the fireplace. "Allow me to introduce you to my mother, who I daresay you remember from long ago, and my sister, Marietta, our cousin Jordan Descartes, and our good friend Mr. Silas Barton."

Gray had assumed others would be present, but hadn't expected Silas Barton.

Deploying his customary urbanely charming mask, Gray bowed over the dowager countess's hand and murmured appropriate responses to her greeting. The countess remained a fashionable, personable, and handsome woman; if he read her aright, she was in two minds over him, uncertain whether to disapprove mightily over his past flight—near enough to a jilting of her daughter—or instead, welcome him back, given he was helping Izzy and was even wealthier than he had been.

He hadn't forgotten her role in his and Izzy's past, but given the passage of years and the current situation, he was willing to let bygones be.

Seated beside the countess, Izzy's sister, Marietta, blithely gave him her hand, her curiosity regarding him and, even more, his connection to her sister undisguised.

He bowed over her hand. "Lady Marietta, it's a pleasure to meet you. I understand you made your come-out this year."

"I did, indeed." Marietta all but bounced on the sofa. "But I understand that you weren't in London at the time."

The words were more question than statement. He smiled. "I believe I was in Boston at that time."

Izzy looped her arm in his and drew him on to meet her cousin, who was standing before the fireplace.

Jordan appeared to be a young sprig a few years older than Marietta and, if his black-and-white-striped waistcoat was any indication, plainly seeking to cut a dash. He grasped the hand Gray offered and shook it vigorously. "I say, Izzy mentioned this dead photographer she stumbled over. Rum business, what?"

"Jordan!" The countess frowned at him. "I told you—no more talk of murder in my drawing room."

Jordan arched his brows. "But I didn't mention murder, Aunt Sybil— you did."

The countess flapped a hand at him. "Dreadful boy! I don't wish to hear more of that matter in any way, shape, or form this evening." She directed a pointed look his way, then skated the same warning look over Izzy and Gray, before leaning sideways to fix it on Silas Barton. "I wish us all to enjoy a pleasant evening of civilized conversation, and I would rather not hear about that subject at all."

Silas—older, solidly built, rather grizzled, and dressed in sober but well-cut clothes Gray would have said had been deliberately chosen to make him appear unremarkable—huffed. "Can't blame the lad for being interested, Sybil. Not every day a murderer comes calling, and I admit to being rather curious myself, but"—he held up a placating hand—"as you wish it, we'll refrain from mentioning the subject."

The countess humphed and subsided, much like a chicken settling ruffled feathers.

Izzy exchanged a look with Jordan and drew Gray on to meet Silas Barton.

The older man started to heave his bulk from the comfort of the armchair, but Gray waved him back. "No need, sir." He bent and offered his hand. "Izzy has mentioned you. It's a pleasure to make your acquaintance."

Silas gripped Gray's hand in a firm clasp, while his shrewd brown eyes studied Gray's face. "Izzy's mentioned you, too. I understand you've recently returned from America and that you're not above involving yourself with trade."

"No, indeed." Gray released Silas's hand and, at Izzy's wave, claimed the chair beside Silas, facing the sofa to which she returned and sank gracefully onto the end. "In truth," Gray continued, "I believe business— the sort I understand you've spent your life engaged in—will become increasingly important to the country's future."

Silas regarded him with interest. "You won't get any argument from me on that score. How did you find it over there, heh? One hears things, but I'm unsure how much to believe."

"Up to a point, I suspect most of what you hear reported is true, but I doubt it gives a balanced view of what it's truly like over there." Gray went on to verbally sketch a picture of American industry that elicited numerous questions from Silas and also a few from Jordan, all of which Gray answered, and that led to more questions—many canny and exceedingly shrewd from Silas—which both tested Gray and, through formulating his answers, clarified his own views.

During one exchange, Silas qualified his dry comments with "If you'll excuse my plain speaking."

Gray grinned. "Plain speaking was one facet of doing business in America that I grew to value. I'm finding having to revert to our less-direct Anglo-European ways more of an adjustment than I expected, so please don't feel you need to cloak your words in furbelows for me. I rather miss the blunt and direct."

Silas chuckled. "It sounds like I could do business over there, then, but truth to tell, I'm too old and fear I lack the energy for the voyage."

Gray was about to ask what areas Silas was interested in exploring, but the countess seized the moment to ask, "And what about American society, my lord? I'm sure you spent a good deal of your time in the drawing rooms there. Is it much the same as here?"

While he could speak about business and industry with authority, Gray was on much shakier ground when it came to society—or at least the upper echelons to which the countess referred. "Yes and no. They lack any form of aristocracy, so the ton per se doesn't exist. However, they do have their principal families, although their status is solely founded on wealth, which, in most cases, has been amassed via endeavors the British would regard as trade."

"Oh." Sybil looked bemused. "I hadn't thought of that."

"They have their grand balls and debutantes and so on," Gray said, "but I suspect you would say that, in that respect, they're still evolving."

"But you must have seen something of the country, my lord." Marietta was keen to hear more. "You mentioned you were in Boston. Did you also travel to New York?"

Cities, he could describe with ease. "I landed first in New York."

Izzy sat on the sofa and listened as Gray entertained the company, capturing both Silas's and Jordan's attention with a few well-placed remarks even while he enthralled her mother and sister with his descriptions of the American cities he'd visited during his years abroad. That list was longer than she'd expected, including, in addition to Boston and New York, Philadelphia, St. Louis, New Orleans, Portland, and San Francisco.

Cottesloe entered and announced that dinner was served, and in pairs defined by age, the company repaired to the dining table. They sat, and the conversation continued unabated.

Izzy ate, watched, and listened, increasingly sure she would not be obliged to intervene and redirect. She'd hoped she could simply introduce Gray and sit back; he'd always had the ability to adjust to whatever company he found himself in. She suspected that was one of the skills fostered in him as a duke's son; in many noble families, it was expected that the sons would develop the facility to rub shoulders with their workers—stablemen, grooms, tenant farmers, farmhands, and so on. When it came to managing estates, having that knack was an advantage.

She wasn't surprised when, with her mother's and sister's questions about American cities exhausted, Gray embarked on an anecdote involving a donkey and a yacht. Whether he'd witnessed the incident himself or merely heard about it—or even made it up—the story was perfect for this audience and had everyone laughing until their sides hurt.

Deftly, Gray turned all attention to Marietta, challenging her to reveal the most outrageous moment of her schoolroom years. That proved to be when, while living in the country and confined to her room with arithmetic she'd hated, she'd escaped from the house and, in order to avoid the family's workers, had gone roaming onto a neighboring estate, only to be chased by a bull into a stream, after which she'd been forced to return home, dripping and bedraggled.

With a smile of remembrance curving her lips, her mother admitted, "I'd forgotten about that."

The moment harked back to better times, before Izzy's father's death had brought their world crashing down.

Gray seemed to realize that and turned to Jordan. "You, next. I'm sure you got up to something deplorable in your youth."

Jordan grinned and promptly regaled the company with a tale from his Eton days.

As the laughter subsided, Gray cocked a brow at Silas. "Any advance on your juniors, sir?"

Silas glanced at the dessert plates, which were sitting empty before them, and her mother took the hint and suggested that the ladies withdraw and allow the gentlemen to savor their brandies.

Silas and Gray exchanged a glance, then both denied any wish for spirits, and Silas proposed that the company entire should return to the drawing room, where he promised to relate a curious tale from his youth.

Within minutes, they were comfortably ensconced in the drawing room, and Silas launched into his story, which fascinated everyone, as he rarely spoke of his youth at all.

Izzy noted that her mother, who, before Gray had arrived, had vacillated between being avidly curious and being frosty about him, had completely thawed, drawn in by his easygoing charm, his storytelling talent, and his subject matter, too. Since Jordan's earlier foray, no one had spoken again of murder, and her mother was pleased about that.

At the end of Silas's amusing tale, her mother seized the stage. "My lord, now you're back in the country, what are your plans? Are you here to stay?"

Given the past, that could have been a barbed question, but her mother's expression and her tone stated she was merely curious in the way of all society matrons, young and old.

Cottesloe chose that moment to wheel in the tea trolley, and the conversation paused while her mother poured and Jordan handed around the cups.

After they'd taken their first sips, Gray replied, "As I explained to Isadora, I found I missed England, so yes, I intend to make my home here." He sipped, then added, "I'm currently searching for a country house, and it's been suggested that I consider standing for a seat in Parliament."

"Is that so?" Silas regarded Gray with even greater interest. "Have you had a chance to catch up with the bills pending?"

"Some, but not all." Gray met Silas's eyes. "I intend to focus particularly on bills that impinge on industry and manufacturing."

Silas leaned closer. "Is that where your investing interest lies?"

The discussion that followed skated over several pieces of pending legislation before veering into investments of various sorts and the prospects for each. While much of it went over Izzy's head—and her mother's and Marietta's—quite aside from Silas's active involvement, Jordan was following the conversation, too.

Intriguingly, while her mother couldn't possibly comprehend much of what was said, she was observing the exchange as if it contained some significant revelation.

Izzy shifted her gaze to Gray and Silas and grasped what her mother had seen; this was the new Grayson Child—a mature, seasoned, experienced gentleman who had come to an understanding about himself and what he wanted to do with his life. There was purpose in his manner and conviction in his voice, neither of which had been in evidence ten years before.

She wasn't surprised because she'd been interacting with him over the past days, but for her mother, this Grayson Child was a new entity very different from the nobleman she remembered.

As for Silas, Izzy had known him for long enough to gauge the signs, and there was no doubt whatsoever that that shrewd and canny gentleman was deeply impressed by what he saw in Gray. She sipped and cynically acknowledged that it didn't hurt at all that Gray's interests and attitudes in business and investment largely mirrored Silas's.

While Gray and Silas continued to entertain each other, Jordan engaged Marietta in a discussion of the few social events looming in their calendars, and that also drew Sybil's attention.

Izzy quietly sipped, watched, and listened; she felt more relaxed and well entertained than she'd dreamed possible—and she suspected everyone else would say the same.

The evening had gone exceedingly well; she hadn't had to leap in and divert the conversation once.

Eventually, the clock on the mantelpiece chimed for ten-thirty, and with the tea consumed and the cups returned to the trolley, Gray declared he should go. He rose and made his farewells with his usual charming grace.

After thanking the dowager and farewelling Marietta and Jordan, Gray turned to Silas and shook the man's proffered hand. "Do send me that information. I'm particularly keen to expand my knowledge in that area."

"I will," Silas promised. "The more like you who understand the evolving situation, the better."

Gray turned, and Izzy waved toward the front door, clearly intending to see him out.

He followed her into the hall. "Thank you for inviting me. It was a thoroughly enjoyable and, at least for me, educational evening."

She met his eyes. "I'm sure the same reflection is passing through everyone's mind. Thank you for bearing with so many questions."

"Did you think I wouldn't?" He accepted his coat from Cottesloe and shrugged it on.

"More that you would grow bored and cut short the inquisition."

"It seemed a reasonable price to pay for making Silas's acquaintance."

Gray accepted his hat from Cottesloe, and on receiving a nod of dismissal from Izzy, the butler retreated, vanishing through the swinging door at the rear of the hall.

Izzy tipped her head, regarding Gray quizzically. "You and Silas got on very well." *Better than I expected* didn't need to be said. "And," she went on, "at a level significantly deeper than the charmingly superficial."

"As the editor of *The London Crier*, you, of all people, should know better than to harbor unnecessary preconceived notions."

"Such as the likelihood of a duke's son taking a genuine interest in the opinions of a millowner?"

He smiled. "Indeed."

She continued to study him as if seeking some physical sign to verify her deduction, namely that he wasn't the same duke's son she'd thought he was; that realization showed clearly in the emerald of her eyes.

Then she blinked and, with her usual haughtiness, refocused on him. "Should I warn Cottesloe you'll be here for breakfast? If you unexpectedly appear, he gets thrown off his stride and worries the kitchen won't have appropriate dishes to serve you."

He laughed softly. "Heaven forbid I rattle Cottesloe." He caught her gaze and inclined his head. "So yes, I plan to be here for breakfast tomorrow."

Her gaze sharpened. "Why?"

He dropped his charming façade and, entirely sober, said, "Because as I mentioned earlier, should the killer learn of *The Crier's* special edition, there's every chance he'll target you."

And? rang in Izzy's mind, but she didn't want to ask. He was watching her, waiting for her to press...and she strongly suspected that if she did, he would tell her his reason.

She wasn't sure she was ready to hear it—to hear him say that she still meant something to him or, alternatively, that he was focused on finding the killer, motivated purely by the investigation, by the thrill of the chase.

In her bones, she knew that something of their past connection still lingered, extant between them, but exactly what that was and how strong or reliable it might be, much less what it might mean...those were questions for another time when she didn't have her mother, her sister, her cousin, and Silas liable to come looking for her at any moment.

Briskly, she nodded—as if having a killer targeting her was unremarkable—reached for the doorknob, and opened the door. "Thank you for your company. Between you, you and Silas made the evening thoroughly enjoyable."

He inclined his head. "The pleasure was mine." He stepped over the threshold, then halted and turned, his amber gaze pinning her. "Do you have a safe in this house?"

Puzzled, she nodded.

"I strongly suggest you put the negatives in it and leave them there. You don't need them to print from, do you?"

"No. Digby said he's already made what they need." She met his eyes and nodded. "I'll do that."

The point brought home the danger of baiting a killer.

Her thoughts must have shown in her eyes. He hesitated, then said, "Quite apart from your Woburn Square subterfuge, whoever he is, he won't suspect the negatives are at your home. Why would they be? The others weren't. I don't believe leaving them in the safe here will result in any threat to this household."

That had been the thought that had risen in her mind. Reassured, she nodded, accepting his reasoning.

Satisfied, he smiled slightly, put on his hat, and raised a hand to its brim in salute. "I'll see you over the breakfast cups tomorrow."

She caught the teasing glint in his eyes.

His smile widened, and he turned and strode away.

She huffed, shut the door, stared at the panels, and reviewed the exchange. It was impossible not to acknowledge that the present situation had fostered a level of direct and open communication between them, resulting in a degree of clarity and understanding that hadn't been there years ago.

She wasn't sure what to make of that. Refocusing on the here and now, she returned to the drawing room.

While she and Gray had been in the hall, Jordan had risen to leave. He'd waited only to make his farewell to her; once he had, Marietta accompanied him to the door.

Izzy claimed the armchair next to Silas, and she and her mother asked about her brother Julius and Dorothy, Julius's wife and Silas's granddaughter, and their burgeoning family. Silas had called in at Lyndon Hall on his way from his home north of Manchester and bore news of the most recent happenings at the hall, which filled the next several minutes.

Marietta returned and joined Sybil on the sofa to listen, smile, and exclaim.

Finally, with his report delivered in full, Silas turned a searching gaze on Izzy. "Now, my girl, what's this about a murder, heh? At the printing works, Sybil said."

There hadn't been time earlier to relate much of the story, and her mother had been adamant she hadn't wanted the dinner blighted by the subject, an approach that had turned out rather well.

But Silas had been instrumental in enabling Izzy to buy the run-down printing works, refurbish the machinery, hire new staff, and establish *The London Crier*. Without him, she wouldn't have got past the first hurdle; he deserved to know of anything that threatened an enterprise to which he'd given so much time.

She started at the beginning—when Gray had walked through *The Crier's* door—and ended with the information that they'd decided that the best place for the crucial negatives was in the safe in the study, a safe Silas had arranged to have installed.

Her mother and her sister kept their questions to a minimum, allowing Silas to voice his often more searching queries.

She answered candidly; she valued his opinion as she did no one else's.

After listening to her account of Gray's reasoning over why the negatives being at Norfolk Crescent wouldn't constitute a danger to the household, Silas nodded approvingly. "I'm glad he considered the possibility and agree with his conclusion. Here is safer than anywhere else and keeps the negatives in your control." Silas's gaze rested on her face. "It appears his lordship is taking a personal interest in ensuring your safety and that of the staff, and of that, I wholeheartedly approve."

Feeling vindicated over agreeing to Gray's suggestion, when Silas rose, made his farewells, and claimed her escort to the door, she delightedly obliged.

As they walked arm in arm into the front hall, Silas patted her hand. "I have to say I'm rather intrigued by this notion of a hue and cry edition. Regardless, one way or another, I have every confidence that, between the pair of you, you and his lordship will see this blighter caught."

"Thank you. I always feel reassured by having your view of things."

"As to that, given his lordship thought your exposé was about him, ergo he's wealthy enough to be the latest Golden Ball, I take that to mean that he's rather wealthier than the typical duke's second son?"

"From his almost-comical conviction that I was referring to him, I would say that's definitely the case. He was no more wealthy than the typical duke's second son before he left for America, and he certainly knows what the term 'the latest Golden Ball' implies."

"Has he given you any inkling of how he came to make his money?"

She grinned. "He said it started with him stumbling upon a gold nugget in California. He used the cash that raised to invest, and his fortune grew to what it is now." That was, in fact, all she knew of how Gray acquired his extraordinary wealth.

Silas allowed Cottesloe to help him into his heavy coat. "From what he and I discussed," Silas said, "he seems to have a sound head on his shoulders regarding industry and manufacturing and investing in the same. Impressive, and not the sort of education one gets at Eton. Only way he could know half of what he does is if he'd studied the business closely, as an investor or owner would."

She smiled, understanding that Silas was reassuring her that as far as he could tell, Gray had, indeed, amassed his fortune via investing.

Once Silas had wound a thick muffler about his throat and set the hat Cottesloe handed him on his head, she stretched up and kissed his cheek. "Thank you for coming and being so helpful."

"Not at all, my dear. Indeed, I found the evening thoroughly refreshing." He caught her gaze and nodded. "Do take care, but with his lordship involved, I expect all will resolve itself in short order."

"I can only hope." She went with him onto the porch and watched him descend the steps. His footman helped him into his coach. Once the door was shut, she waved and, through the coach window, saw Silas raise a hand in salute, then the coach rumbled off.

With a satisfied sigh, she returned to the hall and allowed Cottesloe to shut the door. She paused, hearing again Silas's confident tone as he assured her that Gray was the investor he purported to be. Not that she'd imagined anything else, but it was comforting to have a man like Silas— so very experienced in judging men—give such a favorable report.

"Will there be anything else, my lady?"

She glanced at Cottesloe. "Lord Child confirmed he'll be here for breakfast tomorrow."

"Very good, my lady. I'll convey the information to Mrs. Hagen— she'll appreciate the notice."

Izzy smiled. "Indeed." She walked to the drawing room and, pausing in the doorway, caught the attention of her mother and her sister, who'd had their heads together, chatting. "I'm for bed. Are you coming?"

The pair looked at each other, then her mother waved her on. "In a moment, darling. You go on. We'll be up shortly."

Izzy nodded and turned away to hide her wry smile. They were, undoubtedly, discussing Child.

With free and easy—lighthearted—steps, she made for the stairs. The evening had been significantly more revealing than she'd expected, and indeed, some of those revelations were not what she would have predicted.

All in all, with respect to Grayson Child, she had quite a lot to assimilate.

CHAPTER 9

*T*he following morning, Izzy glanced across the breakfast table at Gray, who was systematically demolishing a mound of kedgeree, and felt a disorienting sense of...domesticity.

Utterly nonsensical!

Seeking distraction, she said, "Last evening, you mentioned you were thinking of entering politics."

He glanced at her, met her eyes, swallowed, and waved his fork. "What's your opinion of Russell's ministry?"

The question almost shocked her. Gentlemen invariably assumed that ladies other than those of political bent—such as the established political hostesses—knew nothing of such subjects. Those gentlemen were wrong, yet...

She wondered if Gray had forgotten the unscripted rules of English society or whether things were different in America.

As if guessing her thoughts, he caught her eye. "Regardless of whether you have any interest in the subject, I'm sure that, as editor of *The Crier*, you keep abreast of the latest news, including the vicissitudes of political fortunes."

Gray watched as, somewhat cautiously, Izzy inclined her head.

"Indeed, that's true." She paused as if collecting her thoughts, then ventured, "For all his reformist zeal, Russell is hedged about and constrained by others in his party. However, the primary source of instability comes from Palmerston's ambitions."

He picked up his coffee cup. "That's certainly the case at the moment. What do you think of Palmerston?"

"Pam, as they've started to call him?" She arched her brows. "As the editor of *The London Crier*, I can testify that he possesses a knack sorely lacking in most of his political peers—namely, an ability to engage with the public. On the whole, the common man approves of him. In many cases, his opinions are theirs." She tipped her head. "Or should I say he reacts to situations in the way they would, so they feel they have a certain bond with him?" She shook her head. "Either way, I would say Palmerston is one to watch. No matter that his peers and the palace distrust him, whatever political future comes, he'll be a part of it."

He was unsurprised to discover that her views aligned with his. "What do you think of this latest brouhaha? Was Russell right in forcing Palmerston's resignation?"

"For my money, that was unwise. Palmerston has a lot of support in Parliament, and it wasn't in session. The move smacked of ambush, even if it wasn't intended as that. But more, Palmerston's congratulatory note to Louis Napoleon was simply a statement of what the vast majority of the British public—and his peers in Parliament—thought. The idea that the note compromised a neutrality Victoria and her advisors wished to preserve is too abstract a concept to carry much weight with the public." She softly snorted. "That's not an argument I would attempt to run in *The Crier*."

He sipped. "That's an illuminating way to gauge things."

She studied his face. "Are you serious about running for a seat in the Commons?"

He met her gaze. "Therese Cader suggested it some months ago. Initially, I shrugged aside the notion, but somehow, it stuck and took root, and now…" He paused, then nodded decisively. "Yes. I'm serious."

He watched her read as much in his face and felt ridiculously buoyed —schoolboyishly buoyed—by the approval he saw in her eyes.

She pushed aside her plate and picked up her teacup. "The way Russell's ministry is going, you might not have that long to wait before putting your case to the people. Have you given much thought to the sort of policies you'll espouse?"

"As I told Silas, I'm interested in supporting industry, but alongside that, I'm also interested in improving the lot for the workers and local communities. I'd rather not have uprisings and revolutions. Leave that to the French."

She laughed and nodded, then glanced at the clock. "We'd better get going."

In pleasant accord, they left the table, quit the house, and rode in her carriage to Woburn Square. There, they didn't dally and were soon opening the printing works' front door.

The staff arrived on their heels.

While Izzy sat at her desk and put the final touches to her lead article, Gray and Mary sat in the office's armchairs and carefully conned the initial proofs of the obituary, Mary's article on the Foundling Hospital, and the listing of "What we know of Mr. Quimby's Movements on That Fateful Day," searching for errors.

Gray was intent on being there when the police came calling, just in case Baines had been further pressured and needed reminding of the forces supporting the hue and cry edition. After Izzy signed off on the three articles he and Mary had proofread, curious to see what came next, he left Izzy correcting the lead article and followed Mary as she hurried out to deliver the approved pages to her father.

Maguire and Matthews had their heads down, filling what Gray had been told were compositing sticks with lines of type. The filled sticks were subsequently set within boxes nestled in the large, page-sized formes. Laid out on the other half of the typesetting table were six formes —rectangular frames constructed of stout wood about two inches high, each the size of a double page. A thick piece of wood ran down the middle of each forme, dividing the area into the two pages, with the six formes accounting for the twelve pages that comprised an edition of *The Crier*.

Digby was sitting farther along from Maguire, swathed in one of the leather aprons and busily working on the blocks that would allow the photographs to be incorporated as part of the printed pages.

The forme that would print the front page, with its banner headline and large-print title, had already been partially filled, and the required type was now residing in the left-hand side of one of the formes, leaving space for the beginning of the lead article to be slotted in. Apparently, the type to fill the right-hand side of that forme would relate to the final page of the edition.

Maguire grunted when Mary set the approved proofs of the three articles by his elbow. He paused in his work and studied them, then glanced at Gray. "The police are going to come and read through everything, aren't they?"

"So they said."

"In that case, I'm going to concentrate on finishing setting the details for the photographs. No sense in us finalizing those articles if there's a chance they'll be reworded."

From the office, Izzy called for Mary, and Gray followed the girl as she rushed to return.

The instant Mary appeared, Izzy held out the sheets of the lead article. "Here—read it over." When Mary took the pages, Izzy slumped back in her chair. She met Gray's eyes. "I think it's done. Could you take a look, too? The more eyes the better."

"Of course." He returned to the armchair as Mary, eyes already scanning the lines of Izzy's neat script, slowly sank into the other chair.

Gray waited patiently, and when Mary looked up and said that she had found no errors, he took the pages and read carefully through.

He was starting to appreciate just how easy it was to miss little words that the mind supplied even if they weren't actually written on the page.

He found no spelling errors within the lengthy article, but queried two verb tenses. Izzy looked, then grumbled at herself as she changed them. That done, she declared the article ready to go to Maguire. Mary had already returned to the front counter, so Izzy rose to carry the pages to Maguire herself, and Gray went with her.

In the foyer, two men were standing at the counter, one speaking to Mary and the other to Lipson, while several others waited impatiently to do so.

As they crossed behind the counter, Izzy murmured to Gray, "Word of the special edition has spread." She tipped her head toward the men. "They're merchants wanting to place small advertisements. Mary and Lipson will deal with them, accommodating the requests as they can and filling up the smaller spaces left between articles, photographs, and the larger advertisements we've already slotted in."

She reached Maguire, and he glanced over the article, and she agreed it would be best to wait just a little longer before typesetting it in the hope the police would arrive closer to ten o'clock than later.

"If they don't show by ten-thirty," Maguire said, "we'll start setting the lead article and work from there."

To everyone's relief, Baines and Littlejohn appeared at ten o'clock on the dot.

Immediately, Izzy fetched the finalized articles and ushered the pair into her office, away from the interested eyes of those in the foyer who were waiting to speak with Lipson or Mary.

Gray followed and shut the office door.

Baines and Littlejohn were standing by the desk, with Baines already poring over the articles. Baines grunted, handed the one he'd finished to Littlejohn, and started on the next.

Gray ambled past and sank into his now-accustomed chair. Izzy was sitting behind her desk, her hands clasped on the blotter, the picture of assurance, but her gaze was hard and sharp as it rested on the policemen.

When Gray saw Baines approaching the end of the last article, he said, "I've read the articles as well. I think they're excellent—they strike the right note and will accomplish what we need them to, namely, galvanize the public and recruit the entire readership in the hunt for Quimby's killer."

Baines looked up, then handed the article to Littlejohn. Baines glanced at Gray, then looked at Izzy and inclined his head. "I agree—they're just what we need. Taken all together, especially with that reward, they're certain to put the wind up the killer."

Littlejohn raised his head, smiled at Izzy, and handed her the sheaf of pages. "They're perfect. Couldn't have done better myself."

That last was said with a twinkle in his eye.

Izzy accepted the sheets with a mock repressive look, but she was pleased. "I'm relieved you agree. Our typesetters are waiting to finalize these." Pages in hand, she rose, went to the door, flung it open, and headed straight for the typesetting table.

Baines and Littlejohn followed her out.

Gray followed more slowly. Even from the office doorway, he saw the relief in Maguire's face as he eagerly took the pages Izzy offered and called Horner to help as Maguire and Matthews plainly set aside everything else and knuckled down to get all the articles typeset.

Meanwhile, Baines and Littlejohn were eying the small crowd about the counter in some puzzlement.

Gray murmured an explanation, and Baines grunted. "We're surplus to requirements here—we'll head off for now, but please tell Mrs. Molyneaux we'll be back to see the final product later this afternoon."

Gray remembered enough of the process to observe, "Only pages for final proofreading will be run today."

Baines shrugged. "Regardless, I'd like to take a look and get some idea of the actual paper."

Littlejohn simply looked eager.

Gray hid a smile as the pair made for the front door. It appeared they were genuinely curious about what the hue and cry edition would be like and, doubtless, even more interested in what it might lead to.

When the door closed behind Baines and Littlejohn, Gray ambled to where Izzy was hovering by the typesetting table, watching Maguire, Matthews, and Horner at work.

Finally, Lipson and Mary finished arranging the smaller advertisements and delivered the sheets with the details to Maguire. He barely glanced at them, grunted, and bent his head once more to his compositing stick.

Mary fetched an apron, donned it, sat on a stool, picked up a compositing stick, and set to work, translating the small advertisements into type.

Meanwhile, Lipson had joined his son, and the pair were working on the press, polishing plates and checking levers.

Gray noted the time and glanced at the staff. All had their heads down, working to get the edition ready to print. He tweaked Izzy's sleeve and, when she glanced at him, bent his head and murmured, "Why don't I fetch pies and pasties and cider for everyone?" He tipped his head toward the staff. "My treat—they need to keep their strength up."

She smiled. "Thank you. I'm sure everyone will appreciate that."

He nodded and went.

Izzy turned her head and watched him go. An offer to fetch sustenance for everyone was…nice. And he hadn't thought about it; the offer had been spontaneous rather than calculated.

She faced forward and, gazing unseeing at the activity in the workshop, dredged her memories of him from long ago; she couldn't recall any similar action, but he'd always been an easy touch for friends, a genially generous gentleman. It seemed that trait had matured and evolved to where he acted out of a pure and simple impulse to help people.

If he's thinking of becoming a politician, that's not a bad trait to have.

Maguire straightened and pointed at a word. "Is that 'intentional'?"

Recalled to her purpose in remaining by the table, she stepped closer, read, and confirmed that it was.

∼

At Izzy's decree, everyone took a break to consume the pies, pasties, sandwiches, and cider Gray had fetched, but immediately after, everyone knuckled down again. The only sounds from the typesetting table were the soft clicks as type was set into compositing sticks, while elsewhere in the workshop, the Lipsons, father and son, muttered constantly as, assisted by Digby, they got the press ready to run the printer's proofs.

It was familiar Wednesday work, getting the week's edition typeset, running the completed formes through the press for a few sheets each, then everyone poring over the proofs to spot any errors, but the excitement of creating such a different edition as the hue and cry had everyone more tense than usual, determined to be extra careful and attentive with respect to every detail.

Finally, late in the afternoon, all was set, and the Lipsons, between them, rolled the press by brute force, generating four copies of each of the six double-page sheets that, eventually, would be printed on three double-sided sheets and folded to create the latest edition of *The Crier*.

As soon as the sheets were dry enough to handle, Izzy took one set and headed for her office. The staff divided up the other sheets, and everyone settled to stare at the pages, looking for typesetting errors or misprints.

Izzy sat at her desk, spread the sheets over the top, and started scanning.

After a moment, Gray ambled in, sat in the armchair, and claimed one of the sheets.

They were immersed in their search for errors when a tap on the door had them looking up to find Digby hovering in the doorway.

Izzy arched her brows. "Yes, Digby? What is it?"

Tentatively, he said, "I was just wondering, ma'am, if you was thinking of hiring another photographer yet, and whether you'd like to hear about this bloke I came across at the Society of Photographers meeting last night."

She beckoned him in. "You met this photographer at the meeting?"

Digby nodded. "He gave an exhibition and a talk about his methods, and I reckon he's as good as anyone. He—the new bloke, Mr. Donaldson —isn't near as old as Mr. Quimby was, but he's been in Paris for two years at some place called an atty..." Digby's tongue tripped, and he frowned.

"An atelier?" Gray suggested.

Digby's face lit. "Aye, that's it. At some at-tel-ier of some famous photographer, learning all the tricks of the trade. Not that he's French—he's as English as I am. But he's come home now, and he's looking for work." Digby sobered and looked at Izzy. "All of the other photographers were surprised Mr. Quimby wasn't there, and they asked me where he was. I didn't know what to say—far as I know, the hue and cry'll be the first time his death'll be spoken of outside—so I just said he'd gorn off. Then one of the regulars asked if that meant he wouldn't be working for *The Crier* no more, and well, I said yes. So later, Mr. Donaldson—Timothy Donaldson, he is—came up and asked if there was an opening, like, at *The Crier*, and...well, I said I'd ask."

From Digby's expression, he was half expecting to be upbraided for his temerity.

Izzy smiled reassuringly. "Well, we are looking for a photographer." She glanced at Gray, wondering what he thought.

He caught her eye, then looked at Digby. "You hadn't met or heard of this Donaldson before?"

The lad shook his head. "But quite a few of the photographers knew him. Seems he was a member from long ago, before he went to France, and he's got a reputation as an up-and-coming man."

That answered the question of Donaldson's bona fides, at least in terms of the Society of Photographers. When Digby looked back at her, she asked, "Tell me what you thought of Donaldson's photographs—the ones he showed at the exhibition last night."

Digby's face lit, and she didn't really need to listen to the superlatives that fell from his lips to understand the answer.

When Digby ended his paean and regarded her hopefully, she hid a smile. "Well, we need another photographer, and the sooner the better. Do you know how to contact Donaldson?"

"Aye, ma'am. He said he'd drop around at home tonight, just in case you was interested."

Knowing that Donaldson was keen and hungry for the position was reassuring and potentially helpful. She nodded decisively. "Very well. Tell him to come around for an interview tomorrow and that I'll expect to see his portfolio and any references he has."

"Yes, ma'am." Almost bouncing on his toes, Digby snapped off a salute and rushed off to whatever chore was waiting.

Izzy grinned. "He's probably scanning the photographs to see if everything's come up as it should."

"Hmm." Gray stared unseeing at the empty doorway, then looked at

Izzy, who had gone back to poring over the printed pages. "About this Donaldson."

She glanced up. "What about him?"

"He couldn't possibly be involved in Quimby's murder, could he?"

She frowned. "Meaning have we gone off on an irrelevant tangent with our hypothesis about the photographs and overlooked a far simpler explanation?"

"Exactly. Killing a rival to take his job is hardly an unknown motivation."

Her eyes narrowed, then she shook her head. "I can't see it. Why go to the bother of—and take the risk involved in—wrecking all the daguerreotype plates if his only motive was to remove Quimby and create an opening? And if Donaldson is as up with the latest techniques as he sounds and had some other motive for destroying Quimby's negatives, he would have known to search for the calotype negatives as well."

Gray wrinkled his nose. "True." He looked back at the page he held. "Forget I said anything."

He felt more than saw Izzy's affectionate smile before she, too, returned to her scanning.

Not long after, Baines and Littlejohn returned, driven, Gray suspected, more by curiosity than anything else. He looked at Izzy. "The police are here."

She sighed, rose, and went into the foyer.

Gray set down the sheet he'd been checking and followed.

After glancing over the printed proofs Mary spread on the counter for them to view and being assured by Izzy that there had been no changes to the articles since they'd "approved" them, both policemen declared they had no further need to squint at the proofs.

Izzy promptly returned to her desk, and after exchanging glances, Baines and Littlejohn cautiously made their way past the counter and deeper into the workshop, looking around curiously.

From near the office door, Gray watched the pair. Eventually, they retreated to stand against the darkroom wall, from where they could study the hulking press, the steam-driven motor, and the wide belt that had been set into place, connecting the two.

Gray shared the pair's fascination. Rather than following Izzy into the office, he ambled down the workshop.

On reaching Baines and Littlejohn, Gray nodded at the press. "Quite something, isn't it?"

Littlejohn confided, "I'm eager to see it in action. Lipson said it can be set to print both sides of the paper in a sort of double pass—they don't have to take the paper out and turn it. The machine can do that itself."

"German made, it is," Baines said. "Very clever with machines, the Germans."

Gray smiled. "Am I to take it you plan to be here tomorrow?"

His gaze on the shining drum of the press, Baines nodded. "Once we explained what was going on and that Winchelsea was behind it, the higher-ups suggested we'd better make sure that nothing went wrong, so either Littlejohn or I, or possibly both of us, will be here from eight to five."

"I see." Gray slotted the information away, but said nothing more at that point.

A few minutes later, Izzy emerged from the office to declare she had found no changes that needed to be made. She checked with Mary, Maguire, Matthews, Horner, Digby, and both Lipsons, all of whom denied having spotted any error or illegible type.

"Right, then." Izzy turned to Lipson and, smiling with satisfaction, nodded. "We're set and ready to roll."

Judging by the staff's universal delight, that was a moment of shared achievement.

Izzy glanced at the clock. "Goodness! It's already after five." She looked at Lipson. "Is there anything more that needs doing?"

Wiping his hands on a rag, Lipson briefly surveyed the press and the boiler and shook his head. "All's well here. We're as ready as we can be to start printing first thing tomorrow."

"Excellent!" Izzy beamed at the staff. "As that's the case, we can call it a day."

Baines and Littlejohn lingered while the staff, Izzy, and Gray found their coats and shrugged into them. Everyone was filing into the foyer, making for the door, when Lipson abruptly halted. "I just had a thought."

Everyone else stopped in their tracks as Izzy demanded, "What?"

Lipson met her gaze and grimaced. "Those merchants had heard whispers about the hue and cry edition. Hardly surprising, given we'd told our regular advertisers. But if the killer hears those same whispers—and by now, after Mary and I spent hours this morning explaining our special edition to so many, those whispers will have spread far and wide—the blighter might come back and try to wreck the press." Lipson turned to view his baby.

"Or wreck our formes," Maguire growled, looking toward his typesetting table where the fully blocked formes sat waiting to be fitted into the press.

Izzy, Gray, and the staff turned to look at Baines and Littlejohn.

Baines read the expectant expressions on their faces. "Littlejohn, arrange to have constables from the local watchhouse stand guard outside tonight. One at each door."

Lipson, who'd been exchanging looks with his son and Matthews, spoke up. "No need for the constables to wait outside in the cold. Tom, Jim, and I'll kip here tonight. We'll have the boiler going to keep the place warm—no reason the constables can't come in and wait with us. That way, if the killer does try anything, the constables will be on the spot, and the three of us'll be here to make sure there's no damage to any of our equipment."

That arrangement met with everyone's approval. The rest of the staff left, followed by Baines and Littlejohn, then Lipson saw Izzy and Gray out of the door and locked it behind them.

The policemen had halted a yard away. As Izzy and Gray came up, Baines turned and said, "I need to get back to the Yard, but Littlejohn will head to the local watchhouse, get two constables, and bring them back here."

Izzy smiled and inclined her head. "Thank you, Inspector. And you, Sergeant."

She waved the pair on, and the four of them walked in a loose group down to Bernard Street, then turned for Woburn Place.

Gray used the time to review the activity planned for the next day.

Frowning, he glanced at Izzy. "After you run the press tomorrow, what happens to all the copies of the newspaper?"

She met his eyes. "They're stacked in bundles and left ready to be picked up for delivery on Friday."

Gray felt his features harden. He raised his voice so the policemen walking ahead could hear. "Stacks of printed paper burn ferociously hot. If I were the killer and heard about the hue and cry edition, I'd be inclined to burn the entire printing works down."

They all halted, and the other three turned to regard him with near-identical expressions of horror.

He met their gazes as the truth of what he'd said sank in.

Baines grunted and beetled his brows at his sergeant. "Littlejohn and I will be at the printing works all day tomorrow, and when Littlejohn speaks with the sergeant at the watchhouse tonight, he'll arrange for a larger force to stand guard tomorrow night—outside as well as inside."

Satisfied, Gray gave an approving nod—one Izzy slowly copied.

"It's a disturbing thought," she said. "But I can't see what more we can do."

The four exchanged glances, then walked on.

They parted in Woburn Place, with Baines hailing a hackney to carry him south while Littlejohn trotted north to the nearby watchhouse.

Gray and Izzy strode on along the north side of Russell Square. With his hands sunk in his pockets, he said, "Yesterday evening, I mentioned I was looking for a house in the country."

She glanced at him. "You'll need a place if you're to stand for Parliament."

"Exactly. I've had a land agent searching for suitable properties, and he's sent word he's found one for me to look at, preferably as soon as possible. Given Baines and Littlejohn will be at the printing works all day tomorrow, and you'll be focused on overseeing the print run, I thought I'd seize the day, take a run into the country, and inspect this place the agent's so keen for me to see."

She nodded. "That sounds sensible."

"I'll be back for breakfast on Friday."

Oh, good. Izzy inwardly frowned at the relief that swept through her.

She pushed the feeling aside and debated asking where the house was, but really, it was none of her business.

They reached Number 20 and went inside. Agatha was waiting, eager to hear their news. As the old lady rarely got out, Izzy sat and, with Gray doing his part, brought Agatha up to date with what, to her, probably resembled an exciting story told in daily episodes.

Thirty minutes later, with Gray, Izzy was in the carriage, rattling along Oxford Street toward Norfolk Crescent. Evening had fallen, and the street lamps had been lit. A cold wind had blown up and was strafing the pavements, snatching at hats and bonnets, reminding everyone of the season.

As they neared Edgware Road, Izzy glanced through the gloom at Gray, seated in his usual elegant manner on the bench seat opposite. They were rather later than usual, and it was a cold and nasty evening...

"Would you like to stay to dine?" The words surprised her nearly as much as they did him. She hurriedly added, "It's after six, and it'll just be us—en famille, as it were. No need to dress. Just stay."

She couldn't make out his expression in the gloom, but sensed his quiet pleasure as he inclined his head in acceptance.

"Thank you." He paused, then confessed, "My gentleman's gentleman is a wonder with clothes and boots, but he can't cook to save himself."

She smiled. "Where in town are you staying?"

"I have lodgings in Jermyn Street, my old stamping ground. Purely temporary until I decide what I'll be doing regarding everything else—the house, politics, and so on."

She nodded sagely. "All such factors will heavily influence which area it would be best to buy in."

The carriage slowed and halted.

Gray opened the door and descended. He handed Izzy down, and they walked up the steps and were admitted to the house by Cottesloe.

Despite being deeply pleased by the spontaneous invitation to dine as if he were part of the family, Gray did his best to mute his pleasure to an acceptable, less-revealing level. Indeed, he wasn't sure why he felt so powerfully uplifted; he only knew he did.

The dowager countess was already in the drawing room when Izzy led him in. With admirable control, the dowager concealed her surprise and welcomed him warmly. She was distantly acquainted with his parents, but after the usual polite queries about their health, she turned the conversation to how he and Izzy had spent their day.

Marietta came in soon afterward and insisted on hearing their news as well, then Cottesloe summoned them to the dining table.

Gray offered the dowager his arm, and she took it with a pleased smile. He escorted her to her chair. She sat and directed him to the chair on her right. Izzy was on his right, and with Marietta opposite, the conversation turned to the usual members-of-the-ton-who-lived-in-London subjects.

It was easy to allow himself to sink into the moment. To laugh, smile, encourage, and enjoy the company of the three ladies and to feel as if, more than being merely welcomed, he had a place there, a comfortable niche that fitted him in their otherwise female world.

By the time the four of them retreated to the drawing room and the tea trolley arrived, he was feeling distinctly mellow. Enough to decide there was no point analyzing the moment; it simply was, and it felt very right.

There was, however, one point he needed to address. Seated in an armchair opposite the sofa on which the countess and Marietta sat, with Izzy in the armchair alongside his, he lowered his teacup, set it on the saucer, and looked Izzy's way. "As I'll be away from London tomorrow, one of my men—a footman—will be here in the morning to escort you to the printing works, and he'll remain nearby during the day and escort you home as well."

He met Izzy's faintly outraged stare and calmly stated, "With Quimby's killer at large and the hue and cry edition about to go out, it would be unconscionable of me to leave you to walk the streets between Woburn Square and the printing works alone."

Her lips tightened, but as he'd anticipated, her mother and Marietta were quick to thank him for arranging such a necessary precaution.

Barely registering her mother's and her sister's predictable comments, Izzy read in Gray's eyes not so much a challenge as a simple hope that she would accept his arranged protection.

Given he'd been clever enough to speak of it in her mother's hearing —although she was faintly peeved that he'd employed such a strategy to effectively tie her hands—there was no point trying to argue against, much less dismiss, the need for such a guard. Aside from all else, she wasn't such a ninny.

But I would have liked to at least make him work for my agreement.

Stifling the urge to humph disparagingly, she regally inclined her head. "Thank you."

She saw his eyes flare slightly; she'd surprised him. *Good.* Such high-handed tactics were acceptable only when she agreed with the outcome.

After that minor moment, the evening rolled on, pleasant and undemanding. He was an easy guest, and by the time he rose to leave, her mother and her sister had grown entirely comfortable in his presence.

He bowed over their hands, deploying his ready charm in thanking them for their company.

She rose before he turned to her; when he did, she waved toward the front hall. "I'll see you out."

They walked side by side into the hall, only to discover Cottesloe wasn't there. She tugged the bellpull, then returned to stand with Gray. Others might be tempted into conversation, but between them, the silence felt relaxed and companionable.

She felt his gaze rove her face and looked up and met it.

His amber eyes captured her awareness and effortlessly held it, even as, his gaze locked with hers, he stilled.

And suddenly, there was more—much more—than simple silence between them.

Something that lured and ached and *wanted* burgeoned and grew, freed by the moment to pulse ever more strongly, linking them as if the past ten years had never been.

She felt herself lean toward him, and he seemed to lean closer to her.

The click of heels on tiles reached them.

They both blinked, drew back, and looked at the swinging door as Cottesloe came hurrying through.

"My apologies, my lady—my lord." With an abbreviated bow, the butler hurried to fetch Gray's greatcoat and hat.

As Gray shrugged on his coat, his eyes found hers with a question—an appeal she had no difficulty interpreting—then he thanked Cottesloe and accepted his hat.

Responding to the unvoiced plea, she said, "Thank you, Cottesloe. I'll see his lordship out."

"Indeed, my lady. My lord." With a bow, Cottesloe took himself off.

She met Gray's eyes and faintly arched her brows, then waved toward the door.

They turned in that direction, their steps very slow.

He bent his head the better to see her face as he lowered his voice and said, "I truly enjoyed tonight. It was relaxing in a way I haven't experienced in…a very long time. Perhaps not ever." He caught her gaze as she glanced up. "Tell me, Izzy, is it possible for us to pick up the strands of what we had, to go back to where we were ten years ago and explore what might lie farther along the road down which we started, but stopped?"

She was stunned by how high her heart leapt at the thought; in instinctive reaction, she forcefully reined herself back. He'd broken her heart once and left her emotionally wrecked and weak. She couldn't afford to have him do so again. Yet… She held his gaze. "As to that…we're two very different people now."

He inclined his head. "Nevertheless…or perhaps that's even more reason to try again."

Perhaps, perhaps… She halted before the front door and conceded, "So much water has passed under each of our bridges, who can say what might or might not be?"

She watched his eyes, his face, as he analyzed her answer.

Then he focused intently on her. "That's not a no."

She tipped her head in acquiescence. "It's not a yes, either."

He smiled. "That's good enough for now."

Before she caught the slightest inkling of what he intended, he bent his head and pressed his lips to hers.

Oh Lord.

She'd forgotten this, the simple pleasure of his kiss. Tingles spread from the first light contact, then warmth welled and spread, washing through her as the pressure firmed.

Yet he kept the kiss gentle—questing, luring, but not pressing, not demanding.

Waiting like a supplicant to see what she wished.

Something inside her blossomed and bloomed, a flower unfurling at the reviving touch of rain—thirsty, hungry, needing, seeking.

Her thoughts suspended; all awareness of anything beyond the contact vanished.

The touch of his lips remained light, enticing.

She leaned nearer, then wanting more, stepped closer, directly into his arms. Her hands rose, and she curled her fingers into his coat and clung.

The sensation of his lips on hers was a drug, but even through the intoxicating miasma clouding her senses, she was aware of how gently his arms closed around her—as if to him, she was the most precious object imaginable.

Then their heads angled, and the kiss deepened, and her awareness was overwhelmed.

With a need more powerful than any she'd known.

With a yearning that came from so deep within her she couldn't have denied it, even had she wished to.

And over and above everything else lay the heady, sparking, thrilling sensations the simple pressure of his lips on hers ignited and fanned, feeding her starved soul.

Fireworks erupting in the hall would have had less impact.

But a simple kiss was all this could be.

Nothing more—not here, not now.

With transparent reluctance, he raised his head as she, responding to the same intuition, drew back.

For a long moment, they stared at each other, then Gray drew in a breath deep enough to have his chest rising beneath her palms. Slowly, he lowered his arms and, his voice rough and low, said, "So...we'll think about that."

She didn't reply; to her mind, the statement was a reasonable summation of where they now stood. She was grateful when, his distracting lips lightly curving, he inclined his head and turned toward the door.

On tremulous limbs, she stepped past him and opened it.

He met her eyes, then smiled in his usual charming fashion but with a light in his amber eyes that warmed her.

Facing forward, he stepped onto the porch, paused to settle his hat on his head, then went quickly down the steps and strode away.

She watched him until he rounded the corner and was lost to her sight.

Then, slowly, she shut the door. After staring at the uninformative panels for several seconds, she turned and, leaving her mother and her sister to think what they would, went quietly upstairs.

Gray reached Edgware Road before he succeeded in wrenching his mind from the mesmerizing events of the past ten minutes.

He hailed a hackney and directed the jarvey to Jermyn Street. The carriage was rattling down Park Lane before he managed to shift his focus to the wider events of the day and all they'd achieved—and all that was yet to come.

From the first, when he'd walked into the printing works and discovered Izzy was the editor he'd come to see, where she was concerned, he'd followed the prodding of his instincts. It was a habit he'd acquired over the years, listening to that inner voice and paying attention to its promptings.

Acting on instinct, he'd kissed her tonight, and plainly, that had been the right thing to do.

And out of that, what had started as an instinctive urge to protect her had transformed into an unshakeable determination to keep her safe no matter what threats confronted them over the coming days.

Them.

It had been a long time since he'd thought of "them"—of her and him or, indeed, of him and any other woman.

After her…there'd never been another who had seized his awareness and focused his senses as she so effortlessly did.

For him and, he hoped, her as well, the writing was on the wall, and he knew how to read it. There was no longer any question in his mind over what he wanted, over what his future should look like. Courtesy of this evening, his desired future had crystalized in his mind.

As the hackney rattled deeper into Mayfair, he realized that, regarding that much-desired future, there was really only one question remaining.

Can I convince her to marry me—the her as she now is and the me as I am now?

CHAPTER 10

*I*zzy sat at the breakfast table, staring at the empty chair opposite, and wondered how it could possibly be that in just a few days, Gray joining her had become her expectation. Enough so that, now he wasn't there, she felt as if she missed him.

She shook her head at herself, dusted the toast crumbs from her fingers, and rose.

After donning her coat and bonnet, she went through the door Cottesloe held open and halted on the porch, blinking at the strapping young man who was holding her carriage door and smiling at her.

Then she remembered; he was Gray's footman-cum-guard.

She descended the steps, and he very correctly offered his hand to help her into the carriage. She grasped his hand, then paused and asked, "Your name?"

He grinned and bobbed. "Tom, my lady. Tom Corby."

Izzy inclined her head and climbed into the carriage.

Tom shut the door carefully, then she felt the carriage dip as he swung up behind, and Fields started the horses trotting.

Resigned to being guarded, she made no demur when Tom dogged her steps through Mrs. Carruthers's house, into Woburn Square, and all the way to the printing works, always a respectful pace behind her, like the well-trained footman he apparently was.

While unlocking the door to the printing works, she glanced at him.

"Do you want to come in? I warn you it will be chaotic, and someone will probably put you to work."

He grinned. "His lordship said you were running the press today. I wouldn't mind seeing that, and I don't mind lending a hand." He shrugged lightly. "Better than sitting in some tavern being bored."

She had to agree. She opened the door and walked in and suggested he sit on the bench by the counter until the staff arrived. Then she found herself being greeted by two young constables, who had been waiting to leave after guarding the workshop overnight. The pair informed her that the Lipsons, father and son, and Jim Matthews had left a few hours earlier, but would return at their usual time to get the press rolling. Izzy thanked the pair and saw them out.

After hanging up her coat and bonnet, she went to her desk, sat, and got ready to do the accounts—her usual chore while the presses clanged and clanked in the workshop. Mary soon joined her, and they opened the ledgers and disappeared into a world of numbers and amounts.

Only when she heard the warning whistle as the heavy press started to turn did she remember Tom Corby. She sprang to her feet, walked quickly into the foyer, saw the bench was empty, and turned to look down the workshop. She spotted Tom, his face alight, working opposite his name-sake—Tom Lipson—as, standing on raised platforms on either side of the massive machine, they carefully fed sheets into its voracious maw. Standing at the nearer end, Maguire and Jim carefully received the printed sheets spat out by the whirring machine.

Clangs and clanks filled the air, and after pausing for a moment to savor the satisfaction she always felt on getting out another edition, Izzy retreated to the office and sank into the ledgers again.

A short while later, the bell over the door caught Mary's attention; being seated on the other side of the desk, she could see who had entered. "It's Sergeant Littlejohn, ma'am, and he's brought another lad with him. Looks to be a young constable, given the way his eyes are on stalks."

Seconds later, Littlejohn appeared in the doorway and nodded to Izzy. "We'll just be keeping an eye on things, ma'am." He cast an intrigued eye toward the press. "If there's anything the lad and I can do to lend a hand...?"

Izzy smiled and waved him down the workshop. "Go and ask Lipson. He always has chores for idle hands."

Littlejohn tried to smother an expectant grin as he nodded and went.

Izzy forced her gaze to the ledger in front of her and resisted the urge to glance at the presently empty armchair. It was truly ridiculous how Gray had somehow imprinted his presence on her mind, even here, and all in such a short time.

You've known he's the only one for you for over ten years.

She shut her mind to the insidious reminder and refocused on her task, yet no matter how ferociously she concentrated, her senses continued to react as if something was missing.

She and Mary finally reached the end of the invoices and expenses. Mary gathered up the ledgers and went to exchange them for those listing the printing works' revenue and income.

That left Izzy with nothing to distract her from thinking of what she didn't wish to dwell on. Such as that kiss last night and what it might mean. She'd already realized the answer was a never-ending prospect of what-ifs, and at this point, she didn't need further uncertainty.

Indeed, in the small hours, she'd concluded that her best way forward was to set Gray and everything to do with him personally on a mental shelf and leave it there while they dealt with Quimby's killer.

One fraught situation at a time.

She was drumming her fingers on the desk and mentally hurrying Mary along when Digby poked his head around the doorway. She arched her brows.

"Timothy Donaldson's here, ma'am, like you asked."

She glanced at the clock; it was just after ten o'clock. "Excellent." Mary loomed behind Digby, ledgers in her arms. Izzy caught her eye. "Let me interview Donaldson first. Then we'll get back to the accounts."

Mary cast a shy glance at someone out of Izzy's sight, presumably Donaldson, and readily drew back.

Izzy nodded to Digby. "Show Mr. Donaldson in."

The man Digby steered into the office was several decades younger than Quimby had been; he appeared to be in his late twenties. He had dark-brown hair and a pleasant, open face with the sort of features that were handsome enough when one focused on them, but in general, were totally forgettable. Donaldson wore a decent overcoat over a neat waistcoat, pressed trousers, clean linen, and a checkered neckcloth. He looked youthful, but not overly young, primarily because of the intelligence that burned in his blue eyes.

He carried a felt hat, along with a portfolio.

Izzy waved him to the armchair Mary had occupied. "Good morning, Mr. Donaldson. Thank you for coming in."

Donaldson nodded politely. "Thank you for the chance to speak with you, ma'am."

Izzy folded her hands on the desk and waited as Donaldson leaned the portfolio against the chair's side and sat. "Now, the first thing you need to be aware of is that your predecessor, Mr. Horace Quimby, was murdered on the premises, in the darkroom here."

Donaldson's eyes flew wide, but almost immediately, shock and surprise were overlaid by speculation. He glanced toward the workshop. "Is that what this hue and cry edition is about?"

"Yes." She waited until Donaldson's gaze returned to her face to say, "I will understand if you no longer wish to apply for the position of photographer with us."

He blinked, then frowned. "Was Quimby murdered because of his work with *The Crier*?"

"Not specifically." She saw no reason not to explain their thinking regarding the seven photographs Quimby had taken on the day he'd been killed.

"So the killer followed him here, stabbed the poor beggar, and destroyed all the daguerreotype negatives he could find, but the relevant negatives were calotypes and were safe in a drawer all the time." Donaldson looked strangely enthused. "That's like something out of a penny dreadful."

Izzy conceded that with a tip of her head.

"And now"—Donaldson's gaze swung toward the workshop —"you're running all seven photographs and urging anyone with information to come forward." He returned his gaze to her. "Frankly, if you offer me the job, I'd be a fool not to take it. *The London Crier* is about to become a sensation."

She fought to stifle a grin. Doing her best to preserve an appropriately serious façade in the face of Donaldson's enthusiasm, she pointed at his portfolio. "Take me through your work."

He leapt to do so, and in evaluating what he placed before her, she concluded that Digby was, surprisingly, a master of understatement. Donaldson's eye was nothing short of spectacular; he had a knack for capturing a moment at its most revelatory, and his subjects were not limited to the tried and true.

Finally closing the portfolio, she met his eyes. "This is—as I'm sure you're aware—most impressive. The terms I'm willing to offer you are these." Succinctly, she outlined the same arrangement she'd had with

Quimby, then went on, "However, if you agree to remain exclusive to *The Crier*, I'm willing to formally employ you and pay you a steady salary on the proviso you provide us with our usual three photographs every week, plus one other of your own choosing. If you come on board as our staff photographer, I'd like you to commence a feature along the lines of 'What a Photograph Can Reveal that the Naked Eye Might Not See.'"

Donaldson's eyes had grown wider and wider. He swallowed, seemed about to speak, then reined himself in and said, "That's very tempting. Perhaps if I could see the darkroom?"

Izzy nodded and rose. "By all means. Come with me."

He followed her to the darkroom.

She opened the door and waved him in, remaining in the doorway as he walked around, examining the fixtures. "Digby is our printer's devil—our lad-of-all-work—but over the past months, Quimby had been training him in photography. If you're willing to take on that training, I'd like to make him your assistant. I can hire another printer's devil, but Digby seems to have a passion for photography, and if it hadn't been for that and his quick thinking, we wouldn't have any means of pursuing whoever killed Quimby. You'll find Digby a very quick study, and his heart is already in this darkroom."

Donaldson flashed her a grin. "I've already heard decent things about him from the other members of the society." He returned to the door and nodded. "So yes, I'll be happy to take him on as my assistant and train him up."

"Excellent. Well, then, Mr. Donaldson, what do you consider a reasonable salary?"

He proposed a figure, and they embarked on a round of negotiations and ultimately shook hands on a deal that, Izzy suspected, they both felt was to their benefit.

"The job is yours, Mr. Donaldson, and this darkroom is now your domain."

He smiled—a boyishly charming smile—but it faded as his gaze, turning shrewd again, went past her. "I'm curious over the police being here, more or less assisting your people in getting out the paper."

"As to that"—she tipped her head toward her office—"let me show you the proofs of the edition."

She led him back to the office and laid the proofs over her desk.

Donaldson pored over them.

Izzy heard the bell over the door tinkle, then Baines's gruff voice speaking to Mary.

Donaldson tapped the proofs. "This is going to capture the attention of every Londoner." He glanced at Izzy. "If this pans out and someone comes forward and you catch the killer, I could photograph the actual arrest. With the latest techniques, my exposure time is down to seconds, not minutes. And you could run those photographs in the next edition— you'd get an enormous boost in circulation from that!"

His enthusiasm was infectious. Izzy battled to hold back a smile. "I like the way you think, Mr. Donaldson."

He grinned at her.

"Well, I'm not sure I do."

She looked up as Baines came plodding into the office with Little-john, openly curious, trailing him.

"Who's this, then?" Baines demanded. "And what's this about photographing arrests?"

Izzy introduced Donaldson and, in what amounted to a trial by fire, left it to him to make the case for being allowed to photograph the capture of the killer.

Baines wasn't convinced, but Littlejohn, who had followed with interest Donaldson's explanation about what could be done with the latest inventions and who plainly had learned a thing or two about communi-cating with the public while knocking about the printing works, ventured to observe, "Sir, I can't help but wonder if the brass wouldn't go for it. You know they're always on about getting positive coverage in the papers. Well, what could be more positive than us actually arresting a killer, all shown on the front page?"

After regarding Littlejohn for several silent moments, Baines returned his gaze to Donaldson and tipped his head Littlejohn's way. "My sergeant's right. The brass are always bending our ear about that. So"— Baines blew out a breath—"let's see if we can't work something out."

"As long as I can be there," Donaldson argued, "close enough to the action to take photographs, I swear I won't get in your way."

Baines humphed and asked several pertinent questions, which Donaldson answered with boyish openness.

Finally, Baines met Izzy's eyes and nodded. "All right. We'll try it and see."

Izzy beamed at all three men. "Excellent!" She spied Mary hovering just beyond the doorway. "And now, gentlemen, if you'll allow me to get back to our accounts?"

Littlejohn said to Baines, "You should come and see the press running, sir. It's a real sight."

With a grunt, Baines nodded to Izzy and followed his eager sergeant out.

Donaldson grinned. "If this works out—"

Izzy held up a hand. "Don't tempt Fate."

Donaldson laughed. "I'd better go and see to the darkroom, then. With luck, we'll have some exciting shots to develop soon."

He walked out, nodding politely to Mary, who blushed and ducked her head but then watched him walk away before recalling her purpose and bustling in, carrying the revenue ledgers.

Normally, Izzy would have sighed at the sight of Mary's distraction, but she was distracted, too, in her case by the prospects opening up for *The Crier*.

As she settled in her chair and Mary opened the ledgers, Izzy endeavored to force her mind back to figures and sums, but couldn't stop a smile from curving her lips at the thought of what Gray would make of Donaldson's zeal and Baines's change of heart.

Then she caught herself, castigated her wayward wits, and ruthlessly focused them on adding up the advertising revenue.

Gray rode through the open gates of Tickencote Grange and drew rein just beyond the gateposts.

He'd lost count of the properties he'd cast his eye over; contrary to his initial assumption, he'd discovered that his prejudices—or rather his instincts over what was the right house for him—made him decidedly picky.

Given how many times his inner voice had saved him from making potentially disastrous decisions and that the sole occasion on which he'd deliberately ignored it had ended in catastrophe, he wasn't about to change what had now become a habit.

If his instincts said no, the house wasn't for him.

He'd taken the train north, putting aside the distrust of rail travel engendered by the accident that had injured Therese several months ago. Although she'd fully recovered, he hadn't felt any need to risk the train, not until today. Given he'd wanted to see the house and return to London within the day, the train it had had to be. Driving up the Great North Road as far as Stamford, then immediately down again wasn't an option; he valued his horses too much. So he'd braved the train to Stamford, hired a nag—a retired hunter who wasn't half bad—and ridden the few miles to the tiny village of Tickencote.

From where he'd halted, he couldn't see the house. A tree-lined drive, the trees mature but currently leafless, led around a curve with winter-brown lawns rolling away on either side, eventually reaching more trees. He tapped his heels to the horse's flanks and rode on.

As he rounded the curve, the house came into view. Built in local pale-gray stone with a steeply pitched lead roof that hosted multiple dormer windows, the house faced squarely north. Gray slowed the horse to a walk and looked around. The expanse of lawn that now stretched to his right ended in unkempt hedges that enclosed a knot garden graced with overgrown topiaries, while to his left, the lawn rolled into an orchard with numerous gnarled, presently skeletal trees.

He returned his gaze to the house. It comprised two full stories as well as the attics evidenced by the dormers. Four double chimneys rose from the central roof, and others were visible at various points around the squarish structure. A flight of stone steps led to a porch before the main door, which was located centrally in the front façade and flanked by long, stone-framed mullioned windows. The walls of the house below the level of the ground floor were covered in some creeper, leafless in this season, which framed low windows that presumably admitted light into a basement level.

Tickencote Grange was a substantial edifice, solid and impressive, with twin square towers jutting forward on either side of the central section of the house. The stone pediment above the front door was finely carved, as was a triangular inset above it.

The style hailed from late in the previous century, but given the simmering excitement that had started to spread through Gray's veins, he wasn't overly concerned with the house's age.

He trotted the hunter into the forecourt. The crunch of hooves on the gravel brought the agent hurrying around the corner of the house.

The portly man saw Gray, beamed, and came forward. "My lord. You're here."

"As you see, Caxton." Gray drew rein and dismounted, then led the horse to where a ring set into the wall beside the front steps provided a convenient hitching point. "Now." Gray turned to the house. "What have we here?"

Caxton seized the invitation, led Gray up the steps and through the double front doors, and proceeded to show him the ground-floor rooms while filling his ears with every last detail the agent had gleaned about the property.

While one part of his mind cataloged the pertinent points in Caxton's monologue, most of Gray's attention was focused on what he was seeing and how he felt being inside the house.

The front hall was tiled in black and white and was paneled in walnut to head height. He studied the plain white walls above, which looked sadly denuded at present. Without comment, he followed Caxton through the rooms, taking note of the plentitude of windows, the pleasing proportions, the ornate moldings, and the continuing paneling, which was the dominant feature of the house's interior. The curtains were heavy velvet, and dustcloths covered the remaining few pieces of furniture. The fireplaces in all the major reception rooms were impressive displays of the woodcarver's art.

Although Gray's nose detected the presence of considerable dust, there was no telltale scent of dampness. He broke into Caxton's description to remark, "You mentioned that the house stands close to a river."

"Indeed, my lord. The rear lawn runs all the way to the bank of the Gwash." The agent urged him on. "If you come through to the ballroom, you'll see how close we are."

Gray allowed the agent to usher him along a corridor to two tall, impressively ornate doors. With a flourish, Caxton flung them wide, and Gray found himself looking across an expanse of polished boards to a wall of windows. He walked forward and saw, as Caxton had said, that the lawn at the rear of the house ran down to a small river, presently running high.

After studying it for a moment, Gray nodded. "It doesn't flood around the house."

"No, my lord. The banks are sufficiently high, and the house itself is still higher."

And the lack of dampness within the walls testified to the solidity of the house's foundations. Gray suppressed a smile. Turning to Caxton, without inflection, he said, "Now I'm here, you may as well show me the rest of the place."

Caxton was keen to oblige. Over the next half hour, he took Gray through the entire house. The first floor, reached via a wide timber stair-case, beautifully carved and elegant, housed nine bedrooms and several bathing chambers, while the extensive attics hosted a nursery as well as numerous rooms for staff. In the semi-basement, the kitchen and associated service rooms were large and easily passed muster.

To Gray, this was *his* house—he felt it in his bones, in his marrow.

Aside from being in an excellent location—readily reached from London via train as well as road and within easy riding distance of Ancaster Park and Alverton—this was the right house for him.

On finally returning to the forecourt, he concealed his excitement and questioned Caxton regarding the land attached to the house. The answer translated to enough and not too much. As he harbored no interest in becoming a farmer, that was precisely what he was looking for.

In answer to Caxton's query of what he thought of the property, Gray glanced around once again and said, "I'll think about it, but unlike the previous houses you've shown me, I'm not instantly crossing this one off my list."

Caxton brightened.

Before he could press, Gray went on, "I'll be in touch if I wish to know anything further, but before we part, refresh my memory—how much is the bank asking for the place?"

Sensing the possibility of a sale, Caxton hesitated for only a moment before confiding, "Actually, my lord, I've heard a whisper that the bank just wants the mortgage paid out."

Given the vendor was a bank, Gray had wondered if that might be the case, but arched his brows as if surprised. "And how much is the mortgage?"

The figure Caxton murmured was low enough to make the property an incredible bargain. "But if you are wishful of buying the place, my lord, I would advise making an offer sooner rather than later, given the bank is letting that whisper get out to us agents. They truly are keen to get this place off their books."

Gray inclined his head in understanding, but he'd learned the hard way to examine gift horses' mouths very closely. "If I wish to purchase the place, I'll be in touch." He nodded in dismissal.

Caxton bowed and left, trotting around the house to where he'd no doubt left his horse.

Gray stood for a moment more, looking around and soaking up the ambience, then untied his horse, swung up to the saddle, and turned the horse's head toward the orchard. From upstairs, he'd glimpsed a rear drive wending past the orchard, and as far as he could tell, the bulk of the village lay that way.

He'd guessed correctly; the drive ended at a gate that gave onto a lane that led down to a mill on the riverbank. In the other direction, more or less east, the lane ran past several cottages to—as Gray had hoped—the local public house. As he walked his horse along the lane, the pub's sign came into focus. The Fox and Hound. Appropriate, he supposed, given this was hunting country.

After tying his horse to a hitching post in the narrow paved area before the pub, he pushed through the door and found himself in a comfortable if low-ceilinged room; he had to duck beneath huge oak beams on his way to the highly polished wooden counter. Other than the barman behind it, there was no one else in evidence, no other customers. Then again, it was not quite eleven-thirty, relatively early for a pub.

The barman nodded in that cautious way of countrymen. Having grown up not that far away, Gray wasn't deterred; he claimed a barstool, leaned on the bar, and in relaxed fashion, ordered a beer.

When the barman set the frothing tankard before him, he handed over a coin. "Nice little village you have here."

"Aye." The barman eyed him with undisguised curiosity. "Quiet, it is. We don't get many outsiders stopping by, not with Stamford so close."

Gray sipped. "I can imagine. I grew up at Ancaster." He tipped his head eastward.

"Aye? That's not so very far. You been visiting there, then?" The barman picked up a cloth and started polishing a glass.

"Not yet." Gray swallowed another mouthful of the surprisingly palatable beer, then lowered the tankard and glanced toward Tickencote Grange. "I've been looking over the grange." He looked at the barman. "I'm thinking of buying it."

"That so?" The barman had already taken note of the quality of his clothes, so the revelation wasn't that much of a surprise.

Gray nodded. "I'm considering it, but the place feels deserted." Until he said the words, he hadn't realized that was, in fact, what he'd noted. "I wondered if you knew anything about the previous owners."

He took another swallow of the beer and, his gaze undemanding and fixed on the barman, waited patiently.

The barman continued polishing the glass. Eventually, he said, "I've only been here for some five, six years, so I can't tell you anything of the family that owned it back when it used to be some nob's estate. I heard they'd moved elsewhere and sold it to some banker gentleman from London, but seemingly, it didn't really suit. 'Bout the time I came here, the banker sold the house to some flashy London gent. A Mr. Hildebrand, he was, but he rarely came up here, and then we heard he'd lost his fancy shirt on some horse race, and the bank took possession. It's the bank itself owns it still and has for nigh on three years."

Gray digested that, then finished his drink and nodded. "Thank you."

He walked out and, while collecting his horse, thought again of the house.

Unbidden, his mind supplied an image of Izzy there. She suited the place—or it suited her; he could readily imagine her coming down that magnificent staircase, strolling through the reception rooms, waltzing in the ballroom, or walking the lawns and the riverbank with him.

The images were deeply enticing.

He reminded himself that, at this time, such images were mere fancies, wishes as yet unrealizable. Gripping the horse's reins, he mounted and turned the horse for Alverton Priory.

～

By midday, it was all hands on deck at the printing works. Even Izzy had joined the small army bustling about the noisy, clanking, clattering press. Donaldson, Littlejohn, and his young constable had been conscripted into service. For once, they had enough hands for the process to flow seamlessly without interruption.

Izzy worked with Mary and Digby at the layout table, checking the sheets Lipson, assisted by Littlejohn and the constable, ferried from the typesetting table where Maguire and Jim laid the pages as they came off the press. At that point, the sheets were printed on one side only; although the press could print on both sides of a sheet in one double-pass, the drying time of the available ink made that impractical; too many pages ended smeared. Once sufficient sheets had been printed and had passed inspection, the forme in the press would be changed, and the sheets would have another two pages printed on their blank side.

The combined scent of hot machine oil and ink was pervasive, overlaying the sharper tang of the coal Gerry constantly fed into the boiler. The rattle of the thick woven belt that drove the huge drum was a constant rumble beneath the solid clanks and thuds as the iron gears moving the forme currently being printed constantly shifted, locked, then shifted again, first holding the inked forme in place for the huge drum to press a sheet to it—printing the sheet with two pages of text and pictures —then lowering the forme for the type to be reinked before relifting and locking it in place again for the drum to roll over it and print the next sheet.

Standing toward the rear of the press, Lipson kept an eagle eye on the rolling drum and frequently bent to check the reservoirs of ink below the machine. Maguire and Matthews, receiving the printed sheets, ran careful eyes over each as the machine pushed it out, checking for any smudging or uneven print.

After toting up all the likely orders and allowing for increased interest, Izzy and Lipson had decided on a first print run of five thousand copies, an increase of six hundred on their usual number. Time-wise, printing and assembling five thousand copies was going to stretch them, which was why even Izzy had donned a leather apron and was assisting as she could. They had to print three double-sided sheets, each side carrying two pages—making up the twelve pages of the special edition—then collate the sheets in the correct order and orientation before folding the stacked pages in half, creating each copy of the paper.

That wouldn't be a small undertaking at any time, but today, with all the excitement, it was extra difficult for everyone to stop themselves from pausing and reading the sheets rather than simply ferrying them on.

After inspecting the press earlier, Baines had left. Izzy had locked the door behind him, a precaution they often took while the press was running, as they wouldn't hear anyone coming through the door.

With the first double-sided sheet done and stacked in piles waiting on the counter, Izzy estimated that they were fast approaching the right number of sheets printed with the first side of the second double-sided sheet. On cue, Lipson called a temporary halt, stopping the press so that he, his son, Maguire, and Matthews could carefully switch out the current forme and replace it with the next. Everyone else seized the moment to eat a sandwich—which Izzy routinely ordered and Mary had brought in that morning—and find a drink of water. On print-run days, there was never time for a proper lunch break.

Izzy nibbled a sandwich and sipped water from a cup. She ran her eye over all those gathered and saw clear interest, a touch of excitement here and there, and beneath all else, an unwavering commitment to getting the hue and cry edition out and, through it, catching Quimby's killer.

There was a sense of comradeship, not just among the printing works' staff but including and embracing all those who were so readily lending their aid, even Littlejohn and the constable. It felt as if everyone there had banded together in common cause; she saw that reflected in the casual glances that tracked Lipson, waiting for his word that the press was ready to roll again.

She leant against the layout table and inwardly acknowledged that she couldn't have accomplished this by herself. Some of it, yes, but without Louisa's idea, Drake's imprimatur, Baines's tacit support, and Littlejohn's enthusiasm, let alone the staff's, the hue and cry edition wouldn't have happened.

And with regard to Louisa's, Drake's, and Baines's very necessary contributions, those had come about through Gray's efforts, through his intercessions on her behalf.

The boiler started to chug again, and the belt rattled to life. Lipson called, and everyone set aside their crusts and cups and dove back into the fray.

At her station at the layout table, Izzy smiled wryly. In general, she had a rather low opinion of the value of gentlemen, but perhaps it was time to revise her stance and agree that some of the species might have their uses.

∾

Gray arrived at Alverton Priory and found Devlin ensconced in his library. Gray had barely walked in, shaken hands, and sat in the armchair Devlin waved him to when Therese came bustling in.

"I heard you'd arrived." She promptly sat in a chair facing him. "How goes the investigation? Do you have news?"

Gray smiled at her blatant inquisitiveness and obliged by describing all that had occurred. "Incidentally, thank you for the recommendation to consult Drake. Without his and Louisa's contributions, I doubt we'd be where we are."

"So," Therese said, "with luck, you'll start to get information in later tomorrow."

"I'm not sure how quickly the distribution occurs, but I suppose that's possible," he allowed.

She glanced at the clock. "You will stay for luncheon, won't you?"

When, brows raised, she looked at him, he smiled. "Thank you."

"But what's brought you this way?" Devlin asked.

"Indeed," Therese said. "With events happening apace in London, this hardly seems a time you would choose to visit your parents."

Gray grinned. "You know me so well."

She nodded. "We do. So?"

"I came up this way to look at a house."

"You did?" She blinked. "Where?"

Just then, Edwards arrived to announce, "My lady, my lords, luncheon is served."

Therese bounced to her feet and, immediately Gray stood, looped her arm in his and towed him toward the door. "Come, sit, eat, and tell us all."

He laughed and, with a fondly grinning Devlin following, allowed himself to be led to the dining room.

Once they'd sat and been served a creamy celery soup, Gray confirmed his intention to stand for Parliament. "Consequently, given the property qualification, a house I must have, and via an agent, I've been looking for a suitable place for months."

"And…" Therese waved at him to continue.

He set down his soupspoon. "There's a house not far away that, I believe, will be perfect." He described why he felt that was so, elaborating on the house itself as well as its highly convenient location.

While he did so, Edwards removed the soup plates and served the main course of mutton, vegetables, and freshly baked bread. They ate as Therese and Devlin asked questions, and Gray replied.

"Northwest of Stamford." Therese frowned. "I admit I'm not familiar with the area." She directed a questioning look at Devlin.

He shook his head. "I've ridden the fields while hunting, and I know the area this side of Stamford reasonably well, but I've rarely ventured to the other side."

Therese shifted her bright gaze to Gray's face. "Does the house have a name?"

He nodded. "Tickencote Grange."

She sat back and looked at him, an odd expression on her face. After a moment, she asked, "Did you know that's Isadora's old home? The original seat of the Earls of Exton?"

Stunned, Gray stared at her. "You're joking."

She shook her head. "Remember I told you that the late earl had broken the entail and mortgaged the estate to the hilt, and after his death, the family were forced to sell the place?"

"I remember you telling me that," Gray admitted, "but I had no idea the estate involved was Tickencote Grange." He related what he'd learned from the publican.

Devlin nodded. "That sounds right. I remember hearing that a banker at the bank holding the late earl's mortgage snapped the place up, possibly for less than it was truly worth."

"Well, by the sounds of it," Therese pointed out, "that didn't do the banker any good, given he eventually sold the place, too."

"And now it's on the market again." Gray frowned. After a moment, he looked at Devlin and Therese. "Do you have any feeling for how the current earl—Izzy's brother—would react to me buying the grange?"

"I doubt he would care," Therese replied. "By all accounts, his experiences with his father soured his affection for the place, and I understand he's very happy at Lyndon Hall—the house his grandfather-in-law bought for him and his wife."

Gray narrowed his eyes in thought. "That fits with what I've gleaned from Izzy and her family regarding her brother—that he's happy where he is."

Devlin concluded, "So from that direction, there's no impediment to you purchasing the place."

Not from that direction, but... Gray looked at Therese.

"Before you ask," she promptly said, "I have absolutely no idea how Izzy would feel about you buying her old home. I can tell you she spent much more time there than Julius did, given he went away to school and university. Other than that"—she grimaced—"it's a subject most of the ton have avoided discussing, especially with the Descartes ladies."

Gray grimaced as well. "Understandable, I suppose."

They had finished the meal and rose from the table.

He'd expected Therese to press him further regarding Izzy and was cravenly grateful when she refrained.

He paused in the hall. "I need to go. I arranged to leave the horse I hired at Uffington and Barnack station for the stable to pick up, and I don't want to miss the train."

Devlin clapped him on the shoulder.

Therese stretched up and pecked his cheek. "Good luck—with every-thing." She caught his eye with such a meaningful look that he had to laugh.

Saluting her and Devlin, he left them for the stable, where he'd left the hired horse.

Soon, he was riding over the fields, on his way to the station.

He'd spent the ride to the priory reviewing everything he'd seen and felt about Tickencote Grange. He'd expected niggles of uncertainty to arise, but they hadn't; if anything, by the time he'd reached the priory, he'd been even more convinced *that* house was the one he needed to own.

Now...he honestly didn't know.

Yet his instincts remained insistent, and despite whatever had happened in the past, given how frequently his and Izzy's attitudes aligned, he had to wonder if she didn't, in her heart, still feel as he did about her old home.

That it was simply the right place to make his—or her—own.

Short of putting the question to her, there was no way he could tell.

Thinking of the house, he resolved to send a message to his man-of-business that evening, instructing him to arrange for a trusted builder-surveyor to examine the place.

For all he knew, with all that paneling, it had woodworm throughout.

First things first; he needed to know if the house was as sound as he thought it was. As solid a prospect as he believed.

If not...there was no reason to potentially cause Izzy pain by even mentioning the place.

～

At twenty minutes past five o'clock, Izzy stood, surrounded by *The Crier*'s staff and the others who had helped throughout the long day, and stared at the massive stacks of copies of *The London Crier*'s Hue and Cry edition.

It was a staggering reality, with one hundred bound stacks of fifty copies each covering the typesetting table, the layout table, and fully half the counter, as well as on the floor, lining the inside of the counter.

She blew out a breath. "That's it. We're ready for distribution at eight o'clock tomorrow."

Digby sent up a cheer, which was taken up by all the males, while Mary and Izzy shared a smiling glance.

There were several loose copies lying about. Donaldson had picked up one and had been leafing through it. "The more I look at this, the more

I'm convinced that no one in London will be able to resist seeing who they recognize."

Maguire smiled at Izzy. "It's a truly sensational edition."

She grinned. "Indeed."

Baines, who had returned about an hour ago to see how things were going and had been promptly conscripted to help with the herculean task of folding five thousand copies, huffed. "I freely admit I've never seen the like, but the proof of the idea will be if it gets us any further with catching this murderer. Speaking of which"—he fixed his gaze on Little-john—"best make sure you have enough men tonight to have a few constables patrolling the street." Baines looked pointedly at the stacked paper, then at the wide front window. "A bottle bomb thrown through that window will set all this alight in seconds, no matter who you have inside."

Littlejohn sobered, as did those who'd volunteered to stay and guard the premises.

"I'll send Blight here"—Littlejohn jerked his thumb at the young constable who had been there all day—"to the watchhouse to make sure they send us enough men."

Baines nodded. "If you need to, draw from other watchhouses as well." He looked at Izzy. "Perhaps mention that Winchelsea's behind this?"

"By all means," Izzy agreed.

Baines grinned at Littlejohn. "That'll get us the men we need."

Izzy looked at Lipson; he, his son, and Gerry planned to remain overnight inside the workshop, along with Littlejohn and at least one constable.

Tom Lipson caught Izzy's eye. "Don't worry, ma'am—we've got plenty of fire buckets. We'll fill them and put them out all around once everyone leaves."

Izzy smiled encouragingly, including Lipson Senior and Gerry in the gesture. "Thank you for agreeing to stay. I'll be able to sleep, knowing you're all here watching over the place."

Not being able to sleep otherwise wasn't entirely an exaggeration. It cost money to buy paper, ink, and coal, let alone pay the staff's wages. Molyneaux Printing Works had a sizeable amount of capital sunk in the copies stacked about the workshop. If they lost those before they could be sold... That really didn't bear thinking of.

With all done and settled, those who were leaving fetched coats and hats and filed out of the front door. Lipson confirmed for Izzy that the rear door was still locked; as far as she knew, other than for taking out the rubbish and fetching in coal, it hadn't been unlocked since Quimby's murder.

She was the last one out of the front door, and Lipson locked it from inside. She went down the steps behind Tom Corby, who, judging by his expression, had had a thoroughly enjoyable day. When, amused, she questioned that, he agreed, launching into a recitation of all he'd found strange and wonderful and eye-opening. While talking, he walked beside her rather than behind as was proper, but she refrained from pointing that out. He was an engaging lad, and she enjoyed his company, and that distracted her from dwelling on whom he'd replaced.

But once she was alone in the carriage, rolling through the streets to Norfolk Crescent, inevitably, her mind turned to Gray and how his house hunting had gone.

A house in the country. The vision that conjured was still painfully sharp and clear and took conscious effort to banish. She replaced it with an image of Lyndon Hall, where Julius now lived—the new seat of the earldom—and thought of how pleasant the country was around there.

She missed living in the country and always had. But…

Beggars couldn't be choosers.

Seeking to divert her thoughts, she wondered what Gray's taste in houses was like. After traveling over half the world, he might be inclined to favor a modern home. She tried to imagine what such a place might be like, then set aside the point as being of no immediate moment.

With the façades of Oxford Street slipping past, she refocused on tomorrow and the release of the hue and cry edition. She wondered what the day would bring and how much closer to capturing the killer they might be by that time tomorrow.

CHAPTER 11

$\mathcal{I}$t was strange how seeing Izzy over the breakfast table had come to seem normal. On walking into the Norfolk Crescent breakfast parlor and finding her at the table, Gray felt something in him relax. Stand down.

Exchanging a smile, he pulled out the chair opposite, sat, and asked, "How went the print run?"

She told him, and with a few well-chosen questions, he had her describing her day in detail, outlining the altered logistics involved in printing a larger number of copies and giving her opinion of Donaldson, the new photographer, and her hopes for what he would bring to *The Crier* and also how well he'd fitted in with the rest of the staff through the ensuing hours.

"It was a real team effort," she concluded as they rose from the table and headed for the front hall.

They shrugged on their coats and retrieved their hats, and she threw him a curious glance. "How did the house hunting go?"

He smiled and escorted her out of the door and into the waiting carriage. Once they'd sat and the carriage had started rolling, he replied, "I'm not as yet sure. That particular house might suit, but I need to do some research first."

Before she could probe further, he said, "I'm curious—did Baines lend a hand, too?"

"Believe it or not, he did, but only at the end, in the last hour or so.

However, Littlejohn was there for the entire day, along with a young constable. They were a big help, as was your Tom Corby."

"He told me he'd enjoyed himself. So what, exactly, will happen today?"

As the carriage rattled across London, she explained how the distributors would send lads to fetch their allocated number of copies. "Most have a set amount, week to week, but I expect, once the distributors themselves see the edition, we'll have reorders coming in. That's why we printed extra, and Lipson and Maguire are going to prepare the formes this morning, so that if we get even more orders beyond the extra copies printed, then this afternoon, we can run off more."

A mounting sense of expectation had gripped them both by the time the carriage drew up at the back of Mrs. Carruthers's house. They stopped to say hello, but didn't dally and went straight through, emerging into Woburn Square and walking briskly to the printing works.

When they turned onto the mews, even though it wanted a good ten minutes to eight o'clock, there was already a queue of impatient lads lined up before the door. Some were alone, but others were in pairs and towed small handcarts.

Several recognized Izzy and bobbed their heads. On gaining the steps before the front door, she surveyed the gathering. "You're here bright and early."

The group exchanged glances, then one of the pair of older lads closest to the door volunteered, "Our gaffers all heard about the special edition. Mr. Hughes warned us to be here good and early and to get twenty copies more than our usual."

Murmurs along the line confirmed that others had similar orders.

Izzy smiled reassuringly. "I'm sure we'll be able to manage that." Confidingly, she added, "We printed extra."

Relieved, the lads grinned.

With a "Won't be long now," she turned to the door.

Mary stood on the other side; she flipped the lock and let Izzy and Gray in, then shut and locked the door again. "Cheeky beggars. The instant we open up, they'll be streaming in."

Izzy, Gray noticed, hadn't stopped smiling. He took in the towers of stacked copies of *The Crier* and owned himself impressed.

All the staff were already there, scattered behind the counter and deeper in the workshop, no doubt having been let in by those who had spent the night guarding the place. Izzy raised her voice and spoke to the workshop at large. "Our distributors have heard about the special edition and are already asking for extra copies."

Everyone brightened.

Scanning the faces, Gray saw signs of the underlying tension he felt, overlaid by hope that the novel tack of a hue and cry edition would work, and today, they would get some clue that would identify Quimby's killer.

That all their hard work over the past days would pay off.

He and Izzy retreated to the office and shed their hats and coats, then somewhat reluctantly, Izzy sat behind her desk.

When he looked at her questioningly, she sighed. "I need to note and issue amended invoices to account for the extra copies they want to take. There isn't enough space at the counter to do it there, so..." She gestured at her desk.

At eight o'clock on the dot, Mary unlocked the front door. With Horner standing beside her, ready to yank any overzealous lad up by his collar, and Matthews lounging against the counter, blocking ready access to the copies stacked there, the youths read the signs and came in quietly and waited their turn to hand in a slip provided by their employers, stating the number of copies to be taken in their name.

Seated in his customary armchair in the office, Gray watched the process of distributing *The Crier* throughout the city get underway, remarkably smoothly. The staff had done this many times before, as had the delivery lads, and it showed. Mary accepted the order slips, and after she logged the details into a ledger and gave the go-ahead, Horner and Matthews loaded the correct number of copies into the waiting youth's arms. If there were more than the lad could carry, he'd cart them out to where his mate waited with a handcart, then return to get the rest of his order. Meanwhile, Mary handed Digby the annotated order slip the youth had tendered, and Digby scampered across to the office and delivered it to Izzy.

She, in turn, wrote out invoices to match the slips and also kept a running tally of the number of copies dispatched.

She saw him taking note of the tally and explained, "Depending on when in the day we get to four and a half thousand copies dispatched, we'll make a decision on whether to run the press again."

He'd seen Lipson, his son, and Maguire working about the press and remembered her earlier comment about running the machine again. "I wouldn't mind seeing the press in action."

She briefly smiled. "I wouldn't mind seeing it in action again myself, as that will signal we're well on the way to making a windfall profit on this edition." She paused, then frowned. "Is it morally wrong to profit from a murder?"

He snorted. "What do you think your competitors would say? And besides, you and the staff here are doing this to avenge Quimby. Your principal motive is to find his killer, and by definition, that can't be morally wrong."

She arched her brows. "It's certainly true that we all want the killer caught."

Digby raced in with another invoice. She accepted it and returned to her task.

Not long after, Baines and Littlejohn arrived. After pausing in the foyer and taking note of the ordered activity there—and being duly noted by the delivery boys—the policemen came into the office.

Izzy briefly glanced up, acknowledged their nods, and waved at the armchairs near the window. "Take a seat, gentlemen. We're going to be busy for some time."

Baines grunted. "Waiting for a case to break is something we're used to."

After exchanging nods with Gray, Baines and Littlejohn retreated to the chairs by the window.

Minutes later, just after Digby, who was popping in and out of the office like a jack-in-the-box, had rushed out again, a man carrying a camera and tripod—presumably Donaldson—tapped on the door frame.

When Izzy glanced up, Donaldson held up the camera. "I was thinking I should take a few shots of the boys picking up the copies, preferably now while there's still stacks of copies on the counter." He glanced toward Baines and Littlejohn. "And perhaps a shot of the inspector and sergeant standing before the counter holding up a copy of the first true hue and cry edition."

Baines frowned, but before he could refuse, Donaldson added, "I could run you each a copy of the photograph. You never know when it might come in handy in the years to come."

Baines paused.

Littlejohn had already shifted to the edge of his seat. "He's right, sir," Littlejohn murmured. "Having such a photograph to show at our next boards won't hurt at all."

Baines shot his sergeant a look, then returned his gaze to Donaldson. "If we agree, we get to see the picture before it's used in the paper."

Donaldson glanced at Izzy, who had paused in her scribbling to follow the exchange.

She nodded. "Just make sure the picture's a good one."

Donaldson grinned, looked at the police, and tipped his head toward the foyer. "We could do it now, if you like?"

Littlejohn looked eagerly at Baines.

Baines sighed. "Might as well." He hauled himself out of the chair and, with Littlejohn, headed for the door.

Izzy caught Donaldson's satisfied gaze. "A moment, if you would."

Donaldson stepped back to allow the policemen through the doorway, then set down his tripod and came to the desk.

Izzy smiled approvingly. "I don't suppose Baines and Littlejohn have had their photograph taken before—it won't hurt to get them used to the process." She waved at Gray. "And this is Lord Child, who was with me when I found Quimby dead and, ever since, has been assisting with the investigation. No doubt he'll be present as matters progress."

Gray held out his hand, and Donaldson, mildly curious, grasped it and shook.

"A pleasure, my lord." Releasing Gray's hand, Donaldson cut a shrewd glance at Izzy. "It would save time to know if his lordship has any objection to being photographed."

Izzy arched her brows at Gray. "Do you?"

He thought for a moment, then said, "Provided the photograph relates to the investigation or the pursuit of Quimby's killer"—he met Donaldson's gaze—"I have no objection."

Izzy looked at Donaldson. "Anything further?"

Donaldson's boyish grin returned. "No, ma'am." He hefted his camera. "I'll get on with it."

Izzy watched him go, then looked at Gray. "What do you think?"

"That he's intelligent and keen to do well, which in such a situation constitutes an excellent recommendation."

She nodded and turned to receive the latest order slip Digby raced in to deliver.

From where he was sitting, Gray could see Baines and Littlejohn posing before the counter, with the stacks of copies of *The Crier* towering behind them. Donaldson was putting a copy into Baines's hands and showing him how to hold it so the front page was fully revealed.

Digby continued to race back and forth, and Izzy's head remained down as she worked through the orders and kept her tally.

Gray uncrossed his legs and rose. "I'm going to take a look around."

She nodded without glancing up.

He ambled to the doorway and halted there. The foyer was a veritable hive of activity, with Mary, Horner, and Matthews continuing to take in the orders and load up the delivery boys. Although the line that had formed earlier had gone, there always seemed one lad at the counter and at least two waiting, impatiently shifting from foot to foot. As soon as one lad weighed down with copies left, another came barreling through the door, which was constantly opening and closing to the extent that someone had disabled the bell.

Closer to the office, Donaldson had set up his camera on its tripod and was in the process of aiming the lens at Baines and Littlejohn.

Gray stepped out of the doorway to let Digby rush past and remained by the wall, watching Donaldson work. When everything was ready and the photographer emerged to say "Hold still now" and pressed a button attached to the camera, Gray counted off the seconds.

Only seven elapsed before Donaldson took his finger off the button, relaxed, smiled, and nodded at the frozen policemen. "That should do it."

Both Baines and Littlejohn looked faintly self-conscious. Baines turned and set the copy he'd held on the stack behind him, then with his sergeant, approached Donaldson.

Smiling, the photographer said, "I should have prints from that by tomorrow. If I don't see you, I'll leave them at the counter, shall I?"

"Mind, I want a look at it before you go putting it in the paper," Baines growled.

Uncowed, Donaldson replied, "Of course."

With a sharp nod, Baines ambled off, going past the end of the counter to prowl through the workshop.

After sharing an understanding look with Donaldson, Littlejohn followed his superior.

Gray left his position by the wall and approached Donaldson, who was fiddling with his apparatus. "That was a remarkably short exposure." When Donaldson glanced at him, he added, "I've seen cameras used quite a bit in America, but I've never seen a photograph taken so quickly."

Donaldson grinned. "It's the latest lenses coupled with the newest medium. In fact, the way I work nowadays, that was a longish exposure, because it's indoors"—he glanced at the wide front window at his back —"and the light in here isn't that strong." He turned back to Gray. "In halfway decent daylight, I can get good results in a few seconds or even less."

Gray considered what that meant. "I imagine that will make photographs and photography much more exciting."

Donaldson's grin widened. "So we—all the photographers—hope."

Gray watched him realign his camera, then walk across to speak with three delivery lads clustered about the counter. Donaldson spoke, and the three lads' faces lit, and they nodded eagerly. He posed them so that one appeared to be about to receive his copies from Matthews, a second was at the counter, speaking earnestly with Mary, who was writing in her ledger, while the third looked on, slip in hand, poised to move in and submit his employer's order.

Digby, ordered not to intrude on the scene, came to hover by Donaldson's elbow.

Noting the intense concentration on Digby's face, Gray smiled.

As soon as the photograph was taken, he started to return to the office, but then the front door burst open, and everyone whirled—hope leaping in every eye that someone was coming in with information—but it was only a gaggle of five delivery lads.

Immediately, a scuffle broke out over which of the five should front the counter first. From the words they flung at each other, each had been sent by their employer to secure extra copies of the hue and cry edition.

"Stop!" Gray's tone cut like a whip and shocked the five lads into stillness. Across the foyer, he held them silent with his gaze and ordered, "Line up and wait your turn, or we'll throw the lot of you out for half an hour."

Baines and Littlejohn appeared at that moment. Baines scowled at the offenders, who immediately looked contrite and sorted themselves into a short queue.

Baines settled as if to keep an eye on things.

Gray nodded at him and was about to turn away when three more breathless lads rushed in. Seeing the queue, they jostled each other to join it.

Mary started frowning as if she was having trouble reading some of the scrawled orders.

With nothing better to do, Gray rounded the counter and offered his services, which were gratefully accepted.

He settled beside Mary, intimidating any presumptuous delivery boys and helping to decipher the rushed orders.

Seeing that Gray had matters at the counter in hand, Horner went to help Matthews load up the delivery lads. As the copies stacked on the counter dwindled, they were replaced by others from elsewhere in the workshop.

At a quarter to twelve, Izzy emerged from her office and walked briskly to the end of the counter. "Lipson?"

The manager straightened from where he'd been poking at the side of the press. "Here, ma'am."

Izzy beamed. "We've already sent out more than four and a half thousand, and the demand for extra copies isn't slackening off. We'll need to run the press again."

A cheer went up from all the staff.

Lipson beamed back. "Right away, ma'am. Gerry, get the boiler stoked. Tom, Digby, get paper ready to roll. Maguire, Matthews, let's get the formes into place."

The summoned staff left what they'd been doing and hurried to their tasks, while Donaldson leapt to set up his camera to take shots of the press being readied for action.

That left Mary behind the counter and Gray and Izzy loading up the delivery boys. After a few moments of hanging back, when still more boys came rushing in and the queue grew longer and wound out of the door, both Baines and Littlejohn also pitched in, counting copies and dumping them into the lads' waiting arms.

Then the press cranked into action, and Gray got a taste of what employment in a printing works was really like. Steam hissed, and iron cogs and gears clattered and clanked. The noise was horrendous; they had to yell to make themselves heard.

But the buoyant spirits only rose higher as more and more lads returned to get still more copies of *The Crier*'s special edition, leaving everyone smiling in triumphant delight.

This is going to work.

Increasingly, Gray felt sure of that.

Izzy glanced at the clock, the hands of which showed the time to be after twelve. "We won't be able to stop for a lunch break—not today."

Gray counted the queue; possibly because the delivery lads were taking lunch breaks, it had dwindled to four. He glanced at Baines and Littlejohn. "Littlejohn, if you can relieve me here, I'll go to the pub around the corner and pick up some food and drink." He tipped his head toward the workshop. "Our crew needs sustenance."

Baines grunted. "I'll come and help carry things back."

With no time to waste—the temporary hiatus was unlikely to last—Gray gave up his position to Littlejohn and, with Baines, left and strode quickly down the street.

In the local pub, the publican and his wife were happy—indeed, honored—to be asked to supply food for *The Crier*'s staff. While the pair bustled about packing pies, sandwiches, pasties, and bottles of cider, Gray and Baines lounged against the bar and idly surveyed the other patrons, intrigued to see that many were poring over copies of *The Crier*.

At one of the nearer tables, three workmen were each reading their own copy. They were studying the photographs, and every now and then, one would squint, point at the paper, and make some comment, to which the other two would either grunt or reply.

Baines mused, "Not the sort of readership *The Crier* would normally command."

"No, indeed," Gray murmured. "But it's an excellent sign."

The instant the victuals were ready, he paid, and Baines helped him cart the packages back to the workshop.

The line of delivery lads had grown again. Gray and Baines hurriedly set their burdens on the table near the darkroom and returned to the counter to assist as before.

When Lipson next paused the press to change out a forme, those working about the machine fell on the food with ravenous intent. Shortly after, the tide of delivery lads slowed enough for Izzy and Gray to man the counter alone, allowing Mary, Littlejohn, Baines, and Donaldson—who had put aside his camera to help Mary—to appease their appetites.

Once the press cranked into gear again and the others, licking crumbs from their fingers and wiping their lips, returned, Gray and Izzy retreated to stand about the table and eat selections from the still-considerable remains.

Izzy took a neat bite of an egg sandwich and held the rest up. "Thank you for this." She surveyed the activity about the counter and also about the press. "I might have hoped, but I had no idea the interest would be this great."

Gray told her of the men he and Baines had seen in the pub. "They're treating it like a community game—spot the murderer."

Izzy swallowed the last of her sandwich. "I don't care what they think, just as long as they look and come and tell us what we need to know." She dusted off her hands. "I'm back to the fray."

His gaze on the press and its many moving parts, Gray nodded.

He heard the smile in Izzy's voice as she said, "We can manage without you for a few minutes if you want to take a closer look."

He grinned and glanced at her. "I won't be long."

He swiped up another sandwich and, with a bottle of cider in his other hand, walked down the workshop, careful not to get in the way of those scurrying purposefully about the giant beast of a machine. To some extent, he'd grown accustomed to the noise and the reek of ink, coal, oil, and other mechanical scents combined, enough to be able to pay full attention to what he was seeing. He halted near the rear door from where he could see the mechanism that allowed the steam from the boiler Horner constantly stoked to rotate the thick, woven belt that powered the huge drum of the press and its associated levers and gears.

That was fascinating in its own right.

After he'd looked his fill, he walked slowly back along the side of the press, noting the precision with which the plate holding the current forme was lowered and a fine, apparently even coat of ink was applied, then the plate was raised again, locking into place, and the huge drum turned, and the next sheet was printed.

Gently shaking his head in amazement, he ate the crust in his hand, then washed down the impromptu meal with the last of the cider. After leaving the bottle with the other empties under the layout table, he returned to the counter.

As the afternoon wore on, the rush of extra orders didn't abate; indeed, the stream of lads coming through the door, some on their third mission, only increased, until the queue before the counter snaked through the door and continued down the street—and the number of copies stacked on the counter and yet to be claimed dwindled to dangerously low.

Then the clatter in the workshop slowed, and steam hissed mightily, and the press ponderously ground to a halt.

Instead of relaxing, the staff rearranged themselves and started collating sheets.

Minutes later, Lipson tapped Gray on the shoulder. "We need two more on the folding table. You and Littlejohn will have to lend a hand." He nodded at Baines. "If you can help the ladies, Inspector, we need to get more copies prepared or"—Lipson tipped his head toward the queue of youths who were growing increasingly agitated as the stacks on the counter shrank—"we're like to have a riot."

His gaze on the restive lads, Gray asked Lipson, "How many extra copies did you print?"

"Another thousand plus."

Gray raised his voice. "There's more copies coming. Be patient, stay in line, and you'll get what you've been sent for."

Baines nodded approvingly and said to Littlejohn, "Go. I'll hold the fort here."

Lipson led Gray and Littlejohn to the typesetting table and showed them what was required. Working alongside Maguire and Matthews, they buckled down and stacked, neatened, and folded like demons.

Soon, the flow of copies out of the door had increased again. Gray heard several lads exclaim over the warmth of the recently printed papers. The term "hot off the press" had never been more accurate.

Eventually, as the clock ticked past four, the queue reduced, and by a quarter past the hour, it was gone altogether. With the last of the new print run folded and stacked, the staff and their conscripts could finally relax.

Under Izzy's direction, Baines reset the bell above the door, and everyone gathered about the table near the darkroom and devoured the last of the food and drink.

Mary and Donaldson hovered by the counter, ready to respond to the few lads still turning up for more copies.

Gray noticed that each time the bell tinkled, everyone looked up and across—hoping that someone would turn up and reveal some useful fact —but on each occasion, the newcomer proved to be another delivery boy wanting more copies for his master.

Then, just after four-fifty, three likely-looking lads, perhaps nineteen years or so old, came through the door. It was instantly apparent they weren't delivery lads; they lacked the focused drive of that species. The trio looked around curiously, then noticed everyone watching them and straightened and, with a show of bravado, fronted up to the counter.

One, presumably the leader, grinned at Mary and Donaldson. "We've come to offer information, like—for the reward."

Eyes widening, hope in her expression, Mary looked across at Izzy.

The entire staff, Donaldson included, looked at Izzy with expectation in their eyes.

Baines, who'd been standing beside Gray, sighed heavily. He murmured to Izzy, "Let me handle this." He started for the foyer. "Littlejohn—with me."

Already drawing out his notebook, but with a disapproving look in his eyes, Littlejohn readily fell in at Baines's heels.

Baines pulled out his badge and waved it at the lad who'd spoken. "Inspector Baines, from Scotland Yard." He held the badge so all three lads could see it, then tucked it away again. "Right, then. What do you have for us?"

The leader blinked, then shot a glance at his mates. "I…er." He swallowed. "We thought we'd be speaking to the man who owns the paper—I. Molyneaux."

Baines nodded amiably. "The owner's assisting us. If you have information to share, son, now's the time to tell it."

"Er…well." After another glance at his mates, the leader blurted, "We saw the bloke."

"And which bloke was this?"

"The photographer fellow—"

"No, it was the murderer," the lad to the leader's left insisted. When the leader turned startled eyes his way, the second lad mumbled, "They know what the photographer looked like. Stands to reason it's the other one they're after."

Baines's expression hardened. "Do you three actually know anything? Or are you just chancing your luck?"

The three protested, but it quickly became apparent that it was the latter description that applied.

Baines sent the three off with fleas in their ears.

As the door shut behind the trio, Gray glanced around and saw disappointment in every expression.

Izzy sighed and voiced what she was sure everyone had thought. "I know the edition has only been out for a matter of hours, but I'd hoped we would have had *someone* come forward with at least a snippet of honest information by now."

Baines grunted and faced the assembled crew. "To have anyone with real information come forward today was, at best, a very long shot. Even if the right people have read the paper by now, I can tell you that members of the public with genuine information always think twice before 'getting involved.' Most often, they'll sleep on it before doing what their conscience prompts them to do, and sometimes it takes even longer for them to work up the backbone to own to what they know. Frankly, if it wasn't for the reward, I doubt we'd see much result, even from all this effort. But sizeable as it is, the reward changes things mightily. And I warn you, come tomorrow, I'm sure we'll have a slew of people thinking to flummox us with spurious information, but amongst all the dross, I won't be at all surprised if we don't get at least a few worthwhile sightings, a few real clues."

Izzy scanned the faces around her and saw Baines's words sink in. She glanced at the clock, then turned to address her troops. "Right, then. You've heard the inspector's experienced assessment, which means we've no cause to feel disappointed, much less dejected. As it's nearly five o'clock, I suggest we get everything squared away and go home for a well-earned rest."

"You're not wrong about that rest," Lipson said, making the others smile. "Usual time tomorrow, everyone, and expect to be busy. Chances are we'll have more orders come in, and we'll need to get the press cleaned and ready for next week."

On cue, the bell tinkled, and another hopeful delivery lad came in. Mary and Donaldson moved to the counter to deal with him, and the rest of the staff dispersed to, among other things, disconnect the boiler and belt assembly from the press and remove the formes and stack them ready to be broken down and cleaned.

Two more delivery lads turned up just as Mary was closing her ledger. She opened it again, and Donaldson quickly counted out the copies the lads had been sent to collect.

Reminded of the chore she'd neglected due to the hectic afternoon, Izzy swooped in and gathered all the order slips Mary had stashed beneath the counter. She carried the untidy pile into the office and placed it on her desk. She eyed the stack; she wasn't looking forward to tomorrow, when she would have to go through all the slips and issue invoices to match.

She returned to the foyer as the staff were collecting their hats and coats. "It seems likely that tomorrow, we'll have more would-be informants flood in, most no more genuine than those three lads earlier." She looked at Baines. "Inspector, are you and Sergeant Littlejohn planning to be here?"

Baines settled his hat on his head. "As it's possible you'll have some genuine information come in tomorrow, you couldn't keep me away." He cast a sidelong glance at his sergeant. "As for Littlejohn, likely you couldn't keep him away regardless."

Everyone laughed, even Littlejohn.

"Very well." Relieved on that score, Izzy turned to the staff. "Before we leave, we should discuss how we'll handle anyone coming in claiming to have information."

"Aye." Lipson nodded. "I suspect we'll have lots."

A short discussion ended with Mary—the least threatening person—being deputized to man the front counter as usual, but actively supported by Lipson and Littlejohn. Between them, they would take down the name and address of anyone offering information, along with the details of that information. Subsequently, only those Littlejohn deemed to have genuine insights pertinent to the crime would be conducted to the office, where Izzy, Gray, and Baines would undertake a more in-depth interview.

With the next day as organized as it could be, Izzy sent everyone off. Now that the hue and cry edition had been distributed far and wide, all had agreed there was no longer any reason for the killer to target the printing works' premises.

Goodbyes were called as the staff departed, and she answered as she fetched her coat and bonnet. With both on, she joined Gray, who had already donned his coat and hat and was waiting in the foyer. The staff had gone, but Baines and Littlejohn lingered; apparently, the pair had been chatting with Gray and had remained to see her safely on her way.

She waved toward the door and led them to it. As she approached, through the glass, she saw three delivery lads crowd onto the steps, tapping desperately.

"Allow me, ma'am." Littlejohn stepped to the door, unlocked it, and patiently explained that as it was after five o'clock, the office was closed.

Izzy glanced at the counter and saw with relief that all the extra copies they still had—several hundred—had been secreted out of sight.

A predictable wail of woe greeted Littlejohn's news, but he was unmoved. "Be here tomorrow when the place opens again."

"At eight o'clock," Izzy called.

Littlejohn nodded to the three. "You heard—eight of the clock, and you'll have your extra copies. That's the best you'll do."

Disgruntled, but recognizing that arguing with the law would do no good, the three reluctantly turned and left.

Baines cleared his throat. "You might want to put a notice in the window." When Izzy turned to him and arched a brow, he said, "Something along the lines of: 'Copies of the latest edition are still available and will be distributed from this office from eight o'clock Saturday morning. Also from that time, the owner of *The London Crier*, I. Molyneaux, will be available at this office to receive any information pertinent to the recent death of Mr. Horace Quimby, as detailed in *The Crier*'s latest edition.'" Baines paused, clearly running the words through his mind, then nodded. "That should do it."

The sense in the suggestion was obvious; Izzy returned to her office, wrote out the notice more or less as Baines had stated, and returned to place the card in the front window, where she propped it up in the corner by the door with a piece of wood kept there for the purpose.

She waved the three men ahead of her through the door, then followed and locked it.

Gray offered her his arm, and she took it, and in the company of the policemen, they walked around to Woburn Place. After parting from Baines and Littlejohn, she and Gray continued toward Woburn Square.

Everything seemed so normal. As they neared Number 20, she sighed. "It seems quite anticlimactic—all the excitement of getting the edition out, but now we have to wait and see."

Gray smiled and caught her eye. "Patience."

She shook her head. "That never was my strong suit."

He chuckled and escorted her up the steps and inside.

They spent a pleasant twenty minutes with Agatha Carruthers, relating the events of the day. Izzy was amused to note that Gray had become a firm favorite with the older lady, who appreciated his ability to tell a tale.

When they finally said their goodbyes and walked through the house to the back door, it struck Izzy that Gray had somehow become a part of even this minor aspect of her life.

The thought would have made her stop and think, except he was following at her heels. She continued down the garden path to the lane where Fields waited with her carriage.

Gray handed her inside, but made no move to follow.

When she arched a brow in question, he smiled. "I've an evening engagement I can't avoid. It's faster if I head south from here."

Reminded of her own schedule, she sighed. "I've got an unavoidable engagement, too." Resigned, she met his gaze and inclined her head. "I'll see you tomorrow."

He grinned. "Buck up. According to Baines, tomorrow will be the day on which everything happens."

"One can hope." She looked at him questioningly. "Will you be around for breakfast?"

He nodded. "Most definitely. Your cook is well worth the effort."

She laughed, and smiling, he shut the door. He stood and watched the carriage roll down the narrow lane, then exit it and disappear.

He started walking down the lane. He would have preferred to go with her regardless of where she had to go that evening, but...

On reaching Russell Square, he headed for Woburn Place, keeping an eye out for a hackney to take him to Jermyn Street. He had just enough time to reach his lodgings and make himself presentable and get to Matcham House, whither he'd been summoned by his paternal aunt for dinner.

Knowing his aunt, she would have music as some part of her evening. He just hoped it didn't involve an impromptu concert of young ladies playing the pianoforte or harpsichord.

He quelled an instinctive shudder and strode on.

CHAPTER 12

*G*ray paused in his aunt's drawing-room doorway. While her butler, Gilchrist, announced him, Gray swiftly surveyed the summoned multitude of ladies and gentlemen, ranging in age from their early twenties to his aunt's elderly years, and concluded that although his aunt's "small dinner party" might include a dinner and might qualify as a party, it most certainly wasn't going to be small.

His social mask firmly in place and with a charming smile curving his lips, he walked in. Aware of the many eyes turned his way, some overtly but many more covertly, he took wary note of the numerous couples with marriageable daughters in tow. Evidently, his aunt was up to her old tricks, and he was slated to feature as one of the principal attractions of the evening while she sought to prod, entice, or simply steer him into matrimony. Railroading, as the Americans so aptly termed it.

The thought of his aunt as a steam-powered locomotive deepened his smile as he approached the sofa on which she sat in splendorous state.

Halting before her, he took the hand she offered and bowed over it, then bent to buss the cheek she angled his way.

"Child. I'm delighted to see you." Lady Matcham pressed his fingers warningly before allowing him to release her hand. With her fan, she indicated the haughty matron sitting beside her and the younger lady standing alongside. "Allow me to present Lady Alberfoyle and her daughter, Marguerite."

He dutifully bowed over the matron's hand, then that of her daughter, an insipid miss who fought not to titter. Smiling urbanely, he exchanged the usual pleasantries and was almost grateful when another matron with two young ladies in tow swept up to claim his attention.

He fought not to look around wildly for help; most of the gentlemen present were the young ladies' fathers and unlikely to come to his aid. Instead, he smiled, let meaningless phrases trip from his lips, and told himself he could cope.

As the minutes dragged by, more couples arrived, some with eligible young gentlemen in tow, no doubt dragged along by their mothers. In this season, with most of the ton in the country, the Marriage Mart was largely in abeyance. Consequently, those still in London wishful of marrying off their young people would view his aunt's event as an opportunity to be seized.

Sadly, the younger gentlemen provided no effective competition for the matrons' and their daughters' attentions. Regardless of not being in line for the title, as a duke's son, Gray trumped them all even before his appearance, experience, and likely wealth were added to the scales.

He soldiered on, feeling grievously misled by his aunt and wishing he were elsewhere. The ineffable comfort of the quiet evening he'd spent in Norfolk Crescent two evenings before loomed longingly in his mind.

A Mrs. Dawlish and her son and daughter cornered him, and he was forcefully reminded that not all sharks swam in the sea. Desperate to escape, he glanced toward the door just as Gilchrist led in a trio of elegant ladies and announced, "The Dowager Countess of Exton, Lady Isadora Descartes, and Lady Marietta Descartes."

Gray's heart rose. Relief and expectation washed through him. Izzy caught and held his attention, a slender figure in aquamarine silk with her hair up in an elegant knot and a touch of fine lace at her throat.

He turned back to the Dawlishes and, without compunction, cut across Mrs. Dawlish's haughty diatribe regarding the lamentable state of fashions in London compared to Paris. "If you'll excuse me, there's someone I need to speak with."

With a half bow to the matron and a nod to the Dawlish son and daughter—a miss every bit as rigid as her mother—Gray set out to inter-cept Izzy, who had greeted his aunt and was stepping away, allowing Marietta to pay her respects.

The dowager countess had claimed the seat next to his aunt, and from the way the two older ladies were avidly engaging with Marietta, he surmised the pair were old friends.

Izzy turned as he approached, and her face lit with a spontaneous smile. "Gray." She held out her hand. "I didn't realize—" She broke off and glanced at his aunt. "I forgot Lady Matcham was your aunt."

"Indeed," he said, the word laden with feeling. He clasped her fingers and bowed over them; he was tempted to press a kiss to the slender digits, but that would assuredly draw attention—even more than they'd already attracted. He straightened and continued sotto voce, "Thank God you're here. I'd reached the stage of seriously contemplating cutting and running."

Her emerald eyes danced. "But this is only a *small* dinner party."

"I'm not sure my aunt knows the meaning of the word." He glanced in that lady's direction, saw she'd noticed his actions, and ignoring her rising brows, wound Izzy's arm with his and turned them in the opposite direction.

Tipping his head closer to Izzy's, with his urbane mask firmly in place, he murmured, "Given my assistance with Quimby's murder and all that's followed, I'm claiming your protection in return. Acting as my guard tonight is the least you can do."

Izzy chuckled, but understood he meant the word "protection" literally. The matrons and marriageable young ladies who continued to approach them—their eyes and intentions brazenly fixed on him—were definitely hunting, and he was their hoped-for prey.

While she was too experienced and knowledgeable about the ton to be surprised by anything that happened within it, she didn't appreciate that predatory attitude any more than he did, and while his tongue had lost none of its glibness, and if anything, his wits had only sharpened with age, having been absent from ton society for the past decade left him at a distinct disadvantage—one she didn't share. Nevertheless, it took several encounters for her status as his preferred companion for the evening to be accepted.

However, once they'd established that, the importuning matrons, although puzzled, desisted, and she and he had a chance to converse.

"I take it"—he glanced at the sofa her mother and his aunt still graced—"that your mother and my aunt are old friends."

"Very old." She glanced at the pair. "They go back a long way. In fact"—she looked farther and located her sister and smiled—"one of their joint aims for this dinner is to encourage a connection between Marietta and Lord Swan."

"Swan?" Gray frowned. "I've come across him somewhere...possibly at the opera?"

"Very likely. He's something of a music aficionado, and Marietta is seriously musically inclined as well."

Gray groaned. "I was right—there's going to be music, isn't there?"

His put-upon tone made her laugh. Trying to school her expression to a mere smile, she patted his arm. "I fear so. In fact, I think one can count on it."

The look on his face reminded her that, while he didn't actually dislike music, he'd never appreciated having to sit still and listen to it.

"All I can say is that I hope we don't have to listen to too much—" He broke off, his expression appalled as, on cue, a string quartet, out of sight in an alcove farther down the room, started to play. "God preserve me!"

Struggling not to laugh again, she tightened her hold on his arm and turned toward where Marietta and Swan stood chatting. "Never mind. Come and I'll introduce you to Swan."

Gray grumbled about not wanting to talk about music, but consented to accompany Izzy to join her sister and Marietta's possible beau.

As they neared, Izzy tipped her head closer to his and murmured, "Be nice. I like Swan. He'll suit Marietta to the ground, and she'll suit him as well."

Thus adjured, he girded his loins and, despite expecting to be utterly bored, when Izzy fetched up beside her sister, he bowed over Marietta's hand and greeted her with genuine pleasure. Then he turned to Swan and, with his social mask firmly in place, offered his hand. "Lord Swan."

Swan was younger by several years and readily grasped Gray's hand. "My lord. I believe we crossed paths in Lady Alverton's box at the opera last year."

Gray inclined his head. "Indeed." Understanding the surprised look Izzy sent him, he explained, "My aunt insisted I attend the event to further my return to the ton."

She attempted, unsuccessfully, to hide her grin. "I see."

Gray had expected Swan to pursue the opera connection, but instead, the young man said, "I saw a fabulous pair of matched grays being driven about town last week, and when I inquired, I was told they were yours, my lord."

Smiling, Gray inclined his head. "They're recent acquisitions." He caught the droll look Izzy and Marietta exchanged and pointedly stated, "And no, I didn't buy them because of my first name. Lord Hoddle had them from some breeder in Ireland, apparently imagining he was up to the task of managing them. Sadly, he was mistaken, and I was able to take them off his hands." He grinned. "His lordship's loss all around."

"Indeed." Appreciation lit Swan's eyes, and he included Marietta and Izzy as he vowed, "Perfectly matched with utterly exquisite lines." He glanced at Gray. "I imagine they run well?"

He nodded. "I couldn't wish for better. Bowling along the Great North Road behind them is truly a pleasure."

Marietta cut in with a comment about a recent offering at the Theatre Royal, and Izzy assisted in steering the conversation away from horse-flesh. With unabashed good humor, Swan played along, as did Gray, and the four of them fell to reviewing recent London events.

By the time Gilchrist announced dinner, Gray had laid to rest his earlier fear that Swan would prove to be an effeminate waste of space. Swan and he had even managed to drag the conversation back to horses by debating the finer points of hunters and riding hacks suitable for the country. As both ladies rode, the discussion had involved them as well.

Gray wasn't the highest-ranking nobleman present—that honor went to the ageing Duke of Perry, who therefore led the dowager countess into the dining room—but to his abiding relief, he was the second highest and therefore escorted the dowager countess's eldest daughter.

Even more fortuitously, whether by design or sheer luck, his aunt had placed him next to Izzy more or less in the center of the long table and thus equidistant from Lady Matcham at one end and the duke and Izzy's mother at the other. Swan and Marietta were seated opposite, a little way along.

Perfect placement. Gray proceeded to make the most of it, with Izzy's ready assistance.

As dessert was placed before them, Izzy caught Gray's eyes. "I'm enjoying this evening much more than I'd anticipated."

Smiling, he held her gaze. "If your mother and my aunt are bosom-bows, then given Aunt Matcham loves to entertain, I imagine you've attended any number of these events over the years."

"Indeed. Over the past twelve years, the number might even top fifty." She tipped her head, regarding him quizzically. "How is it I never saw you at Matcham House long ago?"

His lips curved wryly. "In earlier years, I tended to avoid Aunt Matcham like the plague. I'm sure she itched to get her hands on me, but I was exceedingly elusive."

"And yet, here you are."

He inclined his head. "With my parents mostly in the country, I've found myself relying more and more on Aunt Matcham's knowledge of the ton, and my attendance at events such as this is her price."

"Ah." Izzy nodded in mock-commiseration. "I can imagine she drives a hard bargain."

Others drew their attention as the conversation grew more general. Not long after, one matron leaned forward to ask the company at large, "Did you see that the latest edition of *The London Crier* is by way of a hue and cry? Over some murder! I haven't read it yet, but I made sure my footman fetched a copy."

"Yes, indeed," another lady replied. "I'm dying to read it. The articles are always so entertaining, but this week's edition bids fair to being quite eye-opening."

Izzy caught Marietta's eye with a warning look, at which her sister rolled her eyes, but she kept her lips firmly shut on any impulsive and unwise utterance.

"Have to say," the duke opined from the end of the table, "I could never understand why Gertie"—he nodded down the table to his duchess, who was seated beside Lady Matcham—"was always in such a flap every Saturday to read the blessed rag, but then I read it myself, and well, the stories aren't half bad. Not the typical scandal-ridden offerings."

"I," the duchess intoned, "find the challenge of identifying the various personages in the stories quite enthralling."

Many other ladies agreed.

Gray caught Izzy's eyes and arched a brow.

Thoroughly pleased, she grinned.

Gray had noted the look she'd sent her sister. Under cover of the wider conversation, he asked, "Do you worry that your mother or sister might let something slip?"

"Constantly." She met his eyes, her own suddenly serious. "And as they're my best sources of gossip, if the connection ever got out…"

If her masquerade as Mrs. Molyneaux ever became common knowledge among the ton, the family would be ostracized.

The gentleman on Izzy's other side claimed her attention.

Gray sipped his wine, his mind turning over the conundrum of how, in the future he was slowly constructing, Izzy might manage to continue to run *The Crier*. He suspected she would wish to and decided to allow the matter to percolate in the back of his brain. He was accustomed to finding his way past apparently insurmountable obstacles and felt reasonably confident that, one way or another, he and she would find a way around the potential hurdles.

His aunt tapped her glass with a fork and, when the conversations broke off and everyone looked her way, rose, bringing all the guests to their feet. "Gentlemen, we'll leave you to enjoy your brandies. I trust"— she swept her gaze over the company—"you won't dally overlong. I have further entertainment planned and would be loathe to find us pressed for time."

With that pointed warning, she led the ladies out.

Drawing out Izzy's chair for her, Gray grumbled, "'Further entertainment.' You know what that means."

She laughed and patted his arm. "You'll survive."

He watched her walk away, then returned to the table and joined the general rearrangement as all the men moved closer to the head of the table, where the duke sat, as Gilchrist and his helpers set out the decanters and crystal glasses.

Gray settled and, smiling, nodded as Swan claimed the chair beside him. The brandy decanter made the rounds, and they helped themselves and passed it on, then sipped appreciatively.

Gray studied the amber liquid in his glass. "I once asked Aunt Matcham how it came about that she always had such excellent brandy. She replied that her late spouse had introduced her to the finer things in life—including the best brandy—and even though he's been dead for decades, she didn't see any reason to change her habits."

Others smiled, several laughed, and the duke held up his glass. "To our hostess and her dearly departed lord."

Everyone drank, then resumed or initiated conversations with their neighbors or those opposite. For a time, Gray and Swan were engaged with the gentlemen across the table, discussing the latest boxing match that had recently been held in Surrey.

When that subject waned, prompted by an impulse he didn't stop to question, Gray turned to Swan and, savoring a sip of his brandy, studied the younger man. "Am I to take it your interest in Lady Marietta is more than passing?"

Caught in the act of raising his glass, Swan paused, then sipped and swallowed. Then he lowered the glass, swiveled so their conversation was somewhat more private, and met Gray's gaze. "Lady Marietta is a sweet and lovely young lady with whom I share many interests."

"So I understand. And as she's in her second season and—as you noted—quite lovely, I assume she's a young lady intent on making up her own mind. In that regard, from what I've observed, you're well on the way to fixing her interest."

Swan's veneer of sophistication fell away. "Really?" Then he realized how hopeful that sounded and winced. But after staring at Gray for a second, he asked, "Are you sure?"

Gray waggled his head. "I only made her acquaintance recently. However, she's very much the sort of lady who knows her own mind, and I can't see her bestowing time on a gentleman if she wasn't genuinely interested herself."

Swan considered that, then blew out a breath. "That's…encouraging."

"Given that," Gray smoothly continued, "I assume you're in a position to make an offer."

"Oh yes." Swan seemed to be concentrating on that prospect as he rattled off his status, financially and estate-wise.

But then, eyes narrowing, he refocused on Gray. "In turn, I take it that your interest in my affairs stems from a similar interest in Lady Isadora?"

Gray met Swan's dark eyes and…realized he was correct. Gray hadn't paused to think *why* he felt compelled to sound out Swan over his intentions regarding Marietta, but that, indeed, was the reason. Given her brother wasn't in London, he felt he should stand in lieu of Julius with respect to applicants for Marietta's hand—exactly as a brother-in-law would.

He could deny his aspirations and, instead, claim to be merely an old family friend…

Holding Swan's gaze, Gray inclined his head. "Just so." He drained his glass and, lowering it, admitted, "However, no more than you can I be certain of the outcome of my suit."

"Ah. I see." Judging from his expression, Swan accepted that without further question. After a moment, he cut a hopeful glance at Gray. "Do you know much about the earl? Marietta's brother?"

Gray considered how forthcoming he ought to be, then thought of what he would hope to be told were their positions reversed. "You've heard of Julius's marriage?" Swan nodded, and Gray continued, "Apparently, he and his wife are content to remain in the country, but the family remain close, and that extends to Julius's grandfather-in-law, Mr. Silas Barton. He was the source of the funds that saved the Descartes and is a firm favorite with the family and, from all I've gathered, has been a great help to them over the years."

From the look in Swan's eyes, he was clever enough to read between the lines, and Gray proceeded to paint as clear and truthful a picture of the dowager countess's household as he could.

At the end of the succinct recitation, Swan grew thoughtful.

Gray left the younger man to digest the information in peace and turned to the gentleman on his other side.

Shortly afterward, the duke slapped the table. "Gentlemen, I fear we should return to what awaits us, or our dear hostess is liable to send in the cavalry."

With chuckles and smiles, the gentlemen rose and, in groups of two and three, ambled toward the drawing room—only to be diverted by Gilchrist and the footmen to the music room, deeper in the house.

His worst fears realized, Gray bit back a groan, which proved wise given the way Swan's expression lit.

"Excellent," Swan said. "I had hoped her ladyship would include a musical interlude."

Gray inwardly sighed. If he and Swan did become brothers-in-law, he would have to confess to his aversion to music in a social setting. He wasn't sure his tact was up to the task; he'd have to conscript Izzy to do the enlightening.

He scanned the room and found her not far from the doorway, chatting with three other ladies, two young and one old.

He joined the group, and Izzy introduced him, but before any conversation could ensue, his aunt banged her cane on the floor, much like a judge with a gavel.

"Come along, everyone." She waved toward the straight-backed chairs arrayed in a semicircle before a pianoforte. "Please sit, and we can begin."

Gray hung back as the three ladies excitedly made their way to the chairs.

Izzy dallied by his side.

He met her amused and faintly questioning gaze and resolutely shook his head. "I can't bear it." Concealed between them, he grasped her hand and surreptitiously tugged. "Come and keep me company."

She searched his eyes, then glanced toward the front of the room. "Wait until the first performer starts and everyone's attention is fixed on them."

That was sound advice. As there were more guests than chairs, plenty of others were standing about, although none were closer to the open doorway than they were.

With relief in prospect, Gray watched as a young lady was persuaded to seat herself before the keys. Helpfully, she launched into a resounding rendition of some march.

Izzy glanced his way. "Perfect covering fire, don't you think?"

He grinned, gripped her hand more firmly, and quiet as mice, they slipped out of the room. He glanced back, but no head turned; no one noticed them leaving.

Matcham House hadn't changed in the past ten years; unerringly, he led Izzy to the private parlor his aunt favored when alone and that would, therefore, be deserted as well as unknown to most guests.

He opened the door, and they whisked inside. The curtains were drawn against the night, but as per his memories, a lamp sat on the small table by the door. He quickly lit it, then turned the flame down to a comforting glow.

"That's better." He surveyed the room, finding it much as he recalled.

Izzy was already making her way to the small, well-padded sofa. With a swish of her skirts, she sat and looked invitingly at him.

He drank in her features, took in the open question in her eyes, then slowly walked across and settled in the spot beside her.

Tilting her head, she studied his face. "Is there something specific you wish to speak about?"

Yes. He'd been acting on impulse fed by instinct, as was his wont. Now, however…

He leaned back, angling so he could watch her face as he spoke; she obligingly mirrored the position so they could more easily observe each other's expressions.

He looked at her, appreciating her quiet confidence, her assurance, and the experienced intelligence lurking behind her emerald eyes. His opening words leapt to his tongue. "One change the past ten years have wrought is that we're older and wiser—with the years, we've gained wisdom and insight." He tipped his head, ruefully acknowledging, "Perhaps not of each other but of ourselves and our world. I hope, because of that, we'll be better able to understand and accommodate each other."

She said nothing, simply waited, and he went on, "Given my suggestion of reclaiming what we had ten years ago and, this time, going further and exploring what might be"—he drew breath and searched her eyes

—"perhaps it's time we shared our thoughts on what we want from our lives."

Her brows faintly rose; she looked unsure.

Unable to stop himself, he stated, "That kiss, Izzy. You know as well as I do the connection still exists." He gestured. "So what are we to do about it? Go forward? Or pretend that link between us isn't there?"

"It's not that," she replied rather tartly. "It's just…where do we start?"

He thought for a moment, then surrendering wholly to impulse, said, "How would you feel if I proposed?"

Izzy blinked. He wanted to start there? Then she realized how he'd phrased the question. Put like that, it gave her the chance to put him off before he actually proposed—an easy way out for both of them, one that wouldn't involve a direct rejection and the associated hurt.

Yet they'd been this way before, talking of sharing their lives.

But those lives had changed, and so had they.

"I don't need to marry for money anymore." That was a simple fact.

"You don't need to marry at all. You've already built a life for yourself. What I would offer you is…not an alternative but an added dimension. Me as your husband, children, a home of your own—if that's what you want." He tipped his head. "What do you want, Izzy?"

A good question. Love?

Strangely, she knew that had always been there, between them. Not always comfortable, yet always present, not spoken of but tacitly acknowledged by them both.

Like the fire in that kiss, it simply was. Had been and still was.

If she took the chance and embraced "them," would things end differently this time?

They truly were standing together and looking down the same path after a ten years' hiatus.

Still…

Did he truly imagine that she might reject his offer?

Yes, he did, for the very good reason that he was such a different man to the cocky, brashly confident, second-son-of-a-duke he'd been back then. Yet the man he was now suited the woman she was now far better than before.

Exasperated by her silence, he looked pointedly at her.

She drew breath, paused, then lightly grimaced. "In response to your question, the honest truth is I don't know."

She met his eyes. "Yes, I'm drawn to you. I always have been, and

yes, the connection seems even stronger now than it was. We get on well
—we understand each other, and despite the years apart, I feel closer to
you as a person than I do to any other, man or woman."

She hesitated, absorbing that.

After a moment, he prompted, "So?"

She refocused on his eyes, the same rich amber she'd never forgotten.
"Is that enough on which to build a marriage? For us, as we are now, is
that sufficient foundation to make a marriage work?"

He held her gaze for a long moment, then admitted, "I don't think
either of us can answer that. Who can see the future? But is it *The Crier*
—your role and responsibilities there—that makes you hesitate?"

The question forced her to confront and examine that issue. Eventually, she conceded, "To a point." She trapped his gaze and held it. "If I
were to agree to go forward, then whatever joint future we constructed, I
would want to retain ownership of *The Crier*, but"—she tipped her head
in acknowledgment—"there are ways to satisfy what I want from the
position that would not involve the same time and personal effort that my
current roles do."

Gray nodded. "You're the owner, the editor—"

"And the principal writer and contributor. However, given how established the paper has become and how sound the printing works is as a
business, I could find others to take on all those roles bar that of owner.
Stepping back from the other roles would see me no longer at the printing
works on a daily basis." She met his gaze. "If there were other demands
on my time, I would have space in my days to meet them."

The last sentence was a thinly veiled challenge. She wanted him to
tell her what he wanted, what he wished for.

He held her gaze for several seconds, then said, "If I proposed and
you accepted…I would prefer to live primarily in the country, with a town
house in Mayfair for when we need to be here. Other than that, we both
have lives and occupations we want to pursue, and I foresee us both
supporting the other in those endeavors, our currently separate lives
enriching the other's, with us ultimately acting as a team in both spheres."
He paused, then without shifting his gaze from hers, went on. "And I
would like to have children with you. However many we feel we can
handle."

That surprised Izzy. "You like children?" She hadn't thought children
would rate so highly on his list.

He grimaced. "I didn't know I did, but having become acquainted with the Alverton brood, I've discovered I do. They're"—he gestured —"engaging and entertaining. They remind me of my youth and all the good times I had." Passion sparked in his eyes as his gaze returned to her face. "I want others to know and have what I did—to enjoy life as I did."

There. That.

That was what was new, his drive to share the good things in life with others. She recognized the trait as one aspect of his character that powered the attraction she felt for him now, an almost-irresistible temptation to go forward with him and see where he went, how he developed.

He'd changed. For the better.

And she felt the tug of temptation ever more strongly.

Perhaps it truly was time to see what might be?

"To go forward"—she thought of it—"we need to put paid to our past. I still have questions from that time, and I daresay you do, too."

He held her gaze. "I noticed how shocked you were when I mentioned the conversation I'd overheard between you, your mother, and your aunt."

"I didn't know you'd heard that. I didn't know you'd called that day, that you'd even been in the house."

"I was admitted by a footman. I breezed past him, asked where you were, and when he said the drawing room, I said I'd show myself in. The household was used to me calling by then, so he didn't argue." Speaking as if the moment was fresh in his mind, he went on, "I went up the stairs, and the drawing room door was ajar. I paused before it, settling my coat, and heard your aunt say my name. I stopped and listened." His gaze recaptured hers. "You know what I heard. Your aunt, your mother, and you discussing me as if I was a commodity— no, a valuable creature to be acquired, to be lured, trapped, and caught."

She heard the vulnerability in his voice, a vulnerability she'd had no idea he—so cocky, so confident—might feel, and didn't know what to say.

He continued to look at her, wordlessly demanding a response.

She swallowed and said, "So...you heard what you did and disappeared without a word."

His eyes narrowed. "I assumed someone would tell you—"

She shook her head and, chin rising, huskily said, "No one did."

He paused, then said, "So when I disappeared..."

"I had no idea what had happened—why you'd left or where you'd gone."

He frowned. "I thought you'd realize I'd overheard what I had, and that was why I'd vanished."

"I understand that now. Then"—she raised one hand in a helpless gesture—"all I knew was that you'd disappeared and effectively deserted me." The hurt was still there, buried deep though it was by the passage of the years.

The senselessness, the futility of all the angst that moment had caused both of them and how much it had changed their lives...

The consequences were staggering.

Dazed by her evolving understanding of how far-reaching the impact of that moment had been, she said, "I really don't know what to say. What you heard, all you remember, is correct. That was what was said." She refocused on his eyes. "How you interpreted it wasn't."

His amber gaze pinned her. "Tell me, then. Explain to me, Izzy, because—damn it—I was so in love with you, and hearing you say those words hurt so damned much I ran to the other end of the world."

I was so in love with you...

The words sank into her, spreading like a balm over a heart that had never healed.

When she didn't immediately respond, he continued, "I overheard your aunt talking of how my wealth made me such an excellent catch. I heard you agree. I heard you say enough to be certain you wanted to marry me because of the money."

"*No.*" The word came out with such strength, such forcefulness it made his eyes widen. She fought the urge to lean toward him, to plead. Instead, with simple dignity, she said, "*I* wanted to marry you because I *loved* you. Mama was happy that the man I loved was wealthy enough to satisfy my aunt. My aunt Ernestine..." She drew in a shuddering breath. "Do you remember her? My paternal aunt, Ernestine, Lady Bloxborough?"

"She was a terrible old tartar," he supplied. "That, I remember."

She nodded. "She was old—far older than my father—and a penny-pinching miser to boot. As much as he was a profligate gambler, she was an inveterate miser. For all I know, those traits were connected—one a reaction to the other. I always suspected a large part of her problem with us—Mama and our family—was that she felt excruciatingly guilty over Papa, her younger brother, running the estate into the ground and callously leaving us penniless."

Unflinchingly, she met his eyes, knowing her own were as hard as flint. "Ernestine was aware of Papa's habits and just how close to the wind he'd been sailing. She knew far more than Mama ever did, yet she never said anything. She knew when Papa broke the entail, but not a word of warning passed her lips. And then Papa died, and it was too late, and we'd lost everything."

She paused, trapped in the past. "We papered over the cracks for as long as we could, hanging on as best we were able to reach my first Season in the hope I would attract a suitor wealthy enough to save the family. Ernestine agreed to fund my Season, but in return, she demanded and insisted that I marry for money, and she held the purse strings in an iron fist. Julius was at Eton, and him continuing there depended on Ernestine, and during the months of that Season, everything Mama, Marietta, James, and I possessed, including running our household, we owed to Ernestine. Without her, I couldn't have had a Season, so we all had to dance to her tune. That was her price—and we, Mama and I primarily, had to pay it."

For a moment, she was back in their London house, with her wretched aunt and her peevish ways. Considering the vision, she tipped her head. "I believe Ernestine viewed what she termed 'footing our bill' as enforced reparation for her brother's failings and her own, and she resented it bitterly. But the upshot was that Mama and I had to do as she demanded." She glanced at Gray. "I had to marry a wealthy man."

"You had to keep Ernestine satisfied."

A statement, no question. Recalling how difficult and, at times, excoriating forcing herself to toe her aunt's line had been...

The pain in her eyes was too raw for Gray to doubt—or bear. He reached out and closed his hand about one of hers, and she blinked and refocused on him.

"That's what the conversation you overheard was about," she told him. "Convincing Ernestine that all was progressing exactly as she wished. Obviously, Mama and I did an excellent job—unknowingly, we convinced you as well." She held his gaze, her emerald eyes clear and unshuttered. "And then you left, and my world fell apart."

He tightened his hold on her hand. He couldn't look away from her unshielded gaze. "What did Ernestine do?"

Her lips twisted wryly. "Exactly what you might expect—she pushed and pushed me to accept another suitor."

"But you didn't."

"I couldn't." She looked into his eyes, then sighed and continued,

"Out of that, Mama grew so desperate, she gave in to the creditors' demands and sold the London house. That gave us a buffer, enough to hold on through another Season, and later, once Julius married, there was just enough left for me to buy the old printing works and start *The Crier*."

She met his eyes again. "By then, of course, we'd fallen out with my aunt, and I couldn't think of anything else I could do to earn income. You could say that Ernestine drove me to become the owner and editor of *The Crier*."

He gripped her hand yet more tightly. "Am I allowed to say I'm glad she did? Is she still alive?"

She shook her head. "She died a few years after that. She left us nothing, not that we expected anything. By then, we were well and truly estranged."

He'd already mentally reviewed the comments she and her mother had made that fateful day, the so-hurtful words he'd overheard and taken to heart. In hindsight, he could see each statement for the appeasement it had been; he could see—could accept—that both Izzy and Sybil had been pandering to Ernestine's view of how things had to be.

"I...had no idea your family was in such straits." He focused on her face. "It never occurred to me—would never have occurred to me—that that was what lay behind those comments, but I can see it now."

She studied his face, then said, "I'm sorry you heard what you did. So very sorry it hurt you so deeply." With her free hand, she gestured helplessly. "Yet if I was in that position again, had to play that scene again, I would say the same as I did then. I regret each and every word"—her eyes on his, she shook her head—"but I can't take them back. They might have led to me losing you, but at that moment, those words were necessary, and I had to say them."

"We can't go back and change history." He raised her hand to his lips and pressed a kiss to her fingers. "So let's not try."

Her smile was crooked. "When I think back to that time...I was so full of naive hope and an unquenchable belief in love."

"So was I." He paused, then said, "Perhaps I should have done the dramatic thing and burst into the room and confronted you. Or at least waited and asked you face-to-face what you felt."

"But we can't rewrite history." When he raised his gaze to her eyes, she continued, "We were who we were then—younger, inexperienced, and far less sure of ourselves, no matter how we tried to appear. We reacted—both of us—to the situation as we saw it." She shrugged. "We didn't know to do otherwise."

He sensed there was more to that statement than he'd yet heard. "We?"

She sighed. "You vanished, and I couldn't understand why. I'd thought...I'd hoped... But then you were gone."

When she fell silent, her gaze distant, once more in the past, gently, he pressed, "Tell me."

"I felt deserted." The words fell from her lips, harsh, full of remembered pain. "I felt that the bright future I'd come to believe we would have—such a precious flame that we'd both ignited and, I thought, nurtured—had been cruelly and deliberately snuffed out."

"You thought I'd led you along, then deliberately left you?"

She met his gaze. "I didn't know what to think. I just didn't know."

He drew in a breath, then said, "Because of that one, accidental moment, we were both hurt deeply. Viewing it now, with the benefit of age and experience, we might have reacted differently and avoided the pain—"

"We were who we were."

"And it's easy to be wise long after the event."

She turned her hand in his and gripped. "Looking back, us parting wasn't the fault of either of us, or alternatively, it was both our faults. One or the other. But does that make any difference now, with so many years having passed?"

"The only difference is we now know the truth. Each of us loved the other, more or less to the same degree, and neither of us deliberately hurt the other. All we can do—here and now—is put that time behind us and let our misplaced rancor fade and die."

She held his gaze for a moment, then gave a small nod. "And now?"

"Now..." He tipped his head and found a faintly teasing smile to distract her. "I was shocked to learn that you hadn't married. Why didn't you?"

Izzy tried to stop her answering smile. "No other man"—*lived up to you in my eyes*—"tempted me." Then she sighed and went on, "And then things got even worse, and we had to sell the country house as well, and the fact we weren't flush any more started to percolate through the ton. Just the usual whispers—you know how it happens. My second Season had passed with no suitor in sight, and later that year, Ernestine died, and we went into half mourning, which severely limited the next Season for me, not that I was interested in socializing by then. I could see we were heading for desperation, and I started developing my ideas about publishing a small newspaper focusing on the ton's social events, and then Julius married, and the upshot of that was that I felt free to try my hand at being Mrs. I. Molyneaux, and with Silas's backing, I pulled it off."

He nodded in understanding. "So now you have a very different life."

"A dual life—half in and half out of the ton." When he didn't respond, she seized the chance to ask, "What did you do during the years you were away? Aside from finding that nugget, how did you become so very wealthy?"

Gray hesitated, but it was she who was asking, and given all she'd revealed and what he wanted to build with her... He paused, marshaling his thoughts.

She waited patiently, attentively.

Eventually, he said, "If we're to have any chance of a shared life, then between us, we must have trust—absolute and unequivocal." He met her eyes. "That means I need to bury the past and all I thought and felt about you then and trust you as you are now—the woman I've observed over the past week, the woman I know you are today, one who deserves my unreserved trust. So...to answer your question, I'll tell you what I haven't told anyone else, not even my oldest, closest friend."

She tipped her head and waited.

He almost smiled. "I know what it's like for people like us not to have money. Not to have recourse to something we grew up taking for granted." His mind balked at giving her *every* detail—not yet, too risky. Instead, he said, "After I arrived in America, over a period, I lost all the money I'd brought with me. I was too proud to contact my parents and ask for more, so I was forced to work, to eke out a living using my bare hands in whatever way offered. I worked in fields, helping with the harvest, and eventually, I worked on the railroads being laid across the country. I was almost to the west coast, in a state called Oregon, when news about the Gold Rush in California broke. I hired on as crew on a ship running down the coast and got myself to the gold fields. Trust me when I say it was a hard and bare existence, scraping out the ore with picks and shovels, panning in the streams, living under canvas or the stars."

He held her gaze and quietly said, "By then, I was little better than what Americans call a 'bum.' I had no money, and what I managed to get,

I spent on food and…entertainment. And drink. One night, after leaving the saloon—a tavern—I was so inebriated that on my way back to my tent in the dark, I collapsed in a ditch and…stayed there. I was all but delirious, and at that point, I truly didn't care if I woke or not."

She squeezed his hand. "You'd reached rock-bottom."

"I had. But, it seems, Fate hadn't finished with me. I woke with the dawn, and as I was hauling myself out of the ditch, my hand landed on a rock. Only it wasn't just a rock—it was a nugget. Not a small one, but one of the biggest found to that point."

"What did you do?"

"I seized it, but I also took it as a sign—as having been given one last chance. I cashed in the nugget at the assay office, took the money, and swore to reform. To become the best man I could be. I took the funds and invested them, specifically in ways that would benefit others —in businesses that gave others jobs. Honest and reasonably paid jobs. Once I'd established such a business, others came looking to purchase it, offering me yet more money. So I sold out, took the money, and moved on to my next venture. In that manner, I progressed, company by company, town by town, gradually traveling back across America to the east coast again. When I reached Boston, I stopped and asked myself what came next."

Her eyes on his, she tipped her head. "And what did?"

He smiled briefly. "That was when I finally faced the question of what I actually wanted to achieve with my life. My epiphany was realizing that I was trying to—and possibly needed to—justify myself to my family, to society here, and I accepted that it was time to come home." He paused, then went on, "It was as if my time in America had been about teaching me things I would never have learned while being Lord Grayson Child over here. But given I'd learned those lessons, it was time for me to come home and face my ultimate challenge, namely, to pick up the reins of being Lord Grayson Child and craft a satisfying life for myself here, where I actually belong."

He met her eyes. "That's why I returned—why I came home."

Izzy digested that, then observed, "Both of us have learned lessons of life and of ourselves by being forced to exist without the funds we took for granted in our earlier years. I had to become Mrs. I. Molyneaux, and you had to become the man you are now. In order to survive, both of us shed the trappings of noble birth, and to be perfectly truthful, I don't regret that. As Mrs. Molyneaux, I've learned more about the common hardships and realities of life than I ever could have as Lady Isadora Descartes."

He was nodding. "That's how I feel, too. That time was no picnic, but I gained a great deal from the experience and, I hope, have emerged a better man than I was before."

"I appreciate you telling me your story." She studied him for a moment more, then nodded. "I agree it's time for us to bury our past and leave it behind us, fully and completely."

An almost-imperceptible tension eased from him. "Our pasts don't define us. We are the people we are now, not ghosts from years gone by."

"Agreed. And"—she drew in a breath and forced herself to ask—"returning to your earlier question regarding how I might react if you proposed, is it the lady I am now you wish to offer for or a wraith from our mutual past?"

His smile was slow. "Definitely not the wraith. In fact, given what I now know of myself, I'm not at all sure the Lady Isadora of ten years ago would have been lady enough for me."

She arched her brows. "Really? But now?"

He sobered. "Now, the lady you are is all I want and all I need."

She tipped her head, sensing the ruthless certainty in the declaration. "You sound exceedingly sure."

"I am." His eyes didn't leave hers. "What about you?"

She considered, but could see only one way of adequately answering that. She shifted closer and raised a hand to lightly trace his cheek. Voice low, she murmured, "I'm not *quite* sure…"

Stretching up, she pressed her lips to his. She kissed him, and for a long moment, he let her. Let her fit her lips to his and savor the firmness of his mobile lips against her lusher, softer ones. Then he responded, and the world spun away until nothing else mattered but the simple, honest, candid exchange.

He reached for her, one steely arm sliding about her waist and slowly drawing her closer. His other hand rose to encircle the wrist of the hand framing his face, but he didn't draw her palm from his cheek. Instead, his long fingers artfully stroked the inside of her wrist, a strangely intimate caress that fractured her awareness.

If she'd wanted to know if he desired her, the answer was there in the sudden heat that flared when he angled his head, and instinctively, she parted her lips, and his tongue surged in and claimed.

Ardent and entirely certain, she responded and pressed closer. She slid her fingers from his cheek and speared them through his thick hair, then raised her other hand and, gripping his head between her palms, met his questing tongue with her own.

She matched him in the increasingly ravenous exchange and, captured by the moment, by the surging passion and all it promised, brazenly urged him on.

With lips and tongues and melding mouths, together, they forged deeper into passion's lair, tempting, exploring, inciting.

Giddy and restless, she almost groaned when the hand that had been at her wrist traced along her arm to her shoulder, then skated over the taut silk of her bodice and closed about her aching breast.

Yes. There.

Gently, he flexed his fingers, then kneaded, and when, through the kiss, she signaled her eager approval, he massaged her sensitive flesh, then his fingertips found the tight bud of her nipple beneath the silk, circled teasingly, then closed and squeezed.

Sensation streaked through her, and she forgot how to breathe.

He continued his ministrations, and her head spun, awash in pleasured delight.

Gray couldn't get enough of her gloriously uninhibited responses. Her lips tasted like ambrosia, her mouth was luscious and sweet, and the intoxicating mix of her desire and his swamped his awareness.

Exultant, he explored her curves, knowing, now, that she would be his —that she'd accepted the challenge of placing her hand once more in his and forging a new path together.

He eased back against the sofa's arm, urging her over him. She came readily, eagerly, no more willing to break the heated kiss than he. She settled over him, her breasts pressed to his chest. Her long legs tangled with his, her thighs sliding between his, her hips riding over his in excruciating temptation.

To distract them both from that temptation, he framed her face between his hands and kissed her voraciously, and she responded in kind.

Just how far their passions might have driven them, they were destined never to learn. The clock on the mantelpiece chimed twelve times, loudly enough to penetrate the haze of desire wreathing their senses.

They both registered the problem and, patently reluctantly, eased back from the kiss.

She raised her head and stared down at him with disappointment etched in every line of her face. "Damn!" she muttered.

He sighed. "I couldn't have put it better myself."

He helped her sit up, and they spent a minute rearranging their clothing. He rose, drew her to her feet, and ran critical eyes over her hair and gown. She did the same for him, then reached up and resettled his cravat. Meeting his eyes, she murmured, "Your aunt and my mother don't need any further clues."

"No, indeed." He closed a hand about one of hers, dipped his head, and stole one last kiss, then he straightened, lowered their clasped hands, and resigned, walked with her toward the door.

He definitely didn't want to return to their prescribed evening's activities, yet realistically, they had no choice.

When they reached the door, she halted and tugged his hand.

When he turned and arched his brows, she met his eyes and waved her free hand between them. "Obviously, we need to discuss our next steps, but with tomorrow looming as a critical day in our pursuit of Quimby's killer…"

He grimaced. "Let's agree to go on as we have been, at least until we see what tomorrow brings." He trapped her gaze. "But I give you fair warning that, after delaying for ten years, I'm not inclined to dally over making you mine."

She read his determination in his eyes, and a glorious smile broke over her face. "You'll get no argument from me on that score—indeed, I'll encourage you—but…" A cloud passed over her features. "If nothing useful comes from our hue and cry edition, then the police might revert to their previous stance of considering me the prime suspect and—"

"No." His tone made the word absolute, impossible to contradict. "Trust me. That won't happen."

She took in his set face and sighed. "Yes, well, things might get messy, but hopefully, we'll know one way or another by tomorrow afternoon."

"Hmm." He wasn't as happy as he had been. He frowned at the door. "We'd better get back to the music room."

Without further words, they slipped along the corridor and into the music room in time to witness the final performance—Marietta at the pianoforte accompanying Swan, singing a country ballad.

Even Gray had to admit the pair made very pleasant music; when the piece ended and Marietta and Swan took their bow, he clapped enthusiastically along with everyone else.

Apparently, that brought the evening to a close. The guests rose and, in groups, thanked Lady Matcham, then headed for the front hall.

Together with Swan, Gray joined the Descartes ladies in tendering thanks—for once, entirely genuine—to his aunt.

Apparently sensing that surprising change, she peered at him curiously, but he kept his expression politely bland and offered the dowager countess his arm down the Matcham House steps.

Izzy glided on his other side.

After he'd helped her mother into the carriage, he glanced back, saw Swan and Marietta still chatting to his aunt, and turned to Izzy. Meeting her eyes, he murmured, "Once Baines has Quimby's killer by the heels…"

She smiled brilliantly and squeezed his arm. "We'll return to our recent discussions."

"And bring them to an agreeable conclusion." *Such as a wedding date.*

She noted his unwavering determination, and her smile softened. "Indeed."

She gave him her hand, and he took it. With "I'll see you at breakfast tomorrow," he helped her into the carriage.

Gray stood back as Swan escorted Marietta to the carriage and assisted her up the steps.

After closing the door and nodding to Fields, Swan joined Gray on the pavement, and they watched the carriage rumble away.

Swan turned to Gray and offered his hand. "Thank you for the information you imparted earlier."

Shaking Swan's hand, with a smile, Gray inclined his head. "It seemed the least I could do."

Both patently pleased with their evening, they established they were heading in opposite directions and parted with amiable nods.

As Swan strode off, Gray glanced at the Matcham House porch and found his aunt staring at him, suspicious and knowing at once.

Deciding that everything in his world was close to being perfect—possibly only one day away from him attaining all he most wished for—he allowed his welling enthusiasm for life to light his smile as he saluted his aunt and, with a spring in his step, walked on.

CHAPTER 13

*I*zzy and Gray didn't dally over breakfast the next morning.

They arrived at the printing works at fifteen minutes before eight o'clock to find a line of people, mostly younger men, lined up outside the door. Some were delivery boys, including, at the head of the line, the three who had been too late to get their orders filled the day before, but others weren't.

Izzy was grateful Gray was there to escort her up the steps and shield her as she unlocked the door. Those waiting seemed restless, but after Gray bent a warning glance on them and said, "The door opens for business at eight o'clock and not before," all remained on the pavement, apparently resigned to more waiting.

Inside the printing works, they discovered that the Lipsons had also come in early. Lipson Senior reported, "No sign that anyone's tried to break in."

"That's a relief." She stripped off her gloves.

Lipson nodded toward the door. "We'll have delivery boys coming in as well as those with information. Do we just deal with them one at a time, regardless of what they want?"

She considered, then cast a glance at Gray. "That might be best."

He nodded. "Otherwise, you'll get arguments over who's been waiting longest and so on."

Maguire and Mary appeared at the front door, and Tom Lipson went to let them in.

Izzy waved at the pair as they entered, then walked briskly into her office. After hanging up her coat and bonnet, she took her place behind the desk. Gray lounged in the chair before it, as had become his wont. Determined to get through the backlog of invoices, she buckled down.

The other staff arrived in a steady stream; she was distantly aware of the voices and greetings. From their tone, she deduced that everyone was eager to see what came from all their hard work.

She prayed that something would.

At precisely eight o'clock, Littlejohn called, "Ready?" When an agreeing rumble came in reply, he said, "Right, then. I'm opening the door."

From where Izzy sat, she could see Baines hovering just outside the office. With him and Littlejohn in attendance, jostling in the queue that formed before the counter would be kept to a minimum.

Izzy paused in her scribing and, straining her ears, listened as Mary and Lipson dealt with the three delivery boys who were desperate to get their hands on more copies of the paper. Once the trio had been sent running back to their masters with their respective loads, several would-be informants fronted the counter, and the task of winnowing the grain from the chaff began. After listening for a minute and verifying that the early birds weren't offering any worms worth considering, Izzy returned to her work.

The occasional clatter from deeper in the workshop confirmed that Lipson had the other staff busy with their usual chores of putting the boiler and press to rights, cleaning and oiling and getting the beasts ready to roll again next week, as well as cleaning and re-sorting all the used type.

After a while, Gray, who, from the comfort of the armchair, had been watching the activity in the foyer, reported, "You've had quite a few delivery lads wanting more papers turn up."

"Hmm." Having finished converting yesterday's delivery slips into invoices, while waiting for Littlejohn to appear with some useful infor-mant to be interrogated, Izzy distracted herself by updating her tally of copies sent out.

When Digby arrived with more delivery slips, she smiled and took them. After flicking through the slips, she said to Gray, "If the reorders keep coming in at this rate, the edition, both first and second printing, is going to sell out."

"The hue and cry concept certainly seems to have sparked London's interest." He continued to watch those coming through the door. "Here's hoping something comes of that."

"How are things going out there?"

"All very ordered. The line outside is moving steadily. People are coming in, reporting what they've come to share and leaving their details, then departing. It's going remarkably smoothly."

"No doubt due to the repressive presence of Baines and Littlejohn."

"Very likely."

The steady stream of people gradually waned.

Gray saw Baines cross to the counter. After speaking with Littlejohn, Baines walked into the office.

Izzy looked up and waved him to the other chair before the desk. "Anything of interest?"

Baines slumped into the chair. "Bits and pieces—quite a few names we didn't know, but at this point, most seem innocent enough."

With a soft huff, Izzy returned to writing out the most recent invoices.

By a quarter to nine, the line outside had dwindled to nothing, yet interspersed with the delivery lads still turning up to beg more copies, people—males and now the occasional female—were coming in, most hesitant, curious, and cautious, to offer up what they knew.

At nine o'clock, the bell over the door tinkled, but it was the firm footstep that followed that had Gray looking up. "Drake's here," he told Izzy.

Baines glanced around, but didn't know who "Drake" was.

Drake glanced at the counter, but made straight for the office, his stride discouraging any interception.

Gray rose to his feet, and Baines lumbered to his and turned to face the door.

The instant Drake walked in, Izzy greeted him. "Winchelsea." She waved at Baines. "Allow me to present Inspector Baines of Scotland Yard, who's in charge of the investigation."

Drake nodded to Baines. "Inspector."

His eyes wide, Baines bowed and mumbled, "My lord."

Gray offered his hand, and Drake grasped it. "Child."

Blandly, Izzy inquired, "Were we expecting you?"

Drake grinned at her. "You didn't think I'd miss this, did you?"

She softly snorted. "I'm more surprised that Louisa isn't here."

"You should be. She was most put out that she had an engagement she didn't dare ignore."

A tap on the door frame had them all looking that way.

Glancing warily at Drake, Littlejohn came in, a list in his hands. "We've got several more names of people in the photographs."

"Excellent!" Izzy set aside her invoice ledger and spread over the desk the pages with the photographs attached.

Littlejohn handed her the list, explained how it was organized, then with another glance at Drake, left to return to his duties at the counter.

Quickly and efficiently, Izzy added the names to the relevant sheets.

Drake rounded the desk to read over her shoulder.

When she finished, she glanced up at him, frowned, caught his eye, and imperiously waved him away. "Go, sit, and stop looming."

Gray heard Baines softly gasp, understandable given the man didn't know who Izzy was.

Drake merely grinned and obeyed, compounding Baines's confusion. Returning around the desk, Drake focused on Baines. "I suggest we retreat, Inspector." Drake waved toward the pair of armchairs before the window. "It's possible our presence might inhibit the tongues of informants, and in the circumstances, we don't need that."

Baines obediently trotted after Drake.

The pair had barely settled in the armchairs when Donaldson tapped on the door frame and proceeded to steer Digby into the room ahead of him.

Lipson followed on Donaldson's heels.

Normally irrepressibly cheerful, Digby looked uncomfortable over being the center of attention and, glancing sidelong at Drake, definitely overawed.

Surreptitiously, Gray signaled Drake and Baines to stay back.

Izzy smiled, simultaneously reassuring, welcoming, and inquiring. "Digby?"

When, wide-eyed, the lad glanced back at Donaldson and Lipson, who had halted just inside the room, Lipson nodded encouragingly and rumbled, "Digby has information we think might prove useful."

"Excellent!" When Digby turned back to her, still smiling, Izzy waved to the empty chair before the desk. "Sit down, Digby. You can be the first informant so his lordship and I can practice how to ask the right questions."

The notion of helping with something calmed Digby somewhat, and he came forward and carefully sat, his gaze flicking from Izzy to Gray and back again.

"Now." Izzy clasped her hands on the sheets with the photographs. "What is it that you noticed, Digby?"

"Well, ma'am, I didn't really have a chance to look closely at the pictures, not to study them like, until just now, when Mr. Lipson let me sit and read all the articles."

Izzy nodded. "And what did you see?"

Digby peered at the sheets trapped beneath Izzy's hands. "It's that I recognized one of the men in the photograph of the coffeehouse in Fleet Street."

Izzy rifled through the sheets, located the relevant one, and spread it on top of the others. "Show us."

Digby half rose, scanned the print, then hovered his fingertip above the image of the tall, well-dressed gentleman standing before the coffee-house, apparently talking to a shorter, more rotund man. "It's this man here," Digby said. The tall man was the most prominent person in the photograph. "Mr. Quimby must've taken this photograph on Friday, sometime during the day, and you remember, on Friday, I left a few minutes early and passed Mr. Quimby in the lane?"

When Digby looked questioningly at Izzy and Gray, they nodded.

"Well," Digby went on, "a few steps later, when I was almost at the corner where the lane meets Great Coram Street, this geezer—gentleman —comes around the corner." Digby sat and looked at Izzy. "I didn't think anything of it at the time—he was just a gent walking down the lane—but what are the odds of him being in one of Mr. Quimby's photographs taken that day and then being just a few yards behind Mr. Q as he made for the back door of the workshop?"

"What odds, indeed." Gray made his tone admiring. "That's an excel-lent piece of information, Digby."

Drake, trailed by Baines, had silently left the armchairs and drawn closer. Now, Drake crouched beside Digby's chair, not too close, and in an entirely unthreatening tone, said, "Tell us what happened, step by step. You said you left earlier than the others?"

Digby's eyes, now huge, flicked assessingly over the terribly elegant gentleman. His tone wary—the lad clearly had excellent instincts—he replied, "Aye. Mr. Lipson said we were done and I could get on home. He knows me ma and sister wait on me for supper every night."

Drake's features softened, and he nodded encouragingly. "So you went out of the back door before any of the other staff."

"Well, the other staff use the front door. It was mostly me and Mr. Q used the rear door, because it's closer to our homes, see?"

Drake nodded his understanding. "So you closed the door behind you and walked up the lane."

"And I saw Mr. Q walking down it. We passed and nodded like, and I walked on toward Great Coram Street. I was nearing the corner when the gent turned onto the lane."

"Tell me," Drake said, "when the gent turned onto the lane, do you think Mr. Quimby would have reached the workshop door and gone in already, or would he still have been in the lane?"

Digby paused to think, but the answer came quickly and with certainty. "He would've still been in the lane. Don't see how he could've reached the door by then, not unless he'd bolted, and I would've heard that."

"Good point." Drake glanced at the photograph, now lying exposed on the desk. "It was evening—already dark. Are you sure that's the man you saw?"

"Aye, I'm sure." The simple statement rang with conviction. "He wasn't wearing a hat, and there's a streetlamp at the corner, see, and when he turned onto the lane, the light fell full on his face." Digby nodded at the photograph. "I'm sure as eggs are eggs it was him."

"Good." Drake fluidly rose.

Despite Drake's impassive expression, Gray suspected he was thinking furiously. "That's Duvall, isn't it?"

Tight-lipped, Drake glanced at Gray, then nodded. "I've checked, and he works at the Board of Trade." Reaching across, Drake picked up the photograph of Duvall and scrutinized it anew. "I'm damned if I recognize the man he's speaking with."

Gray rose and looked over Drake's shoulder at the shorter man in the photograph. While also well-dressed, the man was older than Duvall, possibly by as much as ten years. He had a distinctly round head to go with his rotund figure and was wearing an expensive-looking coat with an astrakhan collar. Like Duvall, he was carrying a cane. After a moment, Gray said, "To my eyes, our mystery man doesn't look English."

"Possibly not even British," Drake added. "However, if our suppositions are correct, then Duvall had to kill Quimby because Duvall was desperate to prevent this photograph—which shows him actively consorting with our mystery man—being widely seen."

With his long fingers, Drake flicked the photograph. "We need our mystery man's name."

A heartbeat of silence greeted that statement, then the bell over the door tinkled.

Along with Drake, Gray looked across the foyer, expecting to see the latest crop of hopeful youths.

Instead, three older workers shuffled through the door and stood hesitantly in a group just inside.

Growing weary of not being able to see what most others could, Izzy rose and rounded the desk to stand beside the armchair Digby still occupied. Like everyone else, the lad had twisted around to stare at whoever had come in.

Izzy followed the others' gazes and realized why the sight was holding everyone silent. The three men were of quite a different ilk to those who'd been arriving throughout the morning with nothing more than inconsequential snippets. Aside from all else, they hung back, mangling felt caps in their hands, and seemed unwilling to even approach the counter.

Eventually, Tom Lipson appeared from behind the counter and walked over and inquired what the three wanted.

One cleared his throat and gruffly said, "We saw the notice in *The Crier*, and we've come to speak to I. Molyneaux."

Tom nodded and guided the men to the counter, where Mary and Littlejohn spoke with them. No one in the office said a word; they were all straining their ears, trying to distinguish the men's rumbling answers to the sergeant's questions.

A minute later, Baines, who was the only one in the office with sight of those behind the counter, came alert. "Looks like we might be about to learn something more."

Seconds later, Littlejohn appeared in the doorway. "You might want to hear what these gentlemen have to say."

Izzy nodded. "Show them in, Sergeant."

She turned to Digby. "Go with Baines and his lordship for the moment." She shooed the three back toward the windows, then whirled and returned to her chair, noting that Lipson Senior and Donaldson had backed into the corner by her filing cabinets in an attempt to make themselves inconspicuous.

Gray had already signaled to Drake to bring up one of the chairs from the windows to add to the pair before the desk.

After lining up the three chairs, Gray stepped back to lean against the bookshelves to Izzy's right.

She looked toward the doorway as Littlejohn ushered in the three workers. She smiled invitingly. "Good day. I'm Mrs. I. Molyneaux, the owner of *The London Crier*." She waved to the chairs. "Won't you come in and sit down and tell me what information you have to offer?"

Unsurprisingly, the three were somewhat taken aback to learn that a woman was the owner of the paper. But after a momentary hesitation, when her inviting smile didn't fade, they shuffled forward and, caps still clutched tightly, sorted themselves into the chairs, sitting upright and definitely not relaxing.

"Now"—Izzy clasped her hands on the desk and kept her smile in place—"I believe you've already given your names and addresses to my assistant, so all that remains is for you to tell us what you know."

The men exchanged glances, apparently settling on the man in the middle as their spokesman. He looked at Izzy and cleared his throat. "It's like this, see. We're dray drivers for the big papers along Fleet Street, and yesterday afternoon, we was having our tea—"

"Early like, it was," the man on the spokesman's left put in. When the other two looked at him, he said, "Just saying. Quality like her might not understand why we was having our dinner at that time. They don't, do they?"

The spokesman acknowledged that wisdom with a nod. "Aye—right enough." Looking at Izzy, he explained, "We start at four in the mornin'—have to be up afore that, o'course—so we has our tea midafter-noon, 'bout three o'clock or so."

Izzy nodded. "I understand."

"So then, we was having our tea in the coffee house we always go to —the Quill and Feather. We always sit at a table near the back corner— it's quieter there—and we saw two of the gents in the picture that shows the outside of the coffeehouse."

Everyone else in the room came alert.

Izzy unpinned the photograph of the coffeehouse from its sheet and handed it across the desk. "Which two men, exactly?"

She held her breath as the men studied the photograph, then the spokesman leaned forward and said, "These two." His wide fingertip indicated Duvall and his friend. "The tall gentleman and the round one."

"Thank you." Izzy took back the photograph and glanced at Drake, who had drawn closer. He'd seen the men make the identification, and really, they couldn't ask for a clearer result. Izzy looked at the men. "We're definitely interested in anything you can tell us about those men. What did you see them do?"

The spokesman waggled his head. "Not so much what they did as what we heard 'em say." When Izzy held her tongue and looked encouraging, he went on, "They was sitting at a table in a little nook just past us —leastways, they were when we noticed them. Seems like they came in while we were eating. Thing is, that nook acts like a funnel for sound. Although they probably thought they was speaking low, we could hear 'em plain as day. And while we was eating, we weren't talking, so we listened—all three of us."

Izzy nodded her understanding. "And what did you hear?"

Everyone other than the three men held their breath.

"Well, for a start, the tall one"—Izzy held up the photograph, and the spokesman pointed again to Duvall—"he was as English as anyone could be, but the other chap, the dumpier one, he was a foreigner."

All three men nodded portentously.

Gray pushed away from the bookshelves and stood by the side of Izzy's desk. "Why are you sure he's a foreigner?"

"Spoke with an accent, he did," the spokesman said.

The man on his right, who had yet to speak, shifted and said, "Not German or Prussian but maybe Flemish?" When Gray and Izzy looked at him, the man colored and said, "What with the exhibition that was on, we've all got used to hearing lots of accents, and I reckon that fellow was Flemish."

Gray nodded in acceptance. "So what did they discuss?"

Via shared glances, the men gathered their thoughts, then the spokesman said, "Most of the time, they was talking about some place they called 'the installation' at Victoria Park Terrace. Not Victoria Park, mind, nor even Victoria Park Road, but Victoria Park Terrace. They said that more than three times, very specific."

Drake had stiffened at the mention of the place.

Gray shot him a glance. "You know what that is?"

Drake came forward to stand beside Gray, effortlessly capturing the three men's attention. He looked at the trio. "Are you sure that's what they said? The installation at Victoria Park Terrace?"

Slowly but surely, all three nodded.

"We noted it particular like," the spokesman said. "Fixed our attention, it did. We've been dray drivers all our lives, delivering all over

London, and we know there ain't no Victoria Park *Terrace*. Not in town, leastways."

Drake nodded. "That's correct. What did the men say about the place in Victoria Park Terrace?"

Once again, the men—picking up on Drake's escalating tension— exchanged glances, then the spokesman volunteered, "Sounded to us like they was planning on demolishing it, whatever it might be."

The man on his right added, "Seemed like whatever was there was going to need explosives to move, so it must be some big old place."

"They mentioned explosives?" Drake's diction had grown so clipped it could cut.

The dray drivers stared at him and simply nodded.

Gray almost expected Drake to explode into action, he was so on edge, but instead, he kept his reactions rigidly contained and, in formal language, thanked the men for coming in and sharing their information and suggested the three should return with Littlejohn to the counter and confirm their names and addresses were correctly noted, as they would definitely be receiving some part of the reward.

Relieved and pleased, the men readily rose, bobbed politely to Izzy, then went out with the sergeant.

Drake's gaze swung to Digby, and he nodded at the lad. "You're in line for a share of the reward, too. Without your eyewitness account, we couldn't connect Duvall to Quimby's murder."

Izzy signaled to Lipson to shut the door. The instant the latch clicked shut, everyone looked at Drake, who was standing staring at a point on the floor and transparently thinking at a rate of knots.

"So what does all that mean?" Gray asked. "What's going on?"

"I wish I knew." Drake raised his head and glanced at the circle of avidly interested faces. "The house in which the under-Channel telegraph cable terminates is located at one end of Victoria Park Terrace in Dover."

Baines pointed at the photograph. "So these two—Duvall and his friend—are planning to blow up the new telegraph to the Continent?"

Drake looked nonplussed. "So it seems."

Izzy frowned. "But why?"

"That's my question, too," Drake said. "I'm not sure what that would accomplish, other than being a dashed inconvenience for a short time."

"I know very little about cabling and so on," Gray said, "but surely they would simply lay it in again—connect it up again?"

"So one would think," Drake replied.

The bell over the door jangled; it had fallen silent with the passing hours, so even muted by the closed door, the sound drew everyone's attention.

Izzy again came out from behind her desk to peer through the glass panel in the office door and saw a burly man in an overcoat step into the foyer.

At a guess, he was in his early forties. He paused, taking in the three workmen at the counter, talking with Mary and Littlejohn. The newcomer scanned the area, saw the office, and before any of the staff appeared to question him, walked toward the office door with the stride of a man who knew where he was going.

Curious, Izzy went to the door and opened it. She halted in the doorway, fixed the man with a commanding look, and inquired, "Can I help you?"

The man stopped a yard away, briefly glanced past her—no doubt taking in Drake, Gray, Baines, and the others visible inside—then refocused on her. "I'm looking for I. Molyneaux. I've information about the dead photographer's photographs."

She arched her brows. "And you are?"

"Neil Hennessy, ma'am." He fished out a card from his waistcoat pocket and handed it over. "I'm senior reporter with *The London Courier*."

Izzy went on full alert. *The London Courier* was a major daily paper, not a competitor but a far larger enterprise. More, she knew of Hennessy's work; he was an experienced ace reporter, known for exposing the secrets of powerful men. She verified the information he'd given was what the professionally printed card declared, then cast a questioning glance at Drake.

At his nod, she returned her gaze to Hennessy, met his eyes—he wasn't much taller than she was—then with a swish of her skirts, stepped back, turned, and beckoned him to follow. "Come in, Mr. Hennessy. Please have a seat."

She reclaimed her chair behind the desk and indicated Hennessy should avail himself of one of the armchairs before it. From the corner of her eye, she saw Littlejohn slip into the room in Hennessy's wake and quietly shut the door.

After taking in the small crowd gathered in the room, his gaze lingering for a moment on Drake, Hennessy walked to the central armchair and sat.

The instant he looked at her, she said, "I presume you're here because you've recognized someone in the photographs."

"I have."

Rather than ask whom, she unpinned and gathered the seven photographs and, across the desk, offered them to Hennessy. "Show us, if you would."

He leaned forward, took the stack, then sat back and sorted through them. "This one." He flashed the photograph of the coffeehouse. "And"—setting aside the other photographs, he pointed to Duvall—"that man."

When he fell silent, she prompted, "And your information?"

Hennessy glanced at Drake and Gray, then looked at her and said, "I know his full name and occupation, the name of the man he's speaking with, and I have some insight into what they might be planning. But before I divulge anything"—his gaze shifted briefly to Lipson and Donaldson before returning to her face—"I want an agreement. I want in on this story, whatever it is."

Drake shifted menacingly, but she held up a staying hand, and he stilled—something Hennessy didn't miss.

Eyes narrowing, she studied the reporter. "You've been in this business long enough to know how it works. Given how much trouble these villains have brought to *The Crier* and how much effort we've put into our hue and cry edition, it's only fair that if there is any story to be broken, we break it first."

"You publish on a Friday," Hennessy replied. "I'll agree not to publish my piece until Friday as well."

"Saturday," she shot back.

Drake was fast losing patience; he stirred, but it was Gray who stepped to the side of the desk and asked Hennessy, "Is your contract with *The Courier* exclusive?"

The question made Hennessy blink, then think. Eventually, he admitted, "It's not."

"In that case"—Gray glanced at Izzy in question—"why not write your story, under your byline, and publish it on the front page of *The Crier*?"

That was a viable suggestion—very viable. She immediately offered, "Usual rates with a ten percent bonus."

Gray added, "With all the extra distribution that will accrue to the sequel to *The Crier's* hue and cry edition, there should be more than enough copies sold for you to reap full glory. Indeed, if your story is published in *The Crier*, there'll be no competition at all. And of course, it never hurts to demonstrate to your present employer that you aren't entirely dependent on him."

Hennessy's brows had risen, then risen further during Gray's little speech. After a long moment staring at Gray, Hennessy looked at Izzy. "I assume you're I. Molyneaux, the owner?"

She nodded. "I am."

Hennessy hesitated, then asked, "Is that agreement acceptable to you? Including the usual rates plus ten percent?"

To have a reporter of Hennessy's caliber publish on the front page of *The Crier*... Taking care not to appear overeager, she nodded. "I'll accept those conditions." She arched a brow at him. "Do we have a deal?"

He sat forward and extended a meaty paw. "We do."

She shook his hand, then Drake rather caustically said, "Now we have the formalities dealt with, please enlighten us as to what you know of the gentlemen in question."

Despite the polite phrasing, that was a demand. Hennessy promptly said, "The taller man's name is Henry Mitchell Duvall, and he works as an undersecretary at the Board of Trade. He told me as much, and I confirmed it. He's too far down the pecking order to have access to the minister, Labouchere, but on the other hand, Duvall seems to know the ins and outs of various projects. Details not many people know."

"Go on," Drake directed.

Hennessy threw him a careful glance. "Duvall approached me—" He broke off and drew a notebook from his coat pocket, flipped it open, flicked through several pages, paused, read, then said, "Last Monday. At the Hound and Whistle—the pub I favor in Fleet Street." Hennessy looked at Drake and Gray. "Anyone with a story knows to find me there."

Gray and Drake nodded in understanding. Drake asked, "And did Duvall have a story to sell?"

"Not so much sell as give, in the hope of using me to get his story to the masses. He was offering information for free"—Hennessy glanced at Izzy—"and that always makes me suspicious. I wasn't sure I believed him, so I took the information, but I haven't done anything with it yet—well, until today."

Hennessy's expression hardened, and he spoke directly to Izzy. "What Duvall had to say boiled down to this. The materials that make up the telegraph cables the government is laying beneath the Channel to various countries on the Continent—for instance, the cable recently laid from

Dover to Calais—are highly unstable and dangerous. Much more dangerous than the government wants anyone to know." Hennessy glanced at the others. "The implication I was supposed to draw was that the telegraph station itself, where the cables are supposedly most exposed, constituted a very real danger to the populace at large."

Drake swore beneath his breath and tensed as if to leave, but Hennessy held up a hand. "Before you race off, there's more you might want to hear." Hennessy fixed Drake with a level look. "You're Winchelsea, aren't you?"

Tight-lipped, Drake nodded.

"Then you'll want to hear the rest." Hennessy looked at Izzy. "I hadn't done anything with Duvall's information because I didn't trust it, but when I read *The Crier* and saw that picture"—Hennessy nodded at the photograph of the scene outside the coffeehouse—"I thought I recognized the man Duvall was speaking with. So I spent this morning asking around, and it turns out that gent is a very dangerous character. Monsieur Henri Roccard, a Belgian, he's said to be—whispered to be—the principal London contact for several of the major crime families on the Continent. He's the man those families ask to arrange for any 'business' they want done in Britain to be carried out."

Hennessy glanced at Baines and Littlejohn, then looked at Drake. "My informants tell me the authorities have suspected Roccard of being behind several murders, but as the victims are usually criminals and he's always at a good distance from the crime, he's never been fingered for anything himself. Some of his men occasionally disappear, sent back to the other side of the Channel to be replaced by fresh faces."

Leaning forward, Hennessy peered at the photograph of Duvall and Roccard talking before the coffeehouse. "Putting together what I can see here with what Duvall told me, I'd say Duvall is taking his orders from Roccard." Hennessy glanced at Drake. "I've also heard that Duvall is hopeless at the tables and is very deep in debt."

Drake, Gray, and Izzy exchanged glances, then she said, "I assume we're all thinking that, operating under orders from Roccard, Duvall is planning to blow up the Dover telegraph station."

Tersely, Drake nodded. "Because the European crime families want to prevent the British authorities being able to exchange information virtually instantaneously with their counterparts on the Continent."

Hennessy's eyes had widened. "I hadn't heard about blowing anything up, but that makes sense. If the police on this side have a criminal fleeing in a boat to France, they can just telegraph to Calais, and the gendarmes will be waiting when the villain fetches up on the other side."

"Even more pertinent," Drake said, "is the interception of all sorts of smuggling and the traffic of villains and stolen goods both ways." He paused, then added, "The telegraph opened for business—at least official business—in mid-October. Over the past months, the police and other authorities have been actively using the service, exploring the possibilities. I understand they've disrupted several long-established schemes over recent weeks. And I can confirm several more undersea links are planned, connecting Britain with the Netherlands, Belgium, and Ireland."

"Well, there you are, then," Hennessy said. "None of the criminal fraternity are going to like that. It sounds like they're using Duvall as their means to strike at the telegraph and get things back to the way they were. From all I've gleaned, those at the head of the families are old and conservative—they don't like anything changing."

Drake nodded. "The telegraph threatens the crime families' futures, so they've devised a plan they hope will turn the population against the entire idea of the telegraph. You can imagine the mayhem." Drake dipped his head at Hennessy. "If they could get the likes of *The Courier* to push a story of how dangerous the telegraph is to life and limb, and then one of the stations blows up, we'll never get a working telegraph network within England, let alone across the sea."

Izzy straightened. "It'll be the Luddite uprisings all over again."

"Well, then." Baines tugged down his waistcoat. "I guess we'd better get along and have a word with this Mr. Duvall."

Drake met Gray's, then Izzy's eyes and grimaced. "Much as I'd like to have a chat with Duvall, my first priority has to be to report this in all the right quarters and ensure word is sent to Dover, warning them to be on guard." He paused, then added, "I'd better warn those building the official Dover telegraph station as well."

Hennessy frowned. "Isn't that—the official office—where the telegraph station in Dover is?"

Drake shook his head. "Not yet. They were in a hurry, so ran a line from where the cable makes landfall at South Foreland to the nearest suitable building they could lay their hands on. That happened to be a private residence at the southern end of Victoria Park Terrace."

Gray saw Donaldson—who, with Lipson, had until then stood silently and listened—shift and frown. The quality of that frown prompted Gray to ask, "What is it?"

Donaldson glanced at Gray, then looked at Drake. "I hail from Dover. The southern end of Victoria Park Terrace...are you saying that Duvall and his friend are planning to blow up a house that's more or less in the shadow of the Dover guns?"

Drake pulled an unusually expressive face. "That's how it looks, and you can imagine the chaos such an explosion will cause." His expression sobered, and he shook his head. "There's no help for it—I'll have to remain in town to ensure the necessary warnings are issued to all the right places." To Gray, he said, "I'll see who I can find and send them down to help keep an eye out in Dover, in case Duvall slips through our fingers here in town."

"But," Gray said, "what are the odds Duvall will have seen *The Crier* by now?"

"Indeed!" Izzy rose to her feet. "Will he run, do you think?"

"Or," Hennessy said, pushing out of the armchair, "will he attempt to carry out his mission before he runs? His target's in Dover, after all."

Drake softly swore. He stared unseeing at the desk for a moment, then said, "We can't take the risk of assuming he'll just run. In fact, we have to assume he's either on his way to Dover already—which means I have to get to Whitehall and get an immediate warning sent to the Dover tele-graph station—or he's rushing around in town, getting his explosives together before heading down. It depends on how advanced in his plan-ning he was. Our best-case scenario is that he hasn't read *The Crier* and is still in town, obliviously whiling away a normal Saturday."

Drake looked at Baines and Littlejohn. "Can I leave it to you to lay Duvall by the heels?"

Baines, Littlejohn, and everyone else—including Digby—grimly assured Drake he could.

"We've more than enough to take him up for Quimby's murder," Baines pointed out. "We'll get straight along to his house. It being Satur-day, if he hasn't taken flight already, most likely he'll be there, and we can ask him to come along with us to the Yard."

Drake nodded. "When you get him there—if you get him there—keep him there. If anyone makes noises about releasing him on any grounds whatsoever, refer them to me."

"Yes, m'lord."

Littlejohn had been leafing through his notebook. He raised his head. "Where does he live? Anyone know?"

They all looked at each other, then faintly exasperated, Drake said,

"Come with me. I have to go to Whitehall. We can stop in at the Board of Trade, and I'll persuade someone to tell us."

Drake made for the door, and everyone rushed to follow.

Gray saw Donaldson summon Digby with a jerk of his head and hurry out. Gray fetched his and Izzy's coats and her bonnet and helped her on with her coat before shrugging into his.

Her reticule dangling from her wrist, still tying her bonnet strings, she hurried into the foyer, where Drake was impatiently waiting. He saw them and turned to the door. "Let's go."

Drake held the door for Izzy and Gray and followed them out. Baines, Littlejohn, and Hennessy were on their heels as, with Drake and Izzy, Gray strode quickly down to Bernard Street.

A clatter of footsteps behind them had him glancing back to see Donaldson and Digby hurrying to catch up while carrying a tripod, camera, and canvas satchel.

Their procession reached Woburn Place, and between them, they hailed three hackneys. Drake, Izzy, and Gray crammed into the first, Baines and Littlejohn shared the second, while Hennessy went with Donaldson and Digby in the third.

With Izzy tucked snugly beside him, Gray spent the time to Whitehall reviewing all they'd learned. The more he thought, the more concerned he became. Had Duvall seen *The Crier*? So much depended on that. Ironic that the very publication that had brought them the information regarding Duvall might also alert him to impending exposure and push him into enacting his plan.

In Whitehall, Drake directed the jarvey to pull up at the curb outside one of the numerous government buildings. All three carriages halted, and everyone spilled out. Gray called to the jarveys to wait, and he and Izzy followed Drake into the building, which housed the Board of Trade.

Watching Drake wield his power among bureaucrats was a lesson in just how high in the pecking order he stood. In just a few minutes, he'd extracted Duvall's address from a clerk, along with the information that Duvall hadn't been rostered to work that day.

Drake turned to Gray and Izzy. Baines, Littlejohn, and the other three gathered around. "He lives in lodgings at Number sixteen, Adam Street. That's south of the Strand, within easy walking distance of Whitehall and also Fleet Street." Drake glanced round the circle of faces. "I'll have to leave it to you to hunt him down. My first port of call has to be the tele-graph office here, to send a warning to Dover. I'll then have to make the rounds, alerting others in Whitehall as to what's going on." He met Gray's eyes. "After that, I'll see who I can find at Arthur's and send them down to watch and wait at Dover."

Gray understood that meant that Drake would recruit some of the younger members of their set—Drake's brothers or Cynster cousins-in-law—who occasionally acted as his agents.

Apparently, Izzy understood that, too. "Excellent idea."

"We'd best get off, then, and find this blighter." Baines turned toward the street.

"Good luck!" Drake called as Gray, Izzy, and the other three followed Baines and Littlejohn down the long hall.

Without looking Drake's way, Gray waved. When they reached the entrance, he glanced back, but Drake had vanished.

Gray led Izzy down the steps and helped her into the lead hackney. "Adam Street," he called to the jarvey. "South off the Strand."

The jarvey saluted with his whip. As soon as Gray sat, the jarvey set his horse trotting, heading for Trafalgar Square.

CHAPTER 14

They congregated on the narrow pavement outside Number 16, Adam Street. Gray hung back with Izzy, Hennessy, Donaldson, and Digby as Baines, supported by Littlejohn, knocked on the door.

A middle-aged woman, gray-haired and neatly dressed in a rather severe gown, opened the door.

"Police, ma'am." Baines held up his badge. "We're looking for a Mr. Henry Duvall."

The woman looked surprised, but readily replied, "He's not here, Officer. He works at the Board of Trade, you know. He would have left this morning. I don't keep tabs on when my gentlemen come and go, but he often works on Saturday."

"Not today, ma'am. We've just come from his office."

"Oh. I see. Well, no doubt he's out and about with his friends, as you might expect of a man his age." She'd noticed the rest of their company lined up by the curb and was growing increasingly curious.

Baines's shoulders lowered, and he touched the brim of his hat. "Thank you, ma'am."

Gray and Izzy exchanged startled looks, then Gray stepped forward. "Inspector, as we are here and Duvall is not, it might be wise to search his rooms."

Baines's face cleared. He shook his head at himself. "Not used to chasing this sort of villain," he muttered, then turned to the landlady. "If we might trouble you to show us his room, ma'am, we'll just take a quick look."

The landlady hesitated, but now-rampant curiosity triumphed. "Yes, of course." She swung around. "Follow me."

Baines glanced at Hennessy, Donaldson, and Digby. "You lot better stay there."

Gray was a trifle surprised when all three readily agreed. He trailed Izzy as she followed Baines and Littlejohn up a narrow stair to the first floor. One of four small apartments, Duvall's domain filled the front right corner.

The landlady unlocked the door and stood back. "You don't need me, do you?"

Baines assured her they could manage without her, and once the four of them had filed into the room, she quickly went back down the stairs.

They spread through the two rooms—a small sitting room with an even smaller bedroom off it, with a bathing alcove in one curtained-off corner. Littlejohn followed Izzy into the bedroom, while Baines went straight to the desk against the front wall.

Gray spotted the notices and invitations on the mantelpiece above the small grate. He quickly looked through them, but found nothing of interest.

He looked around, but the sparse furniture held little prospect of any useful, hidden information. He glanced out of the window and saw Hennessy, below, notebook in hand, chatting avidly to the landlady. Donaldson and Digby were across the street, setting up to take the woman's photograph before the door of her house.

Gray couldn't help but smile. Clearly, Hennessy wasn't one to miss an opportunity to collect background color for his story.

Izzy and Littlejohn reappeared. "Nothing noteworthy in the bedroom," Littlejohn reported.

"Except," Izzy said, "for the quality of his clothes, which is rather remarkable for a lowly undersecretary."

Bending over the desk drawer, Baines huffed. "That fits with what's here—nothing but tailor's bills. Startling amounts, too."

Gray frowned. "Let me see."

Baines held out a stack of rumpled papers.

Gray took them and quickly scanned them.

Izzy came to stand by his shoulder.

He handed the stack to her. "If these are any indication, he was definitely living well beyond his means, especially for one who, according to Hennessy, is deep in debt."

Baines sniffed. "If he's being paid by foreigners, we're unlikely to be able to trace it."

Izzy handed the bills back, and Gray crossed to the desk and dropped them back in the drawer, which Baines had left open.

Looking down, Gray shut the drawer and froze.

Izzy noticed. "What is it?"

He stooped, reached into the wastepaper basket beneath the desk, and drew out five pieces of torn paper. He straightened and turned them over in his hands, aligning the pieces, which were from two separate wrappers. Face hardening, he looked at Baines and handed him the pieces. "One is a wrapper from a largish packet of black powder. The other is from a packet of blasting fuse."

Baines and Littlejohn confirmed that.

Littlejohn raised his head. "So he has his explosives?"

Grimly, Gray nodded. "Ready to go." He started for the door, and Izzy followed. "I think," he said, "we should assume that Duvall has seen *The Crier* and taken himself to Dover to complete his mission before anyone —like Winchelsea—can stop him."

Baines and Littlejohn clattered down the stairs behind them. "The landlady said Duvall left this morning. He might already be there."

"Or," Izzy said as she followed Gray out of the front door, "he might have gone somewhere else first and still be in town. We just don't know."

With the Strand so close, they hadn't kept the hackneys. Gray nodded to the landlady and, with Izzy, walked a little way along the street, then they stopped and waited for the others to catch up.

Baines and Littlejohn joined them, then Hennessy, Donaldson and Digby, having taken their leave of the landlady, came hurrying up.

"Anything?" Hennessy asked.

Gray explained what they'd found. "We need to decide what we should do next—what would be best for us to do next."

"Drake—Winchelsea—will already have warned the Dover telegraph station," Izzy pointed out, "so they'll be on their guard, which, at this point, is the best we can do at that end."

Gray nodded and met Baines's eyes. "It's Duvall we need to catch— now more than ever. Given he's carrying around the wherewithal to demolish a small building, if there's any hope of catching him before he lights the fuse, we have to seize it."

Baines and Littlejohn agreed.

"At this moment," Baines said, "we don't know if he's already left for Dover." He looked at Gray and Izzy. "He wouldn't have taken the coach, would he?"

"I can't imagine why he would," Gray said, "given the train is so much more convenient. And he isn't wealthy enough to keep horses in town and is unlikely to hire a carriage and drive down, either."

"Right, then." Baines nodded with decision. "The first thing we need to learn is whether he's already gone down on the train or if, for some reason, he's still lurking in town."

"The terminus for the Dover train is London Bridge," Littlejohn supplied.

"Let's go there and ask." Gray grasped Izzy's hand and turned toward the Strand. "Once we know where he is—down there or up here—we can decide what our next move should be."

Their hackneys drew up outside the front door of the South Eastern Railway terminus, on the south bank of the Thames just east of London Bridge.

During the short ride, the members of their party had, apparently, become infected with a sense of urgency; they all but fell out of the carriages in their haste to learn whether Duvall had left London.

Her hand in Gray's, Izzy remained beside him as they pushed through the front doors.

He looked around, then pointed to their left. "Over there."

A sign identified the booking office, and their company descended on one of the two manned windows.

Izzy dove into her reticule, pulled out the photograph showing Duvall, and thrust it at Baines. "Here—ask if they've seen him."

Baines seized the photograph, fronted the counter, and after identifying himself and Littlejohn, stated, "We're hot on the track of a felon."

His rank and that opening had the men in the ticket office gathering on the other side of the window.

Baines held up the photograph and pointed out Duvall. "This gentleman here." He handed over the photograph. "Have any of you seen him over the past hours—say from ten o'clock onward? He would have been wanting to take the train to Dover."

Hennessy, who'd hung back, scanning the overhead sign listing the trains, called, "There was a train at nine-thirty, another at eleven-thirty, and one about to leave at one-thirty."

The five men in the booking office passed the photograph around, and the youngest said, "Oh aye. I remember him."

"What train did he leave on?" Baines reached beneath the grille and beckoned to have the photograph returned.

The clerk came to the window and handed the photograph over. "Well, he hasn't left yet. He bought a ticket for the one-thirty to Dover about half an hour ago." The clerk squinted up at the sign, with its large clock on one end. "Daresay he'll be on board by now—that train's due to pull out in another three minutes."

Baines's expression cleared. "You have to stop that train."

The clerks looked shocked.

"Stop it?" the youngest parroted.

"We can't do that, mate," the eldest said. "Worth our jobs, it'd be, messing with the schedule."

"But it's vital we capture him!" Baines insisted. "You have to at least hold the train and let us nab him."

"Don't know about that, sir—Inspector," the eldest said, with the other four nodding seriously. "Not something we can do, is it?"

Fixated on stopping the train, Baines, joined by Littlejohn, continued to plead their case.

Izzy cast a startled glance at Gray, caught his eyes, and looked at the clock.

Gray nodded and moved with her to the other window.

He attracted the attention of one of the clerks and promptly asked for seven tickets for the Dover train about to depart.

The clerk reeled them off, took Gray's money, and handed over the tickets.

With Gray, Izzy turned.

Baines was red-faced and close to shouting.

Hennessy, Donaldson, and Digby had seen what Gray and Izzy were about and had collected themselves and their equipment and started for the platform.

Gray tore off four tickets and thrust them at Izzy. "Go with the others. We'll catch up."

She took the tickets and went. In her skirts, she couldn't run as fast as the men could.

Following the others, before she rounded the corner, she glanced back and saw Gray grab Baines's shoulder and haul him away from the window, waving the tickets in his face. "Leave it—we'll have to catch the train and pick him up in Dover."

Izzy heard the first warning toot and, picking up her skirts, ran flat out after the other three.

From behind, she heard one of the clerks helpfully sing out, "It's Platform C you want."

Izzy was close behind Hennessy, Donaldson, and Digby when the three ran onto the platform.

"All aboard for Dover!" came the stentorian bellow from the guard at the very rear of the train.

Digby, in the lead, leapt up, caught the lever handle of the door at the end of the last carriage, dragged it down, and swung the door wide.

Puffing, Hennessy nodded at Digby and staggered up the iron ladder, then turned to take the heavy camera Donaldson held up. Hands freed, Donaldson turned to help Izzy up the steps, then grabbed the tripod Digby had been carting and leapt up after her.

The train whistle sounded—one long piercing blast.

"Come on, Digby," Donaldson urged.

"The others are coming—I can see them," Digby reported. Then he looked up and explained, "The conductors can't let a train start if there's a door open."

"Clever boy," Izzy remarked and made her way into the carriage.

Seconds later, Gray arrived, followed by Baines, huffing and puffing and all but pushed up the steps by Littlejohn. Digby nimbly hopped on board and slammed the door after him, just as an irate conductor came running up.

Scowling, the conductor checked the door was shut, then turned toward the front of the train and bellowed, "Stand clear!" With that, he put a whistle to his lips and blew a long, shrill note, then waved a green flag out to his side.

The train gave one last long whistle, then jerked into motion.

Those still standing caught themselves, then as the carriage settled to a steady rattling roll, made their way to where Izzy had slid onto one of the bench seats facing forward. It was a second-class carriage, so had no compartments, but the other passengers in that carriage were seated closer to the other end, sufficiently far away to allow their party to converse in reasonable privacy.

Gray sat beside Izzy, and Baines and Littlejohn slid onto the bench seat opposite. Hennessy had claimed the seat on the other side of the aisle to Gray, while Donaldson and Digby piled their bag and equipment on the seat beside Hennessy, then sat on the bench seat opposite.

For several minutes, they all simply sat and caught their breaths.

Baines eventually looked around their group. "Anyone know the stops?"

Donaldson replied, "Mertsham first, then the track veers to the east and it's Tonbridge, Ashford, and Folkestone, before we get to Dover."

Izzy smiled at her new photographer. "Having you hail from Dover is going to be useful when we get to the other end."

Donaldson smiled back.

They sat in silence for some time, each, no doubt, busy with their thoughts.

After a while, Izzy's mind caught up with events enough for her to raise her head and peer down the carriage, checking who was there. No gentleman of Duvall's height or coloring was among the dozen or so people sharing the carriage.

Then Baines cleared his throat. "Seeing our man is supposedly on this train, should we search the carriages? Use each stop to search through a few, moving forward toward the front of the train?"

From his expression, it was clear he wasn't enamored of the idea but had felt he had to air it.

Izzy shook her head. "I'm not at all sure that would be a good idea."

"We know he's carrying explosives," Gray pointed out. "We know he's had the black powder and fuse with him for several hours before he got on the train. We have to assume he's set up powder and fuse in such a way that igniting the fuse and detonating his bomb will be easy." Gray caught Baines's gaze. "If we corner him, or even if he sees us coming, who can tell what he might do?"

Everyone remained silent as the possibilities sank in.

"He'll most likely be in a first-class carriage," Izzy observed. "There'll be others there as well—ladies, gentlemen, even children, and all of the sort the authorities would especially not wish to see harmed."

Littlejohn nodded. "I agree. Sounds like our best bet will be to follow him once he leaves the train in Dover. At least we know he's on the train and not already down there, blowing the telegraph station sky-high."

That was met by nods all around, including from Baines.

"We can follow him and choose our moment," Gray said. "Preferably once he's away from the center of the town." He glanced at Donaldson. "You said the telegraph station was in the shadow of the castle's guns. I'm assuming that means on the edge of the town."

Donaldson nodded. "That's the last house, really, before Castle Hill Road turns up the hill toward the castle gates."

Hennessy looked at Gray. "Do you have any idea how much damage the stuff Duvall is carrying might cause?"

Gray appeared to mentally calculate, then said, "I can't, of course, be sure, but depending on the size of the house, it'll almost certainly cause extensive damage. Possibly not enough to bring down the walls or roof, but enough to destroy most of the interior."

Hennessy grunted. "So enough for Duvall's—and Roccard's and his masters'—purposes."

Gray leaned back against the seat. "If Roccard and his masters' aim is to cause chaos and sow public panic and distrust of the telegraph..." Grimly, Gray nodded. "More than enough."

Izzy faced forward and pondered that as their company settled, and the train rattled and rocked toward Dover.

When the train pulled into Dover Town Station, by general agreement, Gray descended first, handed Izzy down, and arm in arm, they started walking briskly along the platform as if they were a couple returning from a quick visit to London and had somewhere else to be. As Duvall hadn't seen either of them before, they'd been delegated to follow him most closely.

Izzy scanned the passengers ahead of them. "At least we know he didn't get off the train earlier."

At every stop, Donaldson, his face another Duvall hadn't previously seen, had hung out of the open doorway of their carriage and watched the travelers who'd left the train, confirming that Duvall hadn't done so.

Gray searched the hordes streaming toward the gates. "I wish we knew in which carriage he was traveling."

"There he is." Izzy slowed. "Climbing down from that first-class carriage ahead, behind the lady in the pink bonnet."

The pink bonnet was easy to spot, and sure enough, Duvall stepped down to the platform just behind it. "And," Gray observed, "he's carrying a decent-sized briefcase. I think we can be sure what's in it."

They slowed, tacked, and settled to follow Duvall at a distance of ten or so yards, with several other people between them. Due to his height and his hat, he was easy to track.

Walking confidently, he headed directly up the platform to the exit to the town. Not once did he glance even briefly around; apparently, it hadn't occurred to him that he might be followed.

Gray glanced back and confirmed that the others were coming along, but keeping their distance. Duvall would definitely recognize Hennessy, possibly Digby, and might even identify Baines and Littlejohn as policemen. There was something about their profession that marked them; most Londoners would know them on sight.

Facing forward, Gray steered Izzy into the thickening throng as the disembarking passengers funneled through the open gates onto the station concourse. Once past the constriction, they followed Duvall in turning away from the row of waiting hackneys and joining the stream of passengers walking up Clarence Place, toward the intersection with Snargate and the road to the town center.

By then, Gray and Izzy were more than ten yards behind Duvall with quite a crowd in between. As the line stretched out, Gray spotted Martin Cynster ahead, also behind Duvall. Walking beside Martin was another tall gentleman who, by his features, was also a Cynster.

The Cynster pair were striding along, chatting easily, apparently unaware Duvall was only a few yards ahead of them.

Did they know? Gray thought not.

He lengthened his pace; instinctively, Izzy matched his stride.

He felt her glance at him. Briefly, he met her gaze. "Those two gentlemen a few yards behind Duvall—can you see them?"

She had to weave slightly to see past others, then said, "One is Toby Cynster, and the other looks like another Cynster, but strangely, not one I know."

"He's Martin Cynster—the man whose fortune you were intending to expose."

"Ah." She studied the pair, now drawing nearer as Gray tacked around the intervening people. "He looks younger than I expected."

"He's twenty-four, and if his companion is Toby Cynster—who I understand is one of Drake's occasional helpers—I think we can assume they've been sent by Drake to keep watch for Duvall."

Izzy considered the duo, now four yards ahead. "I don't think they know Duvall is just ahead of them."

"No. Drake didn't take a photograph, so he could have given them only a verbal description, and Duvall is wearing a hat." He considered, then said, "Play along."

He raised his voice and called, "Martin!" When, surprised, Martin glanced around, Gray smiled affably, but caught Martin's gaze and held it. "Fancy running into you down here."

Drake would have told Martin and Toby about those pursuing Duvall. Gray angled Izzy to the side of the path, out of the stream of people heading for the town.

Martin's face cleared, and he smiled. "Lord Child!" He tugged Toby's sleeve, and the pair stepped to the side, halted, and waited for Gray and Izzy to join them.

As they neared, Martin gestured to Toby. "Allow me to present my cousin, Toby Cynster."

Halting before the pair, Izzy nodded to Toby and extended her hand to Martin. "Lady Isadora Descartes."

While Martin bowed over her hand, Gray held out his to Toby. "Grayson Child."

His easy expression belied by the active intelligence in his hazel eyes, Toby shook hands. "A pleasure, my lord. I've heard you've been sighted around town recently." He inclined his head to Izzy. "Both of you."

That seemed to confirm that Drake had filled the pair in. "Indeed." Gray kept his expression mild and engaging. Lowering his voice, he said, "We weren't sure if you were aware that the man ahead of you, the one with the black hat, was the gentleman you've been sent here to hunt."

"He is?" Toby tensed, but stopped himself from glancing around. "He's down here already?"

Martin glanced sidelong. "The man with the case?"

"Indeed." Izzy smiled as if they were exchanging pleasantries. "That's him, and we believe we can guess what's inside the case."

"Namely, explosives," Gray said.

"Ah." Toby's expression blanked, and Martin suddenly looked grave.

Gray had continued to track Duvall, who was walking steadily on in a manner guaranteed to attract no attention.

To the Cynster pair, Izzy brightly said, "Come, walk with us. We can go into the town together." She retook Gray's arm and waved ahead.

Martin and Toby turned to flank Gray and Izzy, and as a foursome, they strolled on in apparently relaxed fashion.

Duvall was now farther ahead, yet with the intervening pedestrians thinning as many hurried on or turned aside to their homes, there was no risk of losing sight of him and, therefore, no reason to close the distance. Not yet.

Gray glanced back and confirmed the others were trailing some yards behind. Unless Duvall had a sudden attack of suspicion and stopped and scanned carefully behind him, he wasn't likely to spot them.

Duvall continued striding along, his pace confident and sure.

Gray said, "There's a group trailing us, about six yards back. Two policemen and three staff from *The Crier*."

Toby and Martin glanced idly back, then faced forward again. "Good-oh," Toby said. "That means we won't have any trouble arresting the blighter and putting him in cuffs."

Izzy smiled. "Just so."

They were well along Snargate and could see the buildings of the town's center ahead.

"So when and how are we going to nab him?" Martin asked.

"Given he's got that case with him," Toby mused, "we're going to have to pick our time."

"It can't be while he's close to other people," Izzy pointed out.

Martin asked, "Do you think he's got the powder rigged to ignite?"

"We have to assume he has," Gray replied. "He had more than enough time to do that before he left his lodgings."

Toby nodded. "I agree. We can't take the chance he'll do something stupid and end up harming a lot of others."

Gray had been studying Duvall. "He really is utterly oblivious. Let's take the chance and get the others to join us. We need Baines and Little-john's input for whatever plan we devise."

Martin, Toby, and Izzy agreed, and Gray turned and beckoned the others forward.

The five rapidly closed the distance.

While they continued strolling in an expanded group, after the briefest of introductions, Gray explained the limitations they faced in capturing Duvall.

"How long do you think that fuse he has might last for?" Littlejohn asked. "A minute? Two? Or less than half a minute?"

"That depends on what type of fuse he's used..." Gray turned to Baines. "You have the wrapper, I think."

Baines dug in his pockets and produced the torn pieces of the packet that had contained the fuse. Gray pieced the scraps together, read the information, calculated, then said, "Assuming he has four inches of fuse leading into the briefcase, then the time from ignition to detonation should be in the order of two to three minutes. Definitely not more."

"So," Toby said, still walking at an easy pace, "just enough time to light the fuse and scarper."

Gray nodded. "That's likely his plan." After a moment, he glanced at Donaldson. "Donaldson, you know the town best. Assuming he's making his way directly to the telegraph station, where en route is he going to be farthest from any crowds?"

Donaldson grimaced. "That depends on which route he takes. Once he reaches the end of Snargate, there are several ways he might go, but if he sticks with the general flow of people, he'll most likely go up to Castle Street and follow it east. That will lead him directly to the bottom of Castle Hill Road. Once he starts up that—as he must given the telegraph station is about halfway up, around the first bend—that's where there's unlikely to be many others about."

Gray glanced at the others. "It sounds as if the best moment to pounce will be once he's on Castle Hill Road."

Agreement showed on most faces. No one argued.

"Right, then." Baines nodded at Duvall, striding on ahead of them. "Let's keep trailing him and see how the land lies farther on."

They broke into smaller groups again, strung out along the pavement. Martin and Toby went ahead, two young gentlemen out to enjoy the day. Gray and Izzy followed a few yards behind, arm in arm, a couple making their way somewhere. Hennessy, Donaldson, and Digby chatted about photography as they followed, while Baines and Littlejohn brought up the rear.

Duvall reached the end of Snargate and strode ahead into Townwall Street, but then stopped and paused as if weighing his options. After a second's dithering, he turned left, along with most of the other pedestrians.

Their company followed. Izzy and Gray remained on the same side of the street as Duvall, with Baines and Littlejohn trailing them. Toby and Martin crossed to the other side of the street, with Hennessy, Donaldson, and Digby keeping farther back on that side.

The street curved to the right, then straightened and opened into a central marketplace. Instead of continuing into the square, Duvall veered right, into a street lined with shops—the Castle Street that Donaldson had mentioned.

It was midafternoon, and there were plenty of shoppers about, providing cover enough to allow their company to congregate again.

Sauntering along ten yards behind Duvall, Toby said, "We need to work out how, exactly, to capture him, and it's occurred to me that it's not illegal to walk around with a case full of gunpowder, even one with a fuse attached." He glanced at Baines. "Is it?"

Baines's sour expression was answer enough. "Much as we might wish it, no, it's not."

"But," Littlejohn said, "surely we can take him up on suspicion and stop him from blowing up the telegraph station—or anything else."

Baines snorted. "Simply pounce on him and haul him off? Once we get him to the station and he insists on hearing the charge, we won't have anything, and he'll just leave. And then he'll catch the first boat to Calais, and we won't be able to stop him doing that, either."

"True," Toby said. "And none of that will satisfy Winchelsea or his masters. If you try to take him up, Duvall is clever enough to keep his mouth shut, and then you'll have to release him, and nothing will have been gained other than a delay. Roccard will keep trying, if not via Duvall, then with someone else—someone else whom we might not learn about in time."

Hennessy looked at Baines. "Can't you arrest Duvall for Quimby's murder?"

Littlejohn nodded and appealed to Baines. "Surely we can do that?"

Baines met Toby's eyes and grimaced. "The evidence is circumstantial. Digby saw Duvall in the lane, and he was in one of Quimby's photographs. So what? Others heard him speaking with Roccard, who I'm guessing parades around as a wealthy foreign businessman." He glanced at Hennessy. "Am I right?"

It was Hennessy's turn to grimace. "From what I've gathered."

"So all Duvall has to do is say they were just making up a story or talking about some place in Belgium." Baines shook his head. "It won't stick."

A glum silence fell, then Gray said, "Regardless of how we feel about Quimby's murder or anything else, we have to focus on the critical element here, and that's exposing the plot against the telegraph."

Izzy saw the light. "Of course. Exposing the plot to blow up the telegraph will alert the public that any such attempt to make the telegraph seem dangerous or to blow up stations is the work of foreign criminals trying to hoodwink the British public into believing the telegraph is dangerous." She looked at Gray, Toby, and Martin. "That's it, isn't it? What's really at stake here?"

All three nodded.

Baines grunted and looked at Duvall, who was still confidently striding on ahead of them. "So we have to make this stick. We have to not only seize him but also make sure we have irrefutable evidence of what he's planning to do."

"That's our challenge," Toby confirmed.

"So," Martin asked, "how are we going to meet it?"

They walked on for several paces, still close enough to talk, then Baines reluctantly said, "As far as I can see, our only option is to allow the blighter to walk into the telegraph station with that bomb and try to light the fuse."

Toby slowly nodded. "I can't say you're wrong. And the telegraph stationmaster was warned by Winchelsea, so they should be on the lookout."

Grim-faced, Martin muttered what they were all thinking. "There has to be a better way."

They wracked their brains as they walked along, trailing Duvall.

When they saw the end of Castle Street ahead and, beyond the next intersection, the rising grade of Castle Hill Road leading up and away to the right, Toby said, "He's heading straight to the telegraph station." He glanced at the group. "Time's up. We need a plan, and we need to agree to it now."

"There's no help for it," Baines glumly said. "We're going to have to allow the devil to go in with his bomb. But we'll need to be right on his heels and grab him before he can actually light the fuse."

Reluctantly, everyone agreed, and in short order, they devised their plan.

Gray and Izzy stepped ahead. They would shadow Duvall most closely and narrow the distance even further as he neared the telegraph station.

Baines and Littlejohn followed Gray and Izzy. Once Duvall rounded the bend in Castle Hill Road and could no longer see the policemen, they would hurry to catch up. From memory, Donaldson estimated the distance from the point of the bend to the telegraph station to be twenty-five to thirty yards. The instant Duvall went through the station's door, Gray would return to the corner and signal the policemen to start running.

Meanwhile, Martin and Toby would approach the telegraph station from the other end of Victoria Park Terrace. Toby had picked up a map of Dover at London Bridge Station, and during the train journey, he and Martin had memorized the various ways to reach the telegraph station. Their aim was to be approaching the house from the other direction or idling outside it as Duvall neared. Donaldson confirmed their idea was sound.

Gray and Izzy crossed the intersection and started up Castle Hill Road in Duvall's wake. Toby and Martin were close behind, but a few yards along, peeled left and started up Laureston Place, which would lead them to the lower end of Victoria Park Terrace. Their way would be more than twice as long; as with Izzy on his arm, Gray paced the narrow pavement bordering Castle Hill Road, distantly, he heard the younger men running.

Duvall toiled steadily up the sharply rising street. While his obliviousness seemed remarkable, in actual fact, behaving as he was and not looking around was exactly the right way to avoid notice. He appeared to be a man who knew where he was going and nothing more—entirely unsuspicious.

As they gained altitude, Gray looked out over Dover harbor, extending his survey to glance behind. In an undertone, he reported to Izzy, "Baines and Littlejohn are three yards behind us, and the others are close behind them."

She smiled up at him as if he'd made some witty comment. "Let's close the distance. That hairpin bend ahead looks steep. We don't want him getting too far ahead."

He nodded. She was right. Duvall was managing the steepness with ease; the same couldn't be said of Baines.

They'd agreed that Toby, Martin, Baines, and Littlejohn, in whatever order, would rush into the station as soon as possible after Duvall, hopefully catching him in the act of lighting a match with his bomb at his feet and preventing him from setting it off. Presumably, the telegraph staff, having been alerted by Drake, would assist in that endeavor. Gray, Izzy, Donaldson, Hennessy, and Digby would remain outside, out of the way.

The timing would be tight, but given how long it took to withdraw a box of lucifers from a pocket, open the box, take one out, strike it, then urge a fuse to catch alight, they should have enough time to stop Duvall from actually igniting the fuse.

Even if the fuse was lit, it could be pulled out as long as they were quick.

Leaning on Gray's arm, Izzy hurried a few steps to keep up with Gray's longer strides.

Duvall was just rounding the sharply rising curve to the left and, for that moment, was able to look down on them, and the action caught his eye.

Izzy laughed and, on Gray's arm, leaned close. "I'm so excited about visiting Felix at the castle. It's been such an age since I saw him."

Gray closed his hand over hers on his sleeve and smiled benignly at her. "I'm sure your brother will be equally happy to see you."

The pavement looped almost back on itself, just significantly higher; on it, above them, Duvall was close enough to hear. He promptly lost interest and continued steadily onward.

Thanking the heavens Duvall hadn't noticed Baines and Littlejohn, who had fallen back as they toiled upward in her and Gray's wake, Izzy forged on even more quickly.

She and Gray rounded the sharp curve, and the telegraph station came into sight, about thirty yards away. The building faced Victoria Park Terrace, and due to the upward angle of Castle Hill Road and the downward curve of the terrace, they couldn't see the building's front door.

They hurried on, and the front of the station came into full view.

Abruptly, they halted, faced with a complication they hadn't foreseen.

With his back to them, Duvall stood holding the telegraph station door for a well-dressed lady clasping the hand of a little girl in pigtails, who was clutching a doll.

His briefcase in his other hand, Duvall inclined his head genially as the lady thanked him and ushered her daughter inside.

"Oh no!" Izzy whispered. "He wouldn't, would he?"

Gray softly swore. "He would—nothing could be better for their scheme."

She was the owner of *The Crier*; she could see the front pages.

Duvall started to follow the woman and girl inside.

Gray whirled and raced back to urge Baines and Littlejohn to run.

Still frozen, staring, Izzy glimpsed a flicker of orange-red near Duvall's chin as he stepped inside and finally recognized what scent had been teasing her senses over the last seconds. "A cheroot."

Duvall had a lighted cheroot clamped between his lips; he must have lit it during the short time he'd been out of their sight as they rounded the curve.

Izzy jettisoned the plan and ran for the telegraph station's door.

She glimpsed Toby and Martin racing up the steeply sloping street; they were too far away to help.

Duvall wouldn't need any time to pull out a box of lucifers and strike one; he was going to hold the lighted cheroot directly to the end of the fuse.

Izzy opened the door, rushed along a narrow vestibule, and pulled up just inside the telegraph chamber.

Time suspended.

Wide-eyed, she took in the counter that ran across the room. Standing before it, to the right, the lady was chatting with one of the telegraph staff. The little girl was leaning against her mother's legs, clutching her doll to her chest.

The girl's eyes were fixed on Duvall, who had apparently sent the other telegraph assistant to fetch something while he bent down and held the burning tip of his cheroot to the end of a short piece of fuse dangling from the top of the briefcase.

The fuse fizzed to life.

Duvall straightened and walked toward the exit, which lay beyond Izzy.

He neared, but she'd lost all interest in him. With a whispered "No," she dashed around him.

Behind her, Gray called her name, then said, "Oh no, you don't."

She swooped on the case, hefted it in her arms, and whirled to see Gray grappling with Duvall.

The woman seized the little girl and, horrified, backed away along the counter.

The assistants were yelling, but Izzy barely heard them.

Outside, outside! Get it outside!

The case in her arms, she raced for the door.

Before she reached the vestibule, the door burst open. She skidded to a halt against the wall beside the vestibule's archway as Baines and Littlejohn thundered past.

The instant her way was clear, she bolted for the open door, through the doorway, and onto the short path before the station's door.

Directly before her stood Hennessy, alongside Donaldson, who was already under his camera's hood with Digby beside him.

She spun away, saw the path leading around the side of the station, and took it.

She rounded the corner of the building, ran down its side, and found herself facing steep stone steps leading to the street—the open and deserted street—which lay higher than head height above.

Ignoring her burning lungs, she hauled in a breath, tucked the case awkwardly beneath one arm, seized her skirts with her free hand, and toiled up the steps as fast as she could.

~

Gray raced out of the station. "Izzy!"

He'd seen her rush out with the case, mere inches of furiously fizzing fuse dangling beside the handle. Desperate, he looked wildly around, saw Hennessy, Donaldson, and Digby gaping at a point to the side of the station, and raced in that direction.

Rounding the corner of the building, he glimpsed Izzy's dark skirts ahead and redoubled his efforts.

He raced into the rear courtyard, saw the steep steps, and flung himself up them.

Glancing up, he saw Izzy standing by the side of the street, the case clutched against her as she tried—vainly—to pinch out the fuse with her gloved fingers.

He leapt up the last steps, seized the case, hefted it like a discus, and flung it high—over the road toward the treed bank on the other side.

"Get down!" He flung himself at her. She dropped to her knees and hunched over, and he draped his body over hers.

The briefcase exploded.

High above the road.

The detonation was as percussive as any bomb, but the force of the blast went upward and outward, and only a rush of displaced air washed over them, raking at his hair and tugging at her skirts.

Smothered by Gray's solid bulk, Izzy could barely breathe. Her ears rang, but regardless, she wouldn't have heard anything over the still-frantic pounding of her heart.

In the split second during which she'd realized the fuse had burned too far into the case for her to snuff it out, she'd stared death in the face.

And understood how much—how very much—she wanted to live.

And why.

Then the reason had arrived and saved her.

Saved them.

She could barely believe she was still alive, and that he was, too.

Slowly, he uncoiled from his protective shell, ending on his knees, and she followed suit.

Whump!

They both jumped as the remnants of the briefcase landed in the middle of the street.

Then several branches and twigs from the overhanging trees rained down.

Her hearing must have been affected; their immediate surrounds seemed preternaturally quiet. There was a commotion somewhere, but it was distant and muted.

After looking around, Gray grasped her hand, got slowly to his feet, and helped her up.

She dragged in a breath and turned to him. "You saved me."

Gray had been staring dazedly around, but her comment jolted his wits into place. He turned an incredulous look on the love of his life, the holder of his heart; that she was that and more was indisputable. "You ran off carrying a live bomb."

He heard the words, even understood them, but a large part of his brain refused to believe them.

He stared at her, then glanced upward and flung out his arms. "I don't know what to say."

His instincts knew what to do.

He seized her, hauled her to him, and kissed her—voraciously, desperately.

Needfully.

She clutched and kissed him back with equal fervor. With an equally urgent desperate determination to cling to the other and never let go.

Relief, hunger, and an immensely powerful joy snared them. They'd nearly died, but they'd survived, and each knew, incontrovertibly, that for them, above all, the source of that joy would forever be their touchstone.

The only thing that truly mattered.

They could face near-insurmountable challenges—and both had—but this, being together, living together, was the essential necessity they would fight to keep, to defend.

A clattering of boots forced them to end the kiss.

Their gazes met and held for an instant, then they turned to Martin and Toby as the pair came up the steps two at a time.

Seeing them standing, patently unhurt, the duo deflated in relief and bent to catch their breaths.

Toby gasped, "Thank God you're all right."

Straightening, Martin looked at Izzy and Gray and shook his head in amazement. "That was the most heroic action I've ever witnessed."

Izzy glanced sidelong at Gray. "I could hardly leave the bomb there, not with a little girl and her mother standing beside it."

Gray shook his head in defeat rather than censure. "I understand why you did it, but I still can't…"

He shook his head again. He couldn't even explain what he meant. What he felt.

Instead, he looked at Martin and Toby. "Duvall?"

"Caught," Toby reported. "Eventually."

Martin grimaced. "We'd misjudged and were too far back when the action started, but as it turned out, that was just as well. Believe it or not, Duvall wrestled free of Baines and Littlejohn and the two assistants who tried to help and raced out of the station, dodged Hennessy and Digby, and ran down the street—"

"Straight into our arms." Toby grinned. "Trust me, it was worth every second to see his face in the instant before Martin slugged him."

Also grinning at the memory, Martin tipped his head toward the front of the station. "Baines came huffing up and slapped handcuffs on him, and Littlejohn has him in hand. As you might imagine, neither are in the mood to be gentle."

"Ho! You there! Stand where you are and put up your hands!"

"What the devil?" Gray turned and, with the others, watched as a company of soldiers, led by their captain and with bayonets at the ready, came rushing down from the side street that led up to one of the castle's gates.

A barked "Hold hard!" came from the opposite end of the street, and they swiveled to see another company, likewise armed, coming up at the run from below the point of the hairpin bend, presumably from the nearby battery.

Gray heard Izzy sigh, then she stepped into the street, clear of him, Martin, and Toby, planted her hands on her hips, and directed a quelling look at first one captain, then the other, then in the refined tones of an earl's daughter, announced, "We four are here at the behest of the Marquess of Winchelsea. Who the devil are you?"

She'd said the magic name. Both captains abruptly halted, and their companies did the same.

Commandingly, Izzy looked from one captain to the other. "Well?"

Very few gentlemen were immune to that tone. The captain from the castle cleared his throat and volunteered, "Captain Sinclair, ma'am."

She glanced the other way, and the captain from the battery came to attention and saluted. "Captain Herries, ma'am."

Sinclair glanced toward the telegraph station. "We—ah—received orders from the marquess to secure the telegraph station, ma'am. We were just on our way to do so when the explosion occurred."

"I see." Izzy swung to face the hapless Sinclair. She folded her arms; Gray couldn't see it beneath her hems, but he thought it very likely she was tapping her toe. "And when, exactly, did you receive those orders, Captain?"

Sinclair colored like a schoolboy, then suddenly paled. He swallowed and replied, "A few hours ago, ma'am."

Izzy extended one arm and pointed imperiously at the remnants of Duvall's bomb. "That, Captain, was what you and your men were supposed to guard against. The next time you receive an order from Winchelsea, I would advise you to jump to it!"

"Yes, ma'am."

"And it isn't 'ma'am,' it's 'my lady.'"

"Yes, my lady."

She looked at Herries. "As you can see, Captain, all is in hand. You may withdraw."

"Very good, my lady." With patent relief, Herries turned to his men, and they retreated in good order.

Izzy refocused—censoriously—on Sinclair. "As you're too late to do anything else, Captain, you and your men can tidy up this mess." She flicked her fingers at the debris from the briefcase and the trees.

With that, she rejoined Gray, Toby, and Martin, who had remained silent observers throughout.

Trying valiantly to smother a grin, Gray arched his brows at her. "Feeling better?"

She nodded. "Much." She looked down at the telegraph station. "I suppose we'd better go and see what's happening down there."

Gray took her hand and assisted her down the steep steps, for which she was grateful. Delayed shock was setting in, and she wasn't, in truth, all that steady on her feet.

They walked around to the front of the station to find Baines and Littlejohn standing over their prisoner, who was sitting on the curb in shackles. The stationmaster and his two assistants had come out and were talking excitedly with the lady, who was holding her little girl tight against her legs.

Izzy barely gave the tableau a glance before looking for her staff.

Hennessy was on the pavement opposite, head down, scribbling furiously in his notebook. Of Donaldson and Digby, there was no sign. She crossed to Hennessy and halted beside him.

He paused in his scribbling and glanced at her. "Best story I'll ever write."

"I'm sure you say that of every new story."

He grinned. "This time, however, it's true."

"Did you happen to notice what photographs Donaldson took?"

Hennessy glanced sidelong at her. "None with you in it, if that's what you want to know. We were all too surprised to do anything when you burst out of the station with the bomb in your arms. Donaldson wasn't ready, but he managed to get a shot of Duvall racing out, looking desperate, and he thinks he might even have one of the explosion." Hennessy nodded toward the station. "We saw the case sail above the roof, and Donaldson pointed his camera up that way, and he thinks, what with his newfangled processes, that there's a decent chance he caught the moment. It'll be amazing if he did."

She arched her brows. "That would, indeed, be a coup. Did he manage to get photographs of the police capturing Duvall?"

"He got one of the other two bringing Duvall down, and once they'd stepped away, he got two shots of Baines and Littlejohn hauling their prisoner along. Should work well with what I'm writing."

She glanced around. "Where are they? Donaldson and Digby."

Hennessy tipped his head toward the road above the station. "They hurried up there to photograph what's left of the bomb and the soldiers. Always goes down a treat, showing men in uniform in action."

She nodded, knowing that was true. Hennessy looked down at his notebook. She followed his gaze. "Incidentally, I'll need to vet whatever you write."

Without looking at her, he murmured, "So no hint of who Mrs. I. Molyneaux actually is slips out?"

She stared at his profile for several seconds, then drew in a breath, let it out, and inclined her head. "Just so."

To her relief, Hennessy nodded. "Whatever it is, your secret's safe with me. As far as I'm concerned, you're the owner of *The London Crier*, and that's all anyone needs to know."

Another portion of the tension that had gripped her eased and fell away.

"One thing, though—just to put it in your diary, so to speak—this exercise and all I've already seen of your operation has firmed up an idea I've had for a while. It's something I'd like to discuss with you once we're back in town and this mayhem is over. I'd like to put a proposition to you"—Hennessy looked across the street at Gray—"and I fancy it might come at an opportune time to be of definite interest to you." He tapped his pencil on his notebook and flashed her a grin. "Especially if this story turns out to be half as good as I think it will."

She laughed. "You don't lack for confidence, do you, Hennessy?"

"No, I don't." He met her eyes and dipped his head. "And you don't lack for courage, ma'am." He glanced up, over the roof of the station. "That was really something."

Standing with Martin and Toby on the other side of the street, Gray saw Izzy head toward him, but as soon as she stepped onto the pavement, the lady and her daughter and the stationmaster and his assistants surrounded her. All had seen her snatch the bomb and rush it outside; although they hadn't seen what had occurred subsequently, they were gushing in their praise.

"My dear, I don't know how to thank you." The lady promptly did her best to do so, extolling Izzy's selflessness and making her squirm. Luckily, the lady was a local and clearly did not recognize to whom she spoke.

The instant the lady wound down, the stationmaster and his assistants took up the baton, raining thanks on Izzy's head, but their curiosity was showing.

Gray tensed to intervene, but Hennessy strolled up to the group, identified himself as writing for *The London Crier*, and asked the station staff what they'd seen of the action.

The three men admitted they hadn't noticed Duvall's case until Izzy had grabbed it, and although they'd all seen Duvall's cheroot, they'd thought nothing of it. He'd asked for a form to send a telegraph message to Calais, then he'd bent and been doing something below the level of the counter while the assistant had gone to fetch the form.

In a soft voice, the little girl piped, "I saw him use the burning part of his smelly stick to make the end of the piece of rope start fizzing." When everyone looked at her, she stared back with wide eyes. "I've never seen rope spark and hiss like that. I thought he was doing a trick."

Izzy smiled at the child, and Hennessy nodded. "You're a smart girl and a good observer."

"I gather"—the stationmaster looked inquiringly at Izzy, then at Hennessy before glancing at the rest of their crew—"that you've been assisting in tracking our villain here to prevent him attacking the telegraph station."

That was the bare-bones story Toby had relayed.

Still smiling, Izzy smoothly said, "Unfortunately, we didn't realize he intended to carry out the attack in quite the way he did, not until he'd lit the fuse. Luckily, however, we were all here, on the spot, and everything turned out well."

On that note, she excused herself and walked on to where Gray, Martin, and Toby were standing to one side, trying to be inconspicuous.

Hennessy promptly distracted the lady, the girl, and the telegraph staff by requesting names and asking for their reactions.

Donaldson and Digby returned from the street above, and in short order, Donaldson persuaded the lady, her daughter, and the three station staff to pose in front of the telegraph station, which they proudly did.

Gray grasped Izzy's hand and tipped his head toward the town. She nodded, and with Toby and Martin, they slipped around Donaldson and started down Castle Hill Road.

Hustling Duvall between them, Baines and Littlejohn followed.

In the lead, Gray and Izzy strolled slowly, and soon, Donaldson, Digby, and Hennessy caught up. Thereafter, they stepped out more briskly, although Donaldson assured them they had an abundance of time to reach the station for the next train, which departed at six-fifteen.

He directed them along a different route, one he said was more direct and which led them along Townwall Street, from where, in the deepening dusk, they could look across the harbor toward the Channel. Gradually, Izzy and Gray slowed, allowing the others to pass, until they were the last of the straggling company.

Gray knew he was gripping her hand too firmly—too possessively—but he couldn't seem to ease his hold.

He'd nearly lost her.

After all the years apart, when they'd just found each other again, come to appreciate—to *love*—each other again, to lose her…would have been devastating.

It would have been the end of the future that shaped his dreams.

That hadn't happened.

A brisk sea breeze, chilly and bracing, reminded him they were alive, yet...

Perhaps by the time they reached London, he'd be able to release her hand.

Speaking to the wind, he said, "I've taken my share of risks in this life."

"I'm sure you have," she murmured. "But risks are a fundamental part of life. I suspect we—you and I—will be taking risks until the day we die."

He glanced at her, saw the love in her eyes, and squeezed her hand. "I can't lose you, not now."

"I don't plan on being lost." She squeezed his hand back. "So we'll go on together and face the world as one. And that, my darling Gray, will, I warn you, be a big enough challenge for us both."

He read the truth of that in her expression, softly humphed, and faced forward.

After a moment, gazing out over the harbor, she said, "I look about, and it's as if all our risks, our endeavors, excitements, and thrills, haven't left any mark. Everything seems so normal."

"That was rather the point, wasn't it? The preservation of normality is our ultimate success. And truth to tell, after my years of wandering and risk-taking"—his tone grew definite—"I've become rather fond of normal."

CHAPTER 15

*T*he following day was Sunday. Gray timed his arrival in Norfolk Crescent so that he could join the Descartes ladies before they left for church.

It had been after eight o'clock when their by-then-weary party had walked off the platform at London Bridge Station to be met by Drake, who Toby had arranged to be informed of Duvall's capture. Drake had been accompanied by guards from the Tower, to whom Baines and Little-john, who were by then heartily sick of their determined-to-be-difficult prisoner, had handed Duvall.

Despite the hour, Drake had insisted on hearing their story, and Izzy had suggested they repair to the printing works to debrief. They'd piled into hackneys and had arrived in the mews to discover that, despite the hour, the Lipsons, Maguire, and Mary were still there, waiting for news.

Everyone had crammed into Izzy's office, and their story had been told.

Thereafter, they'd dispersed, heading for their respective homes. Gray and Izzy had walked to Woburn Square and spent time glossing over what had happened and calming everyone before rattling on to Norfolk Crescent.

Gray had accepted Izzy's invitation to share a late supper, which they had while describing their day to Sybil and Marietta, who had hung on their every word.

When Izzy had seen him to the door, neither he nor she had been in any condition to further address their personal situation. He'd suggested calling on her the next day, and she'd invited him for luncheon. After indulging in a kiss that had held both satisfaction and promise, he'd left for Jermyn Street.

That morning, he'd woken restless and impatient and, instead of waiting for midday, had decided to arrive at ten-thirty and escort the three ladies to Sunday service.

When Cottesloe opened the door to his knock, Gray saw he'd timed his arrival to perfection; all three ladies were in the front hall, tying on bonnets and pulling on gloves.

All three looked at him and smiled in delighted welcome, which was pleasing in and of itself.

After they'd exchanged greetings, he offered Sybil his arm, Izzy took the other, and with Marietta bringing up the rear, they descended to the Descartes carriage, which had drawn up to the curb.

The drive to Hanover Square had been filled with Marietta's and Sybil's questions regarding the likely upshot of Duvall's arrest. Once at the church, Marietta took Sybil's arm, leaving Gray to escort Izzy down the aisle in her mother and sister's wake.

He sat at the end of the pew, beside Izzy, and let the familiar phrases of the service wash over him, almost, it seemed, in benediction.

No matter how far he'd roamed, this land of his birth, with all its traditions and curious ways, was the only place he'd ever felt that he belonged.

He'd returned intent on crafting a satisfying life for himself there, and all the building blocks bar one were in place, although that missing one was the most important, the foundation stone, and with respect to that, he had two hurdles yet to overcome.

At the end of the service, he escorted Izzy, Sybil, and Marietta onto the porch, and they dallied there, chatting with other members of the ton. This was the second Sunday on which he'd attended with the Descartes ladies, and every matron worth her salt had noticed and was intrigued.

His aunt Matcham had also noticed; she came sweeping up, curious and eager and wanting to know whatever there was to know, but suitably wary of treading on any toes.

Reading nothing but encouragement and approval in her comments, Gray seized the moment to mention, "I'm seriously considering throwing my hat in the ring at the next election."

Lady Matcham's eyes widened. She searched his face and confirmed he was serious. "Well! I must say I heartily approve." Her gaze drifted to Izzy. "It could well be the making of you."

"I don't know about that, but I need something to occupy my time, and with my business interests well in hand, I'm inclined to see what I might achieve in that sphere." He paused, then added, "Devlin and Therese seem to think it a sensible idea."

His aunt studied him assessingly, then nodded. "Call on me sometime. I'm not without connections in that world, and I want to hear more of your ideas."

Gray hadn't known she had any interest in politics, but readily agreed.

Apparently satisfied, she took herself off, and he turned back to the ladies and discovered that Swan had joined them.

Izzy watched her mother's face as Gray returned to her side. With Swan chatting to Marietta, and Gray so patently fixed beside Izzy, her mother didn't know which way to look. She was bright-eyed and plainly thrilled at the prospect of marrying off both her daughters in such highly acceptable fashion.

After the years of drama and struggle, Izzy felt pleased on her mother's behalf.

Lady Matcham, who had swanned off, returned in a rustling rush to whisper something into Izzy's mother's ear. As both older ladies' gazes shifted to Izzy and Gray, she suspected she could guess the topic.

She pretended to be oblivious, but with Gray standing tall, strong, and so very much by her side, she couldn't stop her heart from rising, buoyed on burgeoning hope.

This was how she'd expected to feel long ago, to live through a scene just like this with Gray beside her and her heart so light...

He bent his head and murmured, "Am I allowed to ask what has put that glorious look on your face?"

She turned her head and, from a distance of mere inches, smiled even more gloriously, letting her welling joy show. Studying his lovely amber eyes, she said, "Remember our earlier discussion about whether it was possible for us to pick up the reins of where we'd once been and forge onward?"

His expression grew intent. "Yes."

"I believe we've accomplished that. Do you agree?"

His smile was all she'd hoped it would be. Between them, he closed his hand around hers and lightly squeezed. "I do. We've found our right path—the right path for us as we are now."

The right path for us as we are now.

The words echoed in her heart, and she nodded.

"Isadora?" Her mother was waiting to catch Izzy's eye. "I was just saying to Lord Swan that he should join us for luncheon."

Izzy and Gray added their voices in support, and Swan readily agreed.

After farewelling those lingering on the church porch, the five made their way to the countess's carriage and repaired to Norfolk Crescent.

Luncheon passed oh-so-pleasantly, in easy, undemanding fashion.

Afterward, while Sybil dutifully sat with Marietta and Swan in the drawing room, Izzy drew Gray into the back parlor.

She settled on the window seat and, once Gray had sat beside her, said, "Hennessy spoke to me while we were outside the telegraph station. It wasn't the time for discussing business, but he wanted to let me know that once our adventures were over, he hoped to put a proposition to me. I suspect it's something about working at *The Crier* and, possibly, more." She met Gray's eyes. "He thought it was something I would be interested in, especially if there was an ongoing relationship between you and me."

"Regarding your identity, is he likely to be a threat going forward?"

"No. In fact, he said he didn't care who I was, only that I was the owner of *The Crier*."

"So what do you think he's going to propose?"

"It might involve coming on board permanently and perhaps even taking a financial stake. For someone of his ilk, that's not unheard of."

"I imagine it isn't. But how do you feel about such a prospect?"

She met his eyes and imagined and considered, then admitted, "Hennessy's good—very good—and he's experienced. He knows the business. If he wants to become a principal writer and also buy in to the enterprise, I'm willing to listen."

Good. Gray didn't say the word, but he was certain she read his approval in his eyes. He reached out and took her hand in his. "Whatever you settle on, I'll support your decision. I know how important *The Crier* is to you."

She smiled, and he squeezed her fingers.

He wanted to return to the question of what she would say if he proposed, but he hadn't yet decided how to broach the subject of Tickencote Grange, much less how to confront what he saw as his final hurdle—namely, confessing that he, too, had once been addicted to gambling.

He needed a few more days to sort things out. Meanwhile…

He lifted her hand over his thigh and cradled it between both of his. "We're both older, more experienced, and wiser now, and it seems to me that each of us have come to one of those points in life when one's road turns a corner. Looking ahead, you're going to have to find some way of continuing to conceal your identity in the face of the increased attention the story of Quimby's murder and Duvall's treason will bring."

"Stepping behind Hennessy will help."

Smiling, he dipped his head. "True. Meanwhile, I have to finalize the necessary details and take the first steps toward the life I want going forward, namely becoming a member of Parliament."

He met her emerald eyes. "I'm hoping the road beyond each of our corners is one we can share—that once we round our separate corners, we'll find ourselves on the same road."

Izzy had wondered… She drew in a deeper breath and asked, "Assuming we find ourselves walking that same road, you don't see me continuing as the owner of *The Crier* as being"—she waved her free hand —"too difficult to manage?"

His gaze remained steady. "Would you be happy without *The Crier* and everyone there in your life?"

"No." She studied his face. "I wouldn't want to walk away from what I've created. I would prefer to work with Hennessy and develop the business further."

He nodded. "I can understand that—appreciate and even approve of that."

She turned her hand between his and returned the pressure of his fingers. "What I wish for most of all is for you and me to work together and see what we can weave from the separate strands of our adult lives— the lives we now have."

He smiled, raised her hand, and pressed a kiss to her fingers. "We're both the determined sort. Together, we'll knit our lives into a single, strong, cohesive whole."

The door opened, and Marietta looked in. "There you are!" She came through the door, with Swan trailing behind her.

Izzy quashed a spurt of irritation; her sister was so pleased with herself and Swan, it was hard to be annoyed, but she had hoped for at least one kiss…

Glancing sidelong at Gray, judging by the slight tightening of his lips, he had, too.

Marietta and Swan sat, and the four of them chatted about Swan's involvement with the committee organizing the schedule for the upcoming opera season, a position he was justifiably thrilled to hold.

Knowing Gray's aversion to all forms of ton musical events, Izzy hid a grin at his artfulness in avoiding advertising his prejudice while endeavoring to encourage Swan.

All too soon, it was time for Gray and Swan to be on their way.

Izzy and Marietta escorted the gentlemen to the front hall.

After Gray had shrugged on his greatcoat and accepted his hat from Cottesloe, Izzy felt compelled to ask, "Will I see you tomorrow?"

It was damning to realize just how let down she would feel if he didn't appear.

But he smiled a warm, almost-intimate smile and stated, "Nothing could keep me away. Aside from all else, I've a vested interest in learning what Hennessy has to say." He paused as if consulting a mental diary, then said, "I won't turn up for breakfast, but I'll drop by the printing works in the morning to see how matters are shaping up."

She nodded and led him to the door. Holding it open, she met his eyes and smiled. "I'll see you then."

～

The following morning, Izzy turned the corner into the mews a good five minutes before eight o'clock and discovered Donaldson and Digby leaning against the printing works' door. They spotted her approaching and straightened, enthusiasm lighting their faces.

They greeted her and stepped aside to allow her to unlock the door.

"We're keen to see what we captured on Saturday," Donaldson said.

She laughed. "So I see."

She led the way inside, smiling even more broadly as, delaying only long enough to hang their coats and mufflers on the pegs, the pair made a beeline for the darkroom.

"We'll bring you the prints as soon as we have them," Donaldson called, then pushed through the door.

She paused and watched Digby flip the sign to Occupied before following and closing the door.

Smiling, she continued to her desk and scribbled a note to get a formal agreement with Donaldson drawn up and signed. "And I must remember to give him the key to the rear door."

She sat at her desk, opened the side drawer, hunted, and found the key Littlejohn had returned. After setting the key on one side of the desk, she retrieved her pencil and jotted a further reminder to speak to Lipson about hiring a new printer's devil and formally promoting Digby to photographer's assistant. He'd proved invaluable on Saturday, helping Donaldson with the tripod and the rest of his paraphernalia. Besides, Digby had a passion, and she knew how far passion could propel one.

Within minutes, the rest of the staff were coming through the main door, and she rose and went to greet them. They gathered around, and for those who hadn't heard, she duly reported on all that had happened, skating over her role and ending with a commendation to them all for their sterling efforts in getting out the hue and cry edition, which was the essential catalyst for all that had followed.

Although the Lipsons and Maguires had already heard the tale, they'd remained to share the wonder with the others. On hearing of the explosion, Gerry and Jim went wide-eyed, and the news that Donaldson might have got a photograph of the moment caused everyone to look longingly at the closed darkroom door.

Then Lipson said, "And now we've got an even bigger edition to put out, one reporting on the outcome of the hue and cry. Everyone in London's going to want a copy of that—a real-life drama they've watched unfold."

Everyone agreed, and soon, the workshop was humming with the usual Monday sounds of getting the press, the boiler, the formes, and the boxes of type ready to set and print the week's edition.

As she retreated to her office, Izzy considered Lipson's words. He was right; this edition would trump even the hue and cry in sales, and in truth, the story—even her edited verbal version of it—contained all the right ingredients to capture imaginations.

For once, however, it was not up to her to write the piece. As she sat again behind her desk, she owned to rampant curiosity over what Hennessy would produce. Meanwhile, she settled to craft an introduction that would permanently turn readers' minds from the hopefully forgotten exposé to the murder and the quest to identify and catch a killer.

It was stirring stuff, and she enjoyed the challenge. On reaching the end of the short piece designed to lead in to Hennessy's article, she sat back and read it through.

She frowned and laid down the sheet. "Damn it—I'll need to check with Drake."

How much would he and his masters allow to be said about the plot?

"On the other hand," she mused, eyes narrowing in thought, "this could be very neatly exploited to ensure no similar action against the telegraph occurs again. A spiking of the ultimate villains' guns, as it were."

She pondered that until the bell over the main door tinkled. She rose and went to see who had arrived.

Halting in the doorway, she watched as Hennessy glanced around the workshop and cordially nodded to those who looked his way. As she'd mentioned that he was writing the lead article to run in this week's edition, all the staff were curious about him.

When his gaze reached her, she nodded in welcome and beckoned. "Come in and let me see what you have."

He grinned and, as she retreated behind her desk again, came into the office.

She directed him to the chair facing her. As he sat, she said, "First things first. I've just realized that we'll need to check with Winchelsea regarding what details we include in any piece."

Hennessy grimaced expressively and reluctantly nodded. "But you're not going to hold the story?"

"Good God, no! I'm prepared to gloss over any details that might be sensitive, but we're going to run enough to satisfy the most avid reader."

He grinned. "Excellent. You're a lady after my own heart." He drew out several sheets and handed them across the desk. "This is what I've got so far. Still in draft—see what you think."

Already reading, she held out the single sheet of her introduction. "This is such a departure from a normal edition, we'll need an introduction to your report."

He took the proffered sheet and read, while she pored over his longer article.

Then they proceeded to confirm every fact and every paragraph they thought should be in there, while she noted in the margins which points were, in their view, essential and which were details they could, if necessary, condense or skip over.

A tap on the door frame had them looking across to see Donaldson and Digby with prints in their hands and beaming smiles on their faces. "We thought you should see these immediately," Donaldson said.

At her wave, the pair hurried in. She cleared a portion of her desk, and Donaldson carefully laid out the prints. Hennessy rose and came to stand on her other side and peer over her shoulder as Donaldson proudly pointed to the first print. "This is the shot I hoped to get—it's an utter fluke. The briefcase exploding above the roof of the telegraph station."

It was, indeed, a remarkable photograph, sharp enough that they could make out the tiles on the roof. Given the relatively dull light, the explosion stood out clearly against the canopies of the trees on the other side of the street.

After scrutinizing the print, Izzy glanced at Hennessy. "I say we put that on the front page, under a headline saying something like 'Attack on the Dover Telegraph Station Foiled.'"

"'Foreign Attack,'" Hennessy corrected. "No sense not playing to our deeply entrenched patriotism."

"Indeed," she agreed.

They continued examining and selecting prints to match the written article. Over the years, both she and also Digby had developed a good sense of what photographs reproduced best on the printed page.

Another tap on the door frame heralded Lipson and Maguire.

Lipson was wiping his hands on an oily rag. "We wondered if we could see." Grinning, he tipped his head toward the workshop. "We're all eaten up with curiosity."

Izzy saw Donaldson and Digby looking at Lipson's hands, and Maguire's were obviously ink-stained. She pushed back from the desk. "Why don't we lay out the photographs on the counter? Then everyone can see without touching, and Hennessy and I can point out which we think will fit best with the article, and we can discuss and make our final selections."

That satisfied everyone. Donaldson and Digby ferried the precious prints to the counter and laid them along it, while the rest of the staff hurriedly gathered around. Everyone exclaimed over Donaldson's fluke, and its position on the front page was supported by all.

After everyone had looked their fill, Izzy and Hennessy explained which prints they felt would best illustrate the main article.

"I'll need to write a closing piece." Izzy caught Hennessy's eye. "To report the ultimate outcome with Duvall, at least as far as we know it by Wednesday."

Hennessy asked about their deadlines.

Lipson and Maguire explained their preferences, and Hennessy promised to have his lead article in by the end of the day on Tuesday.

Then everyone returned to staring at the photographs, and the male staff asked about the army company, and Mary wanted to know about the little girl and her mother.

The lively exchange abruptly cut off as the door opened and everyone looked, but it was only Gray who, with a smile and a nod to everyone, entered. He saw the prints on the counter as he drew near. "What's got you all in such fine fettle?"

Izzy grinned and allowed Hennessy, Donaldson, and Digby, ably assisted by the rest of the staff, to explain how they proposed to use the quite amazing collection of photographs.

Gray was duly impressed and said so.

Then Maguire told Digby, "We'll need those prints blocked up."

"I'd like to learn the process," Donaldson said, and everyone dispersed to return to their chores.

With Hennessy and Gray, Izzy retreated to the office. She returned to her chair while Gray made for his usual seat. Izzy signaled Hennessy, the last through the door, to shut it. As he came to take the other chair before the desk, she fixed her gaze on Gray. "We realized we need to speak with Drake before we set anything in type. Can you arrange a meeting?"

Gray's brows rose, but then his expression cleared, and he nodded. "Yes, of course." He sat up and gestured. "Give me a piece of paper and a pen, and I'll write a note now."

He proceeded to do so. Signing, folding, then addressing the missive, he said, "I'm sending it to Wolverstone House and putting Louisa's name on it as well. If Drake's not there, she'll read it and get it to him, wherever he may be."

Izzy nodded. "Good thinking." She held out a hand for the note and, when Gray gave it to her, rose and took it out for Lipson to arrange delivery.

When she returned, she found Hennessy waiting to catch her eye. "There's not much more you and I can do until we get the go-ahead from Winchelsea. While we wait, I was wondering if now might not be a good time to discuss that proposition I mentioned on Saturday."

Understanding he was asking if he could speak in front of Gray, she shut the door and returned to her chair. "That's an excellent idea." She tipped her head toward Gray. "It will help if his lordship can hear your proposal directly as well."

Hennessy had clearly been expecting that answer. "Right, then. It's like this. I'm well established in my current place, as lead writer for *The Courier*. But I've been there for nigh on eight years now, and frankly, the work's grown a bit stale. I've been casting about for something more." He looked at them both. "For the next challenge, if you take my meaning."

Izzy and Gray assured him they understood the sentiment perfectly.

Heartened, Hennessy went on, "You see, there's a big difference in writing for a daily and writing for a weekly. Even just over the past few days, I've seen and heard with my own eyes and ears that you, here at *The Crier*, have a very different outlook and aim to what I've grown used to at *The Courier* and even before that. I've worked dailies all my writing life." He paused as if marshaling his thoughts.

Izzy and Gray waited patiently.

Eventually, Hennessy continued, "Writing for a daily is all about grabbing the readers' attention with something sensational and lurid, day after day. That means you move on every day to the latest incident, and everything you write, almost by definition, remains superficial. You point out something, but you never have time to poke and pry. Writing for a daily, you never have the luxury of exploring a subject in any sort of depth. You report on what happened that day and move on."

He looked at Izzy. "I've read what you write, and you're a good storyteller. You have the knack. But if you don't mind an old hand telling you what's what, I think you could put your talents to even better use—and do a lot more good—if you aimed that pen of yours at some subject more serious than the social round. I'm not saying society reporting doesn't sell papers—it does—but there's no reason to limit yourself to that. You could do both—as you did with that Foundling House article, only in greater depth."

Hennessy drew breath and barreled on, "Which brings us to the here and now. With the attention garnered by the hue and cry edition and, even more, what this week's edition will generate with the news of us tracking and capturing Duvall and his arrest for murder and treasonous mayhem, *The Crier* will have a much higher profile—at least for a little while." He held Izzy's gaze. "The question you need to consider is, having captured the attention of the masses, how are you going to keep it?"

Izzy studied his dogged expression. "I've a feeling your proposition will go some way toward answering that."

Hennessy grinned. "Yes, well, that is my intention." He glanced at Gray, then looked back at her. "So here it is, then. I've got a good bit put by. I never married, and I've no one to leave it to. If you're willing, I'd like to buy into *The Crier*. Along with you, I'd become one of its two senior writers." He tilted his head toward the workshop. "You have the makings of an excellent crew, and Donaldson's taken the entire enterprise up a notch, as we've just seen. Using his talents in conjunction with mine and yours… I'm thinking that, every week, alongside the social column, we could run a piece examining"—he waved—"something of real interest to the wider public."

She arched her brows. "Such as?"

He'd come prepared. "How about the Crystal Palace—where it is now, what is going to be done with it—and at the same time examine some of the benefits the nation got through running the exhibition. I'm sure a lot of captains of industry would like to get a mention, especially given *The Crier's* new prominence, and would give us their inside stories and also allow us to take photographs."

Gray stirred and sat up. "If I might make a suggestion, there's the new chamber of the House of Commons. You could interview the architect about how it's all been done and use that to see if you can get Donaldson inside."

Izzy sat straighter. "That *would* be a coup."

"We'd still cover some crimes," Hennessy said. "I'll still have my snouts, but we could choose which crimes to showcase and go deeper than the surface reporting the dailies do." Eagerly, he met her eyes. "We might even convince some of Baines's colleagues to work with us—to use us as a mouthpiece sometimes, as with the hue and cry edition."

She nodded in agreement and encouragement.

"Most of all," Hennessy went on, "I think you need to seize the opportunity afforded by what happened with Quimby and Duvall to create a solid base for *The Crier* to leverage upward from. Winchelsea would never have learned what Duvall was up to if it hadn't been for *The Crier* asking readers for help. That's new—it's something no other paper has done, not in such an open and definite way. And most importantly of all, *The Crier* delivered the goods. If the story's treated in the right way, the public will lap it up and stay engaged."

She smiled. "I can see that." She studied Hennessy for several seconds, then sat forward and clasped her hands on the desk. "Obviously, we'll have to work out the details, but in principle, I'm in favor of your proposal. However, becoming a partner and senior writer here would mean being exclusive to *The Crier*. You'd have to walk away from your position with *The London Courier*. Are you prepared to do that?"

Hennessy drew in a deep breath and nodded decisively. "It's time for me to move on to the next thing. You can't live your life standing still."

How true. "No, you can't." She discovered her mind was already made up. "Think about how much you're willing to commit financially to *The Crier*, and meanwhile, I'll work out what seems fair to me, and we can meet here tomorrow morning and see if we can devise a mutually satisfactory arrangement."

Hennessy's smile was as bright as her own. "Excellent."

"But"—she pinned him with a warning look—"our agreement regarding the article for this week's edition stands."

He chuckled and rose. "You'll get no argument from me about that. Now I've seen Donaldson's work, my piece will run better in *The Crier* than anywhere else."

The door cracked open, and Mary looked in. "Sorry to interrupt, ma'am, but you have visitors." Breathlessly, she confided, "The Marquess and Marchioness of Winchelsea."

Mary stood back, and Louisa swept in, followed by Drake.

Already on his feet, Hennessy stepped around the desk and put his back to the wall—possibly in the hope of making himself invisible.

Louisa smiled brightly at him.

Izzy quickly intervened by standing and saying, "How delightful to see you, Louisa."

After directing brief nods and pained looks at Izzy and Gray, Drake diverted to fetch one of the chairs from near the window.

Izzy extended her hand across the desk to Louisa, and they clasped fingers.

"Welcome to the home of *The London Crier*." Izzy gestured at Hennessy. "This is Mr. Hennessy, who will be writing the lead article." She waited while Hennessy bowed and received a gracious if curiosity-laden nod from Louisa, then waved Louisa to the vacant armchair. "Please—do sit."

Gray had, of course, come to his feet. He nodded in greeting. "Louisa."

Drake set a chair beside his wife's, and as both ladies subsided, he and Gray sat.

Izzy promptly took charge. "Now we have the preliminaries out of the way"—she looked inquiringly at Drake—"have you learned anything more from Duvall?"

Drake smiled the smile of a satisfied predator. "I spent most of yesterday interrogating him. He confirmed what we'd surmised about his mission regarding the Dover telegraph station and also divulged that he'd been working for Monsieur Roccard for the past eighteen months in various relatively minor ways. Destroying the cross-Channel telegraph was his first major mission." His gaze flicking from Izzy to Hennessy, Drake paused, then, as if accepting their right to know, went on, "Even better, Duvall has agreed to trade his testimony implicating Monsieur Roccard and the criminal fraternities he represents for leniency in sentencing, which will amount to transportation rather than hanging."

"So you have Roccard?" Gray asked.

Drake's smile grew almost blissful. "We have." After a second, he explained, "Others have been pursuing Roccard for some time—the Home Office, the Foreign Office, even the Board of Trade. But while they've suspected the man for several years, they've never found anyone —at least, not anyone alive—willing to testify against him, and as he's a Belgian national, their hands have been tied. Duvall's testimony has solved their problem, and I believe Roccard's already gracing a cell in the Tower."

Seeing how deeply pleased Drake was, Izzy decided the time to strike was now. "The reason we requested this meeting was to run past you what we wish to print in this week's edition." Concisely, she outlined the points she and Hennessy had agreed should be in the lead article, detailing the findings identifying Duvall as Quimby's killer, the motive behind Duvall's action, and consequently, Duvall's attempt to carry out his mission and demolish the telegraph station at Dover, all to further the ends of foreign criminals.

Drake grew palpably cooler as Izzy's points progressed. By the time she reached the triumphant end, his features had set. When she lowered the draft article and arched her brows at him, he said, "I have no quibble over publishing the details regarding the murder and Duvall's actions connected to that. However, I do not believe it will be in the nation's best interests for the source of his motive—namely, the involvement of a foreign gentleman acting on behalf of Continental crime families and their wish to sabotage the international telegraph links—to be made public."

She'd expected as much and was prepared to argue her case. "Drake, there is no way to keep the attack on the Dover telegraph station from the public. Even if we don't mention it, news of the explosion will seep out. Given that, I would have thought it would serve the nation best to use the incident to swing public sentiment behind the need for governments and —most pertinently—police forces on either side of the Channel to be able to swiftly communicate."

Hennessy offered, "And surely the best way to ensure it doesn't happen again would be to lay it all out and explain how dastardly foreign criminals had tried to attack a prime example of British inventiveness because it threatened their schemes—schemes that swindle money from the British public."

Louisa had been unusually silent. Now, in the tone of one who had seen the light, she brightly said, "Ah—of course! If you explain the criminals' ploy to hoodwink the public into imagining there was something dangerous about the telegraph—inflaming the public to act against their own best interests—that will render such an approach unusable in the future, because the public will be wise to manipulation of that ilk."

She looked encouragingly at Drake.

"Exactly!" Izzy stated. "Explaining this incident to the public will alert them to the fact that there are foreign forces who behave like this, and that will put them on guard against such schemes in the future."

"We could," Hennessy suggested, "stress that—make it clear in a simple, easy to understand way."

Louisa nodded. "The phrasing would be key."

Hiding his amusement, Gray watched as Izzy and Louisa, aided by Hennessy, set about swaying a nobleman not given to being easily swayed.

Drake's position reflected the commonly held view among those who ruled that the less the general population knew of such attacks, especially from foreign sources, the better. But times were changing; Gray suspected the increasing reach of newspapers was going to force a significant shift in such attitudes.

Izzy, Hennessy, and Louisa made an eloquent case, leaving Drake clearly uncertain, something Gray suspected Drake rarely was.

Nevertheless, Gray was surprised when Drake turned to him and asked, "You've sat there listening to all sides of the argument. How do you see this? Are they"—he waved at Hennessy, Izzy, and Louisa—"correct in predicting how the public will react?"

Gray nodded. "I believe they are. Times have changed and are still changing, and taking the population with you by allowing them sufficient information to understand what's been going on will serve the nation better than clinging to the outmoded notion of keeping everyone in the dark. That might have worked in times past. It will not work in the future."

Drake regarded Gray for half a minute, then grunted. "Can I second the push for you to stand for a seat in the Commons?" Then he turned his dark gaze on Izzy and nodded. "Very well. Explain the lot."

Izzy and Hennessy were patently thrilled.

"But"—Drake held up a finger—"only if I get to see the articles before they're typeset."

Izzy assured him they would abide by that caveat.

Drake nodded, reached for Louisa's hand, and drew her to her feet, bringing Gray and Izzy to theirs. "We must get on. I've several people I still need to report to regarding Duvall, Roccard, and the incident in Dover."

With Izzy, Gray accompanied Drake and Louisa to the front door, with Louisa plainly intrigued by the fact that Gray was there. After seeing the pair out, Gray trailed an energized Izzy back to the office, noting the buzz of activity throughout the workshop as the staff prepared for the coming week.

He entered the office to find Izzy seated at her desk and Hennessy in the chair Louisa had vacated. Both were focused on the draft of the lead article, going over it line by line and adding snippets, polishing others— making the piece shine.

Izzy glanced at him. "Can you ask Donaldson, Digby, and Maguire to come in? And we'll need the selected photographs, too."

Gray smiled, swung around, and ambled into the workshop. He didn't mind being a messenger boy; it was part and parcel of being a member of the team at *The Crier*. That team had only grown stronger in the aftermath of Quimby's murder and looked set to go on to greater things. Strength built through adversity; this was surely an example of that.

He delivered his message, then strolled back through the workshop, amazed at feeling so much at home in a world that, until ten days ago, he'd known nothing about.

Smiling to himself, he halted in the foyer. The more he rubbed shoulders with those who hadn't been born to the privileges he had, the more clearly he understood the needs of the populace as a whole. *The Crier* would help him with that.

Feeling compelled to make some contribution to the pervasive sense of expectation and impending triumph welling throughout the printing works, he looked into the office and announced, "I'm going out to fetch lunch for everyone." He grinned at the eager looks. "In celebration."

Everyone laughed and urged him on, and with a smile on his face, he turned and went.

CHAPTER 16

he week flew by in a flurry of activity as the staff of *The Crier* knuckled down to produce their most important edition yet.

On Thursday afternoon, with the boiler chuffing and the press clanking and clanging non-stop, Izzy was at her desk, busily tabulating early requests for extra copies, when the sound of brisk footsteps impinged on her awareness. She looked up and saw Gray walking through the office doorway.

She smiled delightedly and put down her pencil. He'd been off in the country over the previous days.

Smiling in return, he halted before the desk. "How are things going?"

"Excellently well." She waited while he sank with his usual grace into his now-customary chair. "Hennessy and I thrashed out the details of our agreement so we both get what we want, and the solicitors are drawing up the papers." Gray had been present for the initial round of negotiations on Tuesday morning. "As for the upcoming edition, everyone's thrilled with how it's turned out."

She waved at the orders spread before her. "Our circulation's gone up again. We started the press rolling on Wednesday afternoon and expect to run it tomorrow as well, just to supply the orders we already have. The advertisers are ecstatic and clamoring for more space." Smiling broadly, she flung out her hands. "These last two editions have elevated *The London Crier* to dizzying heights."

Lowering her hands, she continued, "On that note, however, we—Hennessy and I—called a staff meeting on Wednesday, after we'd settled on how we wanted to run things. We've agreed to keep *The Crier* small and focused and to continue with the other side of the business as well. We might eventually need larger premises, but for now, as far as *The Crier* is concerned, we're going to concentrate on capitalizing on our increased circulation and locking in those gains by refining our offerings to both entertain and educate our readers."

Gray smiled. "It sounds as if everything's shaping up well. That leads nicely to my question."

She arched her brows. "You have a question?"

He nodded. "Given everything here is bowling along smoothly and Hennessy is about should an owner be required, can you steal away for the day tomorrow? I'd like to show you something and get your opinion."

She couldn't read much from his expression or his eyes. "What do you want me to see? And where?"

"It's in the country. There's a deal I'd like to finalize, but I want your opinion on several aspects first."

The "something" had to be the country house he'd been looking at. Her heart fluttered at the evidence of how serious he was over linking their lives. "This 'something.' Can't you tell me what it is? So I can consider what might be important in forming my opinion."

He held her gaze, then shook his head. "You'll see it tomorrow, and once you do, I'm sure you'll know exactly how you feel about it."

She frowned. "It's not a horse?"

He laughed and assured her it wasn't.

In her mind, she heard her mother repeating the exhortation she'd voiced only the evening before.

Follow your heart and live your life.

Her mother had insisted that, having fought for so long to secure the family's well-being, now the chance for Izzy's own desired life had come her way, she should seize it.

Gray arched his brows, a hint of vulnerability in his eyes. "So, will you come?"

She smiled reassuringly. "Of course."

A tap on the open door had them glancing that way.

Digby flung a grin at Gray, then said to Izzy, "Ma'am, Mr. Donaldson's wondering if you have a moment to talk about what photographs you and Mr. Hennessy want for next week. We've been looking over the old stock, but as Mr. Donaldson says, if the paper's heading in a new direction, you might want different pictures."

"Indeed, we will." She pushed back her chair and rose.

Gray joined her, and they followed Digby to where Donaldson and Hennessy were standing at the layout table. A brisk discussion ensued, and any doubts Gray harbored regarding how well Hennessy and Izzy would get on were laid to rest; their attitudes over what sort of stories they wanted to pursue and the direction in which they wanted to take *The Crier* were closely aligned.

It was finally decided that Donaldson, assisted by Digby, would go and take pictures of the remnants of the Crystal Palace, now in the process of being dismantled and carted who knew where.

Meanwhile, Hennessy would lean on his sources to see if he could learn where the structure was slated to go. "Then," he said, "I'll contact some of the businesses who participated in the exhibition and find some success stories to run alongside." He nodded to Donaldson. "Once I have the stories, I'll get you a list of businesses to go and photograph."

With that settled, Izzy introduced Gray to the new printer's devil, Eddie, a lively looking lad presently working closely with Lipson and very much under the manager's eye, yet Eddie's grin at his good fortune never left his face.

"He'll do," Lipson gruffly mumbled.

Allowing Izzy to retreat to her paperwork and sums, Gray hung around the workshop until it was closing time.

After farewelling the staff—and being farewelled in turn, very much as if they counted him one of them—he waited while Izzy locked the door, then offered his arm, which she took, and in comfortable accord, they walked to Woburn Square.

Mrs. Carruthers was delighted to see Gray as well as Izzy. They spent ten minutes satisfying the old lady's bright-eyed curiosity, then walked to the lane, climbed into the carriage, and rolled around to Norfolk Crescent.

As the carriage turned onto the crescent, with a smile in her eyes, Izzy looked at Gray. "Are you free to stay for dinner? Silas is in town and should be joining us, and Swan might as well."

Gray grinned and, through the dimness, met her eyes. "Thank you— that would be delightful."

The evening that followed was truly that—pleasant, relaxed, and filled with quiet laughter and cheer. Silas was in excellent form, and he and Gray spent a good half hour discussing business while Swan entertained the ladies.

In return, after dinner, Gray and Silas put themselves out to engage Izzy and Sybil, leaving Swan to Marietta and she to him.

While all were distracted in handing around the teacups, to Gray's surprise, Marietta fetched up beside him.

She caught his eye and quietly said, "I don't know what drove you and Izzy apart all those years ago, but it's plain as a pikestaff you two should be together."

When Gray merely arched his brows and waited, Marietta frowned and, with unaccustomed fierceness, said, "Make it happen, Child. I want to see Izzy happy—truly happy."

Battling a smile, he inclined his head. "Rest assured I'll do my humble best."

Marietta humphed. "You'd better." With that, she glided away, leaving him to sip his tea and reflect that everything in his life was settling into place.

One last but central and essential piece to go.

Supported by Silas, he continued to entertain Sybil and Izzy until it was time for him to take his leave. He did so with his usual charm and was entirely content when Izzy took his arm to steer him to the front door.

She didn't resist when he diverted them to the empty parlor, whisked her inside, closed the door, framed her face, and kissed her. Ravenously.

Being Izzy, she responded in kind, and the exchange spiraled into a hungry give and take, fueled by complementary cravings.

This, between them, was so very real.

So potent and powerful and so utterly addictive.

Her lips and mouth were lush fruits he longingly savored, while her fingers tangled in his hair and gripped as she plundered his lips in reply.

His hands wandered, sliding, stroking, caressing, and claiming, and hers followed suit.

Desire rose, powerful and compelling. The ache of need that consumed them both was a passionate heartbeat that drove them.

They wanted, yearned for, and needed so much more, yet...

They were where they were, and no amount of desperation could change that.

Gradually, reluctance in every incremental movement, they eased back from the all-consuming vortex of sensations the kiss had become.

Bringing it to an end was hard.

He raised his head, rested his forehead against hers, and sighed—then dove back for one last, lingering, infinitely gentle kiss, one of unrestrained promise.

Her lashes rose as he drew away. She met his gaze, the emerald of her eyes rich and deep, then softly sighed.

They stepped back, rearranged their clothes, then he gave her his arm, and they resumed their interrupted stroll to the front door.

They halted in the hall, and he shrugged on his coat and picked up his hat.

She cleared her throat. "Tomorrow?"

"I'll call for you at eight. In a hackney. Dress for the train."

"The train?" She sent a surprised look his way.

He caught her hand, raised it, and kissed her fingers. "Yes, the train." With a grin that plainly stated he wasn't going to tell her anything more, he released her, opened the door, cast one last look her way, and said, "Until tomorrow."

Then he left.

Gray felt Izzy's gaze as he walked along the pavement. Only once he'd turned the corner and was out of her sight did he allow himself to think of how much he had riding on tomorrow.

If he'd thought of that earlier, she would have seen just how nervous he was over how his last ploy and his looming revelation would play out —for them both.

Gray managed to buy the train tickets without Izzy overhearing their destination.

She sat by the window in the first-class carriage; the constant rattling of the wheels made conversation too difficult, so he sat opposite her and watched her face as she gazed at the passing fields.

As the train slowed to draw into Stamford, he rose and offered her his hand.

She looked up at him in surprise. "Here?"

He grasped her hand and, as the train hissed to a halt, drew her to her feet. "Ancaster Park isn't far away."

She allowed him to lead her out of the compartment and down the corridor to the carriage door. "Your parents' estate?"

He nodded, went down the steep steps to the platform, and held up his hands to help her down.

She joined him and glanced around, but didn't say anything.

He wound her arm in his and led her out of the station to where a groom was waiting with a hired curricle. "We'll be returning to catch the afternoon train."

He helped her into the curricle, then took the reins, tipped the groom, climbed up, and sat beside her. From the station forecourt, he tooled the curricle north, over the bridge across the river Welland, and on through the town, eventually striking west along the main lane that led to the Great North Road. On reaching the highway, he turned the horses' heads north and flicked the reins, setting the curricle bowling along.

Izzy hadn't said a word, but she was gripping her hands tightly in her lap.

They rattled across the bridge over the river Gwash and came to the tiny hamlet of Tickencote. Gray slowed and turned onto the lane sign-posted to Empingham. Almost immediately, a pair of gateposts appeared on their left, the wrought-iron gates between them set wide, and he turned the horses through.

Izzy was so preternaturally still, he would have sworn she'd stopped breathing.

He kept the horses to a walk until they rounded the bend and the stately bulk of Tickencote Grange faced them.

Abruptly, Izzy reached over and closed her fingers tightly about his wrist.

He drew the horses to a halt and looked at her.

She was staring at the house, then she turned her head and met his eyes. "What are we doing here?"

Her voice was weak, thready.

Izzy looked back at the house; she could barely breathe past the hard knot that had formed in her chest.

Joy, sadness, relief the house still stood, and countless other emotions and memories warred within her.

She glanced at Gray, and he met her eyes.

"I searched for months for the house that would suit me and whoever I married. Of more than fifty houses, this is the only one that called to me."

Unable to bear looking at her old home, she kept her gaze fixed on his face.

His lips twisted wryly. "I've learned through experience to follow my instincts—that they rarely, if ever, guide me wrongly, no matter what my rational mind sometimes thinks—and when it came to this place, from the first time I sat here and looked at it, it seemed to be the answer to my prayers.

"Then I ventured inside and knew beyond question that my instincts hadn't lied." He looked at the house. "No matter that I subsequently learned that this was the house your family once owned, the house your father lost through gambling it away, my instincts keep insisting that this is the right place for me to put down roots and thrive."

He stared at the house a moment more, then simply said, "But I can't thrive without you, Izzy."

She'd followed his gaze to the well-remembered façade; she watched it draw nearer as he drove on down the drive.

He drew rein in the forecourt, tied off the reins, and climbed down, then rounded the horses and offered her his hand.

She gripped it, and as he helped her down, he said, "When I first visited, I had no idea it had once been your family home. Since the Extons were here, it's been through several owners and ended in the care of a bank."

She looked at the ornate panel above the front door. "And now, you're thinking of buying it." He wouldn't have brought her there otherwise.

She glanced at him.

He was gazing at the house with a longing she recognized, then he met her gaze. "Only if you will be happy living here with me." He tightly squeezed the hand he held. "But before we get to that, I've a confession to make."

Gray saw wariness seep into her eyes and rushed on, "I have to tell you about my gambling."

"What?" She stared uncomprehendingly at him. "What gambling?" She swung to face him.

Lips thinning, he took her hands in his and looked down at her slender fingers. "I told you earlier that the scent of adventure lured me to America. What kept me there…wasn't gambling but the outcome of it."

He drew in a rapid breath and forged on. "At Matcham House, I told you that after I reached America, over a period of time, I lost all my money. As you might imagine, I'd taken quite a bit with me, and in less than a year, I'd lost it all." Briefly, he met her eyes. "At the tables, mostly."

He didn't try to conceal his self-disgust. "I was a fool. An arrogant, thought-I-knew-my-way-around-the-world fool. My only saving grace was that I came to my senses before I got into impossible debt."

After a second's pause, he continued, "I was naive, overconfident, and reckless. And looking back on those months, I would say I was addicted." He drew a tight breath. "You decreed we should put our pasts to rest, and I agreed, but this is a part of my past that you need to see, to know."

He finally raised his head and met her shocked gaze. "I didn't know about your father's gambling until Therese told me and didn't truly appreciate the whole until you revealed that he'd made your family destitute through being addicted to gambling."

Gripping her fingers more tightly, he held her gaze. "After the hardship, heartache, and sorrow your father brought to you and your family, I know gambling has to be a deeply difficult issue for you. On my honor, I swear that since that time—just over a year after I left England, when I found myself without a single cent in my pocket—I haven't gambled in any way. Not socially, not professionally. Not for anything would I go back to the tables or permit myself to participate in any form of wagering again."

He paused, then, still holding her gaze, said, "The truth is, after a time, the craving died. I learned my lesson the hard way, but learn it, I did. From having nothing, I clawed my way back to at least existing on my own terms—being able to pay for food and shelter. For years, I lived at that level, until I found that nugget."

Her fingers curled, gripping his. Sharp and measuring, her gaze searched his face. "That's why you viewed the nugget as Fate giving you a second chance."

"That was the only way I could see it, and I knew I had to seize the chance and make the most of it." He held her gaze. "And I did. That nugget and what grew from it saw me return to England. And it was instrumental in bringing us together again—it created the wealth that made me think I was the target of your exposé."

Izzy studied his eyes while she absorbed what he'd told her and aligned that with what she knew of the man he now was. "You've trusted me with this because you want me to trust you."

"Not just want—I *need* you to trust me. I want you as my wife more than I can say, but without trust...without you believing that I would never jeopardize our future, much less the future of the family I want to have with you..." He shook his head and let the sentence trail into silence.

There was a vulnerability in his face she'd never expected to see—not in him—and he was braced in anticipation of...her rejection.

With no further protestations, he stood, silently waiting for her judgment. She read as much in his amber eyes.

She held his gaze. "No one else knows of this, do they?"

He shook his head. "I was ashamed of it at the time. Now..." He lightly shrugged. "I would rather walk barefoot over broken glass than tell Devlin I was such an utter ass."

"You didn't have to tell me," she pointed out.

He frowned. "Of course I did. Given your past with your father, I couldn't *not* tell you."

She finally allowed her expression to soften, her lips to gently curve. "And that, dear Gray"—she freed one hand and cupped his cheek—"is why I believe you. Why I trust you when you say you've finished with gambling, now and forever."

He looked puzzled, so she went on, "You didn't have to say anything —you could have left me in complete ignorance in the hope I would never find out. Instead, you cared enough about what I might think and feel to make a clean breast of your past failing, even though you've put it behind you."

She allowed her smile to deepen. "And just so you know, you would never have passed Silas's assessment if you harbored any vestige of a liking for gambling—he has antennae that are beyond sensitive when it comes to detecting that particular vice."

He caught her raised hand, brought it to his lips, and pressed a kiss to her fingertips. "And Silas knows, as I do, that the subject matters to you."

"Indeed. Yet far from denouncing you, he's talking of going into business with you. In that respect, there can be no higher accolade as to your trustworthiness."

He tipped his head. "I hadn't thought of it like that, but you're probably right."

"Trust me, I am. I've watched that old man navigate the shoals of England's businessmen, and he never puts a foot wrong."

"Hmm. I might just push to become his apprentice."

"You could do a lot worse."

He met her eyes. "We've strayed from the critical point. Can you accept me as I am now and overlook what I once was?"

She tightened her grip on his fingers and unwaveringly held his gaze. "The man I see before me now is the man I always hoped you would be— just ten years older and ten years wiser. As for any inclination to gamble, you stand before me as wealthy as Croesus, proof positive that you haven't been frittering away your fortune but, instead, growing it. That's not the hallmark of an inveterate gambler."

His features finally eased, and his lips curved wryly. "No, that's true. But I should probably warn you that, to some extent, I've swung the other way. When it comes to parting with money, you'll discover that I'm rather careful."

She laughed. "I believe I can live with that."

"Good." Gray exhaled, and it felt as if a massive weight had slid from his shoulders. For several moments, he luxuriated in her laughing, loving gaze, then keeping his eyes on hers, gestured toward the house. "Next subject. I fell in love with this place before I knew it was your old home, but I don't know whether, for you, it holds good memories or bad." Keeping his tone even, he added, "I did hear that your brother wasn't all that bothered about selling it and moving away."

"No, he wasn't." Her smile grew only more dazzling as she looked at the house. "But he wasn't our grandmother's favorite. I was. I used to spend so much time here—with her and Mama, too—when I was a child and even later. My memories of this house are wonderful. That was why I was so cut up when we had to sell."

Relief swamped him, and he grinned like a schoolboy. "Thank God for that."

As one, they walked toward the house.

He swung the hand he still held. "I take it you're willing to look over the place."

She beamed. "Oh yes."

They climbed the steps to the front porch. Gray fished out the front-door key from the back of the urn where the agent had said it would be, then opened the door and ushered Izzy inside.

She knew her way; she kept hold of his hand, and he let her lead as she explored her old home.

"Very little has been changed," she murmured.

They went down, then up, and eventually, she led him into the sunlit ballroom. Once inside, she slipped her fingers free and went to the central window. She stood before the large glass pane and looked over the lawn to the river and the fields beyond.

He joined her, standing shoulder to shoulder and looking over the sweep of land to the south. After a moment, he found her hand with his, raised her fingers to his lips, and pressed a soft kiss to her knuckles. "I mentioned that Ancaster Park isn't far away. Although I never ventured in this direction, this area is my home. It's the electorate I'd like to stand for —the local member is retiring, and he's encouraging me to put my name forward. And in this district, being a Child counts for quite a lot."

She glanced his way, curious and encouraging, and he continued, describing his intention to work to make life better for as many people as he could. "Politics offers the prospect of reaching further and making a difference for more people than just those I represent."

She dipped her head in agreement, then asked, "Why this house?"

He had his reasons, including location, ease of access from London, size, spaces both inside and out, and the right mix of reception rooms for the events a member of Parliament would be expected to host. After elucidating those, he studied her face. "If you would rather not host such events here, we can buy a house in London as well and entertain there."

She laughed and shook her head. "I know as well as you do that the most important people to build connections with are those who live in the electorate. Local entertaining will need to be done here, and"—she met his eyes—"I don't mind in the least."

He tipped his head, studying her face. "Can you see it? Us here, living the sort of life we want to live."

She held his gaze for several heartbeats, then looked out of the window. "You're proposing to make me mistress of Tickencote Grange."

"The position is yours if you want it."

She looked to the east. "My ancestors are buried in that churchyard— you're offering to allow me to re-establish my roots."

He didn't know what to say to that.

She glanced his way, then smiled a rather secretive smile and grasped his hand. "Come with me."

Izzy's heart was thudding as she led Gray through the house, out of the front door, and along the side of the front lawn to where hedges protected the old knot garden.

It was overgrown and in dire need of tending.

Undeterred, she drew him toward the circular central bed. "This is the place, above all others at the Grange, that was my favorite. Not just because of the glorious scents in spring and summer but also the cooing of the doves and the soft sounds of the river."

She cast him a smiling glance. "I used to spend hours here with my grandmother and Mama. Even when my siblings were born, for some reason, they rarely came here. It became my special place."

They reached the raised central bed, and she halted and faced him. "Years ago, I had a vision of my future that I cherish to this day—of me, here, with my own granddaughter, teaching her the names of the plants and how best to make them grow."

She met and held his gaze. "When we were forced to sell the house, I thought that dream was dead and gone. Now you..." She held her arms out to her sides and, laughing, unable to keep the beaming smile from her face, whirled in a circle. "You've brought me here, and you're offering me this, and giving me back my dream. You're set on making it possible. And yes, I can see how our lives will fit together, how we can meld our individual lives into a single, solid reality."

Stilling, she looked into his amber eyes and, surrendering to impulse, grasped his hands, one in each of hers, and with her eyes locked on his, asked, "Grayson Child, will you please do me the honor of asking me to marry you?"

Gray threw back his head and laughed. Then he looked at her and, smiling unrestrainedly, freed one hand, hunted in his pocket, then went down on one knee. Looking up at her, his expression open and, like hers, filled with joy, he asked, "Isadora Descartes, will you do me the honor of becoming my wife?"

He drank in her expression of untrammeled happiness and couldn't resist adding, "I've waited ten years to say those words."

Her smile deepened. "And I've waited ten years to say yes!"

She tugged at his shoulders, and he rose and opened the jeweler's box he held. "I saw this and thought it would be perfect for you. I hope it fits."

Her eyes lit as she plucked the ring, with its marquise-set emerald surrounded by smaller diamonds, from its velvet bed.

He took it from her fingers and, when she offered her hand, slid the ring onto her third finger.

Izzy raised her hand and admired the ring. "It's fabulous, Gray. And it fits."

"Just as we do." He closed his hand about hers, slid his arm around her waist, and drew her to him. "And this is something else I've been waiting ten years to do—to kiss Lady Isadora Child-to-be."

He suited the action to the words, and she met him with unfettered joy in her heart.

Heady strands of passion and desire wound about them, and they clung to the exchange, eager and glorying, as a lifetime of promise opened before them.

How long they stood there, locked in each other's arms, exploring the connection that now bloomed bright as any star, neither could have said, yet eventually, both drew back, laughing softly, breathless as they leant their foreheads against each other's and fought to find some semblance of balance.

"Sadly," Gray said, once he could speak, "this is neither the place nor the time. That seems to have been a recurring theme over this past week."

Izzy sighed and raised her head; when her gaze met his, her eyes were the deepest emerald he'd ever seen. "I don't understand why, after waiting ten years, it seems so hard to wait a few more weeks." She glanced toward the house. "Nevertheless, between us, I'm certain we'll ensure that our wait will be worth it."

He laughed and took her hand, and they walked out of the knot garden and onto the lawn.

They halted directly before the house. Izzy stood in front of Gray and leant back against his chest, and with his arms wrapped around her, they gazed on the place they would make their home and, in whispers and murmurs, shared their hopes and dreams.

∼

Saturday, February 14

They were married in St. Peter's Church, the local village church that lay beyond the grange orchard, the same church that, for centuries, had seen Izzy's ancestors from birth to grave. The minister, a longtime local who remembered the Descartes family, had been beyond delighted to be asked to officiate at a wedding that would bring the well-regarded ladies back to their ancestral home.

It was too early in the year for blossom, but throughout the orchard, Christmas roses spread like a carpet, raising their white, pink, magenta, and crimson heads to wave in the light breeze as Izzy, attended by Marietta, her brother Julius, and her mother, walked from the house, across the old orchard, past the lily pond, and on through a small gate to the church.

The crisp, clear air lent the scene an almost-magical quality, something the select gathering of guests invited to witness the nuptials of Lord Grayson Child and Lady Isadora Descartes had already noted.

As Izzy walked confidently beneath the stone pillars that formed the church's porch, the sun broke through the light clouds to beam down in unexpected blessing.

She paused in the foyer, haloed in the beam of light while her mother and Marietta fussed with the folds of her ivory silk gown with its overlay of delicate lace. Holding the bouquet she'd fashioned for herself from white Christmas roses, hyacinths, and ivy picked from the knot garden that morning, Izzy looked down the nave, smiling with unrestrained joy at those gathered in the pews of the old stone church with its amazing carvings and impressive chancel arch.

Beneath that arch stood a man with burnished brown hair, waiting for her to join him, and even from that distance, she could see his amber eyes were brimming with love.

Then her mother, finally satisfied, slipped past her and walked quickly down the aisle to the front pew, and the organ swelled, and Julius offered his arm. Smiling at her brother, who was more nervous than she was, Izzy placed her gloved hand on his sleeve. "Just follow my lead," she murmured as she raised her head and stepped out.

Julius smothered a laugh. "Just as I have all my life. You've been an inspiration, Izzy. I'm so pleased Gray came back to you."

She was as well. This might be occurring ten years later than first planned, but he and she had grown so much in the intervening years, there was no sense of wasted time. They'd needed those years to become who they now were, so that as strong, experienced, tried and tested individuals, they could join forces and, together, go on.

Smiling radiantly, she met the many eyes turned her way. Some belonged to Gray's family—cousins and connections—as well as several staff from Ancaster Park, while others represented the Descartes family, yet those she smiled most brightly at were the staff of *The Crier*.

She and Gray had elected to set aside all anxiety over her true identity becoming more widely known in order to have all the staff, who had supported her through the years and whom he had come to know, join them on their special day.

They'd been as one in decreeing theirs would not be the usual ton wedding and had limited their guest list to family, indispensable connections, and close friends.

Gray waited for her with Devlin Cader, his groomsman, beside him.

As she neared, she glanced along the front pews, meeting Gray's parents' pleased gazes, the approving yet reserved expressions of his brother and sister-in-law, and the openly admiring gazes of his nephews.

Therese Cader sat just behind, enjoying herself hugely, and Martin Cynster was there as well, smiling broadly. Beside Martin sat Lady Matcham, her eyes alight with curiosity and approval, and beyond her sat Louisa and Drake, both relaxed and smiling.

On the Descartes' side, Sybil, already dabbing at her eyes, sat by the aisle, with James, Izzy's younger brother, beside her, and beyond him, her sister-in-law, Dorothy, and Silas, both beaming. Julius and Dorothy's children sat in the pew behind, along with Lord Swan. To the delight of everyone in both families, Swan and Marietta, presently following Izzy down the aisle, planned to announce their engagement at the start of the upcoming Season.

With Julius, Izzy reached the end of the aisle, and Gray met her gaze and held out his hand.

Flown on happiness, she lifted her hand from Julius's sleeve and laid her fingers across Gray's and felt them close, strong and firm and undeniably possessive, about hers.

Together, they turned to the beaming minister, and the service began.

They'd decided to keep the service as short as possible, and the hymns they'd chosen were ones everyone knew and were happy to sing with gusto.

After the minister pronounced them man and wife, at his recommendation, Gray and Izzy shared their first kiss as a married couple while the sun poured down to bathe them in golden light.

They surfaced to discover that Donaldson and Digby had captured the moment. The pair rapidly drew back as, laughing and smiling joyfully, Gray and Izzy faced the congregation. Then they shared a swift glance, saw their eagerness and enthusiasm for getting on with their now-joint life mirrored in the other's eyes, and faced forward and, hand in hand, started up the aisle.

The guests mobbed them, squeezing Izzy's hands and slapping Gray's back, their faces split by grins and smiles.

After tendering their congratulations, many guests poured outside to gather about the porch steps, and when Izzy and Gray finally emerged, a shower of rice rained down upon them.

Then Donaldson and Digby arranged Izzy and Gray in pride of place in the porch archway, with Devlin and Therese and Marietta and Swan flanking them, then begged everyone else to gather around. All the guests gladly obliged, and Donaldson took several exposures to commemorate the occasion.

Thereafter, the crowd—all invited to the wedding breakfast— streamed out of the side gate and along the path past the pond and on through the orchard. The staff Izzy and Gray had put together to man the Grange had been at the back of the church and had hurried to return to the house. They now stood proudly waiting to greet what were, in effect, the first guests to grace the old house in its new incarnation as Izzy and Gray's home.

While the guests flowed through the house to the ballroom at the rear, Izzy and Gray dallied in the orchard, and Donaldson and Digby, both resplendent in dark suits with white Christmas rose boutonnières, took photograph after photograph, primarily at Gray's behest.

He smiled at Izzy. "I want to be able to look back at this moment when we're eighty years old."

She smiled delightedly. "Preserving our memories in black and white. Not many have that chance."

He nodded. "We do, and I'm seizing it."

Soon after, they joined their guests, and the wedding feast began. The food was delectable—their new chef was on his mettle—and the champagne and wine flowed freely. The speeches, led by Devlin and Therese, aided by Swan and Marietta and Julius, with special appearances by Silas and Lady Matcham, were both touching and hilarious.

Then the musicians started playing, and to the delight of all present, Gray and Izzy shared the first waltz, then everyone was up and dancing.

At one point, Izzy's hand was claimed by her younger brother, James, all of fifteen and acutely aware of it. They'd arranged the ceremony to coincide with the short leave toward the end of the Lent term, and James would return to Eton on Monday. However, having expected to spend the days in London with some of his friends, he wasn't overjoyed at missing out on the likely hijinks.

For her part, having overheard several of James's comments to his cousins, Izzy wasn't the least sorry that James was in the country, far from the temptations of town. Not that she allowed that to show, but instead, complimented him on his dancing, which made him smile and almost preen.

Subsequently, Gray claimed her hand for a slow waltz, and when he asked for the source of the frown in her eyes, she shared the concerns she and her mother harbored over her father's propensity for gambling emerging in his younger son.

They circled the room, then Gray observed, "James is nearing a critical age." He met Izzy's eyes. "Why not arrange for your mother not to be available to host him in town and, instead, have him divide his time between Lyndon Hall and the Grange? Between us and Julius and Dorothy, I doubt James will have time to develop a taste for that particular sport, and if you wish it, when the time is right, I'm willing to speak with him about my experiences." He met Izzy's eyes. "I'm certain the picture I paint will make James think three times before engaging in any serious game of chance."

Relieved, she smiled. "Thank you." When he urged her closer, she obliged and laid her head on his shoulder. She studied his profile from close quarters, then breathed, "I'm very glad you came home."

He cast her a sidelong glance. "So am I."

Earlier, Donaldson had taken several photographs of the wedding high table and of Gray and Izzy ceremonially cutting the tiered wedding cake. Now, set up in one corner by the windows, Donaldson and Digby were taking photographs of those of the guests who wished to pose.

Seeing some of those participating, Izzy grinned. "I had no idea the older generation would be so taken with being photographed."

Gray was smiling at the sight of Lady Matcham settling herself on the posing chair as if it were a throne. "They want to leave something for their descendants to remember them by." He tipped his head. "It's not a bad idea."

Inevitably, Gray and Izzy found themselves with their peers—Devlin, Therese, Martin, Louisa, and Drake—discussing Gray's plan to stand for the local seat.

"I'm fairly certain we'll see a declaration within the next few weeks," Devlin said. "Lansdowne is making concerned noises, and he's one you can be sure will read the wind correctly."

Drake nodded. "Russell's ministry is on its last legs—he'll be gone inside of a month—and that means we'll be heading to the polls sometime in the middle of the year." He nodded at Gray. "You'd best get ready."

Gray had made the decision to stand as an independent, and with everyone there, including his parents and brother and sister-in-law, ready to support him, along with the additional backing Izzy could bring to bear, while he felt sensibly nervous, he was also reasonably confident he would win through. He inclined his head to Drake and Devlin, then shared a smile with Izzy. "We'll be ready. I'm looking forward to the challenge."

Standing on the edge of the group, Martin surreptitiously tugged his sister's sleeve. When Therese glanced questioningly at him, he lowered his head and his voice to ask, "Do you have any idea where Gregory is? I tried calling at his lodgings twice, but no one seemed to be there, and none of the others in town have seen him recently."

"Ah." Therese turned to face him. "I heard from Mama that Timms —" She broke off and looked inquiringly at Martin. "Do you remember Timms?"

"Of course. She always fed me ginger biscuits. She's Minnie's companion."

"Was." Therese squeezed Martin's arm. "Minnie passed on years ago, just after you went off. In her will, she left Bellamy Hall and much of her wealth to Timms, more or less in a caretaker capacity, on the under-standing that when Timms passed, she would leave the hall and the funds to keep it up to whichever of Mama's or Uncle Gerrard's children Timms judged was most in need of the legacy. Timms died just before Christmas, and she willed Bellamy Hall and the funds to Gregory."

Martin blinked. "Well, that makes sense. Of the four of us, he's the one with the least other responsibilities, and Frederick and William are far too young."

"Indeed. So I suspect that Gregory has gone off to Bellamy Hall to see what he has to deal with." Therese's lips curved. "And no, he really has no idea."

Reading her tone and the tenor of her smile, Martin asked, "What doesn't Gregory know?"

Therese's smile bloomed into one of delighted anticipation. "From all I've learned, I rather think our dear brother is going to find laying his hands on the reins of Bellamy Hall to be the biggest challenge of his life."

The wedding breakfast rolled on in joyous vein, with not a wrinkle or hiccup to mar the day.

Eventually, however, all the guests left, driving to their houses in the surrounding countryside or heading back to London via the Great North Road, or alternatively, crowding into the charabancs Gray had hired to ferry guests back and forth from Stamford Station.

The last to leave were Sybil, Marietta, James, and Silas, who departed in Sybil's carriage for Lyndon Hall, following Julius, Dorothy, and their three children in Julius's coach.

At the top of the porch steps from where they'd waved everyone off, Izzy leant against Gray and sighed with unalloyed happiness. She glanced up and met his amber eyes. "Everything went off perfectly."

Smiling, he raised her hand and pressed a kiss to her fingers. "A wedding day to remember."

"And thanks to Donaldson and Digby, we'll have indisputable proof of that."

"Indeed." Gray grinned, and together, they walked inside.

Corby, transplanted from London to fill the post of butler of Tickencote Grange, was waiting to shut the door and report, "Everything is in hand, my lady, my lord. The staff are clearing the ballroom, and we'll have it and the rest of the reception rooms in good order within the hour."

Gray had ended his lease on his lodgings and dispatched his small household staff to the Grange, and Izzy had added several locals eager to join the servants' hall at the "big house."

"Thank you, Corby." Izzy directed a teasingly speculative look Gray's way. "If you don't need his lordship or myself, then I believe we'll…"

It was far too early to retire.

Catching her gaze, Gray smoothly supplied, "Retreat to our apartments so we won't be in your way."

Corby bowed. "Indeed, my lord. That would be much appreciated."

With Izzy grinning delightedly, Gray steered her to the stairs. Halfway up the first flight, he paused and looked back. "Oh—and Corby?"

About to disappear down the hall, Corby halted and looked up. "Yes, my lord?"

"If we don't appear again today, don't send a search party."

Corby looked faintly affronted. "Of course not, my lord!"

Izzy couldn't help her laugh. She caught Gray's hand and tugged. "Come on and stop teasing the poor man. He's coped wonderfully given he's never had to butler a gathering such as today's."

Despite their years of waiting, neither, it seemed, saw any reason to rush. Instead, they prolonged the anticipation by ambling, exchanging comments about this and that, remarking on the new furnishings they'd installed to soften and brighten the corridors and make the house more definitely theirs.

Eventually, they reached the door at the end of the upstairs corridor, the door that opened to the master suite. Gray set it swinging, and smiling, Izzy led the way inside, waiting only until he followed and shut the door to boldly walk into his arms.

They closed around her as she stretched up and, framing his face with both hands, set her lips to his.

The passion that had simmered for ten long years ignited.

Heat raced through them, and the years fell away, and they were the eager young couple they once had been, driven by their natures and their physical needs. Needs they could finally unleash.

Their lips melded. Their tongues dueled—seeking, exploring, and claiming.

He lured, and she followed without hesitation, eager and brazenly wanton in her desire to venture and learn.

Encouraged, he caressed her, sculpting her curves, still tightly encased in silk and lace.

She murmured in incoherent dissatisfaction and reached behind her to undo the tiny buttons that marched down her spine. Blindly, he helped, then she broke from the kiss to shed the delicate gown, closely followed by her ruffled petticoats. She kicked off her ivory slippers, and before he could do more than stare at the sight of the curvaceous figure defined by her corset, she launched herself at him, kissing him as if she were starving and he was her only hope of succor.

Need hit him like a train, driven and unstoppable.

He gripped her hips and fell into the kiss, into the raging torrent of desire and wanting she'd called forth and set free.

In short order, clothes flew, and with hands reaching, searching, stroking and possessing, they waltzed their way across the room.

Then they fell on the bed, hot skin to searing skin, and the jolt to their senses shocked them to stillness.

Darkened by passion, their eyes met.

Their gazes locked and held.

Both were breathing in shallow gasps, gripped by a yearning so powerful and intense they all but vibrated with the compulsion to rush on.

But they weren't the youthful would-be lovers they once had been.

She might not be experienced in this sphere, yet he knew she knew there was more.

Lost in the glory of her eyes, he drew in a huge breath.

And more or less in concert, they drew on their reins.

Moving much more slowly, he lowered his head, and once again, their lips melded. But this time, they held the heat and driving urgency at bay and tasted each other, supped and sipped and savored.

Instinct—his and hers—flared and led them on, and together, like musicians following the directions of a conductor's baton, they embarked on a slow, sensuous journey into intimacy.

Beat by beat, the pleasure mounted, and soft gasps and murmurs of appreciation became their symphony, one to which they both contributed.

Explorations were steeped in reverence, discoveries treated with worshipful awe.

Through the increasingly heated moments, knowledge of each other was their currency, and pleasuring the other became their ultimate and overriding aim.

The heady scent of passion wreathed about them as, finally, they joined, and for one shining moment, that scintillating sensation of being one, locked together in true intimacy, in the ultimate physical harmony, overwhelmed them.

Fingers clutching, gazes locked, they hung, suspended for an indefinable instant, no longer solely in this world, then the irresistible compulsion welled, swelled, and washed over them, and they surrendered to the compulsive tide.

Joy and delight, pleasure and sensation danced like magic beneath their skins. Passion and desire seared and burned and branded, and through it all, that elemental conflagration grew, undeniable and all-consuming, until it subsumed their senses and swept them from this world.

Into the heart of the sun of their creation.

They shattered, her, then him, nerves unraveling and senses expanding as light and glory filled them, and a connection so profound it linked their souls glowed in their minds.

Then aftermath rolled over them, and oblivion issued her commanding call.

They slumped, exhausted, yet with exhilaration still coursing through their veins.

Head bowed, he lifted her hand to his lips and brushed a still-burning kiss to her fingertips. "Thank you," he murmured, soft and low.

She raised her lids, revealing intensely emerald eyes that still glowed with the fires of desire. She met his gaze, steadily held it for several heartbeats, then her lips, lush and swollen, curved, and on an irrepressible chuckle, she said, "And you. And yes, that was, indeed, worth waiting ten years for."

EPILOGUE

TICKENCOTE GRANGE, RUTLANDSHIRE.
AUGUST 27, 1853.

*I*zzy knelt on a cushion on the gravel path in her knot garden and busily weeded and clipped. The herbs were a riot of scent and color; everything she'd sown had taken and grown.

A gurgle of laughter had her looking up in time to catch her daughter, Sylvia, almost one year old and just starting to toddle everywhere, leaving her nursemaid running in her wake.

Said nursemaid, Ginny, came puffing up. "I'm sorry, m'lady—she got away from me again."

"No harm done." Izzy hoisted Sylvia and settled her on her hip, from where the little girl could more easily see into the garden bed. "Mama is cutting mint to make a sauce for tonight's roast lamb." She plucked two leaves, crushed them lightly in her fingers, and held them to her nose, then to Sylvia's. "Smell—mint."

Sylvia dutifully sniffed in lungfuls, and her button nose wrinkled, then her features lit, and she squirmed to get down.

Having also heard the approaching footsteps, Izzy grinned and obliged, warning Ginny, "Stand back. His lordship is coming."

Released, as fast as her chubby legs would carry her, Sylvia rocketed toward the green archway giving access to the front lawn, simultaneously shrieking and waving her arms in the air.

Forewarned, Gray walked into the garden and smoothly stooped and hoisted the little girl in his arms.

"Dadda! Dadda!"

He kissed Sylvia on the forehead. "Yes, my darling daughter, I am, indeed, here."

Smiling, Izzy pushed to her feet. She was pregnant again, but was thankfully having a much easier time with it than when she'd carried Sylvia. "Are you coming to help weed?"

Gray glanced around. "Ah, no." He waved the papers he was carrying. "I've come to ask your opinion on this bill I'm supposed to be drafting. Lord knows, you're better with words than I am."

"Hmm." Dusting her fingers, Izzy walked to him and took the pages. She started to read, then waved to the stone bench, set in one corner to allow her to sit and appreciate her efforts. They retreated to the spot, and she sat and read while Gray played peekaboo with Sylvia.

On reaching the end of the closely written pages, Izzy glanced at Ginny, who promptly came forward to take Sylvia from Gray.

Wisely, Ginny mentioned the possibility of getting some bread from Cook to feed the ducks on the river, and Sylvia went peaceably; feeding the ducks was her favorite pastime.

Relieved of their distracting daughter, Izzy pointed to one of the clauses in the bill. "Is this really what you want to say?"

Gray took the page, read, and frowned. "You're right—it's convoluted to the point of being indecipherable."

He fished a pencil from his pocket, and with their heads together, they worked through the bill, correcting, amending, and clarifying.

They'd just reached the end and relaxed and shared a satisfied smile when the sound of carriage wheels on the gravel had them glancing through the archway.

A familiar coach rumbled along the drive.

Izzy rose with a smile, as did Gray.

"They're here already. Come on." She swiped up her basket of herbs, and Gray took her hand, and together, they walked through the archway and onto the lawn.

Seeing a young gardener trimming the hedges, Izzy paused to hand him her basket. "Can you run this to Chef? He needs it for tonight."

The lad grinned and bobbed. "Yes, m'lady."

He took the basket and trotted off, bearing Izzy's harvest, while she and Gray angled toward the forecourt where Julius's coach horses were being drawn to a halt.

Julius, Dorothy, their children, and Silas were there to dine, along with Sybil, Marietta, and Swan, who were currently staying at the Grange.

Aside from the usual catching up, the family planned to discuss the details of Marietta and Swan's wedding, slated to take place before the end of the year.

Gray and Izzy reached the graveled forecourt as Julius and Dorothy's children spilled from the coach. Two boys and a girl, all three looked around, saw Gray and Izzy and, beaming, pelted their way.

The hellos and hugs and kisses were barely exchanged before the elder boy asked, "Can we go down to the river and see the ducks?"

Izzy laughed. "Your father was always down there. I believe you might find Sylvia there, and her nursemaid might even have bread!"

"Good-oh!" the boys exclaimed.

"So can we go?" Emmy, the girl, asked.

Gray and Izzy nodded, and the trio streaked off.

Izzy called after them, "But no getting too close and falling in!"

"Well," Julius said, strolling up with Dorothy on his arm with Silas beside her, "they haven't fallen in yet, but thankfully, all three can swim."

Smiling, Izzy angled her cheek for Julius to kiss, then embraced Dorothy and Silas, while Gray and Julius shook hands, then Gray kissed Dorothy's cheek and clapped Silas on the back.

Sybil hurried out of the house, closely followed by Marietta and Swan. "You're here!" Sybil came down the steps, with Marietta and Swan close behind.

Standing beside Gray, Izzy watched as, with laughter and teasing and relaxed and happy smiles, her family embraced, kissed, and exclaimed.

The westering sun bathed the company in golden light. For years, she'd believed she would never see this again—her family, the descendants of those who built the house, congregating there on a late summer afternoon. The squeals of the family's children drifted up from the riverbank while carefree chatter enveloped the adults.

She'd never expected to reclaim this—this anchored, solidly rooted family joy.

As the company turned toward the house, she glanced at Gray. They fell in behind their guests, and she found his hand and squeezed. "Thank you for making my most precious, impossible dream come true."

He met her eyes, his own glowing with a love she would never—could never—doubt, then he raised her hand, pressed a kiss to her fingers, and softly said, "You don't have to do anything except be you, because you are my dream come true."

Dear Reader,

From the moment he walked onto the page in the previous novel, *The Games Lovers Play*, Grayson Child was plainly destined to feature in his own story. And even as I penned that teaser for the upcoming exposé in *The London Crier* that appeared at the end of the previous novel, I knew who the mysterious I. Molyneaux, editor, would prove to be.

I had fabulous fun learning about newspapers, printing presses, the first telegraph stations and Continental connections, about Dover and the railways to north and south of London. Much of what is included here is accurate, barring the actual location of the private abode that was the initial Dover telegraph station—try as I might, I could not find the location of that house, other than that it was somewhere in the Dover of that time.

For those who might wonder, in describing my characters moving about towns, for instance Dover, wherever possible I work from maps of towns from the correct period, so in many instances, especially when speaking of the center of towns and cities, the names of streets and even the actual position of roads may now be very different.

I hope you enjoyed reading of Gray and Izzy's renewed journey into love.

As usual, the last pages in this novel flag the character who will feature in the next book in the series—in this case, Gregory Cynster, who, as Therese informs Martin, has gone to claim his inheritance, namely Bellamy Hall. That book, as yet untitled, will be with you in March 2022.

But before that, by popular demand, *The Meaning of Love*, the long-awaited romance between Miss Melissa North, one of Lady Osbaldestone's granddaughters, and Julian, Earl of Carsely, previously Viscount Dagenham, will be released on October 14, 2021—yes, later this year! Although it's not a Christmas-set work, there are, of course, echoes of their past appearances in the various volumes of *Lady Osbaldestone's Christmas Chronicles*, and I hope it will prove a treat for you to enjoy in the lead up to the festive season.

With my best wishes for continued happy reading!

Stephanie.

For alerts as new books are released, plus information on upcoming books, exclusive sweepstakes and sneak peeks into upcoming novels, sign up for Stephanie's Private Email Newsletter http://www.stephanielaurens.com/newsletter-signup/

Or if you don't have time to chat and want a quick email alert, sign up and follow me at BookBub https://www.bookbub.com/authors/stephanie-laurens

The ultimate source for detailed information on all Stephanie's published books, including covers, descriptions, and excerpts, is Stephanie's Website www.stephanielaurens.com

You can also follow Stephanie via her Amazon Author Page at http://tinyurl.com/zc3e9mp

Goodreads members can follow Stephanie via her author page https://www.goodreads.com/author/show/9241.Stephanie_Laurens

You can email Stephanie at stephanie@stephanielaurens.com

Or find her on Facebook
https://www.facebook.com/AuthorStephanieLaurens/

COMING NEXT:

Connected to Lady Osbaldestone's Christmas Chronicles
THE MEANING OF LOVE
To be released on October 14, 2021.

Julian, Earl of Carsely, decides he'd best be proactive in finding himself a wife before the grandes dames do that for him. So after an absence of

eight years, he returns unheralded to the ton's ballrooms, only to find himself compelled to rescue the one young lady he's never forgotten from the clutches of his ne'er-do-well, predatory cousin. In the past, Melissa North and he had both been too young to envision forming a lasting connection, but now... Neither he nor she are the youthful souls they'd been. Now, they are so much more.

Available for pre-order from mid-August, 2021.

RECENTLY RELEASED:

THE GAMES LOVERS PLAY
Cynster Next Generation Novel #9

#1 New York Times *bestselling author Stephanie Laurens returns to the Cynsters' next generation with an evocative tale of two people striving to overcome unusual hurdles in order to claim true love.*

A nobleman wedded to the lady he loves strives to overwrite five years of masterful pretence and open his wife's eyes to the fact that he loves her as much as she loves him.

Lord Devlin Cader, Earl of Alverton, married Therese Cynster five years ago. What he didn't tell her then and has assiduously hidden ever since—for what seemed excellent reasons at the time—is that he loves her every bit as much as she loves him.

For her own misguided reasons, Therese had decided that the adage that Cynsters always marry for love did not necessarily mean said Cynsters were loved in return. She accepted that was usually so, but being universally viewed by gentlemen as too managing, bossy, and opinionated, she believed she would never be loved for herself. Consequently, after falling irrevocably in love with Devlin, when he made it plain he didn't love her yet wanted her to wife, she accepted the half love-match he offered, and once they were wed, set about organizing to make their marriage the very best it could be.

Now, five years later, they are an established couple within the haut ton, have three young children, and Devlin is making a name for himself in business and political circles. There's only one problem. Having attended numerous Cynster weddings and family gatherings and spent time with Therese's increasingly married cousins, who with their spouses all embrace the Cynster ideal of marriage based on mutually acknowledged love, Devlin is no longer content with the half love-match he himself engineered. No fool, he sees and comprehends what the craven act of denying his love is costing both him and Therese and feels compelled to rectify his fault. He wants for them what all Therese's married cousins enjoy—the rich and myriad benefits of marriages based on acknowledged mutual love.

Love, he's discovered, is too powerful a force to deny, leaving him wrestling with the conundrum of finding a way to convincingly reveal to Therese that he loves her without wrecking everything—especially the mutual trust—they've built over the past five years.

A classic historical romance set amid the glittering world of the London haut ton. A Cynster Next Generation novel—a full-length historical romance of 110,000 words.

The fourth instalment in Lady Osbaldestone's Christmas Chronicles
LADY OSBALDESTONE'S CHRISTMAS INTRIGUE

#1 New York Times bestselling author Stephanie Laurens immerses you in the simple joys of a long-ago country-village Christmas, featuring a grandmother, her grandchildren, her unwed son, a determined not-so-young lady, foreign diplomats, undercover guards, and agents of Napoleon!

At Hartington Manor in the village of Little Moseley, Therese, Lady Osbaldestone, and her household are once again enjoying the company of her intrepid grandchildren, Jamie, George, and Lottie, when they are unexpectedly joined by her ladyship's youngest and still-unwed son, also the children's favorite uncle, Christopher.

As the Foreign Office's master intelligencer, Christopher has been ordered into hiding until the department can appropriately deal with the French agent spotted following him in London. Christopher chose to seek refuge in Little Moseley because it's such a tiny village that anyone without a reason to be there stands out. Neither he nor his office-appointed bodyguard expect to encounter any dramas.

Then Christopher spots a lady from London he believes has been hunting him with matrimonial intent. He can't understand how she tracked him to the village, but determined to avoid her, he enlists the children's help. The children discover their information-gathering skills are in high demand, and while engaging with the villagers as they usually do and taking part in the village's traditional events, they do their best to learn what Miss Marion Sewell is up to.

But upon reflection, Christopher realizes it's unlikely the Marion he was so attracted to years before has changed all that much, and he starts to wonder if what she wants to tell him is actually something he might want to hear. Unfortunately, he has set wheels in motion that are not easy to redirect. Although Marion tries to approach him several times, he and she fail to make contact.

Then just when it seems they will finally connect, a dangerous stranger lures Marion away. Fearing the worst, Christopher gives chase—trailed by his bodyguard, the children, and a small troop of helpful younger gentlemen.

What they discover at nearby Parteger Hall is not at all what anyone expected, and as the action unfolds, the assembled company band together to protect a secret vital to the resolution of the war against Napoleon.

Fourth in series. A novel of 81,000 words. A Christmas tale of intrigue, personal evolution, and love.

PREVIOUS CYNSTER NEXT GENERATION RELEASES:

THE INEVITABLE FALL OF CHRISTOPHER CYNSTER
Cynster Next Generation Novel #8

#1 New York Times *bestselling author Stephanie Laurens returns to the Cynsters' next generation with a rollicking tale of smugglers, counterfeit banknotes, and two people falling in love.*

A gentleman hoping to avoid falling in love and a lady who believes love has passed her by are flung together in a race to unravel a plot that threatens to undermine the realm.

Christopher Cynster has finally accepted that to have the life he wants, he needs a wife, but before he can even think of searching for the right lady, he's drawn into an investigation into the distribution of counterfeit banknotes.

London born and bred, Ellen Martingale is battling to preserve the fiction that her much-loved uncle, Christopher's neighbor, still has his wits about him, but Christopher's questions regarding nearby Goffard Hall trigger her suspicions. As her younger brother attends card parties at the Hall, she feels compelled to investigate.

While Ellen appears to be the sort of frippery female Christopher abhors, he quickly learns that, in her case, appearances are deceiving. And through the twists and turns in an investigation that grows ever more serious and urgent, he discovers how easy it is to fall in love, while Ellen learns that love hasn't, after all, passed her by.

But then the villain steps from the shadows, and love's strengths and vulnerabilities are put to the test—just as Christopher has always feared. Will he pass muster? Can they triumph? Or will they lose all they've so recently found?

A historical romance with a dash of intrigue, set in rural Kent. A Cynster Next Generation novel—a full-length historical romance of 124,000 words.

A CONQUEST IMPOSSIBLE TO RESIST
Cynster Next Generation Novel #7

#1 New York Times bestselling author Stephanie Laurens returns to the Cynsters' next generation to bring you a thrilling tale of love, intrigue, and fabulous horses.

A notorious rakehell with a stable of rare Thoroughbreds and a lady on a quest to locate such horses must negotiate personal minefields to forge a greatly desired alliance—one someone is prepared to murder to prevent.

Prudence Cynster has turned her back on husband hunting in favor of horse hunting. As the head of the breeding program underpinning the success of the Cynster racing stables, she's on a quest to acquire the necessary horses to refresh the stable's breeding stock.

On his estranged father's death, Deaglan Fitzgerald, now Earl of

Glengarah, left London and the hedonistic life of a wealthy, wellborn rake and returned to Glengarah Castle determined to rectify the harm caused by his father's neglect. Driven by guilt that he hadn't been there to protect his people during the Great Famine, Deaglan holds firm against the lure of his father's extensive collection of horses and, leaving the stable to the care of his brother, Felix, devotes himself to returning the estate to prosperity.

Deaglan had fallen out with his father and been exiled from Glengarah over his drive to have the horses pay their way. Knowing Deaglan's wishes and that restoration of the estate is almost complete, Felix writes to the premier Thoroughbred breeding program in the British Isles to test their interest in the Glengarah horses.

On receiving a letter describing exactly the type of horses she's seeking, Pru overrides her family's reluctance and sets out for Ireland's west coast to visit the now-reclusive wicked Earl of Glengarah. Yet her only interest is in his horses, which she cannot wait to see.

When Felix tells Deaglan that a P. H. Cynster is about to arrive to assess the horses with a view to a breeding arrangement, Deaglan can only be grateful. But then P. H. Cynster turns out to be a lady, one utterly unlike any other he's ever met.

Yet they are who they are, and both understand their world. They battle their instincts and attempt to keep their interactions businesslike, but the sparks are incandescent and inevitably ignite a sexual blaze that consumes them both—and opens their eyes.

But before they can find their way to their now-desired goal, first one accident, then another distracts them. Someone, it seems, doesn't want them to strike a deal. Who? Why?

They need to find out before whoever it is resorts to the ultimate sanction.

A historical romance with neo-Gothic overtones, set in the west of Ireland. A Cynster Next Generation novel—a full-length historical romance of 125,000 words.

The first volume of the Devil's Brood Trilogy
THE LADY BY HIS SIDE
Cynster Next Generation Novel #4

A marquess in need of the right bride. An earl's daughter in search of a purpose. A betrayal that ends in murder and balloons into a threat to the realm.

Sebastian Cynster knows time is running out. If he doesn't choose a wife soon, his female relatives will line up to assist him. Yet the current debutantes do not appeal. Where is he to find the right lady to be his marchioness? Then Drake Varisey, eldest son of the Duke of Wolverstone, asks for Sebastian's aid.

Having assumed his father's mantle in protecting queen and country, Drake must go to Ireland in pursuit of a dangerous plot. But he's received an urgent missive from Lord Ennis, an Irish peer—Ennis has heard something Drake needs to know. Ennis insists Drake attends an upcoming house party at Ennis's Kent estate so Ennis can reveal his information face-to-face.

Sebastian has assisted Drake before and, long ago, had a liaison with Lady Ennis. Drake insists Sebastian is just the man to be Drake's surrogate at the house party—the guests will imagine all manner of possibilities and be blind to Sebastian's true purpose.

Unsurprisingly, Sebastian is reluctant, but Drake's need is real. With only more debutantes on his horizon, Sebastian allows himself to be persuaded.

His first task is to inveigle Antonia Rawlings, a lady he has known all her life, to include him as her escort to the house party. Although he's seen little of Antonia in recent years, Sebastian is confident of gaining her support.

Eldest daughter of the Earl of Chillingworth, Antonia has abandoned the search for a husband and plans to use the week of the house party to decide what to do with her life. There has to be some purpose, some role, she can claim for her own.

Consequently, on hearing Sebastian's request and an explanation of what lies behind it, she seizes on the call to action. Suppressing her senses' idiotic reaction to Sebastian's nearness, she agrees to be his partner-in-intrigue.

But while joining the house party proves easy, the gathering is thrown into chaos when Lord Ennis is murdered—just before he was to speak with Sebastian. Worse, Ennis's last words, gasped to Sebastian, are: *Gunpowder. Here.*

Gunpowder? And here, where?

With a killer continuing to stalk the halls, side by side, Sebastian and

Antonia search for answers and, all the while, the childhood connection that had always existed between them strengthens and blooms...into something so much more.

First volume in a trilogy. A Cynster Next Generation Novel – a classic historical romance with gothic overtones layered over a continuing intrigue. A full-length novel of 99,000 words

The second volume of the Devil's Brood Trilogy
AN IRRESISTIBLE ALLIANCE
Cynster Next Generation Novel #5

A duke's second son with no responsibilities and a lady starved of the excitement her soul craves join forces to unravel a deadly, potentially catastrophic threat to the realm - that only continues to grow.

With his older brother's betrothal announced, Lord Michael Cynster is freed from the pressure of familial expectations. However, the allure of his previous hedonistic pursuits has paled. Then he learns of the mission his brother, Sebastian, and Lady Antonia Rawlings have been assisting with and volunteers to assist by hunting down the hoard of gunpowder now secreted somewhere in London.

Michael sets out to trace the carters who transported the gunpowder from Kent to London. His quest leads him to the Hendon Shipping Company, where he discovers his sole source of information is the only daughter of Jack and Kit Hendon, Miss Cleome Hendon, who although a fetchingly attractive lady, firmly holds the reins of the office in her small hands.

Cleo has fought to achieve her position in the company. Initially, managing the office was a challenge, but she now conquers all in just a few hours a week. With her three brothers all adventuring in America, she's been driven to the realization that she craves adventure, too.

When Michael Cynster walks in and asks about carters, Cleo's instincts leap. She wrings from him the full tale of his mission—and offers him a bargain. She will lead him to the carters he seeks if he agrees to include her as an equal partner in the mission.

Horrified, Michael attempts to resist, but ultimately finds himself agreeing—a sequence of events he quickly learns is common around Cleo. Then she delivers on her part of the bargain, and he finds there are benefits to allowing her to continue to investigate beside him—not least being that if she's there, then he knows she's safe.

But the further they go in tracing the gunpowder, the more deaths they uncover. And when they finally locate the barrels, they find themselves tangled in a fight to the death—one that forces them to face what has grown between them, to seize and defend what they both see as their path to the greatest adventure of all. A shared life. A shared future. A shared love.

Second volume in a trilogy. A Cynster Next Generation Novel – a classic historical romance with gothic overtones layered over a continuing intrigue. A full-length novel of 101,000 words.

The third and final volume of the Devil's Brood Trilogy
THE GREATEST CHALLENGE OF THEM ALL
Cynster Next Generation Novel #6

A nobleman devoted to defending queen and country and a noblewoman wild enough to match his every step race to disrupt the plans of a malignant intelligence intent on shaking England to its very foundations.

Lord Drake Varisey, Marquess of Winchelsea, eldest son and heir of the Duke of Wolverstone, must foil a plot that threatens to shake the foundations of the realm, but the very last lady—nay, noblewoman—he needs assisting him is Lady Louisa Cynster, known throughout the ton as Lady Wild.

For the past nine years, Louisa has suspected that Drake might well be the ideal husband for her, even though he's assiduous in avoiding her. But she's now twenty-seven and enough is enough. She believes propinquity will reveal exactly what it is that lies between them, and what better opportunity to work closely with Drake than this latest mission with which he patently needs her help?

Unable to deny Louisa's abilities or the value of her assistance and powerless to curb her willfulness, Drake is forced to grit his teeth and acquiesce to her sticking by his side if only to ensure her safety. But all too soon, his true feelings for her surface sufficiently for her, perspicacious as she is, to see through his denials, which she then interprets as a challenge.

Even while they gather information, tease out clues, increasingly desperately search for the missing gunpowder, and doggedly pursue the killer responsible for an ever-escalating tally of dead men, thrown together through the hours, he and she learn to trust and appreciate each other. And fed by constant exposure—and blatantly encouraged by her—their desires and hungers swell and grow…

As the barriers between them crumble, the attraction he has for so long restrained burgeons and balloons, until goaded by her near-death, it erupts, and he seizes her—only to be seized in return.

Linked irrevocably and with their wills melded and merged by passion's fire, with time running out and the evil mastermind's deadline looming, together, they focus their considerable talents and make one last push to learn the critical truths—to find the gunpowder and unmask the villain behind this far-reaching plot.

Only to discover that they have significantly less time than they'd thought, that the villain's target is even more crucially fundamental to the realm than they'd imagined, and it's going to take all that Drake is—as well as all that Louisa as Lady Wild can bring to bear—to defuse the threat, capture the villain, and make all safe and right again.

As they race to the ultimate confrontation, the future of all England rests on their shoulders.

Third volume in a trilogy. A Cynster Next Generation Novel – a classic historical romance with gothic overtones layered over an intrigue. A full-length novel of 129,000 words.

If you haven't yet caught up with the first books in the Cynster Next Generation Novels, then BY WINTER'S LIGHT is a Christmas story that highlights the Cynster children as they stand poised on the cusp of adulthood – essentially an introductory novel to the upcoming generation. That novel is followed by the first pair of Cynster Next Generation romances, those of Lucilla and Marcus Cynster, twins and the eldest children of Lord Richard aka Scandal Cynster and Catriona, Lady of the Vale. Both the twins' stories are set in Scotland. See below for further details.

BY WINTER'S LIGHT
A Cynster Special Novel
Cynster Next Generation Novel #1

#1 New York Times bestselling author Stephanie Laurens returns to romantic Scotland to usher in a new generation of Cynsters in an enchanting tale of mistletoe, magic, and love.

It's December 1837 and the young adults of the Cynster clan have succeeded in having the family Christmas celebration held at snow-bound Casphairn Manor, Richard and Catriona Cynster's home. Led by Sebastian, Marquess of Earith, and by Lucilla, future Lady of the Vale, and her twin brother, Marcus, the upcoming generation has their own plans for the holiday season.

Yet where Cynsters gather, love is never far behind—the festive occasion brings together Daniel Crosbie, tutor to Lucifer Cynster's sons, and Claire Meadows, widow and governess to Gabriel Cynster's daughter. Daniel and Claire have met before and the embers of an unexpected passion smolder between them, but once bitten, twice shy, Claire believes a second marriage is not in her stars. Daniel, however, is determined to press his suit. He's seen the love the Cynsters share, and Claire is the lady with whom he dreams of sharing *his* life. Assisted by a bevy of Cynsters —innate matchmakers every one—Daniel strives to persuade Claire that trusting him with her hand and her heart is her right path to happiness.

Meanwhile, out riding on Christmas Eve, the young adults of the Cynster clan respond to a plea for help. Summoned to a humble dwelling in ruggedly forested mountains, Lucilla is called on to help with the difficult birth of a child, while the others rise to the challenge of helping her. With a violent storm closing in and severely limited options, the next generation of Cynsters face their first collective test—can they save this mother and child? And themselves, too?

Back at the manor, Claire is increasingly drawn to Daniel and despite her misgivings, against the backdrop of the ongoing festivities their relationship deepens. Yet she remains torn—until catastrophe strikes, and by winter's light, she learns that love—true love—is worth any risk, any price.

A tale brimming with all the magical delights of a Scottish festive season. A Cynster Next Generation novel – a classic historical romance of 71,000 words.

THE TEMPTING OF THOMAS CARRICK
A Cynster Next Generation Novel

Cynster Next Generation Novel #2

Do you believe in fate? Do you believe in passion? What happens when fate and passion collide?
Do you believe in love? What happens when fate, passion, and love combine?
This. This...

#1 New York Times *bestselling author Stephanie Laurens returns to Scotland with a tale of two lovers irrevocably linked by destiny and passion.*

Thomas Carrick is a gentleman driven to control all aspects of his life. As the wealthy owner of Carrick Enterprises, located in bustling Glasgow, he is one of that city's most eligible bachelors and fully intends to select an appropriate wife from the many young ladies paraded before him. He wants to take that necessary next step along his self-determined path, yet no young lady captures his eye, much less his attention...not in the way Lucilla Cynster had, and still did, even though she lives miles away.

For over two years, Thomas has avoided his clan's estate because it borders Lucilla's home, but disturbing reports from his clansmen force him to return to the countryside—only to discover that his uncle, the laird, is ailing, a clan family is desperately ill, and the clan-healer is unconscious and dying. Duty to the clan leaves Thomas no choice but to seek help from the last woman he wants to face.

Strong-willed and passionate, Lucilla has been waiting—increasingly impatiently—for Thomas to return and claim his rightful place by her side. She knows he is hers—her fated lover, husband, protector, and mate. He is the only man for her, just as she is his one true love. And, at last, he's back. Even though his returning wasn't on her account, Lucilla is willing to seize whatever chance Fate hands her.

Thomas can never forget Lucilla, much less the connection that seethes between them, but to marry her would mean embracing a life he's adamant he does not want.

Lucilla sees that Thomas has yet to accept the inevitability of their union and, despite all, he can refuse her and walk away. But how *can* he ignore a bond such as theirs—one so much stronger than reason? Despite several unnerving attacks mounted against them, despite the uncertainty racking his clan, Lucilla remains as determined as only a Cynster can be to fight for the future she knows can be theirs—and while she cannot command him, she has powerful enticements she's willing to wield in the cause of tempting Thomas Carrick.

A neo-Gothic tale of passionate romance laced with mystery, set in the uplands of southwestern Scotland. A Cynster Second Generation Novel – a classic historical romance of 122,000 words.

A MATCH FOR MARCUS CYNSTER
A Cynster Next Generation Novel
Cynster Next Generation Novel #3

Duty compels her to turn her back on marriage. Fate drives him to protect her come what may. Then love takes a hand in this battle of yearning hearts, stubborn wills, and a match too powerful to deny.

#1 New York Times bestselling author Stephanie Laurens returns to rugged Scotland with a dramatic tale of passionate desire and unwavering devotion.

Restless and impatient, Marcus Cynster waits for Fate to come calling. He knows his destiny lies in the lands surrounding his family home, but what will his future be? Equally importantly, with whom will he share it?

Of one fact he feels certain: his fated bride will not be Niniver Carrick. His elusive neighbor attracts him mightily, yet he feels compelled to protect her—even from himself. Fickle Fate, he's sure, would never be so kind as to decree that Niniver should be his. The best he can do for them both is to avoid her.

Niniver has vowed to return her clan to prosperity. The epitome of fragile femininity, her delicate and ethereal exterior cloaks a stubborn will and an unflinching devotion to the people in her care. She accepts that in order to achieve her goal, she cannot risk marrying and losing her grip on the clan's reins to an inevitably controlling husband. Unfortunately, many local men see her as their opportunity.

Soon, she's forced to seek help to get rid of her unwelcome suitors. Powerful and dangerous, Marcus Cynster is perfect for the task.

Suppressing her wariness over tangling with a gentleman who so excites her passions, she appeals to him for assistance with her peculiar problem.

Although at first he resists, Marcus discovers that, contrary to his expectations, his fated role *is* to stand by Niniver's side and, ultimately, to claim her hand. Yet in order to convince her to be his bride, they must plunge headlong into a journey full of challenges, unforeseen dangers, passion, and yearning, until Niniver grasps the essential truth—that she is indeed a match for Marcus Cynster.

A neo-Gothic tale of passionate romance set in the uplands of southwestern Scotland
A Cynster Second Generation Novel – a classic historical romance of 114,000 words.

And if you want to discover where the Cynsters began, return to the iconic
DEVIL'S BRIDE

the book that introduced millions of historical romance readers around the globe to the powerful men of the unforgettable Cynster family— aristocrats to the bone, conquerors at heart—and the willful feisty ladies strong enough to be their brides.

ABOUT THE AUTHOR

#1 *New York Times* bestselling author Stephanie Laurens began writing romances as an escape from the dry world of professional science. Her hobby quickly became a career when her first novel was accepted for publication, and with entirely becoming alacrity, she gave up writing about facts in favor of writing fiction.

All Laurens's works to date are historical romances, ranging from medieval times to the mid-1800s, and her settings range from Scotland to India. The majority of her works are set in the period of the British Regency. Laurens has published over 75 works of historical romance, including 40 *New York Times* bestsellers. Laurens has sold more than 20 million print, audio, and e-books globally. All her works are continuously available in print and e-book formats in English worldwide, and have been translated into many other languages. An international bestseller, among other accolades, Laurens has received the Romance Writers of America® prestigious RITA® Award for Best Romance Novella 2008 for *The Fall of Rogue Gerrard*.

Laurens's continuing novels featuring the Cynster family are widely regarded as classics of the historical romance genre. Other series include the *Bastion Club Novels*, the *Black Cobra Quartet*, the *Adventurers Quartet,* and the *Casebook of Barnaby Adair Novels*.

For information on all published novels and on upcoming releases and updates on novels yet to come, visit Stephanie's website: www. stephanielaurens.com

To sign up for Stephanie's Email Newsletter (a private list) for heads-up alerts as new books are released, exclusive sneak peeks into upcoming books, and exclusive sweepstakes contests, follow the prompts at http:// www.stephanielaurens.com/newsletter-signup/

To follow Stephanie on BookBub, head to her BookBub Author Page: https://www.bookbub.com/authors/stephanie-laurens

Stephanie lives with her husband and a goofy black labradoodle in the hills outside Melbourne, Australia. When she isn't writing, she's reading, and if she isn't reading, she'll be tending her garden.

www.stephanielaurens.com
stephanie@stephanielaurens.com

Lightning Source UK Ltd.
Milton Keynes UK
UKHW022244170821
389016UK00013B/2590

9 781925 559484